THE IDEAL HUSBAND

A new wife

        A new life

                A dead body

A. K. ADAMS

Novels by A. K. Adams

An Unknown Paradise

Searching for Juliette

Shouldn't Have Done That

They Fade and Die

The Locked Room

Down a Long Dark Road

In the Dead of Night

Outlive the Lie

'A great marriage is not when a perfect couple comes together.

It is when an imperfect couple learns to enjoy their differences.'

Dave Meurer

For my parents

Arthur and Gladys

With love

Prologue

It seemed a good idea. The more they talked about it, the more exciting it became. The legal bit shouldn't take long, and they'd agreed the plan between themselves while they'd been on holiday in Spain - over two bottles of Rioja. Give it twelve months or so and they'd both be set for life. There wasn't anything that could go wrong. If they took it nice and slow, told their friends that they'd decided on the divorce because of 'irreconcilable differences,' and then went ahead, it would be like taking candy from a baby. He agreed to be the cause of the marriage breakdown, the philanderer, and she would act the role of the mistreated wife.

Of course, they'd keep in touch; they'd be neighbours anyway, and when an opportunity presented itself, they could get together to review progress. But they'd have to be careful; they knew that. Even their closest friends wouldn't suspect anything.

The family of his new bride would be upset, that was bound to happen, but he had ideas to placate them – at least to start with. He wasn't going to be controversial, or rub anyone up the wrong way. No, he was going to be 'Mr. Nice Guy,' and show them that she'd made the right choice. But slowly, ever so slowly and almost imperceptibly, he would change things. He hadn't done any acting before, but he'd learn quickly, and was clear in his mind exactly how it was going to work out. And how was that?

By being the ideal husband.

1

There's the monthly statement for the gas!" said Tom Ball to his wife, Liz, after opening the mail that the postman had delivered to their semi-detached bungalow. The couple had been married since August, 2011. "Look! Eighty quid and fifty pence every month!" Liz had just come downstairs, still in her pink candlewick dressing gown, the matching belt loose around her waist. Her blonde hair was tousled and in need of a wash. Liz checked the calendar - it was Saturday, 10 April.

"We are not borrowing anymore from that loan company. They'd skin you alive if they could. We'll just have to raid the holiday money tin. It's just as well we've paid for the holiday to the Costa del Sol. And there's the fifty quid our Mary owes me for that sideboard she bought off us last month. We will manage, Tom." Liz was usually philosophical about money matters, and would always cope . . . somehow. Tom checked the other post - a pamphlet from Weight-Watchers, a mail – order catalogue from a clothing company, and a letter with a Southend postmark.

"Looks like a letter from Mary," said Tom, putting the mail on a small table near the front door. Liz's sister, Mary, had lost her husband, Keith, a year ago in an industrial accident. The company accepted the blame for some scaffolding that had collapsed during building work in Rayleigh, and Mary received a decent compensation payment. "I'd better get going. I do not want the gaffer moaning again," chirped Tom. He gave Liz a kiss on the cheek as he left the property.

Tom checked his watch. 7.25 am. He got into his white Peugeot Boxer van parked on the drive, turned the key, and headed off to the builder's merchants where he worked as a delivery driver. Twenty minutes later he was parking in front of the main block, Corbett and Perkins writ large in green letters across the top of the front façade. The head office of C & P had been in Basildon since 1969.

"Morning, Tom," said Harry Phillips, the manager. "How are you this morning?" He always said the same thing to Tom, and Tom gave his usual reply.

"Fine thanks, Harry. And you?" Harry smiled and grunted. That meant he was OK. Harry wasn't one for small talk, and wanted to get on with the business of the day. He handed Tom a delivery list.

"Today's products are on three pallets round the back. Fourteen drop offs. Do the usual with your sat-nav and minimise the mileage, Tom. There's a good chap." Tom winced. His manager was one for efficiency, and the fourteen deliveries had to be done in the minimum mileage possible.

"Yes, boss," replied Tom as he headed for his van, "I always try!" Loading took half an hour, and then Tom was on the road by just after 8.30 a.m.

Tom Ball, now 38 years of age, had been working for C & P for eighteen months. Prior to that he'd been employed as an electrician, and before that as a gas boiler installer with British Gas. He had a City & Guilds certificate in both areas which made him a useful guy to know.

By 12.30 p.m., Tom had offloaded eight of his deliveries and was now parked up in a layby with a pork pie and can of Coke he'd bought from a cafe a mile down the road, the narrow counter had several layers of dried brown sauce and ketchup which gave the surface the appearance of Italian marbling. Tom sat listening to BBC Radio Essex on the van radio as he bit into his crusty pie. A few drops of pork juice dribbled down his chin which he wiped with the sleeve of his blue, grey and white check shirt that he'd bought from an Oxfam charity shop three months ago. The local radio DJ was doing too much rabbiting for Tom's liking, so he tuned in to Classic fm.

The soothing music gave him time to think. More about the life that he and Liz were leading than wondering about his beloved West Ham United. The Hammers had finished sixth in the league and Tom wasn't certain if David Moyes was the right man for the manager's job, but he'd do for now. Things might improve next season at the London Stadium, and some new blood could even see the team finishing in the top four . . . if Moyes put his hand in his pocket.

Tom and Liz lived from hand to mouth. She worked three days a week as an office cleaner in Basildon, looking after a small number of businesses in the town centre. At 36 years of age, Liz was no spring chicken, but she kept herself fit on the exercise bike in the back bedroom. They'd decided soon after their wedding ten years ago that neither wanted children, and Liz asked Tom if he'd have a vasectomy. It meant that she wouldn't get pregnant, even if she forgot to take her the pill after a night on the town.

Their joint wage kept their heads above water, spending-wise. The 54" LG television and both Apple i-phones were paid for monthly by direct debit, the Netflix and Amazon Prime subscriptions added to their outgoings, and after the utilities bills and food shopping, it resulted in them having about £150 a month to spend on clothes and eating out. Thankfully there was no mortgage. Tom's parents had left the semi-detached bungalow to them when they went into a Care Home together six years ago. Shortly after that, both died a month apart.
Three years ago, Tom and Liz had borrowed three grand from Loans-For-You to see them pay off a few bills, but ended up repaying a little over five thousand pounds. Right now, the couple were on an even keel, both careful

in what they bought on a daily basis. Tom's pie and Coke lunch set him back £1.80, and his check shirt was £2.50. However, his Doc Martens work boots had cost him almost £40, but they were his pride and joy - the dark maroon surface always polished to a mirror-like finish.

2

It was one of Liz's days off, and after Tom had left for work, she busied herself around the bungalow doing some washing and dusting. After the washing was dry, Liz got the ironing board out and spent an hour on the shirts and blouses, as well as one of Tom's overalls that he wore to work. She listened to a talk-in show on the radio as she moved the iron from left to right, then back again. But the radio was only wallpaper music and chat. Her mind wandered to their forthcoming week to soak up the Spanish sun in Benalmadena. They were booked into the hotel Puerto Marina close to the sea front. They'd been before, and loved nearby Torremolinos and Mijas. There were some lovely parts to Benalmadena, the marina being especially beautiful. Further along, nearer to the sea beyond a car park, was the American paddle steamer, *Willow*, that was listing badly. It had once been a nightclub, but when it began to leak, the owner couldn't afford to get it fixed. It was now in a sorry state, but Liz often wondered what it had been like in its heyday.

The day wore on, and after a sandwich for lunch, and the ironing finished, Liz decided on some gardening. Neither the front nor rear garden was very big. Each one was about nine yards square, but there was sufficient to keep her busy. No grass meant relatively easy maintenance, the gravel a good base for the multitude of potted plant that Liz had spread around. Geraniums, fuchsias, hollyhocks, hardy jasmines . . . they all added to the variety of colour and perfume that she enjoyed so much. Three hanging baskets added to the whole ambience of their small property, and the thing that pleased Liz most of all was that the total cost of all of this was less than a tenner. The hanging baskets had been salvaged from the local tip, two neighbours had donated seed plants, and when Liz's sister had visited from Southend, she'd brought two small plants with her. The compost was from the garden of Gertrude Heseltine, their elderly neighbour from the large house next door, albeit, twenty yards away. Free of charge.

    At 81 years of age, Gertrude was still quite nimble on her feet, but Liz had noticed the early signs of dementia. She was becoming more forgetful, and would tell Liz and Tom stories on the same topic several times over. But they went along with it. There was no point in saying that they'd already heard about the milkman having his float stolen and been killed in a back alley, or how she'd mislaid her handbag at the supermarket. No, they'd listen to the slightly different versions over and over. But Gertrude's heart was in the right place. She'd told Tom and Liz her late husband, Nigel, had owned a jewellery store in Saffron Walden after he'd left a senior role at Hatton Garden in London. Gertrude liked to call the store an 'emporium.' Before that, he'd worked for DeBeers managing a South African diamond mine in the Northern Transvaal, and later made his fortune trading in the precious gems. Their three children were all born in South Africa. Gertrude had told Tom and Liz that Nigel had passed away some years ago but she couldn't remember the year. Liz was about to prune an evergreen shrub in the front garden that was growing out of shape, when she glanced up and saw Gertrude walking toward her.

    "Hello, Elizabeth," said Gertrude. She always called Liz by that name, and Liz never commented on it. It was typical of her neighbour, who'd been well educated at a private school and then at Cambridge. "I don't know if it's me, but my boiler doesn't seem to come on when I turn on the hot water tap. It always does, you know." Liz smiled, saying nothing. "Do you think Tom could have a look at it for me when he gets in?" Liz put down her secateurs.

"Of course, Gertrude. He'll be home soon. I'll ask him to pop round as soon as he arrives. How's that?" Gertrude agreed it would be fine. This wasn't the first time her boiler had gone on the blink, not to mention a dozen other things over the past six months. It wasn't as if she couldn't afford to phone a gas engineer, or get a plumber when a tap leaked, or a locksmith when she'd locked herself out of the house last month. But asking if Tom could help out had become a habit. At least that was Liz's theory. Gertrude had simply decided in her own mind that if something needed attention, her neighbour Tom, who could turn his hand to tackle most domestic jobs, was the man to ask.

But one issue was payment. When did Tom charge Gertrude for fixing a tap, or catching a mouse in the attic? So far, he'd never needed to ask. Whenever he'd finished mending something, Gertrude was there, purse open, and offering him forty or fifty pounds. Of course, Tom would refuse, occasionally suggesting a lower figure like a tenner or twenty. But Gertrude was adamant. In fact, whatever the job, her payment these days was £50. Tom's moral dilemma didn't exist, however. He knew that for his neighbour to get a qualified person in to do most of what he had done for her, it would be a darn sight more. Her large purse often contained a wad of £50 notes.

"By the way, Elizabeth, did I tell you that the milkman had his float stolen yesterday? His body was found in a back alley," said Gertrude before she left.

"Do you think we'll ever need to consider a care home for mum, Di?" asked Kathryn, Gertrude's eldest child, who was the manager of a health food store in Chelmsford called *Nature's Harvest*. Kathryn was phoning her sister, Diane, a primary school teacher who lived in Rush Green near Romford.

"I don't know, Kath. The last time I went over to see her she'd forgotten where the milk was – it certainly wasn't in the fridge – and there was an ice cream tub in the bread box. Thankfully it hadn't started to thaw and I put it back into the freezer." Kathryn sighed.

"I'm certain that if we suggested care for her, she'd blatantly refuse, and we couldn't do anything about that. But if things get worse, or dangerous even, we'd have to get together with Mike and talk about it." Mike Heseltine, aged 28, was the youngest of the three siblings, and he and his Thai wife, Pyong, ran their own kennel business, *Pooches*, in Brentwood. Mike had previously worked as a vet's assistant in the town, and Pyong had a certificate in animal care from the University of Bangkok. She had been caring for dogs in a canine rescue centre when she met Mike, who was in Thailand on a singles holiday seven years ago. He persuaded her to come to England and they married a year later which was when they decided to set up their business.

"Yes, that's a good idea," agreed Diane. "I know when Mike popped over to see her recently, she went out to the local Londis shop for a packet of digestive biscuits for them to have with a cup of tea. While she was out, Mike checked a couple of kitchen cupboards and saw at least ten packets of biscuits. I mean . . ." Diane's voice trailed off, a hint of exasperation in it.

"Maybe we should keep a diary, to plan visits. We could take it in turns to go over and see how she is and share anything out of the ordinary. Even use the diary as a notebook to record anything unusual?" Kathryn had made her point, and Diane agreed. "Let's leave Mike out of this for now, but I'll pop in soon. I'm planning to meet an old school friend near Basildon and I'll call by the house." So, the daughters ended their conversation, both happy that they'd keep an eye on their mother in the coming months.

Gertrude's slow mental deterioration hadn't been noticed by many. At the age of 81 people were expected to begin to slow down, take longer to get dressed, need to sit down more. But when Diane had noticed her mother struggling to use the TV remote to make a telephone call, and her mother getting anxious when the numbers she pressed weren't showing on the remote anywhere, the alarm bells began to sound. How dangerous could things become at home? Sometimes the oven had been left on, but thankfully it was electric, or bread had stuck in the toaster, potentially setting fire to the cupboard above it? At only five feet two, Gertrude had to use a stool to reach for many items above her, whether it was in the kitchen or bedroom, or elsewhere. A fall off the stool, a broken wrist or arm, and she could lay unnoticed for days.

Diane was aware of Mr and Mrs Ball who lived next door. Her mother spoke fondly of them, especially when Mr Ball had been in and mended a faulty switch, or stopped a tap from leaking. But to be fair, Diane had never really bothered with the neighbours. Maybe she ought to say 'hello' next time she was there . . . perhaps suggest that they be aware of her mother's activities without it being a burden, and giving them her mobile phone number in case of emergencies. Kathryn had placed a NO COLD CALLING sign inside the window of the porch in the hope of deterring any salesperson who wished to knock and sell her something she didn't need. Her mother's left hip was also beginning to play up.

When Diane had proposed the fitting of two white support handles on either side of the front door, Kathryn had poo-pooed the idea, suggesting they would be a magnet for anyone wishing to prey on the elderly. 'Come and knock at my door, I'm frail and old' was the message Kathryn had sarcastically stated could be put up in lights above the entrance. Diane felt like kicking her sister at the time, but agreed that it was best left for the time being.

4

"Gertie's been round, Tom. Says her boiler isn't working. She asked if you can have a look at it for her?" Tom's eyebrows raised. "I think she fancies you really. Suppose she actually altered something on the boiler on purpose? Made it look as if there was a problem when there wasn't?" Tom pecked Liz on the cheek.

"You've been reading too many crime novels lately. I'll have to have a word with your psychiatrist," chuckled her husband. "How long before the meal?" Liz gave him an hour's notice. "I may as well go straight round before I go and have a wash and get changed," said Tom, heading for the small utility room at the rear of the kitchen where he kept his tools.

"Have you had a good day?" enquired Liz, genuinely interested in what he'd been up to.

"It was all right. A couple of awkward customers over in Purfleet, and one in Epping who claimed he hadn't ordered some of the items on the invoice. But, you know, it's a job!" Liz grinned. His response was what she expected, and it seemed pretty much an average day for Tom. "Anyway, I'll go next door and see what she wants. If I'm not back in an hour, call the police," joked Tom as he went out of the back door. A minute later, and after four raps on the brass knocker, Gertrude Heseltine opened her front door.

"Oh, hello, Thomas. How are you today? What can I do to help?" said Gertrude, wringing her dry hands on an invisible towel as if she'd just washed them. Tom was taken aback for a second.

"Hello, Mrs Heseltine. My wife, Elizabeth said you'd been round to let her know your boiler isn't heating the water." Tom used Liz's full name as he knew his neighbour always did. It avoided confusion.

"Call me Gertrude. I've told you before! Now then, boiler? Hmm, let me think. Oh, yes. The boiler. It isn't heating my water. It doesn't make that whirring sound when I switch it on like it normally does. You'd better come in." Tom stepped over the threshold. This was the third time he'd looked at the equipment situated in the large kitchen, and he knew it needed replacing. Should he suggest it, or leave it? He decided to take a look first, then suggest to Gertrude that she invest in a new, more efficient boiler, avoiding any details about digital controls which would very likely put her off. He put his toolbox on the floor and then removed a screwdriver. In no time the front of the unit had been removed and the working parts exposed. He could see that the pressure dial showed a very low reading, and a lead had come away from the fan connection. A recirculation valve was stuck, and a joint was damp.

"Gertrude, I can see what the trouble is. Give me a few minutes and I'll get some parts that'll fix this." Tom looked in a plastic box labelled *British Gas*, a souvenir from his days working with Britain's biggest provider of gas products. He rummaged amongst the items until he found what he needed. "Here we are, Gertrude, I've got what's required to do this," said Tom as he began to strip part of the boiler.

"Required to do what?" asked Gertrude. Tom looked at her. Was she taking the mickey, he wondered? "Oh, yes, fix the boiler! Silly me," she added. Ten minutes later, the problem was solved. Tom turned on the hot tap and in seconds hot water was gushing from the spout. Not wishing to waste water, he switched it off quickly.

"There you go, Gertrude, job done. As much hot water as you want." She sidled up to him. Placing her hand on his arm she spoke in a quiet voice.

"You are a clever boy, aren't you, Thomas? And so handsome, too. I'm glad you live so close, it really is a blessing for me, now that my Nigel isn't here anymore." Tom eased away, slowly enough for it not to appear as if he was rejecting her friendliness.

"You're welcome, Gertrude. I'm always willing to help, you know that," said Tom, quickly glancing at his watch.

"Now, I must pay you, Thomas. Shall we say one hundred pounds?"

"Oh, no, it isn't as much as . . ." Gertrude cut him off.

"Nonsense. You've got my boiler going, and I'm very grateful. I won't hear another word." She took the purse from her handbag and opened it in front of Tom, making no effort to hide the contents. Tom couldn't help but see the wad of crisp, £50 notes. 'Bloody hell,' thought Tom to himself. Gertrude delicately pulled out two with her thumb and index finger, her nails manicured perfectly. "There you are," she said, slipping the folded notes into the breast pocket of his Corbett & Perkins uniform, then lightly pinching his left cheek.

"Would you like a cup of tea before you go? I was just about to put the kettle on when you knocked. I can pop over to the Londis shop for some biscuits if you like." Tom kindly refused.

"Thank you, Gertrude, but I must be going. Elizabeth said our evening meal would be ready soon." Tom felt a sense of relief as he closed his toolbox and walked to the front door.

"Thank you, again, Tom, you're so kind. I must get on. I've cotton to pick and potatoes to hoe," said Gertrude as she slowly closed the door behind him. 'Cotton? Potatoes?' thought Tom. What the hell is she talking about? He felt good to be out in the fresh air again. Breathing deeply, he went through his back door into the utility room and put the toolbox where it belonged. Entering the kitchen, it was time for him to clean up before their meal.

"Are you all right, Tom? You look a bit flushed . . . and there's a mark on your left cheek," observed his wife.

"Yes, fine. I just caught my face with a piece of reinforced tubing I was connecting on the boiler. It's nothing. I'll get washed and changed . . . be through in a minute."

"Did she give you the usual £50?" enquired Liz.

"Yes. Same as she always does," replied Tom.

5

Pyong had finished shampooing three of the dogs in her care at *Pooches*. Currently, she and Mike were caring for fifteen dogs, ranging from a couple of large German Shepherds to a miniature Chihuahua. At £24 per day full board, their income was pretty good, and it kept them at a comfortable level of living.

Most of their customers were easy going normal people, who were quite pleased to let Mike and Pyong look after their pets. But recently they had a guy called Mr Herring bring his Cavalier King Charles in and demanded the best care for it, including specialist dog food with added vitamins, and a daily shampoo. Herring was six foot tall with fair hair and blue eyes. Good looking in a 1950's film star sort of way. He'd pay cash up front, plus a bit extra for the dog food. Mike didn't take to him, but not wishing to get a bad reputation, or any negative comments on Facebook, had agreed to take the Cavalier King Charles for the ten days that Mr Herring was going to be away. He said he had some 'business to attend to,' which made Mike think of something sinister. The customer had sounded like a character from the film *The Godfather*. Mr Herring promised to bring in three packets of the special dog food that he expected Mike and Pyong to provide when he brought the dog in. He'd also spelt out the name of the medicated canine shampoo he wanted them to use.

Mike always asked the owners for their dog's name. It clearly helped in making them settle down quicker. He had to stifle a gasp, however, when Mr. Herring told Mike that his dog was named Carisbrooke. It was only later, out of interest, when Mike had googled that name that he realised King Charles I was imprisoned in Carisbrooke Castle on the Isle of Wight in 1647. 'It takes all kinds,' thought Mike over a gin and tonic that evening.

A little after 10.00 p.m. their home telephone rang. The couple were watching a crime drama on ITV. Mike looked at his wife with eyes that said 'your turn.' She got up and went through into the hall. A Basildon STD code came up on the phone screen.

"Hello? Gertrude?" said Pyong.

"Yes, it's me," replied her mother-in-law. "I'm using the phone box down the road. Can't remember when I last used one of these!"

"What are you doing in a phone box, Gertrude?"

"Well. I came out to buy some milk. I like a cup of cocoa before I turn in, and always prefer whole milk. I didn't have any in, so obviously I came out to buy some. Trouble is, the Londis shop has just closed. I don't where else I can get some at this time of night." Pyong sighed. What were they to do?

"Listen, Gertrude. I make my cocoa with semi-skimmed, then add a spoonful of honey. Do you have any honey?" Thankfully, she did. "It makes for a really nice hot drink, and helps me drop off to sleep in no time," she lied. "Now, go back home and lock your front door."

"Oh, you're a sweetie," said Gertrude, not intending to make a pun. "I'll go home straightaway and try that." She paused. "When are you and Mike coming to see me again?" Pyong thought quickly.

"What about this week-end? Say, Saturday afternoon for an hour. We can't stay long because of the dogs."

"Dogs? Have you got yourselves some dogs? That's nice. Nigel loved dogs. Bring them over with you when you come. Bye for now." Pyong returned to the lounge to see the credits for the crime drama drifting up the TV screen.

"Who was that?" asked Mike. Pyong gave him the outcome of their conversation. "She's losing it, isn't she?" Mike flicked the off button on the TV remote. "Do you think she's safe to be on her own?"

"Not really, but knowing your mother, there's no way she'd want to be in a care home. We can't force her to go to one. It would have to be with her agreement." Mike agreed. He pondered the situation.

"And do you know, as far as I'm aware, she hasn't made a Will." He ran his fingers through his mop of black hair. "Her and dad were independent in that respect. If anything happens to her, there'll be all the legal hassle you read about in the newspapers." Pyong sidled up to him on the sofa.

"Do you think we should brace the subject with her?" Mike rubbed his eyes with the heels of his hands, a sign of fatigue.

"I suppose so, but the best thing to do is for me to talk to Kathryn and Diane." He paused. "I'll do it tomorrow evening." Mike got up and held his hand out. "Come on, time for shut
eye."

6

After Tom had left for work that morning, Liz decided to take a look at their finances . . . work out just how much they had between them. They had a joint bank account for their day-to-day spending, a separate savings account each of them – making next to nothing in interest – a building society account that paid a slightly higher rate of interest, one hundred pounds of Premium Bonds, and an old Black Magic chocolates tin on a kitchen shelf where they put small amounts of cash.

Tom used to spend a few pounds each week on lottery tickets, but not having won anything for well over three months, he'd given up. His so called 'lucky birthday numbers' were about as much use as a chocolate fireguard. They both had a credit card, as well as their debit bank cards, but Tom was one who preferred to pay cash. He knew how much he had in his wallet, and how much he was spending. Liz, on the other hand, simply found putting as much as she could onto her Mastercard made life easier for her. Why pay cash when you could scan the card reader at the supermarket, or in the café, where she'd sometimes meet with friends? And now that the card cash limit had increased, it made things a whole lot easier.

By mid - morning, Liz had done her sums. She had access to Tom's savings account via an app on her phone, and she'd gone through the latest bank and building society statements. The final payment for the holiday to

Benalmadena had been paid. Without a car, there were no outgoings on insurance and fuel for that, or garage bills when something went wrong. Tom was able to use the Peugeot Boxer van as long as he didn't 'abuse the privilege.'

Their socialising was limited. Liz had what she called her Wednesday Coffee Club, when she and half a dozen girlfriends would meet at Costa's in the town centre to catch up on all of their news and any gossip. No babies were allowed, so there was no crying and screaming to interrupt their chat. A couple of the pregnant girls had dropped out over the last two years, but one or two had managed to coax their mums into a morning's baby minding. Both parties benefited from the symbiotic relationship – mothers enjoying their grandchildren, young mums getting a bit of peace and quiet for a couple of hours.

On most Saturday night's they got down to the Crown Inn, a Free House, a ten - minute walk from their bungalow. Liz enjoyed a brandy and pear cider while Tom considered himself a real ale connoisseur and was all for trying the different 'guest ales' that the landlord, Les, had to offer on a regular basis.

Liz felt that their life was much the same as millions of others, living more or less from hand to mouth. They'd struggled to save up for the Spanish holiday coming up soon, but both were eagerly looking forward to the break on the Costa del Sol. Her small income from the cleaning job supplemented Tom's wages from C & P, and they managed to cope.

But wouldn't it be nice to have a big bank balance? Buy a new car. She liked the new hybrid Toyota Yaris that her friend, Sylvia had. To be able to buy clothes from big stores like Marks and Spencer or M & Co - something fashionable, modern and chic. Maybe afford more holidays such as long weekend breaks to the west country, or the Lake District, and stay in smart hotels and eat the best food. Lobster with a glass of champagne had always tickled Liz's fancy. When she went on the amazon web site to buy something, which wasn't that often, Liz always went for the least expensive version. Her mother was the same, and would often come out with a saying about 'cutting your cloth to suit your coat.'

It was time to put the kettle on. Liz picked up a jar of own brand coffee, half the price of Nescafe, and scooped a spoonful into her favourite mug, WORLD'S BEST WIFE printed on the side. It had been a thirtieth birthday present from Tom. With her hot drink made, she sat on a kitchen stool and looked at the piece of paper with her calculations. The bottom line read £1,996. That's what they were worth. Less than two grand in total, but thankfully they'd now cleared that big loan. If there had been a mortgage to pay, too, they'd be struggling.

Liz's thoughts turned to their holiday to Benalmadena. She'd been to the local library, used a computer, and printed off the four e-tickets - two outbound to Malaga, and two inbound to Stansted. The tickets advertised food that could be bought on board, but Liz would do the usual – make sandwiches at home to take with them and a couple of cereal bars. They'd buy a bottle of water at the airport. Closing her eyes, she imagined she could hear the lapping of the seawater up the sandy beach as she and Tom lay sunbathing, two opened bottles of the local beer close to hand. Then she heard a bell, was it a ship out at sea? No, it was her front door! Liz put her mug down and went to see who was there. It was Gertrude.

"Hello, Elizabeth. Sorry to bother you, but I can't seem to find the switch for the electricity – you know, the one that puts it all back on. Do you think you can help?" This wasn't the first time this had happened. Liz had been around several times to re-set the mains trip switch, noticing that when she did so, several electrical devices came on at once.

"Morning, Gertrude. You've probably had too many things plugged in and switched on. Give me a minute, and I'll pop over," offered Liz.

"Did you know that the Londis shop closes at ten o'clock? It's such a nuisance when you need some whole milk, don't you think?"

7

"But it says on that poster that everything is half price this week!" Kathryn Heseltine was dealing with an awkward customer in *Nature's Harvest*. Dressed in a thick woollen suit and wearing a pair of brogues, her voice was getting louder. "Your so-called Senior Sales Assistant here tells me these lecithin capsules, and this apple cider vinegar, are not included!" Kathryn's training had held her in good stead over the four years that she'd been in charge of the Chelmsford branch. This woman, with a wicker basket over one arm, was just another customer who thought they could get one over on the staff, or even relish trying to make them feel small. Kathryn stayed calm.

"My Senior Sales Assistant has a name, and it's Jackie." She paused for a second. "If you had read the poster carefully, madam, you may have seen that certain items are not included. Those marked with an asterisk on the shelf label are *not* half price this week." The customer drew herself up to her full five feet, three - inch stature and stared at Kathryn.

"It isn't clear enough! I've been coming here for ages, and always been a good customer, but I'm going to have to rethink my health food shopping strategy!" *Health food shopping strategy*! That was a first for Kathryn's ears.

"Madam, let me point out those items are we have on offer this week. Would you like to follow me along this aisle and I can show you the items?" Kathryn held a genuine smile, refusing to be ruffled by this woman.

"No, I'm leaving right now. I've been conned by your shop, and I'm going to look for somewhere else to do my shopping, or even use mail order! The Scruples shop just along the High Street has a good selection of vitamins and minerals! Good day." And with that, the irate woman waltzed out of the store and turned left – probably towards Scruples, a value-for-money shop that offered mid-quality brands. She tripped as she exited the wide door, and Jackie stifled a giggle.

"She won't find lecithin nor apple cider vinegar in Scruples," said Kathryn to Jackie. "You win some, you lose some." That certainly turned out to be true. As she headed back to her office at the rear of the shop, three more women came in. They appeared to be new customers as they went from shelf – to – shelf, cooing at what was for sale. Later Jackie told Kathryn that the trio had spent just over £90 between them, and had promised to return.

Kathryn Heseltine was a single woman who lived in a penthouse apartment on Parkway. A woman of principle, who had her own standards of behaviour and ethics. Outwardly, she was an excellent manager, did her job well, and earned a decent salary. Her friends liked her, and the H & B staff respected her professionalism. But there was a dark side to her.

Kathryn had recognised the awkward customer as Miss Asa Briggs, who had always paid using her credit card. The local telephone directory gave Miss Briggs address as New London Road, Chelmsford. Kathryn recalled that Miss

Briggs had mentioned her new Citroen C1 in Pillar Box Red some months ago, of which she was very proud.

In the early hours of the following morning, a red Citroen had burst into flames on the front drive of a property in New London Road. The fire brigade had been called, and the police believed it to be a case of arson. The car was a complete write-off. The perpetrator was never found.

8

"You could always consider getting another job, or longer hours, Liz," suggested Tom over a pizza at the kitchen table one evening. Liz put down her wedge of Domino's Hawaiian.

"Tom, do you realise how much time it takes to do the washing, ironing, cooking and cleaning around here? Obviously not!" She sipped her water from the engraved tumbler, one of a pair she'd bought from a charity shop.

"OK, OK. But having gone over our finances, we aren't exactly rolling in it, are we? I mean, this Benalmadena holiday is costing us what we spend during the rest of the year!" Liz nibbled at her pizza.

"Yes, but we've agreed on all of that, and you know how much we love the place. Heavens knows, we could both do with a decent break, especially after I was laid low with that flu a while back." Liz had caught influenza, probably from one of her cleaning jobs, but she'd never had a flu jab in her life. She was off work for three weeks, feeling like a sack of porridge most of the time. Tom was scoffing his food as if it was about to be stolen. He always ate quickly, blaming his caveman ancestors who gulped their food down before it could be taken from them by a wild animal.

"Yes, agreed. You looked horrible for a few

weeks . . ." Liz gave him a threatening look. He got back on track.

"I'm looking forward to Spain, too. I hope the little bar across the road is still open. Aurelio and his staff do a great job there, and the beer is so cheap. I love the San Miguel." Liz concurred, but preferred the bars alongside the harbour, with good cocktails and better opportunities for 'people watching.' "And don't go getting too friendly with the other inmates. Goodness, that couple we met last time were like leeches. Couldn't shake them off for the whole seven days!" Liz smiled.

"They were all right. Came from North Yorkshire, she said. I thought we watched our pennies but he was tight. Kept asking 'how much' this was and 'how much' that was. When you're on holiday, my thinking is to let your hair down. That's what it's all about, surely?" Tom laughed and agreed.

"OK," he said, "we'll do that, and then when we come back, we must take a long, hard look at our savings and see how we can either cut back, or increase our income."

"Fine, but I'm not increasing my hours, Tom. No way. We'll have to think of something else." The front door bell rang. Tom noticed it was 8.20 p.m. by the kitchen clock.

"Who's that?" asked Tom in a slightly annoyed tone. Liz left the table.

"One of the girls I meet on a Wednesday wants to borrow the House & Home catalogue. I said she could keep it as I won't be using it anymore. I'll get it." Liz padded to the front door, one of her pink fluffy moccasins nearly slipping off.

"Hello, Elizabeth. I'm sorry to bother you, but do you think Tom could take a look at my television? I have to bang the top of it now and again to make it stay on. I think I need a new one." Liz sighed and turned.

"Tom, it's for you. It's Gertrude. She wants a word." Tom obliged. Minutes later he went next door. The co-axial cable on the back of the tv was loose, and the connector needed trimming, then refitting. The mains lead was loose at the plug. Tom had taken a few tools with him, and within five minutes had both aspects sorted. The picture and sound were fine, and it switched on and off perfectly.

"There you are, Gertrude. Good as new!" said Tom. She beamed.

"You are such a handy man to have as a neighbour, Thomas. Here let me get my purse." Gertrude shuffled off. Tom looked around the lounge at the four oil paintings hung on each wall, and the silverware in a display cabinet. The chandelier was glinting through the multitude of crystals surrounding the dozen small bulbs. "Here we are. Let's call it a hundred again."

Tom's eyes widened on seeing the wad of notes. She deftly pushed two fifty - pound notes into his left trouser pocket. "There you are, Thomas. You're a good man. Thank you so much." She squeezed his arm, before turning and seeing Tom out of the front door.

"Did you manage?" asked Liz. Tom nodded.

"Yes, easy peasy. A couple of loose cables. All sorted."

"And another payment?" Tom nodded and tossed a fifty - pound note onto the table. Liz grabbed it. "That's going into the holiday tin!" she said.

Tom slid his hand into his trouser pocket, fingered the other note, and smiled inwardly.

Northern Transvaal - November 1992

The day was hot and sultry. Nigel Heseltine wiped the sweat from his brow as he got out of his Plymouth Sedan at the Venetia diamond mine. The aircon in his American car wasn't working as it ought to be, and his shirt was already damp. It was 7.30 a.m. This was his sixth month at the newly opened De Beers mine. Having spent three weeks at the company's head office in Luxembourg, Nigel had been offered the position of General Manager, running the operation in South Africa. He knew there were things to learn, but he was an acute businessman with an MBA from Cambridge, and had a ruthless streak when it came to man management.

Two months ago, Heseltine had welcomed a new accountant, Pieter Vermeer, who was heading up the Finance Department at the De Beers office. Vermeer, a Dutchman who was single, had been working for the company in Namibia for the past two years where he'd done a good job. His smart accounting skills had streamlined the Namibia operation, and he'd presented the fiscal details, including future projections, at major De Beers conferences. He'd received praise from the company Chairman on several occasions. The problem was that Heseltine and Vermeer didn't see eye to eye on a number of matters, and the Dutchman was making decisions without informing his boss. Heseltine gave the accountant some slack for a few days, but today he'd called Vermeer to a meeting in his office at 11.00 a.m. Heseltine had asked Alice, his secretary, to hold all telephone calls for the duration of the meeting, and to make the coffee nice and strong. By 11.30 a.m. the two men had finished arguing, and Heseltine had given Vermeer an ultimatum. *Change your ways or you'll be fired.*

The General Manager had his own ideas on finance. His MBA degree had included significant emphasis on profit and loss accounts, cost analysis, and FIFO production. Vermeer's methods didn't show the Venetia Mine's business as well as Heseltine felt they could. And he himself was under the microscope, determined to prove that he was worth his salary of 100,000 US dollars, plus performance bonuses.

What had riled Heseltine was that Vermeer mentioned his strong relationship with the Chairman on three occasions, suggesting that he was safe in his role as Finance Director. The GM left Vermeer in no doubt that he didn't give a 'rat's arse' about his friendship with the Board officer. At that point, Vermeer strode out of Heseltine's office, his coffee unfinished.

Two days later, Pieter Vermeer's body was found in the Limpopo River, 32 km north of the mine. He was just beneath the water, wedged under the thick branch of a heavy tree that was stuck in mud on the river bank. The coroner's report stated that Vermeer had died from drowning. How he'd got to the river was a mystery. Tyre tracks found close to the spot did not belong to any of the vehicles that were checked by the police. The coroner's verdict was that Vermeer had taken his own life, particularly as a typed suicide note had been found in his office.

Whoever finds this note needs to know that I have found life too stressful and demanding. I have chosen to end it all by drowning myself. Pieter.

Colleagues said that they felt Vermeer had been under pressure at work, but many were surprised that he'd committed suicide. His handwriting was poor, so some assumed that a typewritten note was his best option.

So that was that. Nigel Heseltine had to appoint a new Finance Director as soon as possible. Martin Baker began work in that role within a month of Vermeer's passing. Baker was a friend of Heseltine's from his Cambridge student days when studying for his MBA, and very good with financial matters. They'd kept in touch since.

The only person who continued to wonder how Pieter Vermeer had come to take his own life was Alice, Heseltine's secretary.

She never told anyone about the argument between the two men two days before Vermeer drowned.

10

Diane Heseltine was writing a letter to the parents of William Smedge. William was in class three at the Sir Tasker Watkins Primary School in Romford. Three days ago, he'd been reported by a girl in his class for tying a piece of string around the neck of a white mouse being cared for in a cage, and leaving it hanging from a door handle. The mouse, whom the pupils had named Snowy, had died. Diane had spoken with William, who showed no remorse, and then with the headmaster, Mr Jones, who'd suggested Diane write to the parents. She would word the letter carefully, and show a draft to the headmaster before asking the school secretary to type it and post it first class.

Diane had met Mr and Mrs Smedge once before, at an outdoor school summer fete. They'd introduced themselves, Mr Smedge saying very little but delighted in showing tattoos down both arms, and his wife chain smoked. They said they were pleased that William was doing so well at school, or at least, that's what he'd told them. Diane knew this wasn't the case, and told William's parents that although he showed progress in some subjects, he tended to be a distraction in class. Mrs Smedge didn't want to hear that, and made her views clear that the teachers were to blame for William's behaviour. Diane had bit her tongue, the summer fete being not the place to have an argument that might develop after a comment like that.

William's teacher had changed the subject, asking about his life at home – hobbies or pets, if he had any. Mr Smedge chirped up that their lovely son had a Persian cat which had been bought for him by a doting aunt. William called the cat Bluey, because of the slightly bluish tinge to its fur. He also collected stamps, and he loved to sort through large packets of a mixed country selection looking for any that were triangular.

After a few minutes of idle chatter, Diane decided to move on, giving a pretend wave to an anonymous person in the distance that she 'simply had to go and talk with.' She excused herself from William's parents, and being honest with herself, was glad to get away. Mr Smedge's body odour was starting to become overwhelming.

So, her darling little boy was telling his mum and dad how well he was doing, was he? Liar.

And now there had been the 'mouse incident.' Diane wasn't going to let this one lie. The letter was destined for William's parents as soon as the headmaster gave his approval. Diane was hoping that he wouldn't make any changes. And he didn't. Mr Jones returned the handwritten letter via his secretary giving it his approval.

That afternoon the letter was posted. At lunchtime the following day, the school secretary entered the staff room to inform Diane that there was a telephone call for her. Diane put down a copy of Country Life magazine and followed the secretary to her office, where Diane then took the call on her own.

It was Mrs Smedge, asking Diane who the hell did she think she was, accusing her William of hanging a bleedin' mouse from a door knob? Her tirade went on for several minutes, using words like 'bitch,' 'asshole,' and 'swine,' at least once. Putting the phone down wasn't an option for Diane; it would have been a sign of weakness. She made an attempt to placate the mother, but Smedge wasn't up for a discussion. In fact, after the tirade, Mrs Smedge slammed the phone down to end the call.

Diane Heseltine was shaken. She looked down at her hands, and both were shaking slightly. Needing to pull herself together, Diane went to the Ladies toilet and rinsed her face with cold water before blowing her nose. Deep breaths . . . slow exhalation, and soon she felt all right to return to the staff room. Diane was going to keep this to herself, and not even tell Mr Jones unless he asked.

'How dare she?' Diane kept asking herself. 'That bloody woman had no right to talk to me like that.' For the rest of the afternoon, Diane remained calm on the outside, but inside her stomach was churning. She managed to get through until the close of the school day at 3.15 p.m., saying goodbye to all of the pupils in her care, including William to whom she gave a special smile.

An hour later, Diane was back in her terraced cottage in Rush Green, two miles outside of Romford. A strong mug of tea was her priority - a little skimmed milk, no sugar. She sat in the window, looking out across the open fields opposite, the mug warming her cold hands which still showed a tremor, albeit slight. The telephone conversation with Mrs Smedge replayed in her head. It was a long time since anyone had called Diane a 'bitch.'

But she wasn't going to let this pass without doing *something* about it. She thought of her father. What would he have done? Not taken it lying down, that's for certain. After finishing her tea, she walked down the road to the convenience store on the corner. Perusing the shelves, she found the cat food section.

"I'll take these please, Mr Patel." Diane placed the two tins of 'deluxe tuna' on the counter.

"Oh. Have we got ourselves a new pet, Miss Diane?" asked the owner.

"No, just for a friend," she replied and put a five pound note down. The till chimed and Mr Patel gave her the change.

After a tuna salad, and Diane saw the irony in that, she decided to go for a long drive to clear her head. It was late, but the roads were quiet at this time of night. She was home before midnight, and surprisingly, asleep by 1.00 a.m.

The following morning Diane was in the staff room early, sorting out some lesson plans and getting some teaching aids ready. The children began filing into the classroom taking their usual seats and looking around at each other in the expectation of an interesting school day. But there was one seat that was empty – and it belonged to William Smedge.

"Does anyone know where William is today?" asked the teacher. A boy sitting in front of Diane spoke up.

"Please Miss, William's pet cat has died. I called for him on the way to school and he was bawling his eyes out. His mam said she was keeping him off school 'cos he was so upset."

"That's terrible! Poor William," replied the teacher. "All right, let's start by looking at the world map on the wall. We're going to talk about America today."

Liz had made a mug of instant coffee for herself and a mug of tea for Tom at breakfast, two bowls of cereal had been eaten, and they'd shared a banana.

"Tom, do you have any idea where Gertie's husband is buried?" She paused. "It's just that one of the girls from the Wednesday coffee club went to the cemetery last week and saw a headstone with the name Heseltine on it. I'd mentioned Gertie to a couple of them, what with you going round to fix things for her. She couldn't recall the first name, but I wondered if it was her husband, Nigel? Didn't she say he'd died a few years ago?" Tom tossed the banana skin into the kitchen waste bin.

"I seemed to think she said he'd died in 2010, so, eleven years ago. It might be his grave. Anyway, I've got to go. Deliveries to load and all that. Don't work too hard. I'll see you later." With that, and a peck on the cheek, Tom left home.

As Liz washed the bowls and mugs, she remembered that Gertie had told them that she'd moved into the big house next door in 2012. But if they'd moved from Saffron Walden, Liz wondered why Gertie's husband would be buried in the Basildon cemetery if he'd passed away in 2010. Maybe they'd lived somewhere else in the town before moving to the current house? If he'd died in Saffron Walden, he wouldn't have been laid to rest down the road, would he? But as Liz, dried the pottery she began to think more about Gertie and her family. She'd seen two young women, and a young man with a female partner, visit her from time to time – and Gertie had told Liz and Tom she had two daughters and a son. So that must be them. But they'd never spoken to Liz, which she thought a bit rude. After all, Gertie must have told her children about the jobs that Tom had done for her?

One daughter had a Ford Focus, the other one drove a VW Polo, and the son and his partner owned a Nissan Qashqai. She'd seen them through her front window when they called, and the two gaps in the privet hedge allowed Liz to see what was going on along the front drive.

Perhaps the next time one of them turned up, she'd make some excuse to go next door and say 'hello' to whoever was visiting Gertie. Maybe say that she was going to plant some bulbs in her garden, and would Gertrude like to have some . . . or that she and Tom were thinking of putting a wooden fence up and would they have any objections?

Unbelievably, the following day, a Saturday, one of Gertie's daughters arrived in the VW Polo – in bright yellow. Liz stuck to her idea, and went out to say introduce herself.

"Good morning! I'm Liz Ball. My husband, Tom, helps your mother out from time to time. He's out the back mending a neighbour's lawnmower. How is she keeping?" Diane Heseltine walked around her car to the gap in the privet hedge.

"Hi, Liz. I'm Diane, but please call me Di. Mum's fine, but she often forgets things. I'm just popping in to see how she is." Diane paused. "Please forgive me, Liz, but I've been meaning to say hello for a while now. Mum tells me, when she recalls the event, that Tom has been round and fixed this or that for her."

"And do you have a brother and sister, Di?" Diane explained about Kathryn and Michael, and briefly mentioned their jobs. "And what do you do, Di?" Her role as a primary school teacher took her ten seconds to describe.

"Do you work, Liz?" enquired Diane.

"Only a cleaner, I'm afraid. Three days a week. Never got enough O levels to do anything as interesting as teaching." Diane glanced at her watch.

"Liz, nice meeting you, but will you excuse me. I need to go and see how mum is doing." Diane began to move away.

"Di, sorry, just one more question." Liz moved closer to the hedge. "It might sound a personal question, but is your father buried in the cemetery here? A friend noticed a headstone with the name 'Heseltine' inscribed on it. I wondered if it was your father?" Diane breathed in, seemingly taking a little while to compose her reply.

"In the cemetery? What here? Certainly, not! My parents got divorced ten years ago. He ran off with his secretary. They live in the north of the county now. The only benefit was that he left mum very well off."

12

Liz and Tom had arranged a lift to Stansted on Thursday with Gordon, one of Tom's friends from work. The departure to Malaga was at 8.30 a.m. so it was an early start. Working out the check - in time, and the journey, plus a little extra for hold ups, meant they needed to leave home at 5.30 a.m. Liz had spent the two previous days getting their clothes ready, laying them out on the bed in the spare bedroom, and making a list of all the other items they'd need. Cosmetics, jewellery, hairbrushes, underwear, bathing items, a couple of paperbacks, phone chargers, and so on. She'd taken that week off work, and Tom had finished on the Wednesday.

"You've done a great job sorting our holiday stuff out for tomorrow, Liz," said Tom over their light evening meal of baked beans on toast and two poached eggs. They'd decided to keep off the alcohol. Both were drinking water. Liz had sprinkled a few drops of lemon juice into hers to give it a bit of jip.

"Thanks. I think everything is in the big suitcase now, then we've got last minute things to go in our hand luggage. It's so long since we've been away that I've got out of the habit of packing. I've rolled up the T shirts and the cotton trousers. I saw that tip in a magazine – stops them getting creased." Tom smiled. His wife had her good points. "I'll take care of the boarding passes and the passports. I checked both last night and we've got another four years on them. And although our EHIC cards will soon disappear, we're still OK to use those if we have to. The government are bringing in another similar card, apparently, you know, all because of Brexit." Tom ran his finger around the rim of the plate, leaving almost no tomato sauce in sight.

"You can put that plate straight back in the cupboard," he joked. Liz gave him a look.

"Why don't you wash up this evening for a change. I'm feeling tired, and there's a programme on telly at eight o'clock I'd like to see." Tom obliged, collecting the two plates, cutlery and tumblers together and managing to get them across to the sink. He put the condiments away, then wiped the table. Tom was quite capable of some domestic chores, but, maybe through habit, had always let Liz do them. He had a good wife, and perhaps he could make the effort to do a bit more around the home.

"What are you going to watch?" he shouted, Liz now settled in an armchair in the lounge.

"It's a programme about Princess Diana, her early years." Tom groaned.

"Not another one! She's getting more publicity now that she's reached what would have been her sixtieth birthday, and she's been dead since 1997."

"Oh, be quiet!" Liz responded. "She was a lovely person who brought a lot of joy into this horrible world." That was Tom's signal to shut up. He'd finished the washing up, tidied around the kitchen, and went through into the lounge. Liz was watching the Diana programme, and Tom's best option was to zip it. He sat looking at the Sun newspaper, and attempted the general knowledge crossword with limited success. After yawning twice, he walked across to his wife, kissed her on the top of her head, and said 'goodnight.' They'd both agreed to an early night before the 5.30 a.m. departure tomorrow.

"I'll be up as soon as this is finished," she replied. Tom was pretty worn out after a long day at work. He was soon in bed, his eyelids heavy. As he lay there, thoughts of their holiday drifted before him. Sun, sea, sand and sangria. Great!

But he was also thinking about his account at the bookmakers, *Hightrack Express*. There'd be a whole week without backing a horse. Terry, his turf accountant, would miss Tom's regular bets.

13

Nigel Heseltine enjoyed his golf. At the age of 78 he considered himself to be reasonably fit, keeping in shape with gym membership and a daily workout on his expensive exercise bike. His second wife, Alice, didn't mind him spending half of his time at the golf club, which had a US professional this year, and a stunning range of malt whiskies in the bar. She had her own agenda. Lunching out three times a week, her painting classes each Tuesday afternoon, and the Audi convertible in Tahitian Blue gave her the freedom to come and go as she pleased.

Their five - bedroom house, called 'Jacaranda,' was situated down a long drive off the main road and gave them seclusion. The part time gardener kept the half acre of shrubbery and plants in good order. Nigel had a large greenhouse in the back garden, and would sometimes potter about with seedlings and nursery plants, just to see how they grew, more than from any horticultural viewpoint. To cultivate a plant with gorgeous, scented flowers to bring into the reception area of the house gave him pleasure, and he'd make a point of telling any guests that *he'd* grown them himself. The part time gardener's role was to keep the garden and greenhouse clean and tidy.

Nigel Heseltine had married Alice Evans ten years ago. Blonde, with high cheekbones and almost six feet tall, Alice originally came from Cape Town. She'd been his secretary when he worked for De Beers in South Africa. They'd stayed in touch after he left the Northern Transvaal, and she eventually moved to a village in Suffolk where they met up regularly when he was in Saffron Walden managing his own jewellery store, *Diamonds Are Forever*. Heseltine didn't think his marriage to Gertrude was what he wanted in life, and, being the kind of man he was, insisted on a divorce so that he could be with Alice Evans. Their three children weren't in favour of their father's proposal, but he was determined to bulldoze it through. He didn't feel, at the age of 68, that it was too late to make the change. Alice was ten years his junior and a had been a model in her younger years. She looked about fifty and still turned heads.

The Chief Constable of Essex, Adam Brightman, was on friendly terms with Heseltine. The police chief's wife had recently been given a ruby ring by her husband for their fortieth wedding anniversary, with a circle of twelve diamonds around the beautiful red stone. Locals said the ring was a gift from Heseltine, but when questioned by the press Brightman denied it and declined to answer any questions on the matter.

At the golf club, situated in Windmill Hill, the AGM was scheduled for Wednesday, 21 July, at which a new president was to be elected. Nigel Heseltine was well liked there, but the ex-mayor of Saffron Walden, Peter Dobson, currently in the role, could be elected for another two years. Nigel felt it was time for him to be given that prestigious position, with the reserved car parking space next to the main door of the clubhouse, where he could park his top of the range Honda CRV, and his name would be in gold leaf on the 'Club Presidents' board near the bar. The financial injection he'd given to the club for an extension to the changing rooms last year could stand him in good stead at the meeting. All he had to do now was be nice to people, persuade them to vote for him, and tell them what a good president he'd make.

But Dobson knew what he was up to, and the ex-mayor had many loyal golf club supporters; far more than Nigel Heseltine was aware of. That presented a challenge to Heseltine, a person known for getting what he wanted. The following weekend, he and Alice were away from the Friday afternoon until the Sunday evening, taking a break on the north Norfolk coast. There was a birthday party being held at the golf club on that Saturday evening, 29 May, for the retiring groundsman, Eric Somersby. Heseltine had left a retirement card for Eric, wishing him all the best, and a small silver model of a golfer in full swing. He'd requested for the club secretary to ensure that he presented the card and the silver golfer to Eric at the appropriate stage in the evening's proceedings.

Everything had gone well at the party, Somersby had received over thirty good wishes cards, and the silver model of a golfer presentation by the club secretary had been given a good round of applause. Copious amounts of beer, whisky and wine had been consumed, and some members who'd driven to the club that evening decided to order a taxi home. But some took the chance to risk driving, and that included Peter Dobson.

Dobson's car, a Kia Sportage, was found in a ditch half way between the golf club and his home, four miles outside of Saffron Walden. The car had left the road on a sharp bend and slid down the embankment. A passing motorist had spotted the vehicle at about 2.00 a.m. by which time Dobson's body was cold. Police asked for any witnesses to come forward. One had said that he'd seen two cars driving dangerously close together at about that time. He recognised one as a Kia Sportage, probably a light grey colour, the other was a dark coloured Mercedes Benz saloon. The two vehicles had made contact about a quarter of a mile before the bend, and the witness assumed both drivers may have been drunk and racing each other. He wished to avoid getting involved, and he'd overtaken both vehicles just before the curve in the road, but didn't use his rear-view mirror after doing so.

Essex Constabulary asked for anyone with any further information to contact them, particularly from any garages in the area that had been asked to do bodywork repairs to any large, black saloon cars. However, the following day, a stolen, dark blue Mercedes Benz saloon was found abandoned on a disused industrial estate, ten miles east of Saffron Walden. The near side was dented and scratched, with traces of silver-grey paint that matched the Kia Sportage belonging to Peter Dobson. The post mortem on Dobson had shown he was under the legal limit for alcohol in his bloodstream, and the police concluded that Dobson had been forced off the road by the Mercedes and died on impact when his vehicle had hit the side of the steep embankment. His skull was severely fractured where it had hit the top of the steering wheel.

The Mercedes was examined by Forensics, and several fingerprints were found on the door handle. A chewing gum wrapper lay in the passenger footwell, and a sealed envelope, which was found to contain £1,000 in used twenty - pound notes, was found wedged down next to the handbrake. On the front of the envelope was written the name *Jimmy* in large letters. Further tests by a calligraphy expert showed that it was very possibly a Mont

Blanc or Parker fountain pen, medium nib, containing blue ink, that had been used to write the name Jimmy.

Police now had something to go on. Who was Jimmy, who's writing was on the envelope, and who owned the pen? Were they Jimmy's fingerprints on the car door, and did he use chewing gum?

Perhaps a DNA sample contained from the envelope seal, if it was licked, would also provide a useful clue?

14

The hotel near the marina in Benalmadena was very comfortable. The bedrooms were a good size, and the bathroom full of extras such as body lotion and terry-towelling slippers. Towels were soft and fluffy. The hairdryer was efficient and quiet, and even Tom used it after his morning shower.

Breakfast was a free-for-all as regards at which table you sat, but dinner was a little more formal, and tables were allocated for the length of your stay at the hotel. As was the waiter. Liz and Tom were served their evening wine or beer by Manuel, a cheery Spaniard with a rounded belly. Tom was never certain if these waiters went over the top with their attention to guests because it was what they wanted to do, or whether they were making a play for a good tip at the end of your stay. Either way, Manuel took care of them very well.

Liz was determined not to be a beach bum every day, and wanted to visit Parque de Paloma in Benalmadena, as well as taking the bus up to Mijas Pueblo for a visit to the village of white-washed houses up in the hills. A bus ride to Malaga itself was also planned with a view to seeing the famous bullring and the Pablo Picasso museum. She loved outdoor markets, and every Saturday the 'mercado' was held on the car park of the Torremolinos football club on the northern outskirts of the town, a ten - euro taxi ride away. Once that was finished, a leisurely walk towards the seafront would let them drop down to the promenade for a stroll back to Benalmadena, passing numerous bars that served cocktails and mojitos.

On the Wednesday night, Tom suggested going out for their evening meal. They'd passed a nice restaurant called Francois El Capricho along the promenade in the opposite direction from Torremolinos whilst out on a walk. It looked clean, and the aroma of barbecued fish wafted in the air. A jovial guy with a large moustache had tried to encourage them to have lunch there on the previous day, but they'd walked on by. 'You try my fish, I give you free bottle of good wine,' he'd offered. When they returned the next evening, Tom reminded him of the free wine offer. Reluctantly, he agreed as he found them a table nestled in a corner with a sea view.

Earlier, Liz and Tom had used Aurelio's bar across the road from the hotel after their evening shower. He'd remembered them from a previous holiday and gave Tom a large beer instead of the regular sized glass, and Liz was served a double gin and tonic when she'd asked for a single. The ambience was perfect. It was a balmy evening, stars were twinkling, and soft music was playing from Aurelio's equivalent of *Alexa*. However, despite the offer of another round, they'd moved on to another bar on the way to their chosen restaurant.

It was now a little after 9.00 p.m. as they sat at Francois El Capricho and began with their shared starter of mixta fritura – a large plate of mixed, battered, deep friend seafood, served warm with a lemon wedge. Both felt happy and relaxed as they picked up the small squid, whitebait or chunky fish pieces with their fingers and savoured each mouthful. Twenty minutes later they'd finished, and asked for a rest before their main course came, the speciality of the house, a Valencian paella. The bottle of white wine was empty, and Tom held the bottle, tilting it to and fro several times to indicate that they'd like another. The waiter nodded. A minute later the cork was pulled from another bottle with a hearty plonk, and poured into their empty glasses with a characteristic 'glugging' sound.

"Liz, I've been thinking." Tom didn't slur his words, but neither did he speak as clearly as usual. She looked at her husband, her vision not as clear as it was three hours earlier.

"Hell. You don't do that very often," she quipped. "You'd better tell me what's on your mind before you forget!" They laughed in unison.

"Well, I've had an idea, but you might not like it. Let me start by saying that I was really surprised when you told me that Gertie was

divorced, and not a widow! Her use of phrases like 'he left me' suggested Nigel was dead!" Intrigued where this was leading, she asked him to go on, as she sipped her wine.

And with that opening line, Tom, during forkfuls of his paella, told Liz about an idea he had for both of them to become richer. But it might take a year or two.

When the following morning dawned, Liz felt as if her head had been through a washing machine spin cycle. Tom lay on his front, naked; his white bottom showing exactly where his swimming shorts fitted. He was snoring as Liz filled the kettle to make a brew. Two headache tablets were shaken onto her hand and gulped down with a glass of bottled water from the fridge. After a shower to help wake her up, Liz went out and sat on the balcony, a mug of tea in her hand. The sun had been up for an hour or so, and it was that tranquil period before other hotel guests began walking about, or the noise of crockery and smell of bacon emanated from the restaurant down below.

Had she dreamt it? Tom's idea to make them richer? She couldn't remember walking back to the hotel after their evening meal, and the complimentary brandy with coffee. The double gin and tonic at Aurelio's . . . yes, that was OK, Liz recalled that. Arriving at the restaurant, yes, and even the second bottle of wine. But after that . . . Her mind was a blank. Except for Tom's proposition. Was he for real? She focused her mind, and what she could recount.

Tom would continue to visit Gertrude when she had problems, and spend longer on each visit. He'd become more friendly, tell Gertrude that he and Liz were at loggerheads, and ask Gertrude if he could move in with her. After all, she had four bedrooms so it shouldn't be a problem. Eventually, when the time was right, he'd suggest that he and Gertrude could live together as partners, and he'd file for a divorce from Liz. The divorce was done through solicitors in their respective home towns, and not in Basildon. Liz was originally from Birmingham and Tom was from Wimbledon, south west London. However, all this was to be Tom and Gertrude's secret, 'their little secret,' and she shouldn't tell anyone – no one at all. Soon he would suggest that Gertrude altered her Will, if she had made one, but once again, nobody was to know. Their secrecy would add to the excitement.

Tom's divorce from his wife would be make-believe, and he'd go round to their place two or three times in the week when he'd tell Gertrude he had to go out for some reason he'd think up as required, but also to collect any mail. Tom knew that Gertrude's state of mind would allow him to do these things and get away with it.

Gertrude's new Will would leave everything to Tom on her death. She was getting on in years, and probably wouldn't live much longer. Tom would prime Gertrude so that when her children visited, she would just say that Tom was having marriage problems and was using a spare bedroom.

Yes, it would all be fine. Tom and Liz would just have to put up with the disruption, but it wouldn't be too long before Tom inherited Gertrude's wealth. After a short while, he and Liz would get back together, tell friends they were having a private marriage ceremony somewhere miles away, and start to think about moving to a big house and buying a really good car. They'd have holidays abroad three or four times each year.

"Good morning!" said Tom in a sleepy tone he had after a night of too much drinking and merriment. He'd stepped into his boxers and eased on a pair of flip-flops. He yawned. "Any chance of a tea?" Liz got up.

"Here, come and sit down. You look like the proverbial bag of camel dung!" Tom managed a smile. Minutes later Liz came back onto the balcony with Tom's tea. He sipped it carefully, then asked for a couple of paracetamol tablets. Liz got the blister pack of tablets and pressed two out.

"Thanks," he said, "for the tablets, that is, not the camel dung compliment!"

"Do you remember what you talked about last night? It started at the restaurant, then continued on the way back here." Tom flipped his tousled hair out of his eyes.

"Yes, vaguely. My plan to make us rich, you mean?" Tom sipped his drink. "What do you think, then?" Liz looked at the blue sky, the promise of another fine day on the Costa del Sol.

"It's too risky, Tom. It's illegal. And what will my friends say, and your workmates? Living with an older woman. There's almost forty years difference between you!" He smiled. "And do I tell my sister?"

"It's not illegal! How can it be? I think the story stacks up. We say we have our marital problems. I lodge next door in the neighbour's spare bedroom, the neighbour dies, she leaves everything to me in her Will. Job done! And . . . you don't tell Mary. At least not the plan."

Liz reflected on the weird plan. How long would it be before she passed away? What would people make of it? Would the police be asking questions? What about Gertrude's two daughters and son, what would they think of it? Suppose Gertrude lived to be a hundred! She would have to tell her sister Mary that she and Tom were getting a 'divorce.'

"Look. We have an opt - out plan. If after an agreed amount of time it isn't working out, we revert to plan B, and go away for a week-end to say we're getting re-married." Liz moved uncomfortably.

"I'm not sure about this, Tom." He leant forward and touched her knee.

"Listen, we don't have to decide just now. Let's enjoy the last few days here, and talk about it again when we get home. What do you say?" Liz sighed.

"OK, OK. But don't go doing anything without telling me first." He agreed, finished his tea, and stood up.

"I'm feeling better already. How's about a look at the breakfast buffet? I'm going to take a quick shower and then we can go down."

15

"Hello, Michael, how lovely to see you!" said Gertrude to her son who was standing alone at the front door. He'd kept his promise to call by and see how his mother was coping. "Do come in, please." Gertrude stood back as Mike walked into the hallway, then on through to the large drawing room. An oil painting of a stag on a Scottish hillside at sunset was hung above the wide fireplace. It had been a birthday present from Mike and Pyong for her seventieth, and it was her favourite picture of eleven paintings that she had in the house. "Tea, coffee?" she asked.

"Yes, a cup of tea would be good, thanks." His mother went into the kitchen while Mike took a seat. "Do you need a hand," he called after her. She didn't. He scanned the room, looking around to see if it was as it should be. Reasonably tidy, things in the right place, nothing needing attention like dead flowers or a mouldy piece of bread under the sofa. A pile of newspapers was laid next to his chair. He picked one up and looked at the date. 18 August 2013. He checked another, then another. All were over seven years old, and turning yellow.

Beneath the television set he spotted three remote controls. Why three, he wondered? Did his mother know which one was used for the set? On the sideboard were four framed photographs of the family, taken on holiday somewhere, but none showing her husband Nigel. Two of them were upside down, and kept in position with blue tack. Within a few minutes she was back.

"Here's your coffee, Michael, but I don't have any biscuits in. I'll just pop along to the Londis shop and buy a packet. Do you like digestives?
Or perhaps, ginger biscuits?" Mike sighed. He'd asked for tea, but would make do with coffee.

"Mother, I don't want a biscuit, and anyway, haven't you got some in the top kitchen cupboard?" She frowned.

"Top kitchen cupboard? If there are, I can't reach them. Who on earth has put them in the top kitchen cupboard?" His mother put the tray down, and Mike got up.

"Come with me. Let's take a look together." Seconds later, Mike reached up and opened a cupboard near to the cooker. There were twelve packets of digestive biscuits laid on their side.

"Look, twelve packets of biscuits! You don't need any more, mother!" Gertrude put her index finger under her chin and looked at her son.

"Well, who has done that? What a pleasant surprise. What kind are they?" He pulled one down.

"Digestive biscuits." She took the packet from him.

"I don't even like digestive biscuits!" she uttered. "Let's leave it, before your coffee gets cold." Prior to putting the packet back in the cupboard, Mike checked the 'best before' date. March 2015.

"Mother, these biscuits are out of date. They'll be awful!" She hadn't heard his comment. Gertrude was now back in the drawing room and sitting in an armchair.

"Now, tell me about your wife and your dogs. How many dogs have you got now? Is it two or three?" Mike explained that he and his wife ran kennels and at the moment were caring for nineteen dogs. "And how's your wife? What's her name, again? Ping pong?" He went on the tell his mother that her name was Pyong, spelt P-Y-O-N-G. Seconds later, she said she remembered that.

"Mother, why do you have three remotes for the one television set?" asked Mike.

"Just in case one doesn't work. It's always best to have more than you need." He groaned. Mike might as well save his breath about matters such as this. He pointed out the two framed photos that were upside down. She'd risen from her chair to take a closer look. "Gosh, you're correct. Fancy that. I wonder who did that?" The best policy right then was to leave the frames as they were. If he turned them the right way up, she may invert them after he'd gone anyway.

"Have you seen the man from next door lately? The one who comes in to do little jobs for you." Gertrude coughed.

"You mean Thomas. Yes, he was in last week to mend the washing machine. He found a plastic bottle in there. It had split in half and jammed against the rotating drum. I don't know who would have put a plastic bottle in there, for goodness sakes!" Was it worth Mike pointing out that it must have been his mother? Probably not. "He's such a good chap. Helps with all sorts of things. I'm lucky to have him and Elizabeth as neighbours."

After further conversation about the weather, Covid 19, Brexit matters, and the state of the Prime Minister's dress sense, it was time for Mike to leave. She moved to the front door with her son.

"Well, it was good to see you, Michael. Thanks for bringing the biscuits, and give my love to Ping Pong," she said as he unlocked his Qashqai with the zapper, the indicators flashing twice. He jumped in.

"What the hell are we going to do with you?" he mumbled to himself as he reversed off the block-paved drive after waving at his mother and blowing her a kiss.

16

"Hi, Kath. How are you?" Mike was calling his sister in Chelmsford. "Had a good day?" She'd not long been home, and was dying to open a bottle of Pinot Grigio inside the door of the fridge.

"Fine, thanks, Mike. Sold lots of vitamins and minerals to the folks of Chelmsford today. And four bottles of the new carrot juice we've just got in stock." Mike laughed.

"Carrot juice! Yuk! I don't mind a carrot, but drinking the juice!"

"I bet you haven't tried it, so until you do, keep those opinions to yourself!" She paused. "But you're not really calling to ask about my day. What's up?" Mike told Kathryn about his visit to see their mother. The next fifteen minutes were spent debating how safe she was to be living on her own in a big house.

"Well, I broached the subject of her going into a care home, you know, sold her the benefits, but you know what she said?"

"Go on . . ."

"Those places are for old people! Old people, I ask you! Bloody hell, she's over eighty!" Kathryn then told Mike that she'd taken a phone call from their sister, Diane, who'd told her that the neighbour, Liz Ball, had a brief chat with her recently.

"I thought you said the neighbour wasn't very talkative?" said Mike.

"Well, Di reckons she's all right, seemed pleasant enough, and her husband, Tom or Tony, does odd jobs for mum. Di also said that this Liz was asking whether a headstone in the cemetery in Basildon belonged to dad. Apparently, someone's buried there with the same surname as us."

"Huh, we know it's not our old man. I think he's alive and kicking and still with Alice in Littlebury. As you know, since he left mum, I don't bother trying to contact him." 'Nor me,' added Kathryn. "I think you and me and Diane ought to meet up soon – talk about mum, see what we think we should arrange for her."

"I think that's a good idea," replied Kathryn.

17

It was Wednesday morning. Liz was getting ready to meet the girls for coffee. She and Tom had really enjoyed Benalmadena, but she wanted to get her story straight before arriving at Costa. After their discussion on 'the plan,' both had agreed that this would be a good opportunity to begin to sow seeds in the minds of their friends on the start of the 'breakdown' of their marriage. Tom was going to mention a 'bust up' on their holiday, and Liz would do the same over coffee when the time presented itself. The 'bust up' was over Tom's infidelity – that seemed an easy and plausible option.

This was how the story would be told.

Tom had been seeing another woman who lived ten miles away, and on the way back from his day's delivery schedule, he was calling in and staying for 'more than a cup of tea.' They decided to call her 'Jane,' surname unknown. Just before going on holiday, Liz had found a receipt for a bracelet in Tom's pocket when she washed his jeans, and he'd explained it away as a surprise gift for Liz. He then said he'd lost the bracelet so couldn't give it to her. After accepting that to begin with, Liz grew suspicious, and late in their time in Spain they'd argued about it and Tom had confessed to seeing a woman called 'Jane.'

So, that was to be their tale. Stick to the script, thought Liz, and everyone will believe it. She didn't look forward to telling her sister, Mary, but for this to work, Liz knew she had to put on a BAFTA award winning performance. At Corbett & Perkins Tom would start to tell some of his pals about his activity, but keep it simple. He'd say he met 'Jane,' five years his junior, during a delivery to one of his customers where she worked part time on Monday, Wednesday and Friday. They got on well from the second he saw her, and she gave him her address. He called in a few days later, then it became a regular thing. 'Jane' wanted to be with him more of the time, and suggested moving away from the area. Tom told her he had to think seriously about that, and 'Jane' was happy to give him more time.

Liz put on little make up before going out, and squeezed a drop of lemon juice into each eye before quickly rinsing them. Looking in the mirror, her eyes were slightly puffy and reddened. Perfect. Liz and Tom had rehearsed the 'Jane' story, and talked it through the previous evening. Liz had commented that it must be like an author writing a novel, planning it out before starting the first chapter, then developing the plot as the book went on. To make things a bit more dramatic, Liz phoned one of her friends, Nancy, an hour before they were all due to meet, and told her in brief detail about her and Tom's situation. Then Liz planned to arrive at Costa at about 10.35 a.m., five minutes after their scheduled meeting time. That would give Nancy a little time to sow the seeds of the marital fall-out, which Liz knew she would do, and for her friends to digest the news before Liz arrived. An extra pack of tissues in her handbag was a necessity for added drama.

"Oh, you poor thing, Liz. Here, come and sit down," offered one of the girls at the table in the corner of the coffee shop. Liz sniffled just at the right moment, as if the film director had said 'roll.' Liz sat between Nancy and Barbara, tissue in hand. She wasn't going to overmilk the situation, and didn't want to be the focal point.
The girls usually chatted about all manner of things from the weather to holidays through local matters, plus some gossip on the side. So, she decided the best was for her to mention it to everyone, as an overview, and get it out of the way. There was her holiday to Benalmadena to mention, too, despite it being blighted by Tom's infidelity and their row over it.

There were seven of them in the café, and two of the girls went to the counter to order drinks. Everyone had the same coffee every week. Today the order was for two Americano's, three flat whites, and two lattes. Liz had recently taken a liking to a flat white.

"You don't have to talk about it if you don't want to, Liz," said Stella. She knew Nancy had 'spilt the beans.' Liz wiped her nose.

"No, it's OK. I've had time to come to terms with it." She paused for effect. "Talk about a bitter – sweet holiday! Gorgeous weather, a trip to Malaga which was lovely, super food and wine, and then near the end of our holiday it all comes out!"

"I can't believe it," added Joyce. "You always seemed such a loving couple."

"We are . . . or were. I just never suspected anything like this was going on. Anyway, I don't really want to talk about it now. I've chatted to my sister, Mary, and she's offered some advice,
but you don't know what it's like until it happens to you." Liz wiped her nose and eyes.

"I don't know if you need any legal advice on things, Liz, but my husband is a solicitor," said Barbara. There was a hush.

"Solicitor? Hell, you kept that quiet, Babs," chirped Stella after sipping her flat white.

"It's all right," replied Liz, "I've made a quick phone call to my solicitor in Birmingham, one I had used before I moved here. He's been helpful. I know that Tom has rung a legal bod he knows in Wimbledon where he's from." There was another pause, and Liz took the opportunity to change the subject. She'd said enough for all of the girls to know that she and Tom were no longer an item. Moira, sitting in the far corner with her Americano, and aware that someone needed to change the subject, chipped in.

"Did you read in the local paper that they're planning to build a new 100 bed hotel near the big Marks & Spencer store?" A couple of the girls raised their eyebrows as if to say 'so bloody what?' but it was an opportunity for the group not to get bogged down in Liz's marital trauma.

"Yes, I heard that. Who needs another damned hotel in this town?" said Phyllis, who'd recently had her hair dyed purple. "Still, I suppose it offers new jobs to the area." A few nods followed as the morning wore on. An hour after sitting down, Liz got up and made her excuses to leave. As she went to the door, Barbara moved alongside.

"Listen, Liz," she whispered. "I'm really sorry about you and Tom, but if you're thinking about a divorce, I can ask my husband how long it takes for these new style 'quickie' divorces to come through." Liz smiled but said nothing. Barbara took that to mean 'OK, go ahead and check.'

Liz suspected that once she was out of the café, the others would be talking about her. Fine. She'd done her bit for today, and the Basildon 'jungle drums' would begin to beat. All she had to do now was keep up the pretence. She couldn't wait to tell Tom what had been discussed, and Liz was keen to know what Tom's mates had made of it.

It was mid - afternoon when the phone rang. Liz wondered who could be calling at that time?

"Hello?" she answered.

"Oh, hi, Liz, it's Babs. Listen, I've had a word with Julian and he says a quickie divorce can go through in about three months if both parties agree to all the terms, etc." Liz thanked Barbara for the information and hung up. She finished some ironing, and then began to get the evening meal ready. Normally, Liz would have been tuned in to BBC Radio Essex at this time, but today the radio was turned off. The silence in the bungalow gave her time to think about her and Tom. At 5.40 p.m. Tom came through the front door.

"Hi, babes, how are you?" asked her husband. She looked at him from the kitchen and spoke in a solemn voice.

"I think we should get a divorce."

It was Sunday morning. Nigel Heseltine had showered and was sipping his coffee in their hotel bedroom whilst checking emails on his smartphone. Alice had risen earlier, and was putting the finishing touches to her make-up before they went down for breakfast. They planned to check out at around 10.30 a.m. and take their time driving back home to Littlebury. Nigel's phone began to make that incoming phone call sound – somewhere between a pig's grunt and a drunk playing a piccolo. It showed on the screen as Bob Atkinson, one of Nigel's golfing pals from the club.

"Morning, Bob," said Nigel.

"I don't know if you've heard, but Peter Dobson was killed last night. Some bastard apparently drove him off the road after he'd left the club following the leaving party. His car was found in a ditch off the main road on his way home." Nigel took a deep breath.

"Oh, my God! Was he drunk? Was his wife with him?" Atkinson went on to tell Nigel that he didn't think Peter had consumed much alcohol, and that Moira Dobson wasn't feeling well and had stayed at home. The police had been to the club half an hour ago to take statements from some of the early risers who were teeing off, and who had been at the party the night before. They had also mentioned that a stolen car found abandoned on a nearby industrial estate was very likely the vehicle that forced Peter off the road. "Anything else, Bob?" enquired Nigel.

"No, that's about it. Two of the Lady members are over at Moira's now, trying to comfort her. They don't have any children, apparently. Moira's brother has been informed, but he lives in Scotland. It's bloody tragic, Nigel!" There was both sadness and anger in his voice. Nigel took another sip of coffee.

"Is there anything I can do, Bob?" offered Nigel. Bob knew that the Heseltine's were away for the week-end.

"I don't think so, but let's wait and see what the two women over at Moira's say. They said they'd be back at the club by mid - morning."

"God, I'm so sorry to hear this news, Bob. Peter was such a good man. We'll be home later today. I'll come over to the golf club this evening." Bob said he'd be there until about

8.00 p.m. Alice had finished applying her lipstick and came out of the bathroom.

"What was that all about, darling?" Nigel was now sitting down.

"Bob's been on the phone from the golf club. Peter Dobson was killed last night, apparently forced off the road on his way home after the party. Police found an abandoned car on some industrial estate which they think was the vehicle that committed the evil deed. I can't believe it. Poor Peter." Alice put her hand on his shoulder.

"Yes." She paused. "What about his wife?" Nigel explained her absence. "Oh, I do feel sorry for his wife. Moira, isn't it? Oh, dear, that's put a damper on things." Nigel tapped her hand in sympathy.

"Look. Let's go and have some breakfast and then check out. We won't rush back to Littlebury, but I told Bob I'd have a run across to the club this evening." He gave Alice a reassuring smile.

After a light, cooked breakfast, the couple checked out of the hotel. Nigel paid for the room with a cheque, something he rarely did these days. Considering the amount of wine they'd drunk, and the liqueurs after dinner on both evenings, Nigel didn't think that £562 was too bad.

"Nice pen," said the receptionist, Angelique, as Nigel signed the cheque. He smiled at her.

"Yes, it is. A gift from a diamond mining company. De Beers, you know." The young lady met his eyes with a quizzical look.

Angelique thought De Beers was a brewery in Ipswich.

19

Once Tom had sat down and gulped a glassful of tap water, he began to settle. A divorce! The words from Liz's mouth had hit him like a karate chop. He was thinking of their discussion on holiday, and recalled that for this to work, they had the option of a real divorce or a 'pretend divorce.' The latter would potentially cause an issue if Tom married Gertrude. If he was done for bigamy there'd be a jail sentence for him, and the whole idea would be blown clean out of the water.

"A divorce . . . for real? Where did that come from, Liz?" She sat next to him on a kitchen stool.

"Well, I've been thinking it through, and . . ." she paused, "a friend of mine's husband is a solicitor. She mentioned it to him, not our plan, but about getting a divorce. She phoned me after talking to him, and I've been thinking about it." Liz carried on to explain her rational thoughts.

If they pretended to divorce, via fictional solicitors in Birmingham and Wimbledon, and Gertrude decided that getting married to Tom was a good idea, and he went through with it, any of her three children might make further legal enquiries. For Tom Ball to be accused of bigamy and tried before a judge, he'd get five years at least.

But . . . if they got divorced after Tom had moved in with Gertrude, he'd be free to move toward his main objective - marry her in secret, then arrange the Will so that upon the death of the first party, the surviving spouse would inherit the whole estate.

Tom and Liz had reviewed their timetable after they'd got home. Clearly, they wouldn't want to let this go on forever, so a time limit had to put on it. Liz proposed twelve months, but Tom proposed a year and a half. She had weighed up Tom's suggestion, then agreed it may be better. She'd see him when he called round, preferably when it was dark, and he'd always use the back door. Tom's idea was to cut a narrow gap in the fence in Gertrude's back garden, whence he could gain access from Gertrude's to his own home. Well, his 'former home.' A tall potted plant, a narrow bush or something, could be put in place to mask the gap.

But there was one thing that was troubling Liz. It nagged at her all the time, like a pressure sore that couldn't be healed. 'What if Gertie lived on to be 85, or 90, or even longer!' She couldn't go on living as a divorced woman for that long – hell, she'd be in her fifties! No, she would pray that Gertie would deteriorate quickly. Liz didn't go to church, but she asked someone 'up above' to forgive her for such an un-Christian thought.

Then she had imagined just how it might be, being a divorced woman. Her Costa coffee friends may want to introduce her to some single men that were pals of their husbands or boyfriends. On her three - day cleaning job, which she would continue, she'd met a couple of guys who were handsome and courteous in two of the offices where she worked. Suppose one of them asked her out for a date? No, that was out of the question! She told herself to stop having such thoughts. Liz had divorced Tom because of his infidelity, but she'd tell her friends, and her sister, Mary, that she still had 'feelings' for him. They'd call her silly, but she would shrug it off.

Liz and Tom hadn't spoken much about the 'secret wedding.' How would Tom go about that, she wondered? However, she'd seen such ceremonies on the TV news, and there'd be some 'certified clerk' somewhere who'd be only too pleased to get the couple to rush through the service, put on the rings, and sign a certificate, followed by wishing the bride and groom all the best for the future. Huh! Thanks for the marriage fee . . . next couple, please! It could be so 'clinical.'

Liz reflected on Gertie's wealth. Neither her nor Tom had any idea what she was worth. But after Tom's stories of oil paintings and chandeliers in her large house, and her divorce settlement from her wealthy husband, Liz considered at least a million pounds would be squirreled away. Maybe two million . . . even five million! Cash at hand, stocks and shares, investments, ISA's, perhaps even an overseas property they didn't know of? So, this then all became a balancing act. 'Risk versus reward' was a phrase she'd heard mentioned on a Martin Lewis money programme. If Gertie left Tom five million pounds in her Will, would Liz accept eighteen months without her husband? You bet she bloody would!

However, there was no guarantee with any of this. Between them, Liz and Tom had made assumptions with most of this plan. But then managers in business had to make *assumptions* about changes in the market, or trends in buying. That's how they wrote their business plans, wasn't it, thought Liz, who'd chatted to one Marketing Manager during her cleaning job one day. A rather dishy young man with a hint of Italian or Spanish about him. Jet black hair, neatly trimmed sideburns, a Rolex gold watch, and a gold tie pin holding his striped silk tie close to his button-down collared pure white shirt.

Liz had also considered the 'after – effects.' Gertie passes away, Will read out, everything to Tom, and a couple of months later, she and Tom are reunited. How would that sound with people they knew?

'It was planned all along...'
'A damned conspiracy, if you ask me...'
'How much? I'd heard over three million...'
'The bloody cheek of it...'

Could she live with that? Well, she could if they moved away from Basildon. The further the better. What about abroad? Start a new life somewhere...get their story straight when people began to ask about them at social events and dinner parties.

'How did you two meet up? What jobs did you have? What do you do now? Do you have any children? How did you earn your fortune, Tom? Blah, blah, blah.'

But Liz could handle that, for five million pounds she could. She'd learn her lines like an
actress and convince all of them that she and Tom were a lovely couple worth knowing.

"So, when are we going to make a start?" asked Tom, jumping up and going to the fridge for a beer.

"You haven't told me about your day. Any comments from the lads?" Tom pulled the tab from the can.

"I pulled Harry Phillips aside first. As my manager it was only right to let him know before the others. He was gobsmacked. Couldn't believe it. Of course, he asked what the problem was, and I said you'd found out I was seeing this other woman. I said her name was Jane who lived five miles out of town, but I didn't say where."

"What about the other employees at C & P?"

"Same thing. Thought I was joking. I said we hadn't been seeing eye-to-eye, been rowing, had a blazing argument on holiday and what have you. They all believed me. OK?" Liz nodded.

"Right. We'll find a solicitor and start the ball rolling," said Liz, with the smile of Mona Lisa.

20

Mike had received a telephone call from Mr Herring whilst the dog owner was away on business. He'd flown to Madeira, but strong winds in that area had resulted in flights being unable to leave the island for seven days. It meant that Mike had to purchase further supplies of the special dog food that Mr Herring had insisted were given to Carisbrooke. He was going to make certain that the cost of that, at £4 per bag, was added to the bill. Also, the medicated shampoo supply had run out, so Mike's wife, Pyong, had made a special journey into east London to buy two large bottles for the dog's daily treatment. In total, Carisbrooke had been looked after for seventeen days, but although Mr Herring had paid cash up front for one week's care, he owed Pooches payment for a further seven days.

Mr Herring had telephoned Pooches from Stansted airport on arrival from Funchal and told Mike he'd be there to collect Carisbrooke later that morning.

"I hope Carisbrooke has been well cared for, Michael," said Mr Herring over the phone, "and that he's had his daily shampoo and been fed correctly." How was Mike to reply to that?

"Of course, Mr. Herring. Better than the other dogs we have been looking after, I can assure you." He didn't feel guilty about telling a little lie. "He'll be ready and waiting for you when you arrive." Mike had glanced at his watch, then made preparations for the spaniel to be looking his best when the owner came to collect him. Pyong had given the dog a double shampoo wash, and used a hairdryer afterwards. His coat was good enough to win gold at Cruft's.

A silver-grey Tesla with darkened windows pulled up in the car park at Pooches a little after 11.00 am. Mr Herring, his left hand bandaged, strode purposefully into the reception area, but there was no one around. A bell, with a small sign saying PLEASE RING FOR SERVICE, was on the desk. He pressed the button. A melodic chime followed. In seconds Pyong emerged from the rear office, followed by Mike who offered to fetch Carisbrooke. Half a minute later, a tail wagging King Charles spaniel was reunited with his owner. Mr Herring looked at his dog, checked his coat and teeth, then raised the dog's eyebrows for an inspection of his big, brown eyes.

"Good," was his only comment. After a pause to take his wallet from his back pocket, he spoke again.

"How much extra do I owe you?" Mike presented the detailed invoice. Extra days, special food, medicated shampoo. Mr Herring glanced at the bill, and peeled off a number of £20 notes. "Here, that should cover it," he said. "Keep the change." Mr. Herring took the leather lead from Mike and moved to the door. He turned before he turned the handle.

"You've done a good job. I like that." He reached into his breast pocket. "Here's my card.
If you ever need anything, anything at all, give me a call." Mike took the gold-edged card.

JAMES HERRING
07977 150911

As the Tesla slowly eased away, Mike looked down at the notes in his hand. The invoice was £255. James Herring had left £500.

"I wonder why his hand was bandaged, Pyong? And I thought he looked a bit stressed, didn't you?"

Pyong nodded.

21

"Good morning, Gertrude. I hope I'm not disturbing you, but do you have a minute?" It was Saturday. 10.30 a.m. Tom's neighbour stood back to allow him inside. He turned as he walked into the large hallway. "I won't take up too much of your time . . ." Gertrude cut him short.

"Nonsense! After all you've done for me. Goodness gracious," she showed Tom into the lounge and pointed to an armchair. "There, take a seat. Oh, move that Tatler." Tom picked up the magazine and placed it on an expensive looking oak coffee table. "The kettle had just boiled. I'm making a pot of coffee. I can add an extra spoonful of the Kenya blend I normally buy." She waited for his response to what Tom thought wasn't a question.

"If it's not too much bother, Gertrude, that would be fine." He smiled.

"And the fruit scones aren't too long out of the oven . . . can I tempt you?" Tom nodded. A fruit scone! He couldn't recall the last time he'd had one of those. He and Liz weren't scone types. Two minutes later, Gertrude came into the lounge with a small tray bearing two cups of coffee on saucers, a full cream jug, two scones on a plate, and four pats of butter. Two silver knives lay on the edge of the tray. She placed the tray on a rectangular table between two armchairs, and passed Tom his coffee. It smelt good.

"Here, try one of these." She passed him a plate with a scone and two pats of butter, along with a silver knife. Tom had to try it, and hoped he didn't make a fool of himself when cutting the scone. He wasn't a big fan of currents or sultanas, but he'd have a go at her baking. It would be rude not to. "Well, what do you want to talk about, Thomas?" enquired Gertrude as she sliced through the still warm pastry. He cleared his throat.

"This is going to be difficult, Gertrude, but I hope you'll understand." Tom went on to explain that he and Liz weren't getting on at all. They argued frequently, had an almighty row on holiday recently, and she had found out that he was seeing another woman.

"She's got a large suitcase out of the loft and told me to pack my things. I'm devastated, Gertrude. On my meagre wage, I can't afford to spend much on accommodation, and I don't seem to have any friends that are willing to put me up." Tom took a bite of the scone. His first impression was that it was hard, and the currents were like tarmac chippings. He swallowed the mouthful along with a gulp of coffee. Gertrude seemed to be contemplating matters for a long time, as she buttered the other half of her fruit scone. At last, she spoke.

"Well, Tom, I certainly wouldn't want to see you on the streets. Not after what you've done for me. There are three spare bedrooms in this house. You could have one of them, if you like." That was music to Tom's ears. This was exactly how he'd planned things, but he continued to be graceful.

"I certainly don't want to be any bother, Gertrude, and put you to any trouble." 'Don't push it too much,' thought Tom to himself. He'd adopted a humble attitude, worthy of Uriah Heep. Gertrude put her plate with the half - eaten scone onto the table between them.

"Don't be silly. It will be no trouble at all. But what will Liz think? I don't want to make an enemy of her." A good question. One Tom hadn't considered.

"I'm certain she won't think any the worse of you. She knows that I can't really afford a B & B somewhere, and a hotel is definitely out of the question. No, I'm positive she won't hold any grudge against you. In fact, if you agree, I can tell her that *you* offered me a room here. What do you think?" Gertrude sipped her coffee as she looked at Tom over the rim of her cup.

"That's a good idea! Yes! Tell her you came round to tell me about your circumstances and I offered you a bedroom here – for as long as you need it." Tom slowly breathed out.

"Phew, Gertrude, that's smashing! I'm ever so grateful. How soon can I move in?" She got up to clear the crockery and place the items on the tray. Then stopped as Gertrude placed a hand on his arm.

"As soon as you like, Thomas. In fact, I'll go and make sure the bed is ready for you now, and tidy the room a bit. It will be the bedroom overlooking the back garden. There's plenty of space up there, and a little desk and chair if you need to sit and do any writing or anything. The orchard is looking nice at the moment, so the views over the garden are lovely." Tom thought she sounded like an estate agent, trying to sell him the property. He got up.

"Gertrude, you're my saviour. I'll go and pack my things and be back in half an hour."
Unexpectedly, she moved closer and hugged Tom.

"Oh, it will be so nice to have some company again." She paused. "I'm sorry about your marriage Tom, but I'll make sure you're comfortable here."

"I'll pay you my rent, Gertrude, you know, I don't expect to have the room for free. The divorce may take a few months so it would not be fair to be here for nothing." Tom was putting it on a bit, being the kind hearted, considerate citizen that he was trying to be.

"Nonsense! You are here as my guest! And that being the case, you will accept my hospitality!" He smiled. This was working so well.

"What about your children? When you tell them . . . what will they say?" She put the tray down.

"Now you listen to me," she said quietly. "I'm not going to tell them anything until they call to see me – which isn't often. No! Why should I? As and when they call, I'll tell them you're staying here temporarily until you get yourself sorted. It's none of their business!" Gertrude was adopting an adamant attitude that Tom hadn't seen before. "Now. Off you go, and I'll get matters arranged here. By the way, what would you like for your evening meal? I've got some salmon, beef and turkey." By now both had wandered to the front door. Tom reached for the handle.

"I love beef, Gertrude. But what about you? What do you like?" He was so thoughtful.

"Anything! I'm an omniscore," she chuckled.

"An omnivore, don't you mean?" Gertrude laughed louder, and acceded to the word she'd got wrong.

"Oh, hark at me! I'm sorry, Thomas, but you'll have to get used to my little foibles. I can see this is going to be fun." A few minutes later Tom was back in his own kitchen with Liz.

"Well? How did it go?" she enquired gently, a slight smirk on her face.

"Perfectly! She's offered me a bedroom overlooking the rear garden and even gave me a choice for tonight's evening meal! I chose beef." Tom pulled himself up, realising he sounded a bit pleased with himself. This wasn't quite how it was supposed to be. "Mind you, she can't bake scones. I had a struggle to eat one, hard black currents and all!" Liz sat on a kitchen stool and folded her arms.

"Listen. We've got to put an act on, right? So don't go getting all excited about things. We are both meant to be unhappy and distraught, so we must act like it. OK?" Liz was right. Tom knew it was all an act, and he had to play the upset husband who had been found out by his wife over his dalliance with somebody named 'Jane' five miles down the road. He also had to decide how long he would be seeing this 'Jane.' He'd explained it to Gertrude, so she was aware. Maybe Tom could use his 'I'm going over to see Jane this evening' as a ruse to pop next door and have an hour or two with Liz? Yes, that was the best thing to do. But he'd have to drive the Peugeot Boxer van away from the vicinity and walk back to his semi-detached bungalow. Gertrude had proposed that Tom leave the van on the large driveway rather than on the road – which made sense. It would signal to everyone that Tom was living with his neighbour, but that would add to the authenticity of the plan.

"Right. I've packed the suitcase. Everything you need is in there – shirts, undies, socks, etc., plus toiletries. You can always pop back in if there is something you want, I'm sure Gertie won't mind." The tone of Liz's voice then altered. "I'm phoning my solicitor first thing Monday morning to file for divorce on the grounds of infidelity. Might as well get the ball rolling on this. I'll check first with my friend Barbara, whose husband is a solicitor, whether the name of the 'other woman' is required. If so, what shall we say?" Tom took Liz's hand.

"Let me see . . . what about Jane Parton? After Dolly. She's one of my favourite country music singers after all. Sounds all right, doesn't it?" Liz removed her hand.

"Please yourself. She's your 'bit on the side.' But we need to get this done as quickly as possible. The sooner it's all over, the better." Liz sounded upset. Tom put his arms around her.

"Listen, babes. We've talked this through. It's going to work. It won't be long before we've got a few million in the bank and we can really start to enjoy life. There's nothing to worry about. Trust me."

22

There were over fifty mourners at the funeral of Peter Dobson. The service was being held at St. Barnabas church, and the presiding minister was the Rev Jacob Clarkson M.A. D.D. Moira Dobson, Peter's wife, was being supported physically and morally by her only son, Dominic. Nigel Heseltine had decided to attend, and brought his wife, Alice. She didn't know Dobson very well, but Nigel had to show they both wanted to pay their last respects. He was a senior member of the golf club, after all. After parking their Honda CRV one hundred yards along the road from the church entrance they slowly walked back toward the wooden gates beneath a stone archway.

Everyone was dressed in black. The coffin was carried into the church by six bearers from Scotstow and Co., the local funeral directors. The church organist, Harry Wigham, was playing a classical piece that the Heseltine's did not recognise. It didn't matter, of course, but it fitted the sombre mood of the occasion. Nigel thought he might have been asked to say a few words, but the request didn't come. It was probably for the best, he thought to himself, as finding the right thing to say would have been a challenge. He'd have to put on his best acting skills.

Rev Clarkson opened by welcoming everyone. Hymns were limited to two and a female singer had been appointed to warble from the front with a microphone. Dominic Dobson spoke the eulogy, and said kind things about his father. A family friend stood for two minutes to add his personal memories and say what a good chap Peter Dobson had been.

Heseltine looked around at the gathered assembly. There were a few he didn't recognise, including two sombre looking men on the back row, both with short hair and clean shaven. One seemed to be wearing an earpiece. Either that, or he was a plain clothes police officer.

After *Abide with Me* and *Amazing Grace*, followed by *What a friend we have in Jesus* by the soprano, a final prayer was said and mourners began to leave the church, starting with the front row and working backwards. Clarkson reminded people of the collection box at the rear of the church in aid of Cancer Research UK, a request from Moira. He also, slyly, mentioned the other collection tray in aid of church restoration funds.

"Church restoration funds my backside!" whispered Nigel Heseltine to his wife. She shushed him. He nodded to several of the mourners as they went out into the bright afternoon sunshine, and made a point of speaking to Moira.

"I was very sorry to get the news about Peter. He was a good man, and I know members of the golf club are going to miss him dreadfully. He did so much for the club." Moira said nothing, but used a damp hankie to wipe her eyes. Before Heseltine could say any more, Moira walked away with Dominic by her side. Other mourners were quick to briefly give their condolences to the widow, who soon was talking with the Rev Clarkson. The wake, as expected, was to be held at the golf club, and wishing to get a decent parking space, Heseltine suggested to Alice that they drive there rather than hang about at the church.

Some mourners began to drift away, apart from the two 'short haircuts' who were standing with their backs to a large oak tree on the east side of the church and seemed to be taking it all in. Being inquisitive, Heseltine waited for the right moment before approaching Rev Clarkson.

"Excuse me, vicar, but do you know who the two gentlemen are over there? I don't recall ever seeing them at the golf club." The vicar, who must have been at least six foot three inches tall, leant forward slightly. He spoke quietly.

"Essex CID. They asked me if it was all right to attend the service, and of course it was." Clarkson then turned around to survey the remaining people in the churchyard who were decreasing by the minute. Heseltine looked at his wife and nodded toward their car.

"Let's go, dear, before the hoards get to the buffet first. Sylvia puts on a good spread at the club and I'm feeling peckish."

Twenty minutes later, with most of the mourners now standing around in the club lounge, drink in hand, Heseltine noticed the two detectives. One was standing at the end of the bar, the other over in the far corner at the window overlooking the eighteenth hole. Each had what looked like a glass of orange juice in their hands. Heseltine was tempted to speak to one of them. Ask them what a detective was doing loitering at a wake? He turned to Alice.

"What do you think those guys are doing here?" She shrugged.

"No idea. They could be keeping a watch over proceedings, make sure a fight doesn't break out!" Alice chuckled. Heseltine ignored the comment as he sipped his white wine.

"But don't you think it's odd. Two coppers hanging about. I mean, what are they looking for?" Alice didn't have an answer. It could be for a number of reasons, she thought, but then began to wonder why her husband was looking a little anxious.

"Why don't you leave it, darling. There's nothing to be gained by getting yourself all hot and bothered about it, is there? Look, people are beginning to get plates for the buffet. Let's get something to absorb the alcohol and find a seat." Heseltine realised his wife was right. Why was he letting the anxiety interfere with the Wake? He had an objective, and that was to subtly begin to mention the forthcoming annual general meeting and start to let everyone know what a good president he'd make if elected. Perhaps now wasn't a good idea? He'd be criticised for being insensitive and uncaring, and that would never do for the new President of Saffron Walden Golf Club.

An hour and a half later, the lounge was almost empty as mourners drifted away. Moira and Dominic remained, with a few wanting to say their last words to her . . . 'and if there is anything I can do, Moira.'

The Heseltine's were about to get into their Honda CRV when Nigel heard a voice behind him.

"Excuse me, sir. Do you have a minute?"

23

"Come on in, Thomas," said Gertrude with a welcoming sweep of her hand. "Go right through. Your room is at the top of the stairs, the one with the tile on the door showing an iris. You may as well take your case up now." Tom heaved the heavy suitcase up the thickly carpeted flight of stairs until he reached the landing. He rested for a few seconds before opening the door.

Inside the room was bright and airy, with heavy curtains held back with a tie at each side. Tom walked over to the window and looked down onto the small apple orchard. A stout wooden fence at least six feet tall ran along the back of the garden, with one corner set to decking and the other with a tall pergola, overgrown with climbing roses. Tom opened the case and began to unpack. A wide wardrobe contained sufficient hangers for his clothes, and a set of six drawers would be ample for his underwear, socks, etc. A dressing table in front of the window held a wide mirror, and there was plenty of room for his hairbrush and comb, deodorants, aftershave, and odds and sods such as nail scissors, nail file and a pair of tweezers. Gertrude had already told Tom that there was an adjacent bathroom for his exclusive use, and in there he'd leave his shower gel, shampoo, toothbrush and toothpaste, as well as the towels that Liz had packed. One thing that Tom couldn't see was a television. He'd have to fix that. He honestly didn't think he could sit in the lounge with Gertie every night, especially if she wanted to watch programmes like 'Strictly' or the 'X-Factor.'

Ten minutes later, sitting on the bed, he felt as if he were on holiday. He was in a hotel room with the bathroom next door, and about to spend a week relaxing and looking forward to a break from routine. But his daydream was broken with a sharp rap on the door.

"Thomas, I've made a pot of tea, but I'm just going over to get a packet of biscuits from the shop. Come down when you're ready and I'll be back in a few minutes." Rather than a hotel, Tom now felt he was in a boarding house, with a landlady telling him tea was ready whether he wanted it or not. He knew that for a while he would go along with almost anything that Gertie suggested. He had to. This was a medium - term plan, and he had to pace himself. There was no need to make any quick decisions on anything, and he was the guest for the moment at least. In time he'd begin to dominate the situation, in a nice pleasant manner. For now, he'd go along with what she proposed.

Then he heard the front door bell. Had Gertie come back, yet? Who was at the door? Blast! He might have some explaining to do if it was any members of her family? Please God. Tom opened the door.

"Hello, Thomas," said Gertrude, "I'd forgotten my key. Silly me! Right, let's get that tea poured and I'll open these biscuits." Tom wondered how forgetful Gertie might be? "Now most men like chocolate, so I decided on chocolate digestives. They're the best type, you know. I don't buy rubbish, Thomas. Not those cheap ones from foreign supermarkets." Five minutes later, Tom was again sitting in the lounge with a cup of tea and a plate of biscuits. He'd have to get used to this, but he already knew the waiting game was going to be worth it. He'd tell Gertie that he had to go out to see somebody, including 'Jane,' from time to time, and be meeting up with his pals down the pub. He just hoped that Gertie wasn't going to be overly possessive – want him home every evening. He couldn't be doing with that. At least, not for a while.

An hour later, up in his room, Tom sat on a wing chair in the corner and put his feet up on a leather stool. He opened his phone and checked for emails, and then Facebook. There were three WhatsApp messages, one of which was from Liz.

I hope you're being a good little boy for Auntie Gertie!

He decided not to reply just yet. He'd do it before he went to bed, then he'd have some news for her on the evening's events, including the meal which promised to be beef. Tom wondered if she was a good cook? Living on her own might mean she only spent minutes preparing meals, or maybe she had them delivered during the week? Was she with *Meals on Wheels* or another one of these meal-delivery companies? And how did she do her shopping, he wondered? Tom couldn't recall seeing any of the big supermarket delivery vans stopping there, and she was too frail to be humping bags of shopping from Morrison's down the road. Not to worry, things like this would all become evident as the days and weeks went on. It would be an interesting time.

Tom checked Messenger on his phone. There was a reply from his bookmaker, Terry. Tom had asked about his turf account. He'd enquired as to how much credit he had. Tom had set up the account so that any winnings on the horses were left to accumulate. He was getting piddling amounts of interest with his bank, so he decided it was as easy to let the winnings grow with *Hightrack Express*. He looked at the message.

Hi Tom, you've got £17,492 in the account. Keep smiling. Regards, Terry.

'Not bad,' thought Tom. 'And Liz knows nothing about it. Well, I don't have to tell her *everything*, do I?' he said to himself.

24

"Hey, Pyong, I've just seen a news snippet on the laptop. You know, one of those daily newspaper ones that flash up in the bottom right - hand corner from time to time." Mike was scooping up the remains of the milk from his bowl of breakfast cereal.

"What this time? News on the Sussex's in California? No, don't tell me, more news on Brexit?" Mike's Thai wife had a sense of humour that could be wicked at times.

"No! A murder on the island of Madeira. Some wealthy businessman, allegedly with Sicilian mafia connections, was murdered in his own home in Santa Cruz. It doesn't say why, except that he allegedly he owed a lot of money to some cartel." Pyong gave a slight huff.

"Huh. It's happening all the time. That's not news. He was probably involved with drugs or gambling. These mafia types, they get mixed up in all sorts of illegal rackets. You know what they say. "He who lives by the sword…"

"Dies by the sword." Mike finished the proverb for her.

"How was he killed? Does it say?" she asked. Mike scanned the news article quickly.

"Strangulation, apparently. Bruising on the neck." He paused as he looked at Pyong. "Hmm. Nice and quiet. No blood so not messy. Just takes a little time to block the airways, the person dies from lack of oxygen." She put the teapot down.

"Don't look at me like that," she added quickly, "I hope you're not getting any ideas! Who'll clean out all the kennels if you got rid of me?"

"I'd have to get an assistant in, wouldn't I?"

The wet dishcloth missed Mike's head by a few inches. He rushed out of the kitchen before any other missiles came his way.

25

Nigel Heseltine had his hand on the car door handle, about to open the Honda. He turned to face one of the two men that he'd seen at the funeral service and the Wake. One of them spoke.

"Mr Heseltine? Nigel Heseltine?" Heseltine nodded and said 'yes.' "I'm Detective Inspector Sandy Matthews and this is Detective Sergeant Chris Hayman from Saffron Walden CID. I wonder if we can have a quick word in our car, sir?" Heseltine looked at his wife. "It won't take long, sir." Heseltine gestured for Alice to get into the passenger seat.

"I won't be long, Ali. Hop in and put the radio on." Alice eased into the front and closed the door with a satisfying clunk. Heseltine turned to follow the DI across the car park to an unmarked BMW 320 police car. He was praying that nobody had seen him get into the back seat, especially with the DS holding the door for him, but if they had it was simply a case of 'helping the police with their enquiries.' DI Matthews sat in the back seat of the BMW, the lowered armrest between him and Heseltine. The DS got into the driver's seat.

"Mr Heseltine, we want to know about your relationship with Peter Dobson. Did you get on well?" Heseltine eased himself toward the detective.

"Absolutely. We got on very well together. He and his wife, Moira, are on our Christmas card list. My wife, Alice, also sends Moira a birthday
card each year. August 21st." Heseltine paused. "What's this all about, Inspector?"

"Well, sir, we've questioned a few guests who were at the leaving party for the groundsman, Eric Somersby, and some say you and Mr Dobson didn't always see eye to eye. Apparently, there's an AGM coming up in a couple of months. At that meeting, the new club president will be elected. Is that correct?" Heseltine swallowed.

"That is correct, Inspector. It's the golf club policy to elect a new president at the AGM every other year, and the president has a tenure for a maximum of four years. I would have thought Peter Dobson would have stood a good chance of being re-elected this time round."

"And were there any differences between you?"

"We debated some aspects of how the club ought to be run. The appointment of the club professional, the catering and use of the bar for non - members, extension of the car park . . . that sort of thing. Nothing untoward, really." The detective looked at his note book.

"Some members we questioned say you deliberately avoided the leaving party. What do you say to that?" Heseltine coughed.

"Nonsense. I'd booked a room at the Links Country Park Hotel in Cromer some weeks before the date for the party was decided. We felt like a break and we enjoy that part of Norfolk." Matthews checked his notes again.

"Do you know anyone named Jimmy?" Heseltine frowned.

"Jimmy? Jimmy Tarbuck, Jimmy Anderson, Jimmy Jewell . . .?" The DI asked the question again, adding the word 'personally.'

"No, I don't. Where's this leading, Inspector. Am I supposed to know a Jimmy?"

"We'd like you to come down to the station during the next 24 hours, if you don't mind. Just for a routine DNA check. A swab taken from the inside of your mouth – nothing more than that. We'll leave it there for now, sir," replied the detective, opening the car door. The sergeant walked round to the passenger side and Heseltine followed suit, smoothing his jacket downwards after feeling cramped in the police car.

"What did they want, darling?" asked Alice as her husband closed the car door heavier than usual.

"Bloody coppers!" He looked at the BMW as it drove away. "Asking me how I got on with Dobson! For goodness sakes, what have some club members been saying to the police? The DI even implied that we avoided the leaving party for Eric. How ridiculous!" Alice put her hand on his left knee.

"Don't go upsetting yourself," she said soothingly.

"They also want me to call into the police station for a saliva swab, and they asked if I knew somebody named Jimmy!" She squeezed his leg gently.

"And did you tell them you did?"

"Of course, I bloody didn't, and you'll keep your mouth shut, too."

26

Tom had fitted the new television in the corner of his room, and was grateful for the tv aerial point next to the double socket. The picture and sound were both clear, and the remote control easy to use. At least now he'd be able to spend some time in his room watching his favourite programmes without having to sit with Gertie in the lounge, although he didn't want to be a hermit, however. If his plan was to work, he'd need to become 'more friendly' with her as time went by.

One thing they hadn't discussed was the laundering of Tom's clothes. Washing and ironing his shirts. Underwear and socks. Or did Gertie expect him to trudge off down to one of the few laundromats in Basildon? He could suggest that he took them back to Liz for her to do, but that would defeat the object in making it clear that the two of them were no longer an item.

"Gertrude, do you think you'd be able to help me with my washing – clothes that is?" asked Tom over a quick breakfast on the first Monday morning after he'd moved in. A bowl of Gertrude's favourite muesli was in front of him, the minimum amount of soya milk in the bowl, along with a mug of tea. He'd buy his own cereal later on the way back from work. He wasn't one for a mixture of what looked like hamster food.

"Of course! I was going to mention that. I can still use a washing machine and an iron, you know! There's a laundry basket in your bathroom. Anything to be washed can go in there, and I'll do it on a Monday. Then, if you don't mind, when I've ironed your shirts, I'll put them on hangers and place them in your wardrobe. How does that sound?" Tom scooped up the last of the cereal and then finished his drink.

"Great! If you don't mind . . ." Gertie smiled at him, Tom noticing for the first time that she still had her own teeth. White, but not perfect, like a set of dentures would have been. She added a consolatory comment about being separated from Liz and how difficult that must be for him. Tom excused himself from the breakfast table. He didn't want to be late for work, nor sit chatting about the intricacies of laundry. He said goodbye to Gertie and went out to his van. Glancing across to the semi-detached bungalow, Liz was nowhere to be seen. Tom turned on the engine of the Peugeot Boxer van and eased off the drive.

On the Saturday, Tom had phoned his manager, Harry Phillips to let him know that he had moved out and was temporarily residing with a neighbour. An elderly divorced lady who lived on her own. Harry hadn't said much. On the way to C & P he thought through all of the ribbing he'd get at work. There'd be some cynical comments, as well as cheeky ones, but he'd be able to handle them. He'd paint a positive picture, tell the truth mostly, but add a few fibs here and there, dependent on what was thrown at him. He'd start by saying it was a temporary arrangement, just until he found somewhere else, but after a few weeks or months, would move to 'well, she says I can stay as long as I like and she is good company.'

The day went as Tom expected. He maintained a fairly sombre attitude but managed to take the ribbing from his work mates. He knew that by the end of the first week all of the banter would have subsided . . . and that was how it turned out. Some good pals said they were very sorry it had come to this, and they looked forward to a pint down at the local anytime he fancied one.

Tom was back at the big house by six o'clock on Monday, reversing the van onto the drive. It was now becoming normal for him to do it, and not having to park out on the road was a bonus. He'd stopped off at Tesco to do some shopping for two main reasons. He didn't want Gertie thinking he was sponging off her, and he had his own preferences for food and hot drinks. In his shopping bag were two boxes of Coco Pops, a large jar of Tesco's own - brand Colombian coffee, three packets of bourbon biscuits, a six pack of lager, and two kilos of apples. Tom loved apples, and as he'd picked up the bag on the fruit display, he realised he hadn't seen any fruit at all in Gertie's house. Not one orange, banana, apple, or pear.

Tom had been given a front door key, with Gertie telling him he could come and go as he pleased. Letting himself in, he called out 'Hello, Gertrude.' There wasn't any reply. More loudly he shouted the same greeting. Nothing. Not to worry. Perhaps she'd popped out to the Londis store for something. Tom put the shopping bag down on the kitchen floor and decided to put his Tesco items away in one of the cupboards. He was certain Gertie would not mind. He opened a large, head - height door and peered in.

Tom counted eighteen packets of digestive biscuits, nine cartons of muesli, eleven tins of peaches, fourteen cans of baked beans and twenty - one packs of cream crackers. And as if that wasn't bad enough, Tom checked the 'Best Before End' dates. Everything was beyond its BBE! He could not believe it! Was Gertie going to be feeding him any of this stuff? He closed the cupboard door and rested his back against the work top. 'Bloody hell,' he thought. 'I knew she was losing it, but . . .'

He reached for the kettle. A strong brew was required. Milk and two sugars. Tom half - filled the kettle and put it on to boil. This was the first time he'd made a pot of tea in the house, but it wouldn't be the last. Before he put a tea bag into the pot, he checked the BBE date on the tea carton. It was OK. A month to go. What about the milk? Tom opened the fridge and lifted a carton from the second shelf down in the door. It had been opened. The date was all right, but Tom sniffed the contents first. No cheesy smell. Nothing to suggest it was off.

Sitting with his mug of tea at the kitchen table, Tom began to realise that this wasn't going to be easy. Living with Liz didn't present any real problems. The odd difference from time to time, yes, but they were similar in many ways and had common interests. Now here he was, living with another woman, who clearly was quite different from his wife, or soon to be, ex-wife. Tom's thinking pattern was broken by the ring-ring-ring of the telephone in the hall. Should he answer it? Hell, they'd never covered the question 'Gertie, shall I answer the telephone when you're not in?'

Tom obviously had no idea who may be calling. A son or daughter? Her ex-husband? A friend? It could be anyone! And what would he say? After five rings he picked up.

"Hello?" said Tom, surprised at the nervousness in his voice.

"Mr. Ball?" Tom said 'yes.' "It's the duty sergeant at Basildon police station here. I've got a Mrs Heseltine at the desk. She wonders if you can come and pick her up? Mrs. Heseltine says she's forgotten how to get home. If it wasn't for the BT letter in her handbag we wouldn't have known where she lived. She couldn't recall her home phone number."

27

"Hello, Di, how are you keeping?" Kathryn Heseltine was holding the phone between her neck and chest as she called her sister, Diane, in Rush Green. It was early evening and Kathryn had been busy in the health food store in

Chelmsford. She had poured herself a glass of wine before making the call. Diane replied that she was fine. "Just thought I'd call to let you know that a customer of ours here in Chelmsford sometimes pops over to Basildon to see an old friend. I mentioned to her a while ago that my mother lives in Basildon, and she actually walks along the same road where mother lives. Anyway, she called in this morning to say that she'd seen a van parked on mother's drive. I wondered if you knew anything about it?" Diane thought for a second.

"I do know that the guy who lives next door owns a van, a white one. Might be a Peugeot or a Ford, I'm not sure. Perhaps it's his?" Kathryn sipped her wine.

"Why would he want to park on mother's drive, though? Next thing is he'll be sleeping there!" Diane laughed, more of a cackle than anything.

"Don't be so stupid! Isn't he the one who helps mother out from time to time? You know, fixing a leaking tap or mending the washing machine. Perhaps she's letting him park there as a favour?" Kathryn felt a little more at ease.

"Yes, you could be right. It just came as a surprise when she mentioned it, that's all. But listen, it's time we visited mother. Are you doing anything this Saturday?" Diane confirmed that she wasn't. "Why don't we meet at that little Italian restaurant in Basildon for lunch at, say, noon. Then go over to see mother after that." Diane thought it was a good idea. It was high time they had another talk with their mum to see how she felt about the possibility of moving into a care home.

"Should we invite Mike?" asked Diane. Kathryn felt it might be best to leave Mike out of the equation for the moment.

"Let's not. We can have a heart-to-heart with mother first, and then let Mike know of anything that comes out of the conversation. She might blankly refuse to talk about it, anyway." Her sister agreed. The daughters made final arrangements to meet at Luigi's at twelve noon and ended their chat.

*

Saturday arrived and Gertrude's two daughters met at the restaurant as planned. Kathryn chose a feta cheese salad while Diane had a mushroom omelette. A bottle of non-sparkling water and two glasses completed the order. If their stomachs allowed, they might go for the tiramisu, the best in Essex, according to Trip Advisor. There was chit-chat between the sisters – arrogant customers and angry parents. In fact, they realised after a short while that they had similar challenges in their work at the health food store and the primary school. People! They chuckled when Diane said their jobs would be fine if it wasn't for demanding customers and damned parents!

Almost two hours later, the two pulled up in front of their mother's house. The white van was on the drive, but there was space for Kathryn's car. Diane eased her VW Polo close to the front of the drive but just off the main road. They hadn't told their mother of the visit, but both were certain she'd be in. Had they phoned ahead she probably would have fussed, tidied up and so forth. No, they wanted to catch her unawares to see how she was caring for herself. Kathryn rang the front door bell. A few seconds later it opened slowly.

"Hello?" said Tom, scrutinising the pair and thinking they were Jehovah's Witnesses.

"Oh, hi," replied Diane, "you must be Mr Ball. Tom, isn't it?"

"Have we met?" asked Tom, trying to recall if he'd ever been introduced to these women.

"I've spoken to your wife, Liz, when I've visited mother on a couple of occasions. You help out with little jobs, don't you?" 'He's obviously fixing something right now,' thought Diane to herself. "Are you doing another mending job for her?" Tom realised that these were Gertie's daughters, and neither knew about him staying in the house. How best to break the news?

"Your mother is in the back garden. I'll get her for you. Please, come inside," answered Tom, deflecting the question. This felt odd to both women. Actually being 'invited' to enter their own mother's home by a virtual stranger! Tom didn't wait for them to get over the step, as he rapidly went through the kitchen and out of the double doors that led onto decking.

"Gertrude, your daughters are here to see you! Now don't forget what we discussed, you know, about me being here." She looked confused.

"Now Thomas, leave it to me," she replied. Kathryn and Diane were now in the kitchen.

"Leave what to you, mother?" said Diane in an assertive tone. Gertrude was taken aback.

"Let's go into the lounge and all sit down. We'll have a cup of tea and talk about matters, shall we?" The four of them, with Tom at the rear, wandered through to the large room that faced the front garden. Kathryn was about to speak when her mother chirped up.

"Now there's nothing for you two to get excited about. Thomas is staying with me on a temporary basis because he and his wife are getting a divorce. He hasn't anywhere else to stay right now, so I've offered him a room. So, that's that. Now . . . who's for tea?" The two sisters stared at each other, both incredulous. Diane was sitting on the edge of an armchair, fingers laced.

"You've offered Tom a room? Here?" Gertrude nodded a 'yes.' She looked at Tom, who by now was feeling very awkward. "For how long, Tom? And what's this about a divorce? The last time I spoke to your wife, which wasn't that long ago, she was saying how much you were looking forward to your holiday in Spain." Tom looked at the carpet for a few seconds, avoiding eye contact with Diane.

"If you must know, I've been seeing another woman. Liz found out and asked me to leave. Simple as that. I can't afford anywhere at the moment, and your mother offered me a room, which I accepted. I'll pay my way, if that's what your worried about."

"And how long are these divorce proceedings going to take? A month, six months, a year?" Diane was clearly irritated to say the least. Tom hesitated.

"We think about six months . . ." Gertrude got up quickly.

"I'll go and put the kettle on. Now you three talk things over and I'll be back shortly." Was this a ploy, wondered Tom, for him to be left alone with the sisters. Into the lion's den? Kathryn took a turn to speak.

"Tom, did mother say what the arrangement is here? I mean, what about your food, washing, things like that? Do you have a front door key?" Tom explained things as best he could. How their mother had said he could have a bedroom in the house, use of a bathroom, she'd do his laundry, and the cooking, and she had given him a key so that he could come and go as he pleased. He mentioned the television he'd bought for his room so that he wasn't disturbing their mother, and that he would do jobs around the house, including washing up and some gardening."

"It sounds a bit too cosy for my liking," said Diane. "To be honest, Tom, I'm sure you're an all - right guy, but we don't really know you, do we?" Tom blushed slightly.

"Of course, I'm OK. What do you want? Date of birth and national insurance number?" He held himself back. 'Try not to get excited,' he told himself. Tom smiled to make a joke of it. "Listen, Liz and I have fallen out . . ., well, more than that. I've already said, Liz found out I was seeing another woman, we argued like hell, and she threw me out. She's demanded a divorce, and we've set the ball in motion. If you want a character reference, my manager is a guy named Harry Phillips at C & P where I work as a delivery driver. I can give you his direct line phone number if you want." The two girls relaxed. The room went quiet. Kathryn stood.

"That won't be necessary, Tom. I'll go and give mother a hand with the tea. But if there's any reports of trouble here, or anything that gets fed back to us, I'm afraid you're going to have to leave. Is that clear?" Tom felt as if he was back in the classroom again. Tempted to say 'yes, miss,' he got up.

"Absolutely. You can be rest assured that I won't go having rave parties here, and bringing all my mates back to wreck the place!" That went down like the proverbial lead balloon. Kathryn left the lounge and went into the kitchen where her mother was struggling to put milk into a jug from a litre carton. Kathryn helped, and a minute later she carried the tea tray through and placed it on a low table in the middle of the room. The offer of a 'cuppa' was accepted by all, and Kathryn did the honours. It was time for a change of subject as Diane spoke.

"The garden is looking nice at the front, mother. The Arthur Bell roses have that glorious golden -yellow colour this time of year." Gertrude smiled.

"Yes, Tom was feeding them with proper rose fertiliser the other day. I usually just put cold tea on them, but he suggested doing it properly." The sisters exchanged a glance, but Tom quickly added to the comments.

"When I was at school, I worked at a plant nursery in the summer holidays for a couple of years. Learnt all sorts of things about plant care, especially roses. Arthur Bell also happens to be one of my favourites, too. I bought some fertiliser, decent stuff, and even now they've perked up quite a bit. I'll do some dead – heading in due course to keep the flowers coming throughout the summer." Half an hour later, the sisters gave their mother a hug and left the house. Both Gertrude and Tom waved them off as the girls got into their cars and drove away.

"I'll wash up, Gertrude," offered Tom as he carried the tea tray back into the kitchen. "You go and sit down." How kind of him, she thought.

It was just as well that Tom had spent five minutes looking at the RHS website a few days ago. It's surprising what information you can get about basic plant care from the internet. Better than the fictional tale about working in a plant nursery. He chuckled to himself as he put the cups and saucers into the washing up bowl. Gertrude called from the living room.

"I forgot to tell the girls that the milkman had his milk float stolen last week. And the poor man was found dead in an alley."

Tom smiled to himself.

28

The mail had been delivered to the home of Mike and Pyong, the dogs in the kennels barking at the sound of the postie's van. Among the letters was one poorly addressed, almost as if written by a child. Mike thumbed it open, leaving a ragged edge along the top of the brown envelope.

"I wonder who this is from?" he asked Pyong, who was busy putting the breakfast cereals away. She stopped what she was doing and looked at him.

"Bloody hell!" he exclaimed. "Look at this!" He held the A4 sheet open for his wife to read.

**YOU DON'T KNOW HOW TO CARE FOR DOGS
YOU SHOULD BE LOCKED UP**

MY DOG WAS TREATED BADLY   WE WANT PAYMENT

£5,000 CASH OR YOUR KENNELS GET BURNT DOWN

DO NOT INVOLVE THE POLICE OR SOMEBODY DIES

I WILL BE IN TOUCH VERY SOON

The ransom note was put together with newspaper cuttings and glue. Pyong gasped.

"Who is this from? Who the hell would do this?" She sat on a kitchen stool and stared at the note. "It says 'my dog was treated badly,' so do we assume it's from somebody whose dog

we've cared for? Mike picked up the envelope and examined the postmark.

"It's been franked *Central Essex*. Let's look at the register and see if we can identify the person who clearly has a screw loose. Pyong reached up to the shelf in the corner of the kitchen where the latest register was kept. She went back for the last six weeks, searching for anyone with an address in the greater Brentwood area. Pyong found three. On the basis that it may be one of them, she tried to recall what the dog owners were like, and if there had been an issue with any of them.

"Here we are," said Pyong, taking a note pad and writing down three names. "There was David Sinclair, Harold Snowdon and William Barker," she added. "I do remember that Snowdon was pretty cheesed off about the state of his dog's coat, saying we hadn't washed the dog during the ten days we had it. Let me see . . . Chippie, yes that was the dog's name. A Pekinese. Do you think it's him?" Mike looked puzzled.

"Well, if it was, why go to this length? Five thousand pounds! And don't tell the police or somebody dies!" he paused. "Mind you, thinking about Snowdon, he did have a look in his eye. He reminded me of Charles Manson, that cult leader who was responsible for numerous murders. Didn't he kill Sharon Tate?" Pyong gave him a look. "What date did we care for his dog?" Pyong read out the dates. 3rd. to the 13th. of August.

"Harold Snowdon gave his address as living in Billericay as per the Central Essex postmark on the envelope. Do you think we should call the police?" asked Pyong. Mike gazed out of the window at the back garden watching a dove on the bird table.

"No! We need to think about this. If the guy has the balls to send this, then he's clearly got some neurosis. In other words, he sounds like a loony!" He paused. "Look, let's get on with the day's work, and we can both think about this. Perhaps when we sit down at lunchtime for a sandwich, we can discuss it further." With that, Mike folded the sheet of paper and replaced it in the envelope. He then put it in a kitchen drawer.

Pyong finished wiping the draining board after putting the crockery away and pushing the two stools under the side unit. In seconds Mike had disappeared to care of the current intake of dogs, fifteen in total, whilst Pyong took another look at the register. Sinclair, Snowdon, Barker. It was one of those three, she was convinced. Her money was on Snowdon – he was the one she could picture in her mind's eye. Not the type of guy she'd want to meet in a dark alley after midnight. She closed the folder and replaced it
on the shelf. It was time for her to get busy with the dogs, too.

Then she had an idea. But it would keep until lunchtime.

29

"Hi, Di. I thought I'd give you a ring to see what you felt about our visit to see mother." Kathryn was using her new Oppo smartphone. "We didn't really have a chance to talk the other day." Kathryn was phoning her sister with some niggling doubts about Tom Ball staying with their mother.

"Oh, hello, Kath. Yes, I was thinking things over, too. But you know, I don't think Tom being there is such a bad thing. If he and his wife are going through a divorce, and he needs somewhere to stay, isn't he providing a number of positives for mother. He knows about gardening, he's adept at fixing all sorts of appliances, and he's there for company, and..." there was a long pause... "if anything happened to mother, like falling over and breaking her wrist, he'd be there to help her." Kathryn quickly admitted to herself that she hadn't considered some of those benefits.

"OK, but don't you think he's playing her along a bit? Taking advantage? I mean, she didn't say how much he was contributing to his keep, but I bet it's a lot less than he'd be paying in some hotel or B and B. Then there's the laundry, and all of his meals, except when he decides to eat out with his mates or his bit on the side!" Diane sighed.

"I feel you're making too much of this. If we keep an eye on things, and call in a bit more often, not necessarily together, we can see how things progress, can't we? One question I have is 'when do we tell Mike?'" It was a fair point.

"You're right. Mike ought to know. Do you want to give him a call when we've finished talking?" replied Kathryn. Diane agreed and said she would. There was another pause, as the sisters were thinking about possible scenarios of Tom living with their mother. "You don't think he's got any sinister things on his mind?" Diane jumped in.

"What! Like sex, you mean. I should bloody well hope not!" She laughed. "I don't think mother and father were doing anything like that for years. She'll have forgotten how to do it!" The two of them giggled like schoolgirls in their first year at secondary school.

"Oh, my sides ache. Stop it! No, I'm sure that's not on the mind of either of them," said Kathryn. "The closest they'll get like that is when their undies spin round together in the washing machine!" There was more raucous laughter.

"Listen, I need to go. Things to do, people to see," chortled Diane. "And before you say it again, yes, I'll phone Mike and let him know mother has a lodger. If I put it like that, it sounds less intimidating. And I'll say he's paying his way."

"OK, Di, now you take care and we'll talk again soon. Bye." The call was ended, but it left Kathryn still feeling a little unsure about matters.

After all, what did any of them know about Tom Ball? He seemed all right on the face of it. But then, so did Adolf Hitler in 1935. The accounts of Ted Bundy, the serial killer who admitted to thirty murders, revealed that some who knew him said he was a nice man, who kept himself to himself. Kathryn wondered if she should play amateur detective . . . do a bit of snooping on this Tom Ball character. But where to start, she wondered. She now knew where he worked, and the name of his boss, and had said 'hello' to his wife, but that was about all. Was he on Facebook? Did he have a twitter account? Was there any other social media activity that might give up something on this Tom Ball? Did he have a police record, or had he ever been imprisoned? What was he like at school? A bully, a nice kid, a loner or a team player?

By the time Kathryn had finished thinking things through, it was abundantly clear that neither she, nor Diane nor Mike really knew this guy at all. And that wasn't healthy. Not for a man aged 38 living with their increasingly frail mother who was showing even further signs of dementia.

It was time for Kathryn to do some digging.

30

Mike had come in from walking three dogs at the local park. All on leads, of course. He loved his job at the kennels, and that morning he'd taken a German Shepherd, a Cockapoo and a Greyhound out for a long trek. He got some odd looks, but that didn't matter. People passing by probably wondered why a guy would have three pet dogs of such different types? He knew the old adage that owners start to look like their pets, or was it the other way round? No matter. He'd also shampooed two others, a Golden Labrador and a Beagle, and had the local vet arrive to check out a Yorkshire terrier that wasn't eating his food.

"Don't forget to wash your hands thoroughly, Mikey!" shouted Pyong as she heard the door shut. 'I always do!' said Mike to himself. Pyong sometimes called him Mikey when giving him instructions, it eased the harshness of the comment a little.

"Yes, dear," he replied with a hint of sarcasm.
Pyong had made two ham and cheese sandwiches for lunch, with a stick of celery and two tomatoes on each plate. A small tub of avocado dip lay next to the salt and pepper pots.

"How was the park?" she enquired after they had both sat down. Mike told her about the dog walk along the usual path, alongside the boating lake and back past the bandstand. She knew the route well. It was one they used frequently. The dogs got used to it, too.

"I saw that man again. You know, the one we've both noticed before. Just loitering. I don't like the look of him at all. He had a bag of bread. He was feeding the ducks, but staring at some of the mums who were there with little kids. Oooo." Mike gave a mock shiver to emphasise his concern.

"I've been thinking," said Pyong, changing the subject, "about the note we received. Mike took a large bite of his sandwich and looked at his wife. "Well, tell me if this is a bit off the wall, but there is something we might consider. Really consider . . ." Mike put his sandwich down.

"Yes?" he asked. Pyong leant forward, elbows on the table. She looked him in the eyes, a focused stare, then placed the card of James Herring in front of him. Mike glanced at the card. "So?"

"If you need anything, anything at all, give me a call." She paused. "Those were his exact words, Mike. When he left here with, dare I say it, Carisbrooke." Mike sat up, alert as if ready for battle.

"Oh, come on, you're not thinking of . . .?" Pyong smiled with her eyes.

"Why not? Here's the threatening letter. I took another look at it, and on the bit that says DO NOT INVOLVE THE POLICE OR SOMEBODY DIES I noticed the name of a newspaper and the date had been partially cut through. The Daily Mail. Monday 16 August." Pyong placed it in front of Mike.

"We don't know Herring. Hell, he could work for the government, or be a solicitor, or even MI5, for goodness sakes!" Pyong jumped off her chair and walked over to the kitchen window. She looked out onto the garden, her back toward her husband.

"Mike, if you don't do something about this, I will!" She turned. "Here's some maniac asking for five thousand pounds and threatening us! Well, where I come from nobody gets away with this kind of thing." Mike reflected on that for a few seconds. Pyong was from Thailand, where the culture was different. They had their own moral standards that were a million miles away from how most Brits felt across a wide
range of issues. "Nobody, you hear?" She thumped the worktop with the heel of her fist. Mike's ham and cheese sandwich was half eaten.

"All right, all right. What do you propose, then?" Pyong came back to the table and sat down. Taking in a deep breath, she spoke in a calm manner. She went on to explain her plan.

Pyong would list the address and contact telephone number of the three persons that could have sent the letter – Harold Snowdon, David Sinclair and William Barker. A phone call would be made to James Herring asking for a meeting over coffee, for which she would pay. Pyong would suggest The Bluebird Café in the local park, near the lake. At the meeting she'd sound him out to start with, so as not to embarrass herself, and perhaps ask for his opinion on the letter that she would show him. Pyong would come across as being in despair and ask Herring what she could do, and then probe to enquire whether Herring knew anybody that could 'sort things out.' She had a strong feeling that James Herring could help – just from his demeanour, what he'd said when he collected his dog, the 'tip' he'd left, and his body language. She'd met men like him in Bangkok. Pleasant on the outside, ruthless inside. It was worth a chance.

"If I didn't love you, Pyong, I'd say you were bloody crackers . . . in fact, *you are* bloody crackers!" She laughed.

"Yes, prawn crackers," she giggled as Mike chewed on a stick of celery.

31

Nigel Heseltine had been to Saffron Walden police station and provided a sample of saliva for a DNA test. The duty sergeant thanked him and informed Heseltine that the results would be made available to DI Matthews within 24 hours.

The following day, DI Matthews called at the home of Heseltine to let him know that an envelope containing one thousand pounds in used twenties had been found in the abandoned Mercedes Benz identified as the vehicle that had collided with Peter Dobson's car. On the envelope was the name Jimmy, and Matthews then revealed why he'd asked Heseltine about that name when they'd spoken at the golf club. The good news for Heseltine was that the DNA sample he'd provided did not match that taken from the envelope seal. Matthews also told him that a blond hair had been found in the same envelope along with the cash. Not Heseltine's colour.

"Surely Inspector, you don't think that I had anything to do with the accident that caused the death of Peter, do you? It's preposterous! I was miles away in Cromer, in any case." Still standing in the hallway, the DI took his hands out of his trouser pockets and knitted his fingers in front of his stomach.

"I'm not saying that, sir, but just as we seek out the perpetrators of crime, we also eliminate those who may have had any connection. As I told you before, we had a number of witnesses that said you and Mr Dobson didn't always get on. You argued and had your differences. So, if you do happen to know anyone who goes by the name of Jimmy, now is a good time to tell me." Matthews held his focus on Heseltine, eyes locked. Heseltine looked away briefly.

"I'm sorry, Inspector, but I do not know anybody of that name, neither a Jimmy, nor a James, nor a Jim. And as far as Peter and I go, or should I now say, went, I told you we had our own opinions on club matters, but, hell, there's no way I would have done anything like that!" Matthews' hands went back into his pockets.

"Or arranged something like that?" asked the detective. Heseltine stared at the DI.

"Absolutely bloody not!" fumed Heseltine.

"I believe that whoever drove the Mercedes that forced Dobson's car off the road had been paid one thousand pounds to do it. This 'Jimmy' must have been in such a rush to get away from the abandoned car that perhaps the envelope had dropped out of an inner jacket pocket, or simply dropped it. That's my theory, sir, and I shall find out who it was. The rightful owner of the Merc has been located but Forensics are giving it a last check. It's surprising what they can find. Every contact leaves a trace." With that, Matthews turned to the front door. Heseltine opened it for him. "Thank you for your time, sir, and if you recall anything that may be of use to the police, please let us know. You've got my number." The DI smiled weakly as he walked back to his unmarked BMW. In seconds he was gone.

"What was that about, darling? What did he want?" asked Alice coming down the stairs. Nigel had gone into the lounge, tempted to reach for the whisky bottle in the sideboard.

"Bloody coppers!" He slumped into an armchair. "He thinks I had something to do with Dobson's death. I'm not bloody having it. It was nothing to do with me." Nigel looked from Alice to the fireplace and back again. "I can't say I'm upset about Dobson. He was a prat, and it means

I've a better chance of getting elected to be President at the AGM, but that detective had the eyes of a vulture. I wouldn't be surprised if he called again." Alice put her hand on his shoulder as if to console her husband.

"Don't worry, darling. Your DNA didn't match that on the envelope seal, nor the hair they
found, so I can't see there's anything for you to worry about. I'll put the kettle on and make some coffee. I bought some of that Kenya blend that you like."

Alice had heard every word of the conversation in the hallway.

32

She switched on her laptop computer. As soon as she had typed the letters 'f' and 'a' in the search bar, facebook.com came up. Kathryn used this social medium now and again, but not as often as some of her friends whose fingers seemed glued to the keyboard of their smartphones. In the top left - hand corner, she typed the name 'tom ball.' Six people with that name came up. She peered closely at the photos attached to each name. There he was, the third one down. She put the cursor over the photo. Up came Tom Ball with all of his details. Secondary school, where he worked, when he started there, current interests, who he was following on social media, and his 'friend' listing.

There wasn't much to go on. It was all pretty basic stuff. Date of birth 10 December 1982. Educated at St. Teresa Secondary School in Basildon. Occupation listed as a driver with Corbett & Perkins since February 2020. Hobbies include real ale and cricket and he seemed to be interested in Kylie Minogue and Kim Kardashian. Tom Ball had 87 friends on facebook.com

Kathryn scrolled through his friends list. There weren't any she knew . . . why would she? She continued going down the names and faces. Mary Smith, Harry Smythe, Elaine Roberts . . . and then she saw Angela Parker. Kathryn peered closely at the photo of Angela Parker. Yes, it was her. One of her customers at her health food store, *Nature's Harvest*. She was a regular visitor to the store in Chelmsford. Seconds later, Kathryn closed the facebook.com site and switched off her laptop computer.

She decided to keep an eye out for Angela Parker, who hadn't been into *Nature's Harvest* this week as far as Kathryn was aware. But she needed to be careful. If Kathryn came across as too inquisitive, Angela may well message Tom Ball to let him know questions were being asked about him by the manager of a health food store in Chelmsford. It wouldn't take much for Tom to find that the person was Gertrude's daughter! Maybe Kathryn should take a different approach?

Four days later, Angela Parker walked into Nature's Harvest and began perusing the various products on offer. When the shop was quiet, and Angela the only customer, Kathryn approached her.

"Hello, Angela. How are you today?" asked the manager with a smile, pretending to adjust the layout of some packs of multivitamins. She recalled another name on Tom's Facebook friends list. June Slater. It was worth a try. "By the way, Angela, I was chatting to an old school friend of mine recently who knows June Slater. She said something about some guy on Facebook who has moved in with an old lady in Basildon. I said she had to be joking! He's about forty years younger! Can you believe it?" Kathryn hoped she'd pitched her comment to elicit a response – of some sort, anyway. Angela picked up a pack of vitamin D tablets and held it whilst maintaining eye contact with Kathryn. She sighed.

"I heard that, too. His name's Tom Ball. In fact, he's getting a divorce, that's the news on the grapevine. He's got a lovely wife called Liz. He's moved into the neighbour's house . . . I can't remember her name . . ." Kathryn interrupted.

"My friend said it was Gertrude – at least that's what I think she said."

"Yes, that's it, Gertrude. What an old - fashioned name, don't you think?" Kathryn smiled in response. "He's only staying for a short while, I've heard, but you never know. He might enjoy being there! Feet under the table and all that. Knowing which side your bread's buttered, or whatever the phrase is." Angela Parker grinned. Kathryn could have smacked her face hard right there and then. She resisted.

"So, what type of a guy is this Tom then?" probed Kathryn casually whilst moving several large packs of multivitamins and ensuring their labels were facing the customer. Parker hesitated, then glanced over Kathryn's shoulder, checking to see if anyone else was within earshot. She lowered her voice.

"Well, you didn't hear this from me, but Tom Ball was involved with the murder of a teenage girl about twenty years ago. Julie Thornton's body was found in a ditch. He appeared in court but there was insufficient evidence to convict him and the jury found him not guilty. It's more-or-less all been forgotten by people hereabouts. Apart from Julie's parents that is, who still live in Basildon." Kathryn's heart missed a beat. She said nothing more as she turned and headed back to the till to serve an old lady who wanted to buy two packs of muesli and a large bag of prunes. Minutes later, a Senior Sales Assistant named Norma had dealt with Angela Parker, who then left the shop without another word.

33

When Tom had left Gertrude's that morning, she'd asked him what he would like for his evening meal. Gertrude didn't always ask, and generally, Tom found her choice of meat or fish to be acceptable although some meat dishes occasionally needed a bit of spice.

"A nice piece of fillet steak," he replied. "If that's OK?"

So that was Gertrude's objective for that evening. She always tried to time it so that she and Tom sat down together at 7.00 pm. Gertrude had suggested to her lodger that 7.00 pm was a good time, and that it would be nice to eat at the same time and to catch up on any news from their day's activities. Tom didn't have an issue with this. By the time he got in from work, cleaned himself up and checked his smartphone for messages, that became a sensible hour to sit down to eat.

Tom also found it a refreshing change for Gertie to ask him questions about various aspects of his job as a delivery driver. It was something that Liz rarely did. 'How many delivery drops did you do today? Did you meet any interesting people? Were the roads busy?' By the time Gertie's queries had been answered and discussed, an hour had flown by and their meal – main course and a dessert – had been eaten.

It had been some time since Tom had enjoyed a fillet steak. The last one was at Spooner's bar - restaurant in town nine months ago where the 'Tonight's Special' was listed as prime Aberdeen Angus fillet steak from grass-fed cattle reared in Scotland. Not inexpensive at £20, but in truth it was only fit for soling his work boots. And he had no hesitation in telling the waiter the truth when asked if everything was to his liking. He'd never been back since.

It had been a hectic day for Tom. The Peugeot Boxer van had broken down on the A127 by-pass and taken an hour to sort out, a customer refused to accept an order because of the damage to the packaging, and he'd spilt half a can of coke on his trousers when parked up in a lay-by at lunchtime. Hell! What a day. So, when he drove back to Gertie's place, he could sense the knife slicing through his fillet steak like a hot knife through butter, brown juices slowly seeping out. Some caramelised onions spread across the top of the well - cooked steak, with a pile of thick-cut chips, and two fried eggs to the side. He almost dribbled as he parked the van on the drive and his stomach rumbled. He unlocked the front door with his key and closed it carefully. Gertrude was known to take a late afternoon nap and Tom didn't want to wake her. At least, not by slamming the heavy door. He went up to his room quietly, got undressed and decided on a shower.

By 6.55 pm, Tom had checked six emails, looked at facebook.com, and seen the racing results from Cheltenham. He had three winners! All at good prices, too. Minutes later, Gertie's voice was heard from the bottom of the stairs.

"Tom? Dinner's ready!" Tom turned his phone off and left his room. The expected smell of a cooked fillet steak didn't greet him as he walked into the dining room. "Here we are," said Gertrude enthusiastically, "white fish as agreed!" Tom looked at the plate laid on the table.

Boiled white fish, mashed potatoes, braised leeks and a white sauce. Laid out on a white plate. A smaller plate was laid with slices of white bread. Yellowish-white butter sat in a white butter dish. A tumbler of water stood on a small square drinks mat.

"This looks lovely, Gertrude. You shouldn't have gone to all this trouble," he lied. His hunger pangs had disappeared. "Aren't you having yours, too? Where's your plate?"

"I had mine earlier," she replied. "I got myself a piece of fillet steak. It was delicious." Gertrude walked out of the dining room and headed for the kitchen. "Enjoy!" she shouted as she walked away.

Tom sat alone and silent for a second. He wondered how the expensive wallpaper might look if he flung his plate at the far wall. A fling that could be a combined shot putt and javelin throw all in one. And he wondered how quickly his divorce papers were being dealt with.

It was time to talk to Liz.

34

"Hello, James," said Pyong as she greeted James Herring a few yards away from the entrance to The Bluebird Café. "I'm glad you could meet me. Shall we go inside, it's a bit draughty out here?" Herring held out his hand as a gesture for Pyong to go in first. They found a table in a corner, with nobody else close by. "I'll get these. What would you like?" asked Pyong. Herring stood and looked at her.

"I've never let a lady buy the drinks in my life and I'm not starting now. You sit down and I'll order. What'll it be?" Pyong asked for a flat white. 'What a considerate man,' thought Pyong. Herring was soon back with a small tray. "Flat white and an Americano with hot milk. I wasn't sure if you took sugar, but there are a few sachets here." He placed the flat white in front of Pyong and his coffee across to the side. He laid the tray against the wall behind his chair.

"No Carisbrooke today?" enquired Pyong as she opened a sachet of brown sugar.

"I'm afraid he's at the vets for a couple of hours. He's got a tiny growth on the inside of his mouth." Pyong wished the dog a speedy recovery. After stirring her coffee, Pyong looked straight at Herring.

"As I said on the phone, there's something that Mike and I are concerned about. Now, let's get this clear . . . if you can't help us, just say so. It'll save any embarrassment on both sides."

"I'm intrigued," replied Herring. "Go ahead, I'm listening." He poured the whole of the small jug of hot milk into the Americano.

Pyong told James Herring about the threatening letter, and then showed it to him. She had narrowed the likely sender down to one of three. She produced another sheet of paper that contained three names, addresses and telephone numbers.

"What do you want me to do, Pyong? How do you think I can help?" She asked Herring if he could prevent them having to pay the ransom. It was a lot of money to Mike and Pyong just now. He pondered the situation. "Are you asking me to do what I think you're asking me to do?"

"When you came to collect Carisbrooke, you said something to the effect of 'if there's anything I can do to help you, let me know.' Well, there is something you can do to help, but I don't need to know the details." Herring sipped his coffee. He looked at the list of three names.

"Are you certain it's one of these three?" Pyong nodded confidently. "The ransom note. It states '*We want payment.*' Do you know if these guys are married?" Pyong didn't. "I'd say the sender is, hence the plural 'we.'"

"OK. Leave it with me." Another pause. "The next time I go away on business, you'll care for Carisbrooke for free, won't you? Is that a deal?" Pyong had to agree. If Herring could 'arrange' something for her now, she would be happy to waive the fees for looking after his King Charles spaniel at some future date.

"That's fine. And listen, we haven't had this conversation," she added.

"What conversation?" asked Herring as he drained his mug. "You stay here for three minutes while I leave. It's best if we're not seen together. I'm not sure about CCTV cameras around here, but you can't be too careful." He pulled up the hood on his grey sweatshirt as he walked to the door. Pyong glanced at her watch. 10.52 am. She checked her phone for messages. There weren't any. There were some news items on Kabul, and issues with the Met police, but nothing important to her. Herring had long gone, and Pyong wrapped her scarf around her lower face as she left the café.

By 3.00 pm that afternoon, James Herring had contacted each of the three on the list. A telephone call from a 'market research agency' that was gathering information on canine care, and wouldn't take more than two minutes, was made to Snowdon, Sinclair and Barker. The 'agency' had a list of dog owners that had been compiled from a variety of sources, and the 'research' would be kept confidential. No details of the respondents would be shared with any other parties.

Have you had canine care for your dog recently?
Do you recall the name of the kennels that looked after your dog?
On a scale of 1 to 10, how would you rate those kennels?
Which single aspect did you rate best?
Which single aspect did you rate the worst?
Are you married?
And finally, which daily newspaper do you read, if any?

Of the three men he spoke with, only one was married, gave Pooches 1 out of 10 and read The Daily Mail.
Harold Snowdon.

*

James Herring watched as Harold Snowdon left his terraced home after dark. Herring had kept an eye on Snowdon for two evenings. It was no trouble. Snowdon visited his local for a drink most nights. The route to the Black Swan took Snowdon along a dark alley behind a row of shops.

"Excuse me, but have you got the time?" asked the old man, hunched over his walking stick. Snowdon looked at his watch, straining to read the face in the murkiness. Before he could tell the old man the time, Snowdon's neck was in an armlock. The old man pulled his arm up quickly in one deft move. Two cervical vertebrae snapped instantly and Snowdon dropped to the tarmac. Dead. The old man lifted the green lid on a five feet tall rectangular waste bin, then heaved the body inside. The lid was closed quietly.

Three minutes later, the old man heard the sound of a council waste disposal lorry, it's orange lights spinning and cutting through the dark night like a laser beam.

35

"Liz, it's me. Open up." Tom tapped on the door of the French window leading from the lounge to the back garden. She was watching a television police drama. Liz jumped. She was part way through viewing a tense crime scene, and Tom had inadvertently caught the glass with his metal watch strap. She pulled the curtain aside. Tom was standing, half crouched, with his hands under his armpits. Liz unlocked the door.

"What do you want?" she whispered. Tom didn't wait to be invited inside. He stepped over the base of the window frame. "It's nearly eleven o'clock," said Liz, now in a louder voice.

"I know. But I wanted to see you for a few minutes. Gertrude has gone to bed, but I told her I was popping out for some fresh air before she went upstairs." Liz looked at her husband, her arms folded.

"Is something wrong? You've got that worried look in your eyes."

"No, nothing's wrong. Well, nothing serious. It's just that it's taking longer to get used to living with her than I thought. And when she asked me what I wanted for tea, and I said a steak, she ended up giving me fish and then told me she'd had steak! I ask you!"

"Come and sit down for five minutes," offered Liz. "Do you want a cup of tea or anything?" Tom declined.

"No, I'm fine. Have you heard anything from your solicitor about the divorce because I haven't?" Liz shook her head. "Neither have I. Perhaps we ought to get in touch. Get it all sorted. Are you still OK with what we planned?" She looked at the floor. Liz was pensive.

"I suppose so, but I didn't realise it would be like this."
"Like what?" enquired Tom.

"Well, me being on my own isn't any fun, yet you have someone for company. She cooks for you, does your washing and ironing . . ." Tom had to play this down. He didn't want Liz thinking he was actually enjoying it.

"You can say that, but I wouldn't say I enjoy it particularly. I put up with it, for the sake of our plan. Come on, Liz, we discussed this on holiday. You knew the score. She's worth millions, and when she croaks, I'll be the sole beneficiary of her Will. I'm going to arrange that when the time is right. In fact, I intend to make some enquiries this weekend. Ask her about the children, what she might leave to them in the future. Be ever so casual." Liz looked at him coldly. Tom continued. "I'll also probe a bit on her husband. Nigel. Ask her whether she ever thought of getting married after their divorce. It'll be fine. She enjoys a glass of red wine, so I'll make sure we've at least a couple of bottles in the rack. A glass or two of a decent Merlot might loosen her tongue a little." He gave a gentle laugh.

"You'd better go back. We don't want Gertie shouting your name and you not being there for her, do we?" There was cynicism in Liz's voice. Tom held her arms.

"Listen, hon, this will soon be over. I know it's a bit of a drag right now, but when it's over we'll look back and think how quickly it all went by. Let's agree to phone our solicitors tomorrow, ask them to quicken the pace – you know, chivvy them along – and ask them to give us an estimated date for the decree nisi. And don't forget, all that money in the bank for us two when we get back together again." Tom leant to kiss her on the lips, but Liz turned her head at the last instant, and he planted a kiss on her right cheek.

"You'd better go," were her last words as she opened the French window and Tom slipped out into the darkness. She locked the door and pulled the curtain across. A minute later, Tom was in his room, having crept as quietly as possible up the stairs, avoiding steps four and seven, which creaked with the least weight on them. Back in his room, he felt unsettled. Liz was decidedly cool about their brief meeting – not what he expected, and she certainly wasn't going to invite him upstairs to look at the new bed linen.

But he had to ignore that. They had a plan. Liz knew what it was, and she was in on it. By living with Gertie for a while, and getting to understand her, there was the chance that all this would work. It wasn't going to be an overnight success, either. The divorce papers had to come through, Tom had to 'propose' to Gertie, and they would live together as man and wife until such time as she passed on. Tom was convinced it would work.

He had to believe it would work.

Otherwise, what was the point of all of this?

Ten minutes later Tom was in bed. He had checked a few horse - racing results, got a couple of WhatsApp messages, and wished an old friend a happy birthday on Facebook. It was time to get some sleep, but sleep wouldn't come. Tom laid on his back, then on his right side followed by the left side before he got cramp in his leg and had to reverse his posture. His eyes became accustomed to the light in his room, just enough for him to look at the oil painting on the far wall. The majestic stag stood on a hill top, master of all it surveyed, the remains of snow laying around in small gullies.

He couldn't recall dropping off to sleep when his phone alarm buzzed at 7.00 am. Tom got up and went through his normal routine. Sometimes Gertie was in the kitchen in her housecoat or dressing gown, but if she wasn't, he'd grab some cereal or toast, make a brew, and get out of the front door by 7.30 am.

There wasn't any sign of Gertie, and as Tom sat at the kitchen table, he wondered about the value of the stag painting in his room. He'd noticed a scrawled signature in the bottom right - hand corner. Difficult to make out, it looked like Reynards or Rennolds. Before he'd gone downstairs, Tom had taken a photo of the whole painting on his phone, and a close up of the artist's name. There was an antique shop in Basildon that often had a small number of oil paintings for sale, as well as a number of other items that Tom had seen on the Antiques Roadshow TV programme. It had to be worth a visit. If he got his schedule sorted for the day, he could make time on the way back later to call in.

'I wonder if you could help? My elderly father has this oil painting which he wants to sell. Do you think you could give me a valuation on it?'

36

Saturday, May 12, 2001

"I won't be late in, mum. Be about ten," said Julie Thornton to her mother, Margaret, as she left the high rise flat in Basildon. Twelve floors up, and sometimes the lift wasn't working.

"Now you take care, and don't be walking home yourself. Get one of the security men at that club you like to visit to ring for a taxi." Julie's father, Edwin, was working a late shift at the nearby biscuit factory.

"Don't fuss, mum. It's only a mile and the nights are still light."

"Yes, but you don't know what dodgy characters are out there!" Julie's mum folded her arms to emphasise her point. "Now, get along. You do look nice tonight, Julie, and can I smell that new perfume you bought?" Julie smiled.

"Thanks, mum. Yes, it's that one off the market – a copy of *Joy* by Christian Dior. I don't think you can tell the difference, apart from the price tag!"

With that, Julie Thornton left the flat and descended to the ground floor courtesy of an Otis lift.   And that was the last time Mrs. Thornton saw her daughter. At 12.30 am she was telephoning the Essex police to tell them her daughter hadn't returned home.

By 8.00 am the next day, a jogger had seen the partly clothed body of a young woman in a ditch that ran alongside of the railway line. Her hands had been tied behind her back with a three - foot length of electric cable. A silver elephant on a silver chain was around her neck. She hadn't been sexually assaulted but there was a knife wound in her neck that had severed the carotid artery. Her clothes were found scattered for a short distance along the railway line. Julie's black leather handbag with her initials on the flap was never recovered. It contained her mobile phone and purse. From the description of Julie that her mother had provided, it seemed it was her.

Three hours later the same day, Mrs. Thornton was asked to identify the body, and *it was* her daughter. Police began their enquiries. Julie's friend, Laura, that she met at the Pink Pelican, told police that they'd been in the club until about 11.30 pm. Enjoying themselves, they'd chatted with some young men in the club, and lost track of time. Both felt a bit light-headed when they left the club and Julie was adamant that she was capable of walking home.

Police obtained the names of eight males that witnesses said were seen talking to the two women during the evening. Each was interviewed at Basildon Central police station, and three of them were interviewed a second time. Thomas Ball, Dean Gifford and Ian Slater. All three were seen leaving the club with Julie and Laura. The best estimate of the time was 11.37 pm, one witness saying that they happened to check their watch against the large clock on one wall in the club as they saw the group of five leaving.

Ball, Gifford and Slater were arrested for the murder of Julie Thornton, but Gifford and Slater were later released. The CPS believed they had enough to charge Ball with the murder. Thomas Ball appeared at Chelmsford Magistrates Court on Monday 9 July, 2001 charged with the murder of Julie Thornton.

The case lasted seven days. The judge made a point of asking the jury to consider the circumstantial evidence against the proven evidence. The jury of eight men and four women found Ball not guilty by a verdict of ten to two.

There was minimal news coverage on the case, which was unusual, and within three months, the gossips in the town had found something else to talk about. Some said Julie was a girl with loose morals.

Used to egg men on.

Deserved what she got.

37

"Hi, Kath," said Diane when she picked up her home phone, Kathryn's number showing on the display. "How are you?" Kathryn got straight to the point.

"Di, listen. I've learnt that Tom Ball has a dubious past. I've been asking questions. He was arrested for the murder of a girl twenty years ago in Basildon but found not guilty. We need to think about how we get him to move out of mother's property. She's not safe with him." There was a pause.

"Murder! How do you know this? Are you sure?" Kathryn explained the Facebook information and the chat with one of her customers called Angela Parker. She'd also checked on the case in the archives of the local newspaper. "Bloody hell, Kath. Does Mike know this?"

"No, not yet. I thought I'd call you first. But we need to be careful how we go about things. I was thinking . . . if we tell mother about his history, she won't believe us, and it may make her more determined to have him stay. It might be best to either have a word with Tom Ball in private, or tell him up front that we want him out of the house," replied Kathryn.

"Look, why don't the three of us get together? You two can come to my place on Saturday morning and we can discuss the way forward. What say you?" Kathryn agreed on the plan, and said she'd call Mike once the conversation was finished. The daughters agreed on 10.30

am, and hoped their brother could join them. Diane continued. "Do we want Pyong involved?"

"It could be useful, but they have the kennels and they wouldn't want to leave the dogs alone. I'll suggest it, but I think Mike will come alone – assuming he can make it."

"Do you think we should phone mother between now and then – check how she is?" asked Diane.

"Good idea! If we all ask that basic question 'how are things going with Tom?' we'll have something to compare when we meet.

But nothing was sacred in Gertrude's house anymore. The three siblings had all called their mother the next day, and she was more than happy to share the discussion with Tom.

"I think they're all worried about me, Tom," she volunteered over their evening meal. "I never get three calls within a day. Ever. They're fussing over nothing. Wondering how things are going with you in the house. I feel safer now than I have done for a long time, and knowing you're here has reassured me in case anything happens to me! Next thing is, they'll all be wanting to come round and start interfering with our lives. I don't want that!" Where did Tom begin? He wasn't going to be forced out. He'd have to go through his tactics before any of the siblings came to visit. He reached out and put his hand over Gertie's hand, touched it for a few seconds.

"Now listen, Gertrude, there's nothing to worry about. I'm coming to enjoy living here, and if it makes you feel safe . . . well, that's a good thing, isn't it?" He waited for effect. "We make a good team, don't we?" She beamed.

"We certainly do! I've told you before, you can stay here for as long as you want. Even after your divorce comes through if needs must. I suppose it depends on your lady friend, though?" Tom had recalled he had mentioned a woman that he'd been seeing, but had to play it down.

"Well, to be absolutely honest, Gertrude, I'm not seeing her anymore," he lied. "It wasn't working out, really. Too many differences between us, I fear." Gertie put her hand over Tom's.

"That's good to hear, Tom. Really good to hear." She sat back and placed her knife and fork together on her half empty plate. "Listen, a good friend had recommended a film that's just come out. We can get it on Netflix. Why don't I put these in the dishwasher, and maybe we could sit down and watch it together? What do you think?" For a second, the thought of sitting next to Gertie on the settee wasn't on his radar. But it fitted his overall plan, and would add grist to him staying longer. Long enough for him to suggest they might become a pair.

To become husband and wife when his divorce came through.

Perfect.

38

"Did you hear the radio news earlier?" asked Mike. Pyong had finished tidying the breakfast table as he walked in the back door. "I had the radio on down in the bottom kennels while I was feeding the dogs."

"No, I was putting a few things in the dishwasher. Anything special?" Mike sat at the kitchen table. His face blanched.

"A man's body has been found on a council waste site. He's been named as Harold Snowdon. It was difficult to identify the body and had to use dental records, apparently. Wasn't he the chap we listed as possibly having sent the ransom note? Him and two others?" Pyong put the tea-towel down and sat at the table next to Mike.

"Listen. I told you I was going to see Herring," said Pyong. "See if he could help us. I mentioned the three guys to him, the ones whose dogs we'd looked after. Gave him some info on them. Then I left it with him. We don't know what actually happened to Harold Snowdon, do we?" Mike stared out of the window, a vacant look on his face. Pyong gently shook his arm. "Mike, we weren't going to be bullied into paying anybody five grand. If you recall, Herring said 'if there was anything he could do . . .' and so, as you know, I met with him." Mike pulled his arm away and stood.

"Yes, but I never thought he'd go and murder somebody! Hell, if we get caught up in this . . ."

"Now just wait!" Pyong raised her voice. "We don't know anything. I met with a client for coffee in the park café and had we a chat. We'd had his lovely dog in our kennels, and got on well with both the dog and Mr. Herring. Where's the problem with that?" Mike turned to look at his wife.

"You make it sound so innocent, Pyong. What if the police come knocking? Asking questions?" He was showing signs of agitation.

"They're not going to 'come knocking,' as you put it. What's to be afraid of? It's as I've just said. A client and his Cavalier King Charles had contact with us because the client was away on business for ten days. He was a very satisfied customer who gave us five stars on the Trust Pilot review he completed. You've got to maximise that type of positive feedback. It's called taking care of business." Pyong was wearing her marketing hat. Mike switched the kettle on. "Then he phoned one day and suggested meeting for a coffee in the park. So?"

"I need some coffee," he said with a degree of agitation, taking an upturned clean mug from the draining board and the jar of Gold Roast Blend from the cupboard in front of him. "Do you want one?" Pyong shook her head. This situation didn't sit well with Mike. He'd always been a bit of a worrier, that was the way he was built. He'd spend time getting worked up about things, only to find later that he'd give himself a bout of indigestion for nothing. Mike stirred his mug.

"OK, OK. As you say, we don't know what may have happened to Snowdon. Let's see what the local lunchtime news says about it. I'll take my coffee with me, I've got some kennels to clean out, and we're expecting two customers in soon." Pyong ran her hand up and down his arm a few times providing some solace; reassurance that all would be fine. She kissed him on the cheek.

"OK. I need to get on, too." He walked to the kitchen door. Pyong spoke before he opened it. "Mike, I love you." He smiled.

"Love you, too."

Pyong needed to keep a lid on this. She knew Mike was worried about his mother, and his two sisters had both telephoned about her in the last few days. One of them had arranged a meeting between the three of them. Gertrude and her toy boy! Pyong smiled to herself about the situation as she finished tidying up the breakfast table and putting some crockery away. She'd go and give her husband a hand cleaning the kennels. Keep an eye on him.

She also had to remember to order his repeat prescription from the medical centre. The propranolol capsules would only last another week.

Mike was also due his twice - yearly assessment at the psychiatry department at Broomfield Hospital next month.

The recent Wednesday Coffee Club gathering at Costa's had been interesting for Liz. She felt a bit more relaxed about things. She ordered her usual flat white as one of the girls, Chardonnay, made a list of what each one wanted. Two of the girls had brought their toddlers, despite it usually being adults only, but both fast asleep in their buggies. To begin with it seemed that the conversation covered everything except Liz's divorce. Babies, new films, TV programmes, a bit of gossip on neighbours, but nothing about Liz's situation with Tom. She wasn't going to raise it. But almost half an hour after sitting down, someone mentioned the subject.

"How are you feeling, Liz?" asked Vanessa quietly. Before she could respond, one of the girls who was an earwigging specialist, added a comment.

"Yes, Liz, how are you coping right now, with your husband getting his feet under the neighbour's table?" For an instant, Liz thought about leaving there and then. What bloody cheek! But that would have shown defeat. No, she wasn't having that.

"I'm fine, thanks. Everything's going through with the solicitor. It won't be long now." Liz smiled – as genuinely as she could. "I'm managing better than I expected, actually.
Cooking for one isn't so different, and there's less washing to do!" Some of the girls chuckled as Liz sipped her coffee.

"I was OK, too," added Fiona. "I could watch whatever I liked on TV, and no more dirty football kit on a Saturday. Once I was divorced, I felt the freedom of bird flying high." More giggles. "Then I met Alfie, and, well, I haven't looked back since." Earwigging spoke again.

"Why don't you start looking around for a new man, Liz. Do you good!" Did this woman have to try to rub Liz up the wrong way, Liz wondered? She remained calm.

"My solicitor advised against that. While it's being dealt with, she suggested no extramarital affair – after all, I'm married until the divorce is finalised." Most of the group agreed, and applauded Liz for her stance. Liz felt it was time to change the subject.

"Anybody got any holidays planned?" asked Liz, looking a few of the girls in the eye.

"Paul and I would love to visit France," chipped in Chardonnay, "and practice my schoolgirl French with the good - looking waiters over there. They all put the Chippendales to shame." A couple of the girls looked bemused.

"The chip and what?" asked Rosalind, almost spilling her café latte. More laughter.

"Bloody hell. You're too young to remember them. A bunch of guys with a six pack, rubbed all over with olive oil!" Some other customers in the café began to tut - tut at the group.

"Sounds as if you'd put them on a barbecue!" chirped another. More chuckles. One of the girls excused herself - she needed the toilet before she wet herself.

Forty minutes later, some of the group began to make their excuses to leave. They'd all paid Chardonnay in cash, and Chardonnay had used her credit card and Costa loyalty card - she wasn't daft. As they left, Vanessa gave Liz's sleeve a gentle tug.

"Listen, Liz, if there's anything I can do, you just have to let me know. OK? You've got both my numbers." Liz smiled.

"Thanks, Van. I'm OK really. I keep hoping things will get sorted soon, you know, get the whole thing over with. It's difficult with him being so close, and seeing him arrive back from work each day. I was thinking about moving away, but why should I? And I've still got my part time job. Once the divorce is finalised, he'll be off to see his girlfriend and probably move in with her."

"Then you can get a boyfriend, Liz! Get down to the clubs at the week-end, you know, grab-a-grandad night!" They both laughed.

Liz did a little shopping and was home by 12.30 pm. She wasn't feeling very hungry, but opened a tin of sardines and popped two slices of bread into the toaster. The afternoon was set fair, and some of the shrubs in the front garden were in need of a prune. Liz planned to get that done before Tom got back; she didn't particularly want to see him today. Sometimes it was better if he was avoided, it saved her from wanting to throw her arms around him and give him a big hug. For some reason, that feeling was becoming more less common these days.

Liz hadn't been in the front garden long when she heard Gertie's voice over the fence.

"Hello, Liz. How are you getting along?" What a loaded question, thought Liz.

"I'm managing, Gertrude. Thank you for asking." Liz moved towards a small holly bush, secateurs in hand.

"I've got a little secret." Gertie resembled a squirrel for a second. Liz waited. "My sister has helped me to book a week-end break away, and I plan to ask Tom if he wants to come with me! He doesn't know, yet." Liz nearly dropped the secateurs. A week-end away with her husband!

"Oh, right. Where are you going?" She wasn't really bothered 'where' they were going, more 'why.'

"There's a lovely little hotel in Clacton-on-Sea that my sister found on one of those travel offer websites. The Brompton Court. Right on the sea front and close to a lovely pub that does good food." Liz was so tempted to ask if Gertie's sister had booked two rooms, but she wasn't going to demean herself. "It will be a nice short break away for both Tom and I."

"Well, I hope you enjoy it, Gertrude," offered Liz, almost biting her lip. "Anyway, I must get on – I've got some gardening to do." Gertie took the hint and walked away.

Liz found it difficult to concentrate on pruning. A pheasant berry bush had to be trimmed, and the laurel in a corner of the garden was growing too large for the space it was in.

'Going away for the week-end, are they?' Liz was fuming. 'Did Tom have anything to do with this?' she wondered. 'Would he suggest it, or had Gertie asked her sister to arrange it so that it would be a surprise for Tom?' By the time Liz had finished her horticultural activities, the pheasant berry bush was less than half its size, and the laurel would take a couple of years to grow back to its previous size. But she found it satisfying! Every snip with the secateurs was a release for her pent - up emotions.

At 6.20 pm Liz saw Tom's van reversing onto the drive next door. She went out for a word.

"So, a week-end away, is it? That'll be nice for the two of you. Don't forget to take your slippers. And your Horlicks!" Liz tried to keep her cool. Tom was barely out of the driver's seat.

"What are you talking about? What week-end away?" His response was genuine. He had no idea.

And this was the first Liz had heard of Gertie having a sister.

40

"I've made the coffee," said Diane once the other two had arrived at her place in Rush Green. "Let's take a seat in the lounge." Mike, Kathryn and Diane made their way through from the hall. "I'll pour the coffee in a few minutes." Diane looked at Mike. "Glad you could make it, Mike. Kathryn and I think it's important we all have a say in mother's future. I hope you do, too." He nodded.

"Of course, but I think there are two separate issues here. One – her dementia, and two – her current situation with the neighbour living there." Kathryn said Tom's name, to remind them of it. Diane excused herself and went to the kitchen. A few minutes later came back with a tray. Mugs, cream, brown sugar, and a large cafetiere.

"Where do we begin?" asked Mike. "Shall we talk about Tom Ball first?" Kathryn shook her head and spoke.

"No, let's start with mother's mental wellbeing." Diane busied herself with filling the mugs. "We know she isn't going to get any better, and the time may come when we have to insist that she goes into a home. There's the private one between here and Basildon. It has a good reputation but you're talking about three thousand a month." Mike whistled in surprise.

"Or there's the Mackay & Rose one where you have your own room, and you can come and go as you like, and there's an emergency pull cord in each room if you need to summon help. Best of both worlds really. Full time nurse in residence, too," said Diane.

The three siblings discussed the options of future care for their mother for the next hour before moving onto Tom. Diane had cleared the mugs away.

"He's got to go," insisted Mike. "I've been thinking about it, and I don't honestly think he's doing mother any favours. I mean, if it gets to a stage where she says she can't do without him being there, what then?" Diane made the point about Tom being a handyman, and being able to help out if anything went wrong, but Kathryn countered the point by saying that their mother was quite able to ring for a plumber or electrician if necessary. They carried on debating the lodger.

"Do you think he's taking advantage of her?" asked Diane. "Don't you think that, if he's seeing this other woman, he ought to be living with her?" They didn't know the circumstances, and all agreed that that might not be possible. "But he's got a full - time job, so he can afford to rent a place, can't he?" added Diane, "or find a B and B."

The debate carried on until Mike suggested that they make a decision on Tom Ball, and then approach their mother with a proposal on having him leave the property.

They all agreed. Next Saturday at 11.00 am they would descend on their mother's house and tell her exactly what she should do. Get rid of Tom Ball!

And so, the week came and went. Diane had another set to with some bolshy parents after several pupils had been given detention, Kathryn argued with a few customers who asked for refunds at Nature's Harvest on opened containers because they'd bought the wrong product, and Mike carried on with the kennels whilst having some sleepless nights thinking about Harold Snowdon.

The Saturday came, and Mike and his sisters arrived at Gertrude's home. The gates were closed, and there wasn't the white van on the drive. That in itself was unusual. Their mother never closed the gates. Waiting until they'd all arrived, the three had parked their cars on the road and walked to the front door together. Mike tried the front door. It was locked, so he rang the bell. A few minutes after 11.00 am, Liz came back after doing some shopping. Diane turned as she heard Liz's footsteps. She came straight to the point.

"Hi, Liz, you don't happen to know where our mother is, do you?" Liz smiled as she put her two bags down on the doorstep.

"Yes, I do. She told me she's staying at an hotel in Clacton. Forget the name. Apparently, your aunt booked rooms for her and Tom for this week-end. They left yesterday teatime. Due back tomorrow afternoon sometime."

The three looked incredulous.

They didn't have an aunt.

41

"I wonder if you can help? My elderly father has this oil painting which he wants to sell. Do you think you could give me a valuation on it?" Tom was asking the manager of the Cholmondeley antique shop, Mr Clarence Pugh. The elderly gent, with a Harris Tweed jacket and mutton chop side whiskers, placed his spectacles on the end of his nose. He looked closely at the photograph on Tom's phone.

"It's difficult to tell without seeing the actual painting, Mr er?"

"Ball, Thomas Ball," replied Tom, preferring the full version of his first name. It sounded better.

"Is there any chance you could get your father's permission to bring it in. I'm here until 6.00 pm today if that helps. It could be a Joshua Reynolds which would make it worth something." Tom wondered if he could get the painting out of the house without causing any suspicion. He'd try.

"All right then. I'll call into my father's now and ask if I can let you see it." Tom glanced at his watch. "I'll be back in twenty minutes." Pugh nodded as another customer came into the shop. Tom prayed Gertie would be busy when got back. His prayers were answered. Gertie was in the back garden when Tom opened the front door as quietly as he could. He crept upstairs and removed the painting from the two hooks, then placed it in a supermarket plastic carrier bag. Within less than half an hour he was back at Cholmondeley's, where a vacant parking space greeted him right outside the premises.

"Ah, that was quick," said Pugh, brushing his mutton chop whiskers from his mouth toward his ear with the back of his right hand on each side. Tom carefully took the painting from the carrier bag and laid it on the counter. The manager removed an eye glass from his top jacket pocket and eased it into his eye socket, making his eyebrow look like a hairy black caterpillar. He made humming noises as he scanned the whole painting, including the signature. Twenty seconds later the eye glass was removed.

"I've valued many paintings in my career in antiques. This is one of the most interesting paintings I've had the pleasure to hold. Reynolds painted oils in his lifetime, mostly portraits, between about 1740 and 1790. This one is a lesser - known painting of his. It's called *The Infant Urchin*." Tom almost felt the need to use the toilet; the excitement had got to him.

"So, what do you estimate its value to be?" probed Tom. The manager laid the frame on the counter.

"I'm afraid I've bad news for your father, Mr Ball. This is a copy. A good one, but a copy nonetheless." Tom peered into the manager's eyes.

"Well? *How much* are we talking here?" Tom was almost begging now.

"You'd get thirty to fifty pounds at auction," said the manager, buttoning his Harris Tweed jacket as he walked to the door. He turned the sign to read Closed. "Good luck if you decide to sell," said Clarence Pugh as Tom left the antiques shop.

"Would you and your son like a hand with your luggage, Mrs Heseltine?" asked the hotel receptionist after Gertrude had signed the register.

"No thank you very much. We can manage, can't we Tom?" said Gertie as she picked up a lightweight bag and nodded for Tom to grab the suitcase. There wasn't a lift, and the newly arrived couple were staying on the first floor in adjacent rooms. Soon, Tom had unlocked both doors, and carried the suitcase into Gertie's room. He spread out the folding case support and lugged the suitcase on top. Gertie gave Tom the lighter bag, which in fact contained his clothes for the week-end.

"Can you manage this?" asked Tom eyeing the case after he'd pressed open the locks. Gertrude nodded.

"Yes, not a problem. I'm going to have a little rest after our exertions, so shall I meet you in the bar in, say, an hour?" It was now five thirty. That was fine for Tom. He went next door and took a few things out of the bag and hung two shirts on hangers, along with a pair of chinos and a polo shirt. His stuck two pairs of boxer shorts in a draw, along with a pair of socks, then placed the toothpaste and toothbrush in the
bathroom. An aerosol deodorant and bottle of aftershave completed his unpacking. His tough, dark brown leather shoes would suffice for the next two days.

Tom decided on visiting the bar now. After rinsing his face and putting on a dab of cologne, his fingers combed through his hair. That would do fine. His shirt was fresh on before they left so he'd make that do for the evening. Maybe there'd be some leaflets in reception to browse to give him an idea of filling in tomorrow. He had no idea what Gertie wanted to do, but that would be the conversation for dinner tonight. That, and a few more probing questions about her family, along with legal aspects such as power of attorney and a Will. But he'd have to be careful. No rushing, just a very steady ramble along life's highway, so to speak. Pretend to be interested in her future . . . show he cared.

But another question was 'why did Gertie ask her sister to book two rooms at this hotel?' Who was her sister? Where did she live? And Tom had to smile when he recalled the receptionist asking if Mrs Heseltine and her son wanted help with their luggage! Mother and son! Is that how they looked? Maybe he ought to suggest Gertie spruces herself up a bit. Get a better, younger-looking hairstyle, use a different brand of cosmetics, change her lipstick colour . . .

"And what can I get you?" asked the barman, Roger, in a voice that made Tom think he was gay. He had a slight lisp, too.

"Have you a local ale?" The barman pointed to two hand pumps, each with an enamel tag.

"These are from a brewery south of here. Wallasea Wench and Broadsword. I love both of them," he replied. Tom tapped the Broadsword tag with his finger. 4.7% strength.

"A pint of that will do fine." Two minutes later, and after a wink from the barman, Tom sat at a table with a handful of leaflets on local attractions. He browsed through them, not knowing what Gertie may want to do. He was pretty sure, though, that she wouldn't be up for the amusement park with the 'highest roller coaster in East Anglia.' Before Tom had read very much more, Gertie entered the bar. She had made an effort. Tom stood to greet her.

"Hello, Gertrude. You are looking smart this evening – if I may say so." She smiled. "What can I get you to drink?" Gertie looked across at the bar. Roger caught her eye. He waved at her.

"Oh, hello! Mrs Heseltine! Lovely to see you again! How are you this evening? Is it the usual gin and tonic?"

The telephone rang. Liz picked it up after four rings. She used to give her name once upon a time, but now it was only the six - digit number. The caller's details seemed familiar, but Liz did as usual.

"423789," she said in a neutral voice. It was Vanessa from the Costa coffee group.

"Hi, Liz, it's me. Hope I'm not disturbing anything."

"No. Nothing that can't wait. I've just popped a deep pan pizza into the oven. Twenty minutes to cook. How's things?" Liz wondered what Vanessa wanted. It was unusual for her to ring in the evening.

"Well, you know how you said you were a lapsed badminton player? I've renewed my membership down at the sports club and I can sign another person in free of charge. Just wondered if you fancy trying your hand again later in the week?" Liz wasn't bothered one way or the other, but she wasn't very busy these days, and Vanessa had been a real help to her, so her mind was made up instantly. "Can you do Thursday?"

"That sounds great! Shall I meet you there? Say, 3.45 pm? I know where it is." Vanessa agreed on the suggestion, and reminded Liz that black soled shoes were not allowed on the court. "OK, see you then. Bye"

Badminton! Hell, Liz hadn't played since she married Tom ten years ago. But she loved the game, and enjoyed watching the occasional matches shown on tv. Liz would have to dig out her shorts and top, along with white socks, and thankfully her trainers had white soles. She had two racquets, both in the loft, which she'd need to get down and wipe the cobwebs off. A headband and wrist bands? Maybe not the headband – Liz didn't think she'd sweat that much. A towel, bodywash, deodorant, hairbrush. Yes, that was about it. A sports bag in the garage might need a wipe over, then she would be ready to go!

Sitting at the kitchen table with her four - meat pizza, with added grated cheddar cheese, Liz thought about getting back onto a badminton court again. Wow! It promised to be fun . . . as long as she hadn't lost her touch. Perhaps a few stretch exercises tonight could help loosen some muscles, but not to overdo it. Liz didn't want to pull a hamstring or anything serious like that. Tom had done that once and the bruising lasted for a fortnight. There was a small bottle of Brown's Liniment in the bathroom cabinet. She'd take that too, and a pair of elasticated ankle supports.

The cool prosecco complimented the pizza. Liz had poured herself a large glass. 'Sod it!' she said to herself out loud, then proceeded to sip it long and slow. Sitting in her kitchen gave her time to reflect. Think about what was going on,
wondering if she and Tom were doing the right thing. If their plan came unstuck, and the police became involved, would she say that it wasn't her idea?

'No officer, my husband came up with this silly idea but I had to go along with it because he threatened me. I wasn't in favour of it at all to be honest.'

Could she do that? No, Liz didn't think so. Ten years of marriage had cemented them together after all.

Hadn't it?

Liz realised that she was day dreaming. A slice of pizza in her hand now cool, the rest going cold. But she didn't know what the immediate future held. Tom and Gertie getting married . . . Gertie passing away, Tom down as the sole beneficiary in her Will. A million or two, or more, in the bank. Her and Tom reuniting, husband and wife again with a life of luxury ahead of them . . .

The front doorbell rang. Liz glanced at the kitchen clock. 7.40 pm. Who could be calling at this time? She opened the front door, keeping one foot behind it to stop anyone barging in.

"Oh, hello. It's Liz, isn't it?" said the tall, dark stranger. He smiled at her.

He was holding something, but Liz couldn't quite see what he had in his hand.

44

As Mike, Kathryn and Diane had made the effort to meet at their mother's house, it seemed a waste of time to disperse even though their mother was away in Clacton with Tom.

"There's a little café down the road," said Mike. "Why don't we go and grab a coffee and talk things over?" The sisters looked at each other, and agreed. "This way," he said and walked off. Ten minutes later the three were huddled over their mugs. The café was in need of a damn good clean, but it would do as a meeting point. The flower-patterned table oilcloth was in need of a thorough wipe, if not ready for the dustbin. Red sauce was congealed on the rim of the tomato shaped plastic dispenser.

"Well, where does this leave us?" asked Diane. No one spoke. She sipped her coffee, which was surprisingly good for a place that should have been closed by the local hygiene department ages ago. Kathryn put her mug down.

"Do you think mother has an ulterior motive for taking Tom to Clacton?" she said. "I mean, if Liz is telling the truth, she said that mother asked her sister to book the place for them. What bloody sister?"

"We shouldn't be surprised at anything these days," offered Mike. "We know dementia is setting in, and maybe her mind is in free-fall when it comes to making things up. If she has told Tom that her sister booked it, then he finds out she hasn't got a sister, what's he going to think?" More musings, and deep breaths.

"Kath, what did you mean 'ulterior motive?' asked Diane.

"I don't know, maybe she has a reason to want to get away from Basildon with him. Show him she's still capable of making decisions, not some old fuddy-duddy who's unable to do very much. Maybe she's living in the past, you know, revisiting things in her head. But why Clacton-on-Sea, and who booked it? She bloody didn't, that's for sure," replied Kathryn. Mike suddenly banged the salt cellar on the oilcloth.

"Just a minute! Clacton? Didn't mother used to go there many years ago? It rings a bell. With friends from the WI?" More silence for a while.

"Now that does sound familiar," said Diane. "We're talking twenty years ago, aren't we?" No one was certain. "Anyway, you're right, I think that she did visit the Essex coast a few times. Talked about buying one of those beach huts on the promenade. Painting it bright yellow!"

"OK. OK. This is all very interesting, but what about mother?" Mike brought the focus back onto Gertrude. "We still don't have a plan. I believe we've got to get her alone and tell her that Tom needs to leave. Get rid of him, and she may get back to normal, or as near to normal as can be, and she won't be influenced by him. Hell, who knows what they talk about when they're together?"

"I agree," added Kathryn. "For all we know he may be planning something, have no intention of leaving her home. Mother will fall for anything these days. He might be planning to take advantage of the situation." The three of them didn't want that. This had to be 'nipped in the bud.' Mike leant forward and knitted his fingers across the table top.

"We could always kill him," he whispered. Diane nearly dropped her half empty mug.

"What!" she exclaimed. "Did I hear you correctly, Mike?" He nodded slowly.

"Sure." He looked around him, but nobody was within earshot. "We kill him. Get rid of the body, miles from here, cover our tracks. Nobody will be the wiser." He smiled menacingly. Diane 'mock examined' her nails, buying time.

"Isn't that a bit drastic? If we tell him to leave the property, and he agrees, we don't have to go to those lengths."

"But if he doesn't." Mike's reply hung in the air. "If he refuses to go, we might have to consider some action, drastic as it seems." There was silence for a while. Kathryn fingered her mug as if it was on a potter's wheel. She thought of setting fire to the red Citroen that belonged to Asa Briggs, her awkward customer at *Nature's Harvest*. Diane twiddled her thumbs. Her mind wandered to the poisoning of the pet cat belonging to her pupil, William Smedge. The poisoned tuna had done the trick after the obnoxious comments from his parents. Mike's thoughts brought Harold Snowdon to mind. How he'd been found dead after Pyong had met with Mr Herring.

"If we did anything like that, we'd have to make a pact. Just the three of us. It would be our secret for always," suggested Kathryn. They looked at each other for a few seconds. "Nothing in writing, no texts or WhatsApp messages, nothing that could be traced back to any of us." Diane shuffled uncomfortably. "Only phone calls."

"Listen guys, I'm feeling shivery. We don't have to go down this route. Bloody hell, he's lodging with our mother for a while before he gets a place of his own. His divorce will eventually come through and then he'll be off chasing some young piece of skirt! We're overreacting here!" Mike put the salt cellar next to the pepper pot, lining them up with a sauce bottle. He lowered his voice.

"Maybe we are, but you never know how this is going to develop. Right now, the two of them are having a weekend away in Clacton and even enjoying each other's company! Suppose mother wants him to stay? Offers him his own room, rent-free. He's not going to baulk at that."

"OK.OK. Listen," Diane called the meeting to order as if she was in the school staff room. "Let's leave things as they are for the time being. If we keep in touch with each other, and telephone mother now and again, we can update ourselves, and if there is anything untoward that concerns us, we'll all meet with her for a full and frank discussion. How does that sound?" Mike thought his sister sounded like Margaret Thatcher but he didn't comment.

"Agreed," replied Kathryn, staring into her empty mug. "I've got to do some shopping so must be off. Mike, are you getting these?" she asked, pointing at the three coffee mugs. "You keep telling us how well the kennels are doing!" He laughed.

"Not as well as Nature's Harvest, I bet. Keeping all the coffin dodgers happy in Chelmsford!" he quipped. So that was that. The two girls left the cafe as Mike stood at the counter to pay the bill.

He had an idea about Tom Ball, but he decided to keep it to himself for now.

45

There was a nice pub next door to The Brompton Court hotel. The Pheasant Inn. After a drink in the hotel bar, Gertie and Tom had ventured across the car park and entered the pub. It was moderately busy, with a few spare tables dotted about. Gertie walked straight to the bar, which surprised Tom, and asked for the manager. A man with SIMON on his name badge came from nowhere and greeted Gertie like a long-lost friend.

"Mrs Heseltine! How nice to see you again!" Simon bent to kiss Gertie on the cheek. "The usual table, is it?" She nodded and gave a wink.

Tom tried to make sense of this. First the barman in their hotel, now the manager of the Pheasant Inn. Clearly, Gertie had been here before. But when, and with whom? Tom would leave those questions for now. Best to get settled, order the drinks, and look at the menus. Simon took the couple over to a table laid for four, and deftly removed the cutlery settings from two sides.

"Is it the usual, Mrs Heseltine? We've got a good stock of Galliano." Gertie nodded again. "And sir? What can I get for you?"

"Have you any Broadsword beer on tap?" asked Tom, having enjoyed his pint in the hotel bar. Simon looked as if he'd smelt dog-poo on his shoe.

"Broadsword, sir? Certainly not! We only stock quality beers here," he retorted in an offhand manner. Tom didn't want to argue in front of Gertie and asked for a pint of their best bitter. Simon handed them two menus. "We've got your favourite on this evening, Mrs Heseltine. Liver cooked in red wine, with onions sauteed in butter, and served with fresh asparagus and Dauphinoise potatoes." With that, the manager turned and walked away. *'Nasty little shit,'* thought Tom.

"He's such a lovely man, Tom. Always helpful. Mind you, he gets a good tip from me." She winked again. "What do you fancy from the menu? The steaks are always good here. I know you like a fillet or sirloin." Tom perused the menu. The fillet steak was served with mushrooms, onion rings, a grilled tomato, and chips described as 'railway sleepers.' That sounded fine.

But Tom had a sudden thought. 'Who's paying for all this?' The hotel next door, their evening meal in the Pheasant, and drinks. Two nights. It was going to be around £300 he calculated quickly. Even £400 at a stretch. Was there going to be a moral dilemma here? If Gertie offered to pay, did he pooh-pooh the suggestion and get his wallet out, hoping she would insist? Or . . . if she didn't offer to pay, he'd be obliged to pay anyway. Hell, she'd invited *him*, not the other way round!

"Your Harvey Wallbanger, Mrs Heseltine, and your IPA, sir," said Simon as he placed the drinks before them. "Ready to order?" he asked. The order was placed. Now it was time to talk. Tom gently tapped Gertie's glass and said 'cheers, good health.' He took a long drink of his pale ale. It tasted good.

"Good health. Yes, we all want some of that, Tom. I'm not getting any younger and I've decided to enjoy what time I've left." Gertie sipped her golden yellow drink, a glace cherry on a stick now on a serviette. Tom looked at the cherry. "I hate glace cherries," said Gertie, "but I haven't the heart to tell him." She smiled.

"So, tell me about your family, Gertrude. What did your parents do?" Tom thought the opening gambit was non - intrusive. She put her drink down.

"Both of my parents worked at Bletchley Park. You know, the code-breaking place. They'd both been in the forces. Father was a major, my mother a lieutenant. That's how they met. Married in 1938, and I came along a year later. Born on Christmas Day!" She took another sip.

"Did you get double presents?" Tom immediately regretted the question. He told himself to think before engaging mouth.

"No, everyone told me that whatever I got was for both Christmas *and* my birthday. I felt cheated. But, never mind. I'm still this side of the grass." Tom didn't comment on that.

The food came, on hot plates with the offer of extra sauces and condiments, and soon they were eating. The conversation flowed, this way and that, with Tom chipping in with aspects of his background from time to time, but not giving too much away. He wanted to keep things simple, not have Gertie asking awkward questions, and certainly not wanting his court appearance to surface. The case of Julie Thornton, who's partly clothed body had been found in a ditch near to the railway line, was something he wanted to forget.

"What was your husband's name, Gertrude? Do you ever hear anything from him these days?" Tom knew he was sailing close to the wind with that question. She put her knife and fork down.

"Nigel." She paused. "No, I don't want anything to do with him. He was a liar and a cheat the day I met him, but I never saw it. Used to spend a lot of time away on business with his secretary. Said she kept his diary. I was a fool. He ended up marrying her. Alice is her name." Tom sensed that talking about her ex-husband was difficult for Gertie, so he changed the subject. He mentioned her three children, and Gertie seemed happy to recount times when the children were young. Michael, Kathryn and Diane. Going off on holidays to France and Belgium, staying in pretty hotels.

Tom decided now was the time to take a chance, and after a lull in the conversation, asked Gertie about inheritance. Her children would miss her immensely, and presumably she was going to leave everything to them when she passed away? He quickly added that he would do that if he had children.

"I've no idea," she said calmly. "They're all well off. They don't need anything I've got. The house, I suppose, they can have that and the contents, and share the proceeds of the sale." Tom had finished his steak; three overcooked chips were left to the side of the plate.

"So, you've made a will out then? I've heard it said it's best if you do that. Saves family arguments afterwards." He smiled to take the edge off the frank question. He waited. Gertrude stared into her glass.

"No, Tom, I haven't made a Will out. It's something I need to do soon." He sighed. Waited a few seconds. "I can help you with that, if you want. You know, give you any advice you may need?" Gertie didn't reply to that, and Tom had to let it lie. She continued.

"I used to come here with the Women's Institute, you know," offered Gertie, changing tack. She scanned the dining area of the pub. "We had some good times here, and often with a guest speaker. Always stayed next door at The Brompton Court. Didn't recognise the receptionist, though. She hasn't been there that long. Roger the barman is a nice man, as is Simon here." That satisfied Tom's question. Gertie had been here before with her colleagues from the W.I., and the barman and manager had remembered her! She must have made an impression.

"What sort of guest speakers did you have? Anyone interesting?" enquired Tom, more as a means of keeping the conversation flowing than really being interested. Gertie looked into her empty glass and gave it a slight shake. Tom caught Simon's eye. He came over and looked at Gertrude.

"Can I help, Mrs Heseltine? How were the liver and onions?" No eye contact was made with Tom. Gertrude told Simon to give the chef her compliments, and before Tom could add a comment about his steak, the manager asked if they wanted to see the dessert menu. Gertrude nodded.

"And another Harvey Wallbanger, Simon. I'll need something to help me sleep. I think Tom here will want another pint, won't you Tom?" Tom's wobble of the empty glass meant a 'yes.' The dessert menus appeared and Gertie started to read. "If they still do their own bread and
butter pudding, I'll have that," she said with a twinkle in her eye. Tom's sweet tooth took his eyes down to sticky toffee pudding, with ice cream, before he rekindled the chat.

"So, Gertrude, anything of interest in the W.I. talks?" She paused.

"Well, once there was a Gypsy. Her name was Callie-Rose. All dressed up with a decorated red headscarf and big earrings. She'd brought her crystal ball and gave us a half hour presentation about how she'd got into it, and her background. Callie-Rose was the seventh child of a seventh child. It was very interesting, but then at the end she asked if anyone wanted their future told." Tom leant forward, his appetite for the outcome whetted.

"And? What happened?" He had to wait a little longer for the reply as Simon placed their drinks before them, then tootled off.

"Four of us said we did. I went first, in a private room. That one over there." Gertie pointed to a door behind Tom. He turned to look, then picked up his pint and had a long drink. He felt some hairs on his neck stiffen, and was suddenly chilled. About to ask for more detail, a waiter came up to the table and placed their desserts down. 'Bon appetit,' he said, in a pseudo - French accent reminiscent of Basil Fawlty. Gertie continued.

"I was in there for five minutes. When I came out Callie-Rose had told me three things." She broke into her pudding. Full of sultanas and cream. "One, I was going to get divorced. Two, I was going to meet a younger man, and three . . ." Tom gazed at her, the ice cream on his sticky toffee pudding melting slowly.

"And three?" he uttered, begging Gertie to spell it out.

"And three, that I would live to be one hundred."

46

Detective Inspector Sandy Matthews had asked Detective Sergeant Chris Hayman for a quick word in his office at Saffron Walden Central Police Station. Hayman had bought two white coffees from the machine along the corridor and, nudging open Matthews' door with his foot, had entered and put one on the desk.

"Chris, any news on the Peter Dobson case at the golf club? I've got the Superintendent on my back wanting an update." Hayman remained standing, coffee in hand. He knew the Super, Charlie McLaughlin, was a hard man. Glaswegian, too.

"Well, forensics have gone over the Merc again. Whoever was driving left no fingerprints. Those found on the car belonged to the owner, a Mr Gareth White from Benfleet Road in Saffron Walden. He's not a chewing gum person and says the wrapper wasn't his, and he confirmed he didn't realise the car was missing until the next morning. We've DNA tested eighteen people from the golf club – as a means of eliminating the person whose DNA was found on the tab of the envelope – but with no success. The blond hair doesn't match any of the club members, either. One guy was reluctant to provide a swab, but he eventually did. Something about being concerned he'd throw up with a swab stick stuck down his throat. We've asked club members whether they have a Mont Blanc or Parker pen, and only two admitted to that. We checked and both nibs were classed as 'broad,' and the pens contained black ink and didn't match the writing on the envelope. There were too many fingerprints on the twenty - pound notes in the envelope for us to use them." The DI let out a sigh.

"If Gareth White doesn't chew spearmint gum, we can assume that the thief may have left it? Is there any *good* news, Chris?" The sergeant took along sip of his coffee.

"Well, the envelope that contained the cash was from Barclays Bank. The inner surface has the bank logo repeatedly ghosted on the inside. There are two branches in Saffron, but it may not have come from there. Nor the cash. But I've got DC Grayson checking both banks to see if they can recall anyone withdrawing one thousand pounds recently, and if so, whether the bank put the money into that envelope. I'm hoping if that's the case, that the teller didn't lick the envelope before handing it over to the customer!"

"OK. Anything else?" asked Matthews.

"The notes in the envelope were all facing the same way. It suggests to me that whoever put the cash in there, arranged the notes themselves. There's no way you'd get fifty notes from the bank all neat and tidy like that. Whoever put the money in there may well be a neat and tidy individual. And the name 'Jimmy' on the envelope was written perfectly straight, parallel with the top edge. The writing was probably done by someone who has a leaning toward art. I'd say we're dealing with a very precise, organised person here. You know, someone who measures the top corner edges of an envelope before putting the stamp on!" Hayman laughed, but it wasn't reciprocated.

"Anything on, what's his name . . . Nigel Heseltine? Do you think he had a motive? After all, we know that he and Dobson were in contention for the upcoming President position at the club." Hayman shrugged.

"We haven't got much on him. Worked for de Beers in South Africa, the diamond company, and started his own jewellery business in Saffron Walden when he returned to the UK. Divorced his wife, Gertrude, and married his secretary, Alice. Three kids to his first wife."

"All right, Chris, let's leave it there. Keep me updated on the bank visits, or any other info you find on him. Thanks." The DI turned to face his computer screen – the signal for his sergeant to leave. With his handle on the door knob, Hayman hesitated.

"By the way, sir, Heseltine was one of two at the golf club who own a Mont Blanc pen."

Hayman went back to his desk and entered Nigel Heseltine into the search engine on his computer. Without any luck at first, he added the word 'diamonds' after his name. Soon the sergeant had some more information, and in particular an article from the Northern Transvaal Herald newspaper, dated 20 November 1992.

'Mr Pieter Vermeer was found drowned in the Limpopo River yesterday. He had left a typed suicide note saying that things had become too much for him and that he intended to end his life. At the time Vermeer was working for de Beers where his manager was Mr Nigel Heseltine. Some sources say Heseltine and Vermeer did not see eye to eye. The coroner recorded an open verdict. Mr Heseltine was unavailable for comment.'

The DS paused. Heseltine involved with an apparent suicide of one of his staff nearly thirty years ago. Peter Dobson forced off the road and killed. Was there any link? Just what kind of a man was Nigel Heseltine?

"Hello, mother. How was Clacton?" asked Diane over the phone on the Monday afternoon following Gertrude and Tom's return from their week-end break. The staff room was quiet, and Diane sat near a tall bookshelf. Gertie moved the phone from one hand to the other, then sat at the small table in the hallway.

"It was wonderful, dear. So good to see some familiar faces again in the hotel and the pub next door. Brought back lovely memories from my W.I. visits!" Gertie sounded in a good mood, which Diane was pleased about.

"And Tom? Did he enjoy the week-end? I hope you had two rooms, did you?" Diane asked the question in a light-hearted way. Her mother explained that of course they had two rooms! "And did you book the hotel, mother?" asked Diane, knowing full well that her mother wasn't capable of doing that.

"I could have done, but my sister did it for me. She has a computer, you know, that makes anything possible." Diane had to confront her mother.

"But you haven't got a sister! Someone else must have done it?" suggested Diane. There was hesitation, as Gertie's mind began to wander. "Are you still there? Mother?" Gertie seemed to come out of a trance.

"Did I say sister? Silly me. No, it was one of the WI ladies. What's her name?" Another pause. "That's right, it was Cecilia. We always called her Sis for short. Yes, that's what I meant. Oh, dear, I'd forget my own head if it wasn't attached!" Gertie chuckled.

"Forgive me for asking, but who paid for the hotel and meals? Did you and Tom go halves?"

"Halves? Certainly not. As far as I'm concerned, when a gentleman takes a lady away for the week-end it's his treat. Anyway, it wasn't that expensive. I know my liver and onions were nineteen shillings and sixpence and a gin and tonic two and nine." Diane had heard of pre-decimal currency, but was surprised to hear her mother talk of shillings and pence. "It's finished now, anyway, but we enjoyed ourselves. You can ask Tom next time you come to see me." Diane took a deep breath.

"Kathryn, Michael and I would like to come and see you soon. We're worried about you." Gertie stood up.

"Worried? What do you mean 'worried?' I'm all right. We're all right. Tom's happy here for now. He mended a leaking tap in the utility room last week, and retuned the main TV in the lounge. He's ever so handy. He goes out a few nights a week to see friends, but he's always home by ten thirty. There's absolutely nothing to worry about, Diane!" Her daughter wondered if her mother was becoming too reliant on her lodger. That, too, would be a concern.

"Well, we'd like to see you anyway. Not necessarily all at once. But, you know, from time to time . . . see how things are?" Gertie sighed.

"Look, Diane, I have to go now. I can see a delivery van outside. I'm expecting a new fridge freezer. It was Tom's idea, but he's right. The old one wasn't energy efficient. Something like that. And he likes a cold beer when he comes in after work. And, you won't believe this, he's introduced me to Australian Sauvignon Blanc! Oh, the man's walking up the path. Must fly. Bye." The call finished, and Diane got up from the hard staffroom chair to take in what had been discussed.

The week-end away. Prices in old money. Somebody named Cecilia booking the hotel. Tom picking up the tab. His idea for a new appliance. Cold beer and CabSav. Being a handyman.

This guy wasn't leaving any time soon. But how much of a plan was it on his part? He was sitting pretty, wasn't he? Own en-suite room, meals on the table, washing done, freedom to come and go as he liked.

And she was losing it! Or, more accurately, had lost it! This could become dangerous, thought Diane as she clicked on WhatsApp and tapped on Mike's name.

48

"Er, hello," said Liz, looking at the tall man stood at her front door. He had an earring in his hand, held delicately between thumb and index finger. "I'm sorry, but do I know you? Your face looks familiar." He smiled.

"I'm George, a barista at Costa coffee. George Davison. I've seen you most Wednesdays when you come in with your friends. Last time you were in, I think you may have dropped this?" George held up the earring. Liz was taken aback.

"Heck. I thought I'd lost that! How did you know it was mine?" He gave a slight shrug.

"I served one of the girls who took your orders last time, but you were sat nearest to the counter, and I noticed your earrings. You don't often see pearl earrings that hang low. Then when I was cleaning up later, I spotted it under the cakes and biscuits display cabinet."

Liz looked into his dark eyes, but suddenly pulled herself together.

"How did you know where I lived?" she asked a little anxiously. He smiled; his skin looked soft.

"One of the girls who works there knows you. Cheryl. Said you were an old school friend. She knew where you lived. I don't mean to pry, but she said something about you getting a divorce." So that bit of news was out – probably everyone in Basildon knew. "I'm just on my way home, and I pass your front door, so although Cheryl offered to hang onto it until next week, I said I'd drop it off." Liz felt relieved.

"That's very thoughtful, George. Thank you very much." Liz moved the door towards him, and George got the message. He stepped back. "Well, I've got a couple of things to do," she lied, "so must get on." George nonchalantly slipped his hands into the pockets of his Levi's.

"Yes, sure, I'll let you get on, but, if you're not doing anything next Saturday evening, I've got two tickets for the cinema. Won them in a competition! Not sure what's on, but they've got fifteen screens so there might be something you like?" Liz didn't say anything. Here was a guy she didn't know asking her for a date! Her mind raced. If her husband could spend a week-end with a pensioner in Clacton . . .

"Sure. That would be nice. How can I get in touch, er . . ." George pulled out a card.

"Here, Costa coffee give some baristas these cards. It's got my name on, and a contact number. Give me a call during the week and we can arrange where to meet. I can pick you up if you like." He turned toward the road. "My car's just there, the bright red one." Liz glanced over his shoulder and noticed the sports car. She wasn't at all sure what make it was, but if she'd asked George, he could have told her it was a 1971 Lancia Fulvia sports coupe.

Liz wasn't going to stand at the doorstep to wave him off. She'd noticed that he wasn't wearing a wedding ring.

George Davison. Liz might just make some enquiries about him. She'd lost touch with Cheryl in the café, but Liz could pop in – or better still, possibly find her on Facebook and message her. Yes, she'd do that, but not for a day or two. She didn't want to be seen as eager to know more about George the barista from Costa.

Minutes later, Liz was checking if Cheryl Blake was on social media. There were six people with that name, but Liz found her and clicked on her Facebook profile. Date she joined, school attended, hobbies, previous work experience . . . all the usual. While she was doing that, Liz decided to enter George Davison into the search engine. Again, a long list, but eventually he appeared. A nice photo, along with some personal details. Nothing untoward, at the age of 27 he seemed a straightforward guy with a good education, and included 'classic cars' as his passion. Before joining Costa, he'd worked at Starbucks, and Facebook showed 105 friends on his page.

Liz wasn't going to action anything right now. The pizza she'd been eating when George called had gone cold, and anyway, she'd lost her appetite. There was some prosecco left in the bottle, so, after draining her glass, she had a refill. It was time to get the two badminton racquets down from the loft, and get her kit ready for the visit to the sports club with Vanessa.

Before that, she went upstairs and placed her pearl earring with its twin, nestling in the black velvet - lined box.

And thought of George.

49

Tom and Gertrude had eaten a little earlier than usual. Tom had been thinking all day about how to broach the subject of Will writing. Not only that, but he'd dwelt too long on Gertie's third crystal ball forecast – 'I'll live to be a hundred.'

One hundred! Bloody hell! 19 years to go before she fell off her perch. This wasn't in the plan of Tom and Liz. At 81, their thinking had been that Gertie had a couple of years left at most. Maybe she had? Can you trust a gypsy who looks at a glass orb and tells you what you want to hear? They snaffle your money, give you good news, and pretend that they can 'see the future' in the bloody ball! What a load of tosh, thought Tom.

But . . . what if Gypsy Rose, or whatever her name was, had that forecast correct? No, that would never do. One question in Tom's mind was whether to tell Liz about that? Maybe get her opinion on what might be the best plan. The divorce papers would be through soon, leaving Tom and Liz as 'free agents.' She wasn't going to find another man, Tom decided, so the sooner things were sorted the better. However, what if Liz did believe it? As a single woman she could please herself about what she did. They'd already agreed that Tom would transfer the ownership of their property to his wife and that he'd pay the mortgage payments on it.

After considering matters, Tom felt that telling Liz would have a negative effect. So, he'd leave it for now. He was, after all, best placed in this arrangement to make decisions on what happened during the next few months.

"Gertrude, do you realise that you can make a Will free of charge?" said Tom after their evening meal. The TV was on a low volume, Monty Don telling viewers what jobs needed
doing in the garden as the autumn wore on. Gertie raised her head to look at him.

"No, I didn't. I thought you had to go through a solicitor and they charged you the earth!" Tom sat upright, trying to give Gertie an impression of a knowledgeable comment.

"Well, if you go to a charity – someone like Age Concern or Scope – they go through the details with you, and get it legally approved. All they ask is a donation to their charity when you pass away. So, if you leave £500 to Age Concern and it costs them £100 to handle it for you, they're £400 to the good. Get it?" Gertie put down her magazine.

"Yes, I think I understand that." She paused. "What do you think, Tom?" Perfect! Gertie was asking his opinion. He was going to ride with this as well as he could; it might be his best chance.

"I believe it's a great idea, Gertrude! I know you've got many years left in you, but once it's done, it's done. One less thing to worry about. You've already said your children are sufficiently well off, so you may as well think about leaving your estate to somebody else." Tom hoped he wasn't over-cooking this. He kept smiling. "An aunt of mine used the British Heart Foundation. They sorted it in a few days. Everything was fully documented, all she had to do was sign and date a form, and hey presto! Job done." Gertrude fell silent for a few minutes. Monty Don was half way through pruning a large clematis.

Tom had lied. He didn't have an aunt, but he knew there was a BHF shop in the High Street. He waited, sipping his beer from the bottle. Reaching across, he poured Gertie another glass of Sauvignon Blanc.

"I could make some enquiries tomorrow, couldn't I? Tell you what, I'll pop along in the morning and ask for some details. See what they say." Tom grinned inwardly. 'Bingo' he mused. But he wasn't finished yet.

"Do you have any idea to whom you'd want to leave your estate, Gertrude?" She glanced at the TV for a few seconds.

"You've been very kind to me, Tom. I suppose when your divorce comes through you won't have much left. Now I know you may disagree with what I'm going to say next, but I'm considering leaving it to you." Enter stage left, prepare for the next scene.

"Oh, Gertrude, you can't. I mean we hardly know each other!" Tom prayed his tone was exactly what was required at this moment. He put his bottle down. "But it would be an extremely kind gesture, Gertrude." His fingers were crossed on his lap.

"I haven't told you, Tom, but you're someone who cares about me. More so than my three. Look at all the jobs you've done – never expecting praise or payment. I have a fondness for you that you don't realise." Gertie stopped and wiped a tear from her eye. This is going well, thought Tom. She looked around the living room, taking in the oil paintings and chandeliers as well as the Georgian oak furniture.

"I've no idea what all this is worth. The children won't want paintings, dark furniture and old lights – they're only interested in new - fangled gadgets and white walls everywhere. Stainless steel this and chrome that. I can see them now, a skip on the drive, tossing most of this into it for a council lorry to collect and take to a landfill site. As for the house, well prices are going down, aren't they?" Tom smiled a reassuring smile.

"Gertrude, you don't have to go through with this if you don't want to, you know?" Tom knew he was on the edge of a mind change by Gertie, but he hadn't to come across as too eager.

"No. I tell you what, Tom. When you come home from work tomorrow, I'll have been to see the Heart people and done the deed! What do you think about that?" She took a long sip of her wine.

"Well, thank you so much, Gertrude. You are very kind . . . and thoughtful." She stood up.

"I'm feeling tired, Tom. If you'll excuse me, I'll have an early night. I've left some of that nice blue cheese you like in the fridge, and there are some crackers in the biscuit barrel. Just in case you're peckish before you retire."

Gertrude gave Tom a kiss on his forehead as she left the room. A minute later, Monty Don was replaced by a black and white western starring Gary Cooper.

Tom flicked the cap off the beer bottle. He gulped down half the contents as he looked up at the crystal chandelier.

Finishing his beer, Tom checked his account at *Hightrack Express*, his bookies. £19,245 in his account. He'd place a couple of bets tomorrow. There were three certainties running at Ascot.

50

Hi Mike. We need to do something about Tom now! Suggest I message K to discuss. Let's give it a week from today to think it over. D x

Hi D. OK. Mike x

Hi K. Messaged Mike. Enough talking done about mother. We need to get Tom out of the house. Think it through. Let's talk in seven days. D x

Hi D. Agreed. Can't keep on talking about it.
Action necessary. Message you next week. K x

51

Liz had forgotten how unfit she really was. Moving across the badminton court wasn't as she remembered it. A long time back. Ten years or so. Reaching out an arm with the racquet didn't seem as long a stretch as it ought to be – and that featherweight shuttlecock floated down to the ground quicker than she recalled it used to do. Vanessa was giving her a pasting. But after a quick break, Liz began to feel more confident.

Bam! Liz swung the racquet through an arc and hit the shuttlecock perfectly. Just over the net and the trajectory took it to the far, right hand corner. Vanessa was left floundering. Luck? No way. As the minutes passed, Liz took over the dominance of the match. Where had she found her inner strength? She had no idea, but mentally she was determined to give Vanessa a run for her money.

Booked for an hour, the clock at the end of the hall showed 3.40 pm. Twenty minutes left. Liz had lost the first game by 21 points to 9. But she came back in the second to win a close fought match by 22 points to 20. Vanessa was tempted to ask her opponent where she'd summoned up the fervour and skill that she was now showing but that would have wasted her breath. Vanessa needed every lungful of air to keep her going. She popped an energy tablet in her mouth and held it under her tongue where it slowly dissolved. Maybe it was psychological, but Vanessa felt stronger in seconds.

Thwack! A hard shot skimmed the top of the net and flew across to Liz's right. Point to Vanessa. This was becoming war. Damn the coffee morning companionship . . . Vanessa wasn't going to let this woman get the better of her. Both girls were sweating, the sports hall humidity high. Liz was glad she'd put a thick, absorbent band on both wrists. It was 19 points each in the third game, and Vanessa wasn't backing down. Smack, biff, thwack, it was even. Five minutes left before they had to vacate the court. One last swing of Liz's racquet sent the shuttlecock flying over the net to make it 21 – 18 to Liz. She'd won! Close to tears, she smiled at her opponent and hugged her – a rather clammy affair, considering both had very damp shirts on!

"Bloody hell, Liz, what are you taking? You seem as fit as a butcher's dog!" gasped Vanessa. Liz took a few seconds to get her breath back.

"Well, I had a glass of Lucozade before I came out this afternoon!" They both laughed.

"C'mon. Let's have a shower. The bar's open and I fancy a drink!" said Vanessa, hands on hips. Fifteen minutes later, both were sat in the sports club bar. Two large spritzers in front of them.

"You should play more, Liz. You're good. There's a league here – you'd soon find your way into the top half of the table." Liz took a long sip of her drink.

"I don't know. I played quite a bit when I was younger, before I met Tom. But, you know, you get married and settle into a marriage routine." Liz paused. "But then you begin to realise what marriage can do to you. I should have kept playing, and doing other things, but there was the housework and washing and ironing, then cooking and my part time job . . ."

"However, now that you and Tom are separated, all of that can go out of the window. You're your own boss now. And once the divorce comes through, you're a free woman! Imagine. Parties every week-end, find Mr Right, holidays abroad – the Caribbean, the Seychelles with all that pure white sand and cocktails on the beach. Heaven!" Liz smiled weakly. She couldn't tell Vanessa what was really going on. There would come a time when Liz could lose all her friends, once the truth came out. But maybe if she and Tom kept up the charade, no one would be any the wiser. 'Stick to the plan,' thought Liz. Go through with it as they'd discussed.

Separate, divorce, Tom marries Gertie, she dies, Tom engineers the inheritance, they remarry and live happily ever after.

"Yes, that sounds wonderful, but I'm not sure about finding someone else. I did have a caller this week. One of the baristas from Costa named George. He dropped by to return an earring I'd lost in the café, and he was nice. Gorgeous red sports car, too." Vanessa slowly put her glass down.

"George? Not George Davison, the tall, good - looking guy?" Liz nodded. "He's a member here, in fact, wait a minute . . . that's him over there at the bar. He's seen us and he's coming over," whispered Vanessa. George Davison had spotted Liz and smiled. He walked across to their table.

"Ladies, good afternoon. Hi Liz, I didn't realise you're a member here," he said cheerfully. She had to be honest with him.

"I'm not. Vanessa signed me in this afternoon to play badminton." Vanessa gave Davison a look and said 'hello.' Liz couldn't make out if there was something in Vanessa's attitude toward him.

"Can I get you ladies a drink?" he offered. The two girls exchanged glances. Liz spoke first.

"Thanks, George, but I need to go. I've got someone calling at my place soon." Vanessa declined, too.

"Is that the time? I must fly," she said, standing and finishing her drink. Davison looked put out.

"Well, maybe another time?" He looked at Liz. "Give me a call soon, Liz, and we'll arrange a date to meet." Liz smiled, realising that Vanessa now knew what was going on. Davison said his farewell, and joined a couple of guys at the bar. The girls left together and headed down the stairs and out to the car park.

"What's that look for?" asked Liz, turning to Vanessa as they reached Liz's car.

"Don't tell me you're going to go out with him!" Liz asked why not. "Well, I need to tell you something, Liz, because I'm guessing you don't know." Liz leant back against the driver's door.

"Know what?" she queried. Vanessa hesitated for a few seconds.

"George used to be a Georgina." Liz gasped.

"Are you telling me that he was a she? What the . . .?" Vanessa got closer.

"George Davison was born a girl. The story goes that his mother used to dress him in girl's clothes until he was about ten. He had a sex-change operation some eight years ago. Now, I don't know what's down below, but if you ever go out with him, be prepared for a surprise." Vanessa grinned.

"Bloody hell! If I'd known that . . ." Vanessa interrupted.

"Well, you do now!" Liz had to go, get away from this place. She thanked her friend for the game of badminton, got into her car, and drove off. Liz nearly collided with an oncoming motorcyclist as she sped along the main road in her hurry to get home.

Once inside, she decided on another shower. Running upstairs, Liz stripped off and jumped into the cubicle. She turned the mixer tap to a hotter setting than normal, washed her hair and gave her body an all – over, thorough scrub using a real sponge.

The thought of spending time with George, or 'Georgina' was now the furthest thing from her mind.

She hoped there was still a bottle of prosecco in the fridge.

52

"I'm glad we could get together," said Diane to her siblings. The three were standing at the end of their mother's drive. "His van is here so he'll be in. We've agreed we'll confront him, even if it causes some embarrassment in front of mother. We can point out the potential problems and simply tell Tom it's time to go." Mike and Katheryn nodded. "Let's go!" It sounded like a cavalry charge against Red Indians somewhere in the Arizona desert. Mike knocked, then opened the front door. Gertrude rarely kept it locked during the day. They trooped in, each wiping their feet as they did so.

"Hello, mother, it's only us," Diane said reassuringly. Gertie was sitting in her favourite chair in the lounge, beneath an oil painting of a child blowing bubbles. She was taken by surprise.

"Oh, good afternoon," she replied, lifting her spectacles from her nose. "To what do I owe this pleasure?" Each in turn gave her a peck on the cheek, then took a seat. Diane spoke first.

"Mother, we have been concerned about you living here with Tom for some time now. We don't think it's a good idea. The three of us agree that he has to go. Find somewhere else to live. What do you think? Is he in?" Gertrude put her specs on the small coffee table by her side, and tossed the magazine she'd been reading onto the floor.

"No, he's not in. And what's all this? Have you been planning behind my back? Scheming? I didn't raise you to be furtive like this." Gertrude wiped her nose on a tissue tucked in her cardigan sleeve. Kathryn looked away, a feeling of guilt coming over her. A slight blush. Diane took control of the discussion.

"Mike, how do you feel about all this?" probed Diane, bringing her brother into the conversation. Mike moved somewhat uneasily in his chair.

"Di's right, mother. We *are* worried about you. I'm sure Tom has been a help to you, and is grateful for you giving him a roof over his head since he left his wife, but he can find somewhere else. A B and B, perhaps?" He paused. "We believe he's trying to wangle his way into your life." Gertrude stood.

"Wangle his way into my life! What on earth does that mean?" She walked across to the window and looked out. "Since your father left to live with that woman, I've been lonely. Can't you see that? He came round initially to fix the boiler, or fridge, or something, and been very helpful with a number of jobs. He's good company. And so charming, I mean he's a lovely man. I enjoy him being here." Kathryn spoke.

"Yes, mother, but can't you see he's getting *too* friendly?" Gertrude wasn't going to let them know that she and Tom had discussed a Will, that she was going to the British Heart Foundation in a few days to sort out a Will. It was her little secret.

"This is all nonsense and I won't hear any more of it!" Her voice was louder than usual. "I'm going to put the kettle on and make some tea. If we all sit down with a cup of Darjeeling and a biscuit, I'm sure we can all come to an amicable agreement that Tom will continue to live here!" There was silence as Gertrude went into the kitchen.

"I'll give you a hand, mother," proposed Kathryn who followed Gertrude out of the lounge. Mike looked across at Diane and pointed an index finger upwards.

"I'm going up to the loo," he said, then winked. Minutes later, Mike came out of the upstairs toilet to find Diane standing on the landing. Her view of the rear garden through the tall, ornate leaded window always gave her pleasure.

"What the hell are we going to do, Mike? She not for shifting. Talk about the Iron Lady!" Mike clasped his hands, crunching his knuckles in the process. He lowered his voice.

"Di, we've got to get rid of him. I know someone who can do it." She looked nervous.

"Do what?" she asked timidly.

"Kill him." Diane's jaw dropped. She slowly repeated his phrase. He nodded. "Yes. I know someone who can do it. I can't say too much, but Pyong has a contact. It may sound a bit dramatic, but she arranged for this guy to get rid of somebody who was trying to blackmail us." He paused and cracked his knuckles again. "His name's James Herring. We looked after one of his dogs, a King Charles Cavalier. I don't know much about him, but she met with him and, well, we didn't hear from the blackmailer again . . . if you get my drift." He smiled, relieved to have been able to share this with someone else. Diane stared into her brother's eyes.

"Bloody hell, Mike!" She put a hand on his forearm. "Do you really think we should do this?" He placed a hand over hers.

"Yes. Absolutely. This guy has to go. We've done enough talking. I suggest we have that cup of tea, then share this with Kathryn. Are you on my side with this?" Diane nodded firmly. "OK. Before we part this afternoon, we must all agree on the plan. The three of us have to be in on it."

Mike and Diane went downstairs and entered the lounge where a tray with four cups of tea and a large plate of biscuits was laid on the centre table.

Upstairs, the door to Tom's room was slightly ajar. He'd heard every word spoken by two of Gertie's children on the landing.

James Herring? Tom wondered who this man was. But he knew one thing.

He was going to find out.

53

Tom had left early for work the following morning. After a restless night, he decided the best thing was to get to the depot and start his deliveries sooner than normal. His schedule would be ready for him, and he'd be loaded up by 8.30 am. By keeping busy, he hoped to take his mind off the conversation he had heard yesterday. About the 'plan.'

Checking the racing results, his three certs at Ascot had let him down. One was probably still running! He'd put a grand on each to win, so his account was down to about £16,250. Never mind, with a few good tips from some of the lads at work, he'd soon be quid's in. One of his mates, Geordie from Newcastle upon Tyne, knows a jockey who he went to school with. He's a source of inside knowledge on most races.

Tom was soon heading out of the depot car park with his van loaded - it was going to be a hectic day, with seventeen deliveries planned. His lunch break would be taken after delivery number eight which was in Romford, and he'd park up somewhere and spend time checking on James Herring. Herring! What a bloody name to carry around, and what leg-pulls must he have had at school.

You smell fishy...that's a red herring...are you going to be a kipper when you die...you look all goggle-eyed...finny you should say that...fancy a smoke...?

After an uneventful morning, apart from a grumpy customer who deserved a good slap if Tom could have had his own way, he pulled the Peugeot van into a layby. The stop had its own burger van which Tom had used before. Mario, the owner, was wearing his bandana and looking like someone off the set of a spaghetti western. He got in the queue and ordered a cheeseburger and can of Coke. Minutes later, and armed with two serviettes, he was munching into the bun. Tom wasn't going to get grease on his smartphone, so he finished eating and gave his hands a good wipe. After drinking half of the Coke, he rubbed his fingers again and tapped the 'on' button. He went straight into Facebook and entered the name James Herring.

Nothing. He tried Jim *and* Jimmy Herring. Still no name. 'Fish' followed James . . . then a number of fish types. Cod, Ray, Turbot. After all, he could be using a Piscean synonym, Tom thought. Nothing, zippo, zilch. Blast! Tom was hoping that by the end of the day, he'd know a lot more about this guy. Nope, he was just going to have to leave it.

He threw the empty can, plus used serviettes, into a rubbish bin near to the back of the burger cabin. Maybe there was another way to get to get some information on Mr Herring? Tom wondered if Gertie knew him? Unlikely. But even if she did, there was no way he could rely on anything she told him.

But it's strange how sometimes Lady Luck can throw you a couple of good dice. For his last Corbett & Perkins delivery of the day, Tom stopped off at a small retailer near Brentwood. He loaded three boxes onto a small sack barrow and went in. It was 4.55 pm and the owner, Fred Wright, seemed rushed.

"Hi, Fred, you seem in a hurry? Is your house burning down?" Tom chuckled.

"Oh, hello, Tom. No. It's the annual meeting of the Mid Essex Dog Owners Club tonight. MEDOC for short, and I mustn't be late." Dog owners club?

"Oh? You a dog owner then?" Tom realised the question was really obvious. Fred nodded.

"Yes, a Cavalier King Charles. He's won a couple of awards at Cruft's. I'm fonder of him than the wife, but don't tell her!" Fred grinned.

Tom recalled that Mike had mentioned a King Charles spaniel in the same breath as James Herring when he overheard him talking to his sister. His wife and him had looked after it at their kennels. Tom couldn't let this pass – it was an opportunity.

"Fred. A friend of mine was telling me about a guy who owns a Cavalier King Charles. His name is James Herring. I don't suppose he's a member of your dog club, is he?" This was a very long shot, with odds worse than some of Tom's racehorse certs.

"Ah, you mean Jamek Ingherr. Yes, he is! The rogue! His real name is Ingherr but he always calls himself Jim Herring – at least that's how I know him. James sounds posh. Perhaps he uses that when he's out to impress? He came over from Serbia a few years ago. Some of the boys say he's a bit dodgy but I think he's OK. Pays cash for everything."

Tom had put the three boxes on the counter and Fred signed the delivery note. Tom left the shop and got back into the Peugeot.

'Jamek Ingherr,' thought Tom. 'Well, let's take a look at your social media profile, shall we, Jamek?'

54

The doorbell rang. Liz glanced at the kitchen clock. It almost 10.30 am. She had been up early and doing some baking. It was ages since she'd got her hands covered in flour. A batch of cheese scones had been out of the oven for half an hour, the Victoria sponge cake had cooled, and been sliced across the middle and lathered with jam and cream, and finally dusted with icing sugar. Liz had washed the little-used tea service and thoroughly wiped the dinner plates normally kept in the sideboard cupboard.

Liz was expecting an important visitor today – someone she hadn't seen for a long time. She had looked forward to this, and asked herself why she hadn't thought of inviting the guest sooner. Her visitor lived alone - the tragic accident having robbed her visitor of a loved one nearly two years ago.

*

Why had the gaffer at the site let a newly qualified apprentice erect the scaffolding with a part – time labourer? The investigation showed that of one hundred and eighty bolts, forty - seven were not fully tightened.

The wind speed had increased during that morning but the men continued working. At precisely 11.23 am the metal tubing framework had collapsed like a pack of cards. Despite four workers rushing to help the three injured men, one had died instantly at the scene. The police, then an ambulance, had arrived very shortly afterwards. Despite attempts to save him, another man was pronounced dead minutes later.

"We've got two dead bodies here, sarge," said the PC into his lapel fitted transmitter.

"OK. You know what to do," replied the duty sergeant at Rayleigh police station.

*

The doorbell rang again. 'Coming!' shouted Liz, wiping her hands on her apron and hurrying to the front door. She opened the door as far as it would go, then spread her arms wide. The visitor put the suitcase down and opened their arms, too. They embraced each other on the doorstep for what seemed an eternity.

"Come in, come in," gasped Liz after the long bear hug. "Here, I'll get your case." The pair walked into the front room, then held each other for a second time, only a little longer.

"God, I've missed you," uttered the visitor. Liz wiped a tear from her eye.

"Me, too. I'll put the kettle on. Let's have that cup of tea I promised you ages ago!"

The pair walked into the kitchen, the visitor perching on a high stool at the breakfast bar.

"And here's something I owe you," said the visitor. An envelope was tossed onto the work surface. Liz looked at the tatty, brown packet. "It's the fifty quid for the sideboard I bought off you. It's really come in handy. Hides a lot of rubbish!" They both laughed.

Liz was pleased that her sister Mary had arrived on the train from Southend, and she was there to stay for a week. They had a lot of catching up to do.

"So, what's the latest on that bloody husband of yours?" asked Mary.

"Don't ask," Liz replied. "Been off with his geriatric carer for a dirty week-end in Clacton!" Mary's eyes widened and her lower jaw dropped.

"What? You're having a laugh, aren't you, Liz?" Her sister explained the scenario, telling Mary she didn't really care. She was sure Tom had no evil intentions. After they'd finished their tea Liz stood.

"I'll show you up to your room, Mary. I've put some fresh sheets and a pillowcase on. The small TV works, and the bedside radio is set to BBC radio two. The wardrobe has room for your things, and I've left a few spare hangers in there. Make yourself at home, anyway." Liz led the way upstairs and showed Mary into the back bedroom. "I suggest we go out for a light lunch. There's a nice cafe just opened in the High Street. My treat. We can eat in this evening, and, unfortunately, I'm working tomorrow." Mary put her hand on Liz's arm.

"Right. Shut up," said Mary. "I propose we go out tomorrow night, and it's *my treat*! I saw a nice place on TripAdvisor – The Cowherd's Arms – not too far away. We'll get a taxi." With that, Liz left her sister to unpack and freshen up.

Mary placed some underwear and cosmetics in a bedside drawer, and put her washbag ready to take into the bathroom. As she hung a couple of dresses up, a woollen belt from one of them dropped to the bottom of the wardrobe. Mary bent to pick it up but it had snagged on something -the buckle of a leather strap. She tugged at the strap, realising that it was a handbag pushed right to the back of the wardrobe. The handbag had to be pulled out to get the belt off the buckle.

Mary looked at it. It was leather, black in colour, with two initials on the side of the flap.

J T

55

Tom had stopped off at his bookmakers on the way back to Gerties. His job paid fairly well, but if he and Gertie were going to go away again, he didn't want to be wondering if he could afford a couple of meals and a few drinks. Gertie might just tell him that she wanted another week-end somewhere, or even have got 'her friend' to book something. The balance in his account at *Hightrack Express* was healthy enough, but another few thousand would be nice. He didn't want to have to penny pinch when Gertie eyed up the most expensive dish on the menu. And, of course, he was still putting money into Liz's bank account. Her part time cleaning job wasn't going to keep her in lobster and caviar!

"Hi, Terry. How are you doing? Still ripping off your customers?" Tom joked as he walked in. Terry, the manager, knew Tom's sense of humour. After all, he'd been a client since before he'd left school.

"No. It's my customers who rip themselves off! I don't force anyone to give me their money!" Terry smiled. "Like you, you have the freedom to make choices. It's just that they're not always good ones." There was an evening meeting at Catterick, and Tom searched the runners and riders for each race. A total of five. After several minutes of weighing up the facts he normally used – the name of jockey, race distance, recent performance of the horse, running conditions, and whether it was a left or right-handed track – Tom made out his five bets.

Geronimo's Friend   5/1
Take It Easy   10/1
Zebra Grass   20/1
Little Miss Cumbria   2/1 favourite
Ray's Golden Arrow   8/1

£250 to win on each – on the nose. Tom breathed in the stale air of the shop as he glanced at some of the dropouts that used this place and noticed the flashing lights on three fruit machines. These were the things that excited him. Anyone could hold a smartphone or I-pad and tap in some letters and numbers, sitting in a comfortable chair in a sterile room, cup of coffee at hand.

"You going to place those bets or do you want a bed for the night?" asked Terry with a
wry grin. Tom got up and ambled across to the counter, protected by a bullet proof glass screen, and slid his slips under the narrow gap at the bottom.

"£1,250 from my account Terry, s'il vous plait," whispered Tom with a wink. "I'll look forward to seeing if all five have won later this evening! If they do, I'm looking at about . . ." He hesitated. "Maybe ten big ones?"

"You never were any good at maths!" Terry replied quickly. "Leave that to me. It'll be quite a bit!" Terry gave Tom his betting slip receipt which he carefully placed in his wallet.

"I'll give you a phone call tomorrow, Terry. Hope you've got enough in the bank to pay your debts!" Terry waved his hand in a dismissive manner.

"Never mind about that. How are you getting on with your new landlady? News on the streets is that you whisked her off on a romantic week-end to the coast!" Terry winked and tapped the side of his nose. Tom had no idea why people did that . . . what did the nose have to do with anything, apart from being nosey? Perhaps that was it? Tom blushed.

"Romantic week-end? Do me a favour. She'd arranged it and invited me along. That's all. Come on . . . you don't think . . .?" Terry busied himself with checking something in a file, and Tom took that as the end of the banter.

What was clear to Tom was that tongues were wagging in the town. A man who has filed for divorce living next to his estranged wife with a woman old enough to be his mother. How did people see this? Oddly, perhaps. But when Tom married Gertrude Heseltine the local jungle drums would be making one hell of a noise!

Tom had to keep going along with his plan. He couldn't let his guard down now. It wasn't going to take long. In fact, he and Liz expected to hear about their divorce any day now. Both had chivvied their solicitors, emphasising that they wanted things cleared up as soon as possible. He made a mental note to call his Wimbledon solicitor, Clive Hapgood, later in the week. Tom realised that the divorce was only the starter to the meal, the main course and dessert were to come along later.

"OK, lover boy, I need to lock up now. Time to go home," ordered Terry with a light chuckle. Tom smiled and moved to the door.

"I'll be in touch," shouted Tom, with a reciprocal tap of his nose as he closed the shop door leaving the bell ringing on the loose shackle at the top. He'd be back at Gertie's in twenty minutes, and wondered what meal she had prepared for him this evening. And what news of the day's events.

"Hello, Gertrude," said Tom loudly, as he closed the door.

"In here, Tom," replied Gertie from the lounge. She was sitting with a bottle of Bollinger and two crystal glasses on the table next to her. "Can you do the honours, Tom? I'm not able to open champagne these days. I once did it with a sword! Can you believe that? On holiday somewhere warm. The waiter showed me how to do it, and zap, the blade took the cork out with a good shower of foam everywhere!" Tom unscrewed the wire, then picked up the clean tea – towel on the arm of the chair. He began to ease the bottle open.

"What's the occasion, Gertrude? Have you won the lottery? A million?" She smiled softly.

"No, Tom. I've been to the Red Cross shop today and sorted out my Will. As we discussed. Remember?" Of course, he remembered!

"Really? What happened, Gertrude?" Tom slowly filled the two glasses and handed one to Gertie.

"Good health," she proposed as she raised her champagne flute. Both sipped the delicate, pale golden liquid.

"Sit down and I'll tell you." Tom obliged, realising he hadn't washed his hands, yet. "Well, I did as you suggested. They were very helpful. A solicitor arrived after half an hour and we filled in the forms. One of the staff acted as a witness to my signature. We dated it . . . job done. I couldn't believe it was so easy. They gave me a copy which I've put in the safe." Tom needed some reassurance. He chose his words carefully, but directly.

"So, you've left everything to me, have you, Gertrude?" Her eyes smiled as she nodded.

"As we discussed, Tom. It's all done. Sorted." That was good enough for him. Wow! It hadn't sunk in. Here he was, sat drinking a fine champagne, under the sparkling chandeliers, with the faces of the subjects from several priceless oil paintings looking down on him.

"Bless you, Gertrude. You're very kind," said Tom, taking another sip.

"It's my pleasure, Tom. Drink up. There's another bottle in the fridge, and I've ordered a meal from that nice restaurant up the road. Delivery time eight o'clock." Tom excused himself. He needed a shower and a change of clothing.

Standing by his bed, he began to get undressed.

'Safe? What bloody safe?' he wondered. *'She never mentioned a safe before.'*

He hadn't even given Jamek Ingherr a thought.

56

DS Chris Hayman knocked on his boss's door. DI Matthews shouted for him to enter. Hayman went in, carrying a folder under his right arm.

"A bit of an update in the Dobson case, guv." Matthews managed a weak smile and looked at his sergeant expectantly. "A neighbour of Gareth White, the guy who had his Merc stolen the night Dobson was forced off the road, has just come back from a month's holiday in South America." The DS glanced at his notes. "Richard Dillistone is the guy in question. He checked his front door CCTV footage and says he can see someone taking White's car off his drive. It clearly shows the date and time on the recording, but the images are a bit grainy. It was Saturday, 29 May at 2340 hrs. He's bringing it in for us to have a better look at." Matthews raised his eyebrows.

"Good effort, Chris. Fingers crossed we can get the tech boys to enhance it and get a better look at the thief." Hayman nodded.

"I'll get onto that. Also, DC Grayson tells me that a teller at one of the Barclays branches does recall someone going into the bank and asking to exchange some euros for sterling and asked if the individual was a customer, to which they replied 'yes.' However, no further check was made. The value of the foreign currency was a few quid over a grand. They asked for one thousand to be put into an envelope, and took the rest and slipped that into a coat pocket."

"What do we know about that person?"

Hayman shuffled, cramp beginning to affect his left leg.

"Well, normally the CCTV in the bank is on all the time, but on the day this transaction was made, two days before Dobson was killed, there had been a fault and it wasn't working."

"Bloody typical!" said the DI, exasperation in his voice.

Hayman held a finger up, schoolboy – like.

"However, guv, the bank teller does recall that this person was a female with what he thought might be the slightest hint of a South African or Australian accent. Shortish blonde hair, about five feet ten, and he noticed that she was wearing red leather gloves but it wasn't a cold day." Matthews laced his fingers behind his head.

"So, if we can find a blonde South African or Aussie woman with red gloves, we're in with a chance? Hell, Chris, I've more chance of winning the Euromillions this week!" The DS shrugged.

"It's low priority, sir, but I'll put some feelers out. There might be something we can find." The Inspector knew his sergeant was tenacious, and would be exploring other avenues. But the more time that passed meant less chance of finding that person. They weren't even sure if the woman did have anything to do with the cash found in the Mercedes. However, it was a thousand pounds. Coincidence?

Matthews nodded, asking Hayman if there was anything else. There wasn't. The DI buried his head in some paperwork and his sergeant took the hint. It was time for a coffee, then Hayman had some other enquiries to which he needed to attend.

57

Mary had pushed the handbag further back into the bottom of the wardrobe. She decided not to mention it to Liz. There was no need. It was just a handbag with two letters on it and it was none of her business anyway. Liz might even think her sister had been poking about in there – even going through some drawers. It was Liz's day off work and they'd planned a girlie day out, with a fancy coffee, light lunch, lots of shopping – or at least, window shopping, and out in the evening.

Yesterday, Mary had occupied herself with a reading her James Patterson paperback, watching some TV, and going for a stroll. The visit to The Cowherd's Arms the night before had been disappointing. Mary wondered if she was going to trust TripAdvisor comments ever again. She'd read somewhere that many reviews on web sites were fakes, anyway. The manager of some pub would ask as many mates as possible to put some good comments on Facebook for a free pint.

They had ordered 'Today's Special.' Beef and ale pie, with twice-cooked chips and side salad. In their opinion the pie was at least a day old, the chips were overdone, even burnt, and the salad had been thrown together without a care in the world. Half of their meal was left on their plates and Mary had told the waiter what she thought of the food.

That aside, they'd caught up on their news and enjoyed a few drinks. The gin and tonics were good, with a decent gin and quality tonic water, two chunky ice cubes and a thin lemon wedge. After Mary had complained about their meals, the manager had gone over to their table. He introduced himself as Kevin and apologised for the fayre, commenting that the regular chef was off sick. Not a good sign when you hear that in a restaurant, thought Mary. Was he tasting his own food? On the plus side, Kevin had offered them free gin and tonics for the rest of the evening.

Neither Liz nor Mary could recall getting home that night. A taxi had dropped them off at the gate, and they assumed they'd managed to stagger into the house and get into bed. Dishevelled clothes lay across the floor, and there were mascara streaks across their pillows. If there was a bonus, it was that neither of the women had vomited. Liz hated throwing up . . . speaking into that big white porcelain telephone bolted to the bathroom floor. Getting rid of that acidic, rancid taste.

They'd had dry white toast and tea for breakfast. Thankfully, Liz wasn't working, and it seemed the rest of the day would be quiet for both of them. Recovery time.

"Who was that guy that spoke to us last night, Liz?" asked Mary, sitting at the kitchen table and pulling her toast apart. She slipped a piece into her parched mouth.

"What guy? I don't remember anyone. Oh, except Kevin," replied Liz, tightening her dressing gown. She poured out the tea.

"He was fairly tall, and well spoken. Don't you remember? He came across to our table and recognised you. I'm trying to think of his name." Mary scratched her head as if that would help her to recall events. "Come on, Liz, he knew you!" Liz toyed with her toast, then broke off a small piece the size of a postage stamp.

"I can't think. I vaguely remember somebody talking to us, but it was quite late, wasn't it? Hell, I think we were close to falling over by then." Liz laughed and sipped her tea. Both women sat quietly for a few minutes, trying hard to piece together what had happened in The Cowherd's Arms. Liz's mind was blank. It did occur to her how dangerous that might have been . . . a conversation with a man she couldn't recall. Suddenly, Mary threw her toast down.

"It's just come to me!" It was a lightbulb moment for Mary. "The man said his name was Terry. I asked him if he liked chocolate oranges! Don't you remember? You giggled like a schoolgirl." Liz looked into her mug. Her mind was a blank. "And . . . he gave me a business card!" Liz turned.

"A business card, you say? Where is it?" Mary jumped off her kitchen stool and went upstairs. Seconds later she was back. Mary handed it to her sister. Liz focused her eyes on the small print.

Terence Williams - Manager
Hightrack Express
Swan Street, Basildon SS14 1ET
Tel. 0800 022 3680

That was it! Liz did remember some guy talking to them late in the evening. She tried to concentrate. Little by little the facts started to connect in her brain.

This Terry ambled over to talk with them. Said he thought he recognised Liz and began talking. He'd had a lot to drink, slurred his words a bit. Tom's name was mentioned. The fog was lifting in Liz's head. Would the words come to her?
What was it he'd said? Something about Tom having an account with him? An account? Oh, yes, he'd mentioned the word 'bookmaker.' Liz took a mouthful of her tea.

"Do you recall he said he was a book-maker, Mary?" Her sister nodded. "And Tom goes to this bookie's and he has an account there?" Another nod. "I never bloody knew that!" shouted Liz, throwing a piece of toast across the kitchen. It bounced off the kettle. "Was there anything else?" demanded Liz.

"Well, I'm pretty sure that Terry let slip that Tom had twenty thousand quid in his account," if my blurred memory serves." Liz gasped. "Not only that, but he backed five horses at Catterick. They all won! Your Tom is sitting on over thirty thousand pounds with that bookie."

Liz's mug dropped to the stone floor and shattered.

The words FROM YOUR and LOVING HUSBAND were split clean in half.

58

Tom had been on Facebook. The name Jamek Ingherr was there. Only the one. But no photo. He knew some that registered with this social media site didn't download their photo. Not because they had anything to hide, but because they didn't want to world to see their face. Sometimes an individual would put a pet's photo beneath their name. Like a dog. Some old mut that they'd claim they loved.

No visual identity of this guy was going to make things more difficult. Tom could be anywhere and Ingherr might be watching him. Waiting. Ready to do whatever his plan was. Tom wondered if Mike Heseltine had already spoken with Ingherr - set things up. It had to be assumed that Mike knew where Tom worked, could even get details of his deliveries. There was no doubt that from now on Tom Ball was going to have to be extra vigilant.

Mike could easily get details from his mother if another week-end away was planned for Tom and Gertie. He imagined being in some seaside hotel spending more time looking at the men in there than listening and conversing with Gertie. How would that appear? Tom eyeing up the fellows as if seeking a rent boy for the night!

The Facebook details on Ingherr were scanty. He'd attended a secondary school in Zemun, been a drop-out at college, and his first job was as a forklift truck driver in a factory in Belgrade that manufactured washing machines and tumble driers. He'd listed his hobby as carpentry, and he had forty - two friends. Tom felt that Ingherr wasn't one for communicating much, and maybe used Facebook for 'dark' activities. Posting messages in code, perhaps, or sending photos that were more representative than actual. If only he could see what this guy looked like.

He was going to give it a go. Tom clicked Friends on the bar across the top of Ingherr's page. From a quick scan, most were British names, the others either Serbian or maybe Eastern European. He scrolled down the names on the left - hand side. Tom stopped on Patrick Murray and clicked. This person was a Brit, with photos showing him on holiday somewhere sunny, at a party, and various others. He'd been to school in Birmingham, and occupation was listed as Meat Purveyor. A bloody butcher, thought Tom. No matter, Tom moved to Message, clicked on it and began to type.

Hi Patrick, I'm an old friend of Jamek, although I know him as Jim. I haven't seen him for some time. He used to have a beard so he probably looks a bit different these days. I'm hoping to surprise him with a visit. Can you help? If you could send me a recent photo that would be great. An address would be good, too. Please keep this between ourselves, and I'll let you know how the surprise visit goes! Cheers, Tom.

Tom hit Post. He was aware that this was a risky plan. If Patrick told Ingherr of this message Tom could be in trouble, but Tom had to know what this Serbian looked like. Now all he had to do was wait for a reply. If he didn't get one in twenty - four hours, he'd try it once more with another 'Friend.' But that would be it.

Suddenly, Tom had another idea, and cursed himself for not thinking of it before. His customer, Fred Wright, had mentioned the dog owners club of which Ingherr was a member. Clubs have events and meetings, and often photographs are taken when members get together. If Fred had a group photo on which Ingherr appeared, that might satisfy Tom's need to see what this guy looked like.

This had to be Tom's second approach. He'd give Fred a phone call, say he was in the area tomorrow, and make up reason why he'd love to see any photos of the MEDOC group.

A cousin loved dogs, was interested in joining the club, wondered about the members, blah, blah, blah.

Tom felt Fred Wright would be proud to show him a photo. He was about to go to bed when his phone pinged. It was a WhatsApp message from Liz.

Hello. How are you? Hope all is well. Are you managing OK with money? Liz xxx

It was time for Mary to go back to Southend-on-Sea, known as the seaside town with the longest pier in Britain. They'd talked a lot, and reminisced about old times. Both parents were dead – their mother, a lifelong smoker, having died from lung cancer two years ago and their father had contracted septicaemia following a hospital operation on his kidneys a year before that. Both agreed they'd had a happy childhood, spending holidays on the Essex coast and the occasional long trip to Scotland in father's Ford Cortina.

They laughed about getting drunk at the pub, and the fortunate offer of free G & Ts for the rest of the evening. When they'd gone shopping, most visits were made to charity shops rather than the bigger stores. Mary had bought a smart coat with an M & S label for £3, and a pair of leather shoes stamped Hotters for the same price. She was tempted by a pearl necklace with a central emerald stone but her deceased husband, Keith, had bought her one for her twenty first birthday so it didn't feel right. Liz moved and looked at a range of clothing on hangers but resisted the temptation to open her purse.

"Hey, Liz, there's a nice handbag here," said Mary in the Oxfam shop. She wanted to 'test the water' with her sister.

"Oh, it's black leather. Hmm, yes, nice, but I prefer brown handbags. I think black ones are so drab and funereal." Mary probed further, asking Liz if she had a black handbag? The answer was 'no.'

Yes, they'd enjoyed themselves, but Mary began thinking about the handbag in the wardrobe before she left. J T. Who did those initials belong to? A few minutes before the taxi arrived to take Mary to the station, she popped upstairs to get her suitcase. She opened the wardrobe door and reached down to ease the leather handbag further forward, leaving the strap showing. That would enable Liz to see the bag next time she opened the door. Mary closed the door firmly, the magnetic catches clicking together.

If Liz asked any questions, Mary would deny seeing it. But if Liz did find it, and didn't mention the handbag to her sister, then surely it would mean that Liz was aware of the bag after all. It might belong to a friend of hers, or she could be caring for it for someone. Mary told herself not to get paranoid about it – all those crime dramas she watched on TV. Huh. It was affecting her judgement.

"Taxi's here!" shouted Liz as Mary came down the stairs. They hugged at the front door then Liz walked Mary to the front gate. The cabbie lifted the suitcase into the boot while Mary got into the back of the taxi. As it pulled away, Mary looked out of the rear window and waved her hand off.

'Just like in the tv soaps,' thought Liz.

Certain that her sister hadn't left anything behind, Liz took the precaution of going upstairs and checking the room where Mary had stayed. She looked in the drawers, opened the wardrobe door and checked the hangers, then looked under the bed. No . . . nothing left behind. No, all clean.

In the kitchen Liz switched on the kettle. Time for coffee . . . with a different mug. KEEP CALM AND DRINK COFFEE was writ in large red letters on the white pot. Stirring in the milk, Liz heard her mobile phone ring. It was Tom calling. She was still annoyed after learning about her husband's, soon to be ex-husband's, account at the bookies.

'Hi Liz.'

'Hello, Tom. You alright?'

'Yeah, fine. And you?'

'OK, I suppose.'

'You don't sound sure?'

'Well, I'm a bit short this week. Mary visited and we did some shopping. Went out, too.'

'What do you need?'

'A thousand would be fine.'

'What! I don't have that kind of money, Liz. You know that.'

'How much can you afford then?'

'I can give you two hundred, Liz.'

'I suppose that'll have to do then. Have you heard from your solicitor?'

'No. You?'

'No. I'm going to phone tomorrow.'

'Me, too.'

'Any other news? How was Mary?'

'She was her usual self. What about you? How's Gertie?'

'Fine. It won't be long now. That big house and car, maybe a BMW 5 series, and long holidays, are just round the corner.'

'I'd better go. I've got some things to do.'

'OK. Love you.'

'Bye, Tom.'

The lying sod. He didn't 'have that kind of money.' Thirty thousand in his account at the bookies! And such a truncated conversation on the phone. Liz felt there was no heart in Tom's comments and questions as if they were almost strangers. There was tension in his voice. Was he worried about something he wasn't sharing with her?

Liz began to wonder about Tom. Married to him for ten years.

How well did she really know him?

60

DS Hayman had checked the CCTV footage from Mr Dillistone, the neighbour of Gareth White. There was little that the enhanced film revealed. A man, wearing a dark coloured hoodie, could be seen approaching the Mercedes from the right, stopping to look around, then using some type of device that resembled a smartphone to unlock the driver's door. There was no hesitation, suggesting that the theft of this particular car had been pre-planned. The perp was dressed in dark clothes, but wearing white trainers. The door handle was tried with his left hand, but it was locked. The unlocking was then done with the device in his left hand, the door handle pulled with his right hand. Hayman wondered if the thief was left - handed. The envelope in the stolen car was found wedged down on the left - hand side of the driver's seat, suggesting that the perp may have put the cash inside an inner pocket on his right if the envelope had indeed fallen out and dropped down. Further possible evidence of the thief being sinistral.

There was the possibility that the perp had visited White's property before, and used the unlocking device to clone the car ignition key? Such items were available on the dark web. Had someone called on the house? A sales rep? A bogus meter reader, perhaps? Or were the car keys left in the hallway of the house, close to an outside wall through which the thief could access the car key chip using a transponder?

The registration plate of the stolen car had been picked up on four separate ANPR cameras. The first a quarter of a mile from Benfleet Road, the last a mile from where the accident with Peter Dobson's car happened. There was a 52 minutes interval between cameras two and three, a journey that normally would have taken eight or nine minutes. This indicated to Hayman that the Merc thief had parked up, either biding his time, or weighing up the options to follow Dobson from the golf club on that fateful night.

Had the woman with the red leather gloves drawn the money from the bank to give to the car thief to kill Peter Dobson? It seemed so. But who was the woman, and who had stolen the car? Hayman needed further evidence, a clue, a link. But right now, he was only hitting a brick wall.

"Hello, DS Hayman here." The sergeant was phoning Mrs White. "I was wondering if you'd had anyone call at your property in the weeks leading up to the theft of your vehicle? Anybody that was a cold-caller. Perhaps a man offering double glazing or solar panels, for instance?" Kate White hesitated.

"Let me see. Ah, yes, there was a man who knocked several times in quick succession three days before the car was stolen at about 10.30 am. That's right, it was Gareth's birthday. Wednesday, 26 May. He was quite persistent. Trying to sell cavity wall insulation. Something about the government offering help with the financing of it."

"Did you get the man's name?" asked Hayman. She shook her head, but mentioned an ID tag on a lanyard which was in such small print she couldn't read it.

"Did he enter your home at all?" probed the detective.

"Let me think. Yes, he did. Because it was drizzling, and I suppose I felt sorry for him. He stood in the hallway for a few minutes. My husband, Gareth, had popped down the road to see a neighbour who hasn't been well."

"May I ask where you usually put the car keys, Mrs. White?" She told him that her husband always dropped the keys into a wooden bowl on a side table in the hall. "Did you leave this man alone at any time during his visit?" A few seconds of silence.

"No. Oh, wait. Yes, I did. I had a fruit cake in the oven for Gareth's birthday and went to turn the oven off. I could smell it was baked. You know, that nice wholesome aroma . . ." Hayman interrupted the Mary Berry moment.

"If I visited you, Mrs White, would you be able to give me a description of the man?" Kate White said she was happy to do that. "I'll bring a colleague with me who could produce an identikit picture, if that's OK?" Kate didn't mind at all. She'd met the tall, handsome DS Hayman once before, and he was someone that could visit her any time he liked. "Tomorrow at ten thirty be all right?

"I'll have the kettle on, sergeant," she replied, putting the phone down, then running her fingers through her hair as she looked in the hall mirror.

Hi Tom. Thanks for your message. See attached photo of Jamek. I hope the surprise goes well. I don't have his address. He has a PO box number. He likes to keep his life fairly private. Mum's the word. Good luck. Cheers, Patrick.

Tom looked at Jamek Ingherr's face, staring at him from his smartphone screen. A tall forehead, eyes close together, thickish eyebrows, a nose that may have been broken, a mop of black hair, and an Adam's apple the size of a golf ball. His lips slightly parted, teeth difficult to see. If an author of a book on early prehistoric life in Europe needed an example of a cave dweller, this would do fine.

Tom realised how gullible some people could be. Patrick had fallen for his story about surprising his friend Jamek. However, Tom hoped that this Patrick guy would keep it to himself. Once Gertie's son, Mike, had made arrangements with Ingherr, or Herring, or whatever he wanted to be known as, Tom would have to be on his guard. And his assumption was that Mike, or one of his sisters, had given Ingherr a full description of Tom Ball.

In fact, for all Tom knew, Ingherr may have *already* been stalking him! He didn't have eyes in the back of his head, or jutting out on stalks like a snail, or a chameleon whose eyes rotated when it kept its head still! So, from now on, Tom Ball would have to be alert – more so than ever before. He'd cut down on the booze, and get early nights, especially during the week. If Gertie said anything he'd simply explain that he was feeling a bit run down. Tom would buy a large bottle of a pick-me-up tonic at the chemists to emphasise the point, and take a couple of spoonsful when he knew Gertie was looking.

Now that Tom had the photo of Ingherr he didn't need to bother Fred Wright, but the shopkeeper may come in handy if Tom needed any other information on the Serbian.

This was beginning to occupy Tom's mind more and more. And in a way it was a crazy position to be in. First off, he couldn't be absolutely sure if Mike Heseltine would go ahead with his threat. If he did, what was the timing on all of this? If Tom wanted to nip this in the bud, could he seek out Ingherr and get rid of him? Maybe not murder him, but set him up somehow, get him into a compromising situation? Tom would have to think about it – and soon.

He couldn't talk to Gertie about the matter. She'd think he was losing it. Chasing shadows. No, he'd have to work it out himself. Give it some consideration. On this Saturday morning Tom's thoughts were interrupted by Gertie who shouted from the hallway.

"Tom, there's some mail for you. It looks official." Tom got off his bed and slipped on his shoes after closing the leather case on his smartphone. He was soon ripping open the white, window envelope with his name and temporary address showing through the cellophane.

It was a covering letter from his solicitor, Clive Hapgood, enclosing documents relating to his divorce. Looking at the dates shown, his decree nisi would be come into force in four days. By next Wednesday at noon, he would be a free man! There was a stack of legal jargon about his responsibilities, including who owned what from the house contents split, as well as financial matters. He guessed that Liz may have received similar information. If not, she would soon.

"Are you all right, Tom? You look a bit pale, if you don't mind me saying." Tom quickly folded the forms together and replaced them in the envelope.

"It's my divorce, Gertrude. It will be official next Wednesday lunchtime." Gertie put a hand on his arm.

"Oh, that's good. I'll put the kettle on."

'Kettle,' thought Tom, 'I could do with a bloody drink!'

A few minutes later, the couple were sat watching TV in the lounge with James Martin whittling on about how to cook Yorkshire puddings.

"How do you feel about things now, Tom?" asked Gertie. "You're almost a free man! It must be a relief." Tom took a long sip of tea.

"Do you know, Gertrude, I'm not sure how I feel," he replied in a vacant manner. "How am I supposed to feel? Happy? Sad? I don't know . . ." Gertie wrapped her fingers around her small mug.

"Well, when Nigel and I got divorced it was one of the happiest times of my life. Getting rid of that arsehole was the best thing I ever did." Tom had never heard Gertie swear before.

She may have had a point. Her husband had cheated on her with his secretary, but for Tom and Liz that wasn't the case. This was all a plan, hatched during their holiday in Benalmadena.

He had a loving wife who trusted him. He knew that. She'd never look at another man, which made this charade all the more awkward. Tom put his tea down.

"Gertrude, I must go next door and see Liz. I'll take the divorce documents . . . check if she's got hers, yet. I'll be back soon." Gertie rose from her armchair.

"I tell you what. Let's celebrate! There's a lovely country pub about twenty miles from here. The name will come to me. They do gorgeous fish dishes. The haddock and chips are delicious. While you're seeing Liz, I'll have a look in the telephone directory. Shall we say one o'clock?"

"James, hi, it's Patrick Murray. I think you ought to know that some guy named Tom Ball has been asking about you." Herring stopped, the dog lead slack in his hand. "He sent me a Facebook message asking if I had a photo of you. Said something about wanting to surprise you. I sent him a photo of a guy we met at a party a long time ago. Neanderthal man, you may recall him? I think he emigrated to New Zealand." Herring ambled over to a park bench and sat down.

"Thanks for this, Patrick. I'll do some checking – see what he's up to. If he messages you again, let me know."

"OK, James. Will do. Cheers and take care." Herring snapped his phone shut and got up. He tugged at the dog lead. 'Come on, Carisbrooke,' he whispered.

Mike Heseltine had already spoken with James Herring. Mike had briefed him on the need to 'eliminate' Tom. That was the word Mike had used – 'eliminate,' adding that Herring could interpret that as he saw fit. The clear objective was to prevent Tom Ball getting involved with Mike's mother. Mike, as well as his two sisters, Kathryn and Diane, had finally agreed that everything was telling them that their mother and Tom were getting too close, too intertwined together. And with their mother's mental problems, all three were convinced that Tom Ball was up to no good. He was a 'schemer.' Their mother would be better off without him.

Far better off.

There was just the fee to agree.

63

"Hello, Mary. Hope you got back all right?" Her sister reassured Liz that her journey home to Southend was uneventful and all was well, although the train was half an hour late getting into the station, Mary didn't bother to mention that. Leaves on the line, apparently.

"Thanks for the break, Liz. I needed it. And we had some laughs, didn't we?"

"It cheered me up, especially after these past weeks of going through this damned divorce. Anyway, I've two reasons to be calling you." Mary listened carefully. "One, my divorce papers have arrived, and two, there's someone who I've met for coffee!" Mary smiled to herself.

"Oh, a bit like zen, or some ancient mythological event. You know, one thing is linked to another. Papers arrive, somebody wants to meet you. Ying and yang, or whatever it's called!"

"Yes, I know. It's odd how it's happened, too." Mary waited for the next part. "I decided to phone Terry Williams about Tom's betting account. His memory needed jogging, but I told him he'd spoken to us in the pub and given you his business card. He said he'd vaguely remembered. Anyway, I told him our conversation was in strict confidence, and he agreed to that. Told me Tom has over thirty grand in an account with them. He was pretty open about it, said Tom calls in once or twice a week, or phones his bets in." Mary whistled, a bit out of tune.

"My God! What do you make of that?" asked her sister.

"I'm keeping it between us for now. Tom doesn't need to know that I'm aware of this. So, no letting cats out of bags if he phones you!" Mary smiled to herself. It was rare that Tom called her, but it could happen so Mary would keep stum.

"And what's the yang part of this, then?" enquired Mary. "You said there was a link?"

"Well, as I was finishing my short chat with Terry, he said that somebody that was in the pub that night asked him who I was. He didn't want to give my details away, so he got this guy's number. When I thought about it, I can recall that Terry was at the bar standing near a tall, good-looking fair haired man. Terry checked with the barman, who said this chap was an honest regular. A bachelor, too." Mary's voice showed eagerness in it.

"What did you do?"

"I called him. And do you know, it *was* the handsome guy that I remembered, although I couldn't recall much as you'll agree! He suggested a coffee in Starbuck's in town." Mary's breathing increased slightly.

"Go on! You can't stop there! What happened next?" Liz decided to get to the point.

"Well, Tom's been enjoying himself lately, so I thought 'why don't I get something out of life?' He's a lovely man. Soft spoken, with a sense of humour. He told me to call him Robbo. Said all of his friends do. He lives near Great Dunmow but works away a lot. A company rep or something. He travels abroad, too, so being near Stansted airport is handy for him."

"Liz, you ought to be careful. I think you need to get to know him a bit better before you go too far." Liz took charge.

"Listen, Mary. I've been cooped up in this house, living like a nun, while Tom's been having a good time. Meeting someone for coffee, and maybe dinner sometime, isn't pushing things too far, surely?" Her sister could see Liz's point of view. "And who knows what the future holds for any of us? Don't worry about me, I can take care of myself."

After another five minutes of banter, the telephone conversation ended with the usual 'love you, keep in touch.'

Liz couldn't tell her sister that the whole divorce issue was a set up in order for Tom to win over Gertie. That soon she and Tom would be rich. The sad thing was that the truth would come out eventually, and Liz hoped that Mary wouldn't stop talking to her. She'd have to confess to the whole plan discussed over a paella on the Costa del Sol.

But for now, Liz's mind was on Robbo. He'd called her last night at ten o'clock, apologised for ringing late, to say he'd pick her up on the following Saturday at 7.00 pm. He'd booked a table at a French restaurant called La Moutarde. Liz had checked it out on google. A three - star Michelin restaurant with excellent reviews. Wow! She was going to have to go through her wardrobe to find her best dress . . . perhaps that little black one with sequins, side split, and spaghetti shoulder straps? The hairdresser, Tresses & Curls in the High Street, might be able to give her a cut and blow dry on Saturday afternoon. Liz would have to look at her shoes. She didn't have the Imelda Marcos choice of three thousand pairs, from Marlet to Christian Dior, but there'd be a pair that matched her dress. Liz was surprised by the choice that the charity shops had these days; Oxfam was especially good.

Liz had put Robbo's mobile number into her phone, more for convenience than anything. At least when he called her, she would know it was him. If it wasn't convenient to take a call from him, if she was in company, she would call him back later.

Her doorbell rang. It was Tom, who now had got into the habit of ringing instead of walking in. Liz had politely suggested that it was her preference from now on.

"Hello, Tom." She stepped aside to let him in. Tom walked into the kitchen, the usual place for a quick chat.

"Hi Liz, I was wondering if you've got your divorce documents through the post? Mine came today." She smiled.

"Yes, they arrived yesterday. All seems to be in order. Wednesday at noon, then?" Tom grinned.

"Indeed, it is. So, we'll be free agents from then on! Well, in theory if not in practice, eh?" Liz stared at him.

"Meaning?" she asked brusquely. "Meaning?" Tom was suddenly aware that he was walking on eggshells.

"All I'm saying is that it'll be official . . . at least to the world. But, you know, we can keep going as we are now, can't we?" Liz stood close to her soon to be ex-husband.

"Tom, you need to know that I'm having dinner with a male friend this evening. He's invited me to a restaurant and he's picking me up later. There's nothing romantic in it." Tom sat on a kitchen stool with a thud.

"But I thought . . ." Liz cut him off.

"As I said, there's nothing going on, it's purely platonic. You don't have anything to worry about. Honest. I met him for coffee a few days ago, and he's asked me out. Simple as that. You've got Gertie to keep you company, and you enjoyed your short break in Clacton, I'm sure." Liz was building the emotional balance. Tom looked at the floor, remembering when he and Liz chose the grey, patterned Armstrong covering from the local flooring store. He wasn't up for a fight right then.

"OK, Liz. I trust you. You're right, I've had it quite cushy over the past months and you've kept yourself to yourself." He paused. "Well, enjoy yourself. You've got my number, so if you need to call me at any time, please do." He eased off the stool. "Maybe we can get together on Wednesday teatime? Go through any final items after it's all official. You know, what we tell friends and that."

"And there'll be some financial matters to clarify, Tom." Liz eyed him like a rattlesnake. "How are things with you just now?" He looked out of the window into the back garden.

"Well, I've a few quid in the bank, perhaps a thousand, and there's my weekly wage. That's about it, I'm afraid." Liz bit her tongue, then placed her hand on his arm.

"I'm sure we'll get by, Tom."

64

Kate White opened the door after the melodic chimes had rung. On the path stood D S Hayman with a colleague. Kate had been up early, washed her hair, and put on just enough make-up to be 'presentable.'

"Good morning, Mrs White . . ."

"Oh, Kate, please Detective Sergeant," she interrupted quickly. "Come on in." Kate stood aside to let the men into the hall. Both stood there while Hayman introduced his colleague.

"This is Grant Greenaway, our identikit expert. He'll want a few details of your 'salesman' shortly. But meanwhile, is this where you stood with the man who called to see you about cavity wall insulation?" Hayman pointed to the floor.

"Yes, right here. As I said I had to go and turn the oven off and left him here for, what, about a minute?" Hayman's eyes noticed the wooden bowl on the semi-circular table.

"And this is where you and your husband normally leave the car keys?" He pointed to the bowl. Kate nodded. "You ought to be aware that car thieves are able to clone a car key using an electronic device that copies the chip in the fob of the car key. In other words, any key can be copied, even from a short distance and through a wall in some cases. We think it likely that 'Cavity Wall Man' did just that when he called. A minute was enough time for him to swipe the device across your husband's car key. He then came back a few days later, all prepared to get into your car and drive away in it." Kate was speechless as she led the way into the living room.

"Let me put the kettle on. Tea or coffee, gentlemen?" Both wanted coffee. Greenaway got his laptop computer out and turned it on as Hayman briefly checked his phone for messages. There were none.

"Here we are," said Kate, as she brought a tray in. "I've put a couple of my freshly baked, buttered scones on a plate for you. Sultana. Do have one," she offered. A minute later, Hayman was chomping at his scone but Greenaway was busy setting up the identikit programme. He invited Kate to sit next to him so that she could see the screen. A basic outline of six different head shapes came up.

"What's your best guess at his head shape, Kate?" asked Greenaway. She pondered each one, then pointed at number three. "OK, good. Now hair. I'll show you eight styles and several colours. Choose the one that best fits the man." Again, Kate scrutinised the images.

"That one! Number six. His head was that shape, and his hair – well, it was a thatch! A right ginger mop, it was. Sort of Ed Sheeran on speed." Greenaway returned to the head shape and added the hair style, then hit Save. Greenaway managed a bite of his scone and sip of coffee, before moving to eyes, nose and mouth. Twenty minutes later there was an identikit image of a man on the computer screen. Hayman bent over to take a look at it.

"What do you think, Kate? Does that resemble your caller?" Kate angled her head.

"The eyes aren't quite right. Can you go back to the ones you showed me, Grant?" He did so. Kate chose another pair, slightly closer together. "Yes, that's better!" Soon all three were looking at a photofit image of 'Cavity Wall Man.'

The DS asked Kate to estimate his height, and any unusual features about him. The DS jotted down her comments as Greenaway licked his index finger to clear up the last of the scone crumbs.

"Well, Kate, you've been most helpful. We'll get that image smartened up and then hope to use it to catch our car thief. It is only my assumption, of course, but I'm convinced that the caller you had here was the perpetrator. The one who took your Mercedes Benz. I'll keep you informed of any developments, but you'll realise I can't share everything with you as the enquiry is still ongoing."

Kate White smiled as she opened the front door.

"Thanks for the coffee and scones, Kate. They were lovely." Hayman was barely over the threshold when Kate spoke.

"Oh, Sergeant, there's something else I've just remembered!" There was a sense of urgency in her voice. Hayman looked at her. "A slight accent. I can't place it, but not pure English if you know what I mean?"

"What? European?" Kate shook her head.

"I'm not sure."

65

"I'm certain it's along this road. Just keep going a bit further. I think it's near an old stone bridge, that's why it's called The Stone Bridge." Gertie was trying to give Tom some instructions, but failing with her effort.

"Look, Gertrude, why don't we stop and I'll check it on my phone?" She looked at him.

"How can you do that? You haven't got a number for them." Gertie sounded confused, which was nothing new. Tom pulled into an entrance to a farm track.

"Look," said Tom, showing Gertie his phone screen. "I enter the name of the place and I get their web site, phone number, and directions." Tom wished he'd done that before they'd set off, but Gertie sounded convincing. He ought to have known better! "Here we go . . . The Stone Bridge. Hmm, there's a pub of that name 24 miles from here. Is that the one?" Gertie had a vacant look on her face.

"I'm not sure, Tom. Do they serve fish dishes?" He checked. The web site listed cod and chips as one of their main choices on the menu. Tom nodded. "OK, let's go there. I'm pretty certain that's the place Nigel and I used to go to."

'Nigel and I?' Was this a nostalgia trip for Gertie? Or did it really have a good reputation as Gertie had claimed after they'd set off? Tom could cut their losses and find somewhere closer. 24 miles was a bit of a slog, and it was now just after 1.15 pm. Still parked up, Tom tapped on an app from a restaurant group. There was a decent sounding pub four miles away. He clicked on Directions and placed his phone into the holder stuck to the windscreen.

"Gertrude, there's a good eating place a ten - minute drive from here. I've heard it's very good," he lied. "Let's go there. My treat!" Gertie was looking out of the window, feeling a little embarrassed.

"Oh, dear, I'm sorry, Tom. My mind is going. I can't remember things like I used to. It's good to have you keep me in line. I agree, let's go to the one near here. Forty miles, you say?"

'Forty miles!' mused Tom. Bloody heck!

"No, Gertrude, four miles. Don't worry – let's go." Tom checked the door mirror and pulled away leaving dust in their wake.

'The old woman isn't getting any brighter,' thought Tom. He knew she was getting worse. Going downhill slowly. It was a strain on him, he knew that. And it was at the stage where he either corrected her when she made mistakes, or he'd humour her. That was a difficult one. Tom realised that it was going to be like passing through shades of grey between white and black. From the white end of this spectrum, he was now at ivory come dark cream, moving toward dirty flannel grey.

The other thing bothering Tom was the very important issue of 'marriage.' In their plan, he and Liz had talked of Tom actually walking Gertie down the aisle. That would make it binding and final when it came to the ownership of material possessions when she passed away. But Gertie had already made a Will with the BHF. That would be good enough – she'd signed everything over to Tom. Why go through getting married? Gertie had a signed copy of the Will in her safe at home. That was all Tom needed.

But what if Gertie didn't want to marry Tom? He didn't really know how she would feel about that. Another thing . . . he'd have to put up with some ribbing at work! He'd have the 'urine extracted' something terrible. Tom, in his thirties, marrying a woman aged 81! Then there was the question of a stag night! And a hen night! Hen night – holy moly! Gertie and her geriatric friends going to some hotel to let their hair down – walking frames to be left outside, please.

Marriage would cement his place in the family. Mike, Kathryn and Diane would be his step-children. But he wouldn't have any control over them, would he? Unless they ever needed parental consent to do something? Tom couldn't think of any examples right there and then. But there would be the marriage vows to consider.

'To have and to hold...'
'From this day forth...'
'For richer, for poorer...'
'In sickness and in health...'

And when he came into possession of Gertie's 'worldly goods,' would being her husband give him any more power over matters than if he was her 'partner?'

"Here we are, Gertrude. The Belted Galloway pub. I shall park over there and we'll take a look inside."

"Tom, what are we doing here? I thought we were going to the fish shop?"

66

Ten days earlier

Mike Heseltine licked his lips. His mouth was dry. It was difficult to swallow. The chewing gum he often carried wasn't in his pocket, and the wooden bench in the park was hard on his backside. The Bluebird Café, a quarter of a mile away, was only just opening up. James Herring came toward him, his Cavalier King Charles spaniel lolling from side to side.

Pyong had made a call to Herring the day before and briefed him on what her husband wanted. She gave scant details, but enough to interest Herring. Mike, of course, was aware that Pyong had met Herring in this park shortly before Harold Snowdon's body had been found. The couple hadn't talked much about it – Mike not wanting to consciously think about what Herring might have done to the poor chap who'd probably sent the blackmail threat to the kennels. But after chatting to Pyong in more detail about Tom Ball, she had persuaded Mike that Mr Herring could possibly do a 'good job.'

"Good morning, Michael, nice to see you again. How's the business?" Clearly this was small talk before getting down to the matter in hand, but Mike decided to be polite.

"Hi. Yes, not too bad. We're still in the holiday period, for some dog owners at least, so pretty busy." Mike twiddled his thumbs. Herring read the body language.

"You wife said you had a proposal for me. Something to be discussed in confidence?" Mike half smiled and gave a slight nod and decided to get to the point.

"My mother got divorced some years ago, and recently took in a lodger. The lodger is a guy who lived next door and is going through a divorce. He used to do odd jobs for her in the house, and when he left his wife because of another woman, he asked if he could stay a while until he got himself sorted out. He's been there too long. I get the impression he's wanting to get on *very* friendly terms with my mother . . ." Herring's eyebrows rose. "No, not like that," Mike added quickly, "but make himself comfortable in her property and take advantage of her. He has his own en-suite bedroom, she prepares most meals, does his washing and ironing . . . hell, he's living the life of Riley!"

"Whoever Riley was!" guffawed Herring as he tugged gently at the lead of Carisbrooke. Mike remained stern.

"My sisters and I can't see him leaving, and if he gets too close to our mother, there's the danger that she'll go and leave everything to him in her Will." Herring looked across the parkland as the sun rose higher in the sky, casting shorter shadows across the grass.

"Tell me about the lodger," said Herring. Mike went on to give as much details about Tom Ball as he knew. His wife's name and where she lived. His delivery job at Corbett & Perkins, and the white Peugeot Boxer van he drove, including the registration number. Herring didn't write anything down, but Mike sensed his brain was absorbing every item of information passed to him.

Mike felt somewhat uncomfortable discussing this with James Herring. It seemed as if he were in a film, the cameras rolling as the two conspirators talked quietly about the dastardly deed that was about to be done.

"To be clear, Michael, you're asking me if I can help you to remove Tom Ball from the scene? Is that correct?" Mike nodded. "OK, but sometimes these things come with a price, I'm afraid." Herring paused. "And conditions." Mike's face blanched, he was waiting for this.

"Conditions?" he asked. "What do you mean?" Herring adjusted a cuff-link.

"No one must know about this conversation. Is that understood? Tell your wife as little as possible. The same for your sisters. Never use my name. Only contact me on this number from now on." Herring passed Mike a card with a mobile number on it in red. No name. "This matter has to be our secret. Tom Ball will disappear in due course, but I cannot say when. It may take some time – I need to plan carefully. There is the price to pay, too." The talking stopped when a dog walker passed within a few yards away. Seconds later, Mike spoke.

"The price. How much are we talking?" Herring glanced at his gold wristwatch. It suggested he was ready to go.

"Ten thousand pounds. In used notes. Half up front, half when I the job is done." Herring rose and Mike offered to walk back to Herring's car with him. Minutes later, Mike was admiring the silver Lexus. He wandered around the back of the vehicle, looking at the fine bodywork. He even bent down to take a peek underneath, noticing the pair of chrome, twin exhaust pipes. He complimented Herring on choosing such a classic modern SUV and the Serb smiled – almost a gloat. Mike then walked away without turning around.

Mike swallowed the spittle in his mouth . . . bloody hell! Ten grand. He was going to have to dig deep, but his sisters had to help out. His challenge would be to share this with Kathryn and Diane soon with minimal detail, but choose his time and place. He would have to play the salesman – sell this whole concept to them so that they'd buy into it. With as few questions as possible.

Mike recalled the time, not that long ago, when the three of them were sitting in the café along the road from where their mother lived discussing ideas on how to get rid of Tom Ball. It was Kathryn who's suggested making a pact, but Diane was more reluctant. The more Mike thought of that, the more sense it made for him to speak to Kathryn and then persuade her to talk with Diane. Perhaps they didn't have to meet up? The only thing the girls weren't aware of was right now was that Mike was asking someone to do 'the job,' and that there was going to be a cost involved. Ten grand between them. Cash.

All three would have to withdraw smaller sums of money. Say a thousand pounds over three visits to the bank, and then the balance of another £340 or so. If his sisters had different savings accounts, so much the better. No point in attracting attention to themselves in the unlikely event of an enquiry. His plan would be to collect the cash from his sisters and stash it somewhere at the kennels. Herring wanted half pretty soon, and the rest when he gave Mike the 'green light.'

Mike's bum was numb. The bench not letting up on its hardness on his gluteus maximus muscles. His watch showed 9.15 am. The Bluebird Café in the distance looked inviting. Pyong was managing fine, he assumed, so there was time for an Americano. He'd also treat himself to a doughnut – one of the big ones with a jam and cream filling, the golden coating dusted with caster sugar.

Five minutes later he was sat near the window looking out over the greensward. Mike had picked up three paper serviettes – he knew the doughnut was going to be a sticky job. He was also thinking about his recent annual psychiatry assessment at Broomfield Hospital. The

Consultant, Mr Abdhu Ranji, had recommended that Mike stay on his current medication of propranolol, but he'd also added amitriptyline, a high strength antidepressant. Mike had just taken his second bite of the pastry and wiped his chin when a hand patted him on the shoulder.

"Hello, Michael, I thought it was you! Mind if I join you?" It was Father Reginald Bedworthy, his Roman Catholic minister. "I haven't seen you at church for ages, Michael. Is all well with you and Pyong?"

This was the last person he wanted to be talking to. The interfering old cleric would be asking all sorts of questions. Before Mike could reply, the minister was sat opposite him and had put his cheese scone and coffee down.

"You're looking a little pale, Michael. Is anything the matter?"

67

Tom looked at the photo sent by Patrick on Facebook. James Herring looked a thug – he was rough around the edges and with piercing eyes. This was one guy for whom Tom was definitely going to keep a watch for. If his body matched his face, this guy could tear telephone directories in half with his bare hands, except that those directories were few and far between these days. BT were saving money again. It was all on line.

Wherever Tom went, he'd make sure to scan a room or a group of people, because Herring was probably going to be lurking somewhere. Tom wondered if he should carry a knife? A small one, on his belt in a sheath. Discreet. It could come in handy for protection in a scuffle or a fight. If his life was in danger, perhaps down a dark alley one night, he'd have no hesitation in pulling the knife on Herring . . . where it would do instant harm. Chest? Aim for the heart?

But knives draw blood. A thrust into Herring's chest would most likely result in his blood getting onto Tom's clothes, then Tom would have to destroy his jacket or shirt, or whatever was bloodied, or face the possibility that the police might find traces if there was any enquiry.

The other option was a gun. A small handgun. Tom had gone on line and found a gunsmith in East London. He'd have to go in person after applying for a firearms certificate, but that wouldn't be a problem. He'd tell Gertie that he was seeing a friend in Mile End or Stratford or somewhere; she wouldn't know her East End from her West End. Tom had seen a couple of handguns that were compact enough for a holster on his trouser belt or in a shoulder fitting.

Tom checked his thinking. Wait, was he taking this too far? A knife, a handgun. Bloody hell. Was it really coming to this? Would Mike Heseltine go to this length to stop Tom living with Mike's mother? Tom chastised himself. 'Come on,' he told himself. If Gertie's son wanted to prevent Tom from staying with his mother, perhaps he was using Herring as a frightener? Maybe the outcome would be for Herring to grab Tom and threaten him. A knuckle duster, or a lead cosh or baseball bat could be the weapon of choice? Grab Tom in a head lock like the TV wrestlers used to do, and whisper in his ear 'leave Gertrude alone or I'll break your legs and readjust your face,' or 'do you want to spend the rest of your life in a wheelchair.'

Something nice like that.

But Tom didn't relish this either. When he was young, he'd do something like that to other kids. But not quite as brutal...just some bruises or a black eye. Even when he used to go out at the week-ends, he'd sometimes duff up someone who'd upset him in his local pub or club. It wasn't unusual for his mates, Dean Gifford and Ian Slater, to help Tom to come out best when he got into a fracas down at the Pink Pelican. Like the night Julie Thornton was there . . . the night she went missing.

Tom was going to have to be extra vigilant. Simple as that. And the best thing would to always be in someone's company, whether it was Gertie or some of his mates. That would make it harder for Herring to attack him since the Serb wouldn't want any witnesses to his crime. He'd even considered a bodyguard! Some bruiser with big fists who would hang around him down the pub or the Pelican, and even when he ventured out to the bookies. Was there a web site, Tom wondered, such as Hire-a Thug.com where he could pick some guy who fitted the bill? Like a dating sight . . . searching for the toughest and meanest – looking guy after scrolling through the mug shots. How much would a bodyguard cost was the next question. £10 an hour? £50 an hour? More?

"Thomas. Your meal is on the table! Wash your hands and get down here now." They were Gertie's dulcet tones, non-threatening, and for a second Tom thought he was aged ten and his mum was shouting for him to come down from his room for his tea. He got 'Thomas' when things were important.

68

"Robbo, it's been a lovely evening. I know it's late but do you fancy a night cap?" Liz and Robbo were standing on her front doorstep. She wasn't drunk, at least not with alcohol, and it seemed the right thing to say. He smiled.

"I don't want to put you to any trouble, Liz. I've enjoyed it, too." Robbo had been the perfect host, from collecting Liz in his car, all through the meal, to opening the car door for her and helping her on with her coat. The perfect gentleman, in fact.

"It will be no trouble at all. I've got some decent Kenya coffee and a bottle of single malt that needs opening. I have such a job getting the foil off the bottle sometimes." Robbo wasn't sure if that was true, but it sounded good.

"Well, Liz, I'd be pleased to help," he whispered in her ear. A shiver ran up her spine as she unlocked the door and went in without putting the light on in the hall. A nightlight on a timer had come on in the lounge for added security. She kicked off her high heel shoes – glad to get them off after five hours, and her little toe was in agony.

"You go take a seat in there and draw the curtains if you would. I'll put the kettle on and bring the whisky through." Robbo smiled and nodded. "Oh, and switch that small corner lamp on, too."

A few minutes later, the pair were sat on the three-seater sofa, each with a mug of decent coffee and a half tumbler of single malt. Liz had asked Robbo if he wanted some ice, but he replied by saying it was only 'pagans' that had ice in their drink.

"Someone I know once met Princess Margaret. She liked Famous Grouse, but after her whisky was poured, they realised there was no ice in it! Her aide had clearly stated before she'd arrived at this function that the princess liked two ice cubes in her Scotch. In seconds somebody had rushed off and got some ice. Probably saved him getting beheaded in the Tower!" Liz laughed.

"You do tell a good story, Robbo. You should go on the stage, do a stand-up routine!" Liz sipped her whisky. "But tell me, what is it that you actually do? A rep or something, you said?" Robbo explained that he was an agent for a fine art dealer in London. Some of his work involved getting to meet potential buyers of artworks and making the arrangements for the delivery of a Monet or a Picasso from the seller, usually a dealer in London, to the buyer. There was a lot to consider – the insurance cover, security, method of transport, even helping with the siting of the artwork in the home of the buyer. When a gold framed painting weighed up to two hundred kilos, you couldn't just pop a couple of tacks in the wall. Liz laughed again, throwing her head back and exposing her lovely white neck. Robbo noticed the gold chain that hung low on her chest, the attached gold elephant dangling near the top of her cleavage.

"That sounds so exciting! Goodness. What's the most famous person you've been involved with? Any film stars or footballers?" Liz moved slightly closer.

"Liz, you must realise that the nature of my work is such that I can't tell you much, I'm afraid. I mean, if I said that David Beckham had just bought a Constable for three million pounds for his Los Angeles pad, that would be betraying a confidence now, wouldn't it?" Liz leant forward.

"You've handled a sale for David Beckham? Wow! That sounds great!" Now it was Robbo's turn to laugh.

"No! That was an example, that's all! Silly!" He paused. "I'm sorry, Liz, but most of my activity is confidential. I'm sure you can understand that . . ." Liz smiled, happy that Robbo was at least letting her part way into his role as an agent of fine art.

They carried on talking for another hour, and Liz had poured two more tumblers of Scotch.

"You won't be fit to drive Robbo. Listen, I've got a spare bed. Why don't you stay the night? I can make you some breakfast before you leave in the morning . . ." Her words hung in the air for a few seconds. She found herself getting even closer to him, his aftershave a magnet to her. Putting his arm around her shoulder, she snuggled closer.

"I don't want to put . . ." Before he could finish his sentence, Liz piped up.

"Yes, yes. I don't want to put you to any trouble, Liz. I know. Well, you're not putting me to any trouble," she responded. "Come on, let me show you up to the spare room." Liz held her hand out and Robbo took it. "I'll leave the washing up until morning," she added. Liz showed Robbo to his room, then showed him the bathroom where a spare toothbrush was sitting next to a glass holding a tube of toothpaste.

Half an hour later, Liz was drifting off to sleep in her double bed when she heard the door open further, the light on the landing shining through the gap.

"Are you asleep?" she heard Robbo's voice whisper gently.

"No. Why?" She rubbed her eyes.

"I'm worried I might have nightmares in a strange bed," he said quietly. Liz eased herself up.

"Well, in that case, you'd better come in here, then," she replied, flicking back the bed sheets.

The next thing Liz remembered was looking at her bedside radio alarm clock with heavy eyelids. The green figures showed 07 12. She turned over and moved her arm cross the bed.

Robbo had gone.

69

"Er, no, nothing's the matter, Father. All's well, in fact." Mike faked a smile, hoping the nosy priest wasn't going to give him the third degree. "The kennels are doing well, so can't complain." Father Bedworthy kept stirring his coffee as he looked into Mike's eyes, almost mesmerically.

"It's just that I saw you down there on a bench with another chap. It seemed as if you were in deep conversation. I hope everything is all right." He paused. "I often like to have my early constitutional in the park – get the benefit of the air before the day warms up." He continued to hold Mike's gaze. "I feel closer to God, too. You know, taking in all His works – the trees, birds, nature." Mike wiped his sticky fingers after he'd put the half - eaten doughnut back on his plate.

"Sounds great. I think I know what you mean, Father," he lied. Bedworthy finally took his spoon out of his cup.

"We haven't seen you in church for quite a long time, Michael. Nor Pyong." The cleric hesitated, hoping for a reply. Mike hinted at a nod. "Well, you know that God's house is always open. He invites all of us every week, but of course you can enter His house on any day. All you have to do is accept His invitation." Mike moved on his chair, more from a feeling of unrest than to ease his backside.

"I can't argue with that, Father. I suppose we've been busy during this past year. Looking after the dogs of our clients is a full - time job, of course." Then he took a chance with his next comment. "I don't suppose God would look after our dogs while we went to church!" Bedworthy glared at Mike for a few seconds before composing himself.

"God cares for us all, Michael. I think he would take good care of your canine friends for an hour each week if required!" Mike had to think quickly.

"That may be so, Father, but with Pyong being Buddhist, she just doesn't feel right in a Catholic church." Bedworthy slowly leant forward.

"Our God welcomes everyone, Michael. If Pyong isn't comfortable with some aspects of the service, I won't mind, and God won't mind! She needn't take part in the Eucharist, for example." The cleric was beginning to sound like a salesman – perhaps he was! Needing customers to fill his pews each Sunday, and dig deep when the collection tray came round. The church always seemed to be spending money on something. Mike looked at his watch, holding the dial between finger and thumb to emphasise the fact.

"Goodness. Is that the time? I really must go, Father. Pyong will be wondering if I've got lost!" Mike got up after pushing his plate away, the doughnut only half eaten. Bedworthy rose, too, and took Michael's hand in his.

"Michael, if there's anything I can help you with, you know you can talk to me in *confidence*. Don't you?" Bedworthy emphasised. Mike eased his hand away, without wishing to cause offence.

"Thank you, Father, I'll bear that in mind." With that, Mike got out of the café as rapidly as his legs would carry him without breaking into a trot. Bedworthy sat down again and removed his smartphone from his jacket. He opened it, and tapped on the Photos app. At the bottom of the screen were three shots taken half an hour ago. He touched one of them and splayed his fingers across it. The photo enlarged. Father Reginald Bedworthy scrutinised the image on his phone.

The man that was talking to Michael on the park bench looked familiar. Bedworthy thought he'd seen him before.

He just couldn't remember where.

"It's a shame we didn't find that chip shop the other day, Tom. I felt the flavours of salt and vinegar on my battered fish tickling my tongue for the rest of the day. Never mind. My plan was to celebrate – if that's the word – your divorce becoming official. Did you and Liz manage to agree on things . . .?" Tom put the spanner down, the nut on the washing machine fully tightened.

"Yes, but there wasn't much to discuss. We don't have a collection of DVD'S, CD's or records to split, and she gets to keep everything in the property. I've got my things here, you know, clothes and personal effects, so that's about it." Gertie moved closer.

"Have you got your passport, Tom?" Why was she asking him about that?

"Er, yes. Why? Are you planning something? A trip abroad, maybe?" To be honest, Tom did not even want to contemplate getting on a flight with Gertie, or walking up the gangway to embark on a cruise. If anything, her memory was getting worse. How would he find escorting her on an overseas break? Taking care of virtually all aspects of the holiday – ensuring they got on the right flight, the correct coach, the hotel room. He'd end up being her carer for the duration!

"Well, you never know! I phoned one of my W.I. friends two days ago, and wondered if we could go as a threesome? She sounded excited at the prospect." 'Bloody hell,' thought Tom. A threesome! Would that be three single beds in the same hotel room? A double and a single? Perish the idea!

"I don't want to pour cold water on your ideas, Gertrude, but don't you think it would be better for us to discuss things like that together first?" Tom suddenly became aware that this was the first time he'd taken command of a situation like this.

He felt it was the right time to do it.

Gertie was silent. Tom began to worry that he'd been too harsh. Gertie still had the power to throw him out. He had to tread carefully. He placed his hand on hers. Gently.

"Don't you agree, Gertrude? Don't you see how things would be better if we shared decisions? You know, you have a thought and talk to me . . . then I wonder about something, and I discuss it with you." Tom smiled, as broadly as he could manage. He took his hand away slowly. She grinned.

"Actually, you're right. I hadn't thought of it like that. Sort of like a 'team?' She curled both index fingers to make the single inverted comma marks. Tom wanted to drive this advantage home. He took a risk. Placing his hand around her shoulder he brought her a little closer to him.

"We do make a good team, Gertrude. I'm convinced of that." His fingers curled a bit more into her loose cardigan. She leant over a fraction, accepting his move.

Tom had been thinking about the original plan that he and Liz had discussed in Benalmadena. Divorce Liz, marry Gertie. Gertie passes away and leaves everything to Tom. Tom and Liz remarry. It had sounded so simple, so clear-cut. And Gertie had been to make out her Will with the Red Cross solicitor a few weeks ago. So, Tom had asked himself the question again. 'Do I really need to *marry* Gertie?' Maybe he didn't? But there was something binding about marriage, and the binding gave power. The power to make decisions, to have dominance over Gertie's three children. Mike, Diane and Kathryn would certainly have a lot to say about their mother getting married again . . . and to a man forty - three years younger. Wow! And Tom wondered which one of the three would kick up the biggest stink? Perhaps Mike as the only son...or Diane, that snotty-nosed teacher used to dominating the kids in her care...or maybe Kathryn, the haughty health food store manager who probably ruled the roost with her snooty customers!

Did it matter? No, it did not, but marriage would be the cement between the bricks of their union. And once Tom became her husband, the children could take a hike off Southend pier. That was it, then. Yes, he and Gertie would have to get married. No longer would he simply be the 'lodger.' He'd become the 'man of the house!'

"I like it when you hold me like that, Tom," chirped Gertie. "It makes me feel secure, sort of all enclosed by a castle wall that can't be stormed by the enemy." Tom gently removed his arm and turned to Gertie. Here was his chance.

"Why, then, don't you and I make this a permanent relationship?" His words hung in the air. Gertie gazed into his eyes. "We're both single. We enjoy each other's company. Neither of us want to be alone, I'm sure . . ." Standing in the lounge, Gertie now moved towards a chair and sat down. Taking a small, lace handkerchief from her cardigan sleeve, she wiped her nose.

"Oh, Tom, that would be lovely!" she exclaimed. "There's just one thing." Tom stood next to her.

"And what's that, my dear?" enquired Tom.

"I'd want to get a check - up at the hospital first . . ." Tom frowned.

"A check up? For what?" Gertie rose from the chair, needing a little help from Tom. She walked across to the window and looked out at the back garden.

"My pacemaker. The cardiac Consultant said it wouldn't last forever, and I was told to avoid any excessive stress – both physical and emotional." Tom stood behind her and stared over Gertie's left shoulder at the old stone trough now used as a birdbath. Placing his hands lightly on both of her shoulders, Tom reflected on matters.

"Perfect," he said to himself.

'Hi. I'm sorry I can't take your call right now, but if you leave your name and a contact number, I'll get back to you as soon as I am able.'

Liz recognised Robbo's voice. She'd tried his mobile number twice just to see if he was OK, and was a bit concerned about his early departure. Liz had even bought some extra eggs and a half a kilo of unsmoked bacon.

With his job as an agent to a fine art dealer in London, Liz realised he would be busy. He'd probably had a meeting that he'd forgotten to tell her about. A high - level meeting with a film star who was in the process of buying an expensive oil painting? A Premiership footballer who was checking on a Caravaggio or a Rembrandt? A TV actor wanting to invest in a portrait of some historic character like Nelson or the Duke of Wellington?

She told herself not to worry. He'd probably call her later to apologise. Liz had time to rehearse her response . . . along the lines of 'oh, don't be silly, I know you're busy, but when can I see you again . . . that is, if you can spare the time . . .' Something like that.

But Liz really knew that when she spoke to Robbo, she'd most likely get her words all mixed up. Verbal diarrhoea, Tom called it. She'd end up saying something total insane, or pathetic, then spend time trying to correct herself.

It was best for her to keep busy. There was some grocery shopping to do, the ironing wouldn't do itself, and some of the shrubs in the garden had been neglected for ages. Branches sprouting in all directions on the fuchsia bushes and the pheasant berry bush looked straggly. She really didn't want to call Robbo again. Hell, he'd think she was over the top. No, Liz would wait for Robbo to call her – which he would do, of that she was convinced.

Mid - morning she was reaching up for a cereal packet in the local supermarket when her phone rang. A melody she'd downloaded ages ago. Couldn't remember the name of it. The screen showed 'Robbo.'

"Hello, Robbo!" she tried to stay calm. "Where did you get to this morning?" asked Liz in a light-hearted manner.

"Hi, Liz. Yeah, sorry about that. As soon as I woke, I remembered that I needed to be somewhere. You were sound, so I crept out as quietly as I could." He wasn't giving anything away, and Liz pondered the fact as to whether she ought to ask.

"Somewhere important, I assume?" said Liz as meekly as possible. Non – threatening was best.

"Exactly. The dealer had a client in early. A multi-millionaire, but of course I can't say who. He wanted me to show him a selection of high-value paintings, all good investments, and then take him to lunch later. I'm just having a coffee while he eyes up our stock so can't talk long."

"Thanks for last night, Robbo. I really enjoyed it. Maybe I shouldn't have poured the extra whiskies, though!" Liz wanted to lighten the mood as she stood in the Cereal & Bread aisle. A customer close by, possibly earwigging, gave her an odd look, but Liz ignored her.

"Me too," he replied. "Perhaps we can do it again sometime?" An invitation Liz could not ignore. "Are you around later today?" Robbo asked.

'Is the Pope a Catholic?' Liz said to herself.

"Er, let me see. I haven't got my social diary with me . . . of course, I am! What are you thinking?" Robbo explained that he would be leaving his client mid - afternoon and could be with Liz at around six o'clock. She told him it was fine, and if he was up for it, she'd prepare a meal for them. "What's your preference for wine?" Robbo said he liked a decent red, an Argentinian Malbec or a Cabernet Sauvignon from Chile would be fine.

"OK, Robbo, I'll see you later." The call was ended. Liz now had to extend her purchasing – decide what to cook later, and wander down the Wines aisle to look at the South American selection of reds.

Liz hadn't felt this excited for a long time. It was crazy, she told herself. Tom and her had their plan . . . and although they were divorced, it was all a sham. Wasn't it?

Well. Yes and no. Liz couldn't stop feeling tinges of annoyance about her husband and the neighbour. Weekend holidays! Eating out in nice restaurants! Getting all nice and cosy watching TV together . . . while she was living on her own! Come on, Liz felt she had a *right*, if that was the word, to enjoy herself until she and Tom got back together again. No one was going to get hurt, no toys thrown out of the pram. Just a bit of fun with a man who'd made enquiries about her – for 'company and companionship' as the dating web sites quoted sometimes.

Her afternoon was taken up with food preparation, making things easier for her when Robbo arrived later. She'd checked a wine website, and put the two bottles of Malbec on the kitchen worktop near the boiler with a thermometer next to them.

Serve between 15 & 18 C. Allow to breathe for 30 minutes before serving.

Liz hoped he liked king prawns in garlic butter as a starter, and coq-au-vin for mains. Two expensive chocolate, ready-made desserts were chilling in the fridge. She didn't really know Robbo's tastes, but she prayed her choices were going to be all right – no Marmite dishes, nor brussels sprouts.

Clothes were laid on the bed ready to change into. They'd eat at around 7.00 pm so her dress wasn't going to be a 'little black number,' but maybe a red one that she hadn't worn for a while. Liz did not want to be 'tarty,' but 'presentable.' However, should she be dressed for him when he arrived, or 'help yourself to a drink, Robbo, while I go up and change?' No. Smart casual on his arrival, then change later.

The day wore on. Liz had done some ironing, and used the secateurs successfully in the garden. She'd even cut back the photinia – the Red Robin shrub. At 5.55 pm, everything was as ready as it could be . . . Liz had double checked. Busying herself in the kitchen, Liz turned on the small television in the corner of the worktop. The local news would be on Anglia ITV in a few minutes and she'd watch that until the front door bell rang. Liz pressed the power button. The adverts were closing.

Good evening. I'm Charlotte Green. Here is the news from the Anglia region. A Roman Catholic priest has been found dead in his rooms at the parsonage where he lived near Brentwood. Let's go over to the scene now and to our correspondent, Freddie Lane. What more can you tell us, Freddie?

Father Reginald Bedworthy had lived in this parsonage you see behind me for the past five years. The building is also the home of three other Roman Catholic priests. A cleaner, on her normal rounds, found his body in the sitting room late this afternoon. Police have not released any details about how Father Bedworthy died, but they are asking anyone who may have seen anything suspicious in or near the parsonage here, or who had contact with the priest in the last two days, to phone Crimestoppers on 0800 555 111. We have been told by the police that the mobile phone of Father Bedworthy, which he always carried with him, has so far not been found. Back to you Charlotte.

DS Chris Hayman had spoken with Kate White again once Grant Greenaway had received Kate's approval of the final identikit picture of the man that had allegedly taken the Mercedes Benz from her drive – and probably the one who'd pretended to be selling cavity wall insulation.

Hayman had met with the media officer at Saffron Walden police station and they had agreed a communications strategy following approval by Detective Inspector Sandy Matthews.

The plan was to release the photofit to three regional newspapers, and Anglia ITV and BBC East, along with details that Essex CID wanted to provide to the public. All would be released on the same day – planned for next Monday, 25th October. Hayman was confident that, with this exposure, someone would be forthcoming with information that would lead to the conviction of this man.

The thief had taken the Mercedes without consent, and then used it to run a vehicle off the road. That vehicle was the Kia Sportage driven by Peter Dobson on the night of the retirement party for Eric Somersby, the golf club groundsman. Dobson had been found to be over the legal limit for alcohol, but a key witness had confirmed that the stolen Mercedes had clearly forced the Kia off the road. The DS didn't know if the car thief knew Dobson, or what the motive was.

Because of Kate White's statement, Hayman had given the thief the nickname of 'Cavity Wall Man.' He hoped the white trainers worn by the thief would also help prompt somebody's memory. Magnification of one side of the left shoe had shown a tick symbol indicating the brand was Nike, and two footprints in a flower bed at White's home were a match to the trainers - *Men's Air Max 90* with a characteristic sole design. The same prints had also been found where the car had been abandoned on the industrial waste site. The dark hoodie, either black or a dark blue or grey, worn by the perpetrator was a fairly common style of clothing and less likely to be an identifying factor.

The hair found in the envelope along with one thousand pounds in the glovebox of the Merc hadn't yet been matched to anyone, and the name 'Jimmy' on the envelope had so far drawn a blank. Chris Hayman had been involved with a few similar cases where a tiny piece of evidence ended up in a dead end, a vital clue going nowhere. Simply not able to be linked to anything else and it was the most frustrating aspect of his role as a detective.

But he wasn't giving up on this one. From next Monday he'd be waiting for phone calls that he prayed would lead him to the car thief, and beyond that, concrete evidence that the person was indeed responsible for the manslaughter of Peter Dobson. If the hair in the envelope was a match for the thief, then there would be a link to the cash found in the Merc. Any recoverable fingerprints from the envelope, or a DNA match, might also belong to the perpetrator.

The Nike trainers retailed at around £100 and Hayman hoped that someone would recognise them. It's not everybody who spends that much on a pair of leisure shoes.

He certainly couldn't afford a pair on his salary!

73

Sitting in the small office at Pooches, Mike made two calls to his sisters. Telling them as little as possible, he said that arrangements were in place which would mean Tom Ball would be leaving their mother's house soon. Both Kathryn and Diane had questions, but Mike decided that less they knew, the better. Keep it simple. Their only concern would be to get two thirds of the £10,000 to Mike for him to pay Herring once he got the nod from the Serb.

"So, what are you suggesting? Draw out small amounts? What difference will that make? If you want the cash, I'll withdraw it in one lump," proposed Kathryn. Mike coughed.

"Listen, Kath, by taking that much out in one sum might arouse suspicion. Have you got more than one source from which to withdraw the cash?" He wasn't sure, they'd never talked money matters before.

"As you ask, I've got my flexible savings bank account, a building society instant access account and another bank account that you don't need to know about." That was him told.

"OK," replied Mike. "I suggest you raid each of them for the total amount, divided more or less equally, and then nobody is going to ask any questions." The conversation went quiet for a moment.

"Why does this have to be so cloak-and-dagger?"

"Because it does! If anything goes wrong and there's an enquiry, it'll be easier to justify taking out smaller sums – you could say you wanted to go shopping for an expensive dress, or have improvements made on your property. Something like that." Mike paused. "Listen, please do as I suggest. *Please.*"

"All right, don't go blabbing on at me. How soon do you want the money?" As soon as possible, Mike told her. Delivered to the kennels where he'd put it in a safe place.

"Look. Can you do me favour? I'm pretty busy right now. Could you call Di and go through this with her? The details the same as we've gone through. Yes?" Kathryn agreed . . . reluctantly.

The awkward phone call to his sister was done. Mike knew Kathryn would call Diane and tell her to get her finger out, and not to worry about anything. The main objective in all of this was that Tom Ball wasn't going to get his grubby little feet any further under their mother's table! Or anywhere else, for that matter.

James Herring would put the frighteners on Tom Ball, and Ball would crawl back into the hole out of which he came. Mike knew that the neighbour's divorce agreement had come through, that he was now a free agent, and would now simply have to get himself sorted out with his own accommodation. It was worth the ten grand that Herring had demanded. If Ball had ended up staying with their mother, the three siblings could potentially lose out on their inheritance, which could run into thousands, if not hundreds of thousands. So, what was ten thousand quid in the scheme of things?

Not much, thought Mike.

74

He'd spotted the man wearing the dog collar in the park. Fifty yards away. A vicar? Walking along slowly, then stopping. Looking around at the trees and people going by. Trying to appear to be nonchalant. The vicar took something out of an inside pocket. It was a phone. Was he going to call someone? No. The back of the phone was pointed at him. The vicar's finger tapped the screen three times.

Ten minutes later he saw the vicar sitting in a café. A mug and half eaten scone in front of him. It was clear that the vicar was looking at his phone screen. Maybe he was looking at the photos? The vicar was splaying his fingers on the glass, enhancing the photos. The man wasn't comfortable with what he observed.

When the vicar had gone, the man asked the café owner if he knew who the vicar was. Yes, he did, and he told the man the vicar's name and where he lived. The café owner was kind like that. He sensed that the man needed spiritual guidance.

Two hours later the vicar was dead. He'd been strangled in the sitting room of the parsonage.

75

Tom Ball assumed that Mike and his two sisters knew most things about him, particularly where he worked, his job as a van driver with Corbett & Perkins, and the white Peugeot Boxer he drove.

For the past few days, he'd scrutinised more and more people. Customers in the retail unit at C & P, new employees that the firm took on, those to whom he delivered – even long - standing customers, and members of the general public that might walk by his van when he was unloading. On the assumption that this guy, Herring, or Ingherr, would be wily enough to disguise himself, Mike told himself that he couldn't take anything for granted.

He had to be vigilant for the Neanderthal – looking man, as per the photo that Patrick Murray had sent to Tom after his Facebook enquiry. Tom had to smile to himself. It had been so easy to get Murray to fall for Tom's 'he's an old friend and I want to surprise him' ruse. Looking at the saved image on his smartphone, Tom looked again at the photo of Herring. What a brute! High forehead, heavy brows, small eyes, square chin. He even imagined him wearing a loincloth made from hide or buffalo skin. The only thing that could be different, maybe, was that Herring had grown a beard since the photo had been taken.

Tom had arrived at work ten minutes earlier than usual. The retail unit was about to open, and he needed to collect his delivery schedule for the day. His boss, Harry Phillips, was sitting in the office.

"Morning Tom, here's your list for today. Just printed it off. One point, we've got a new customer. Mr. Graham Ellison. He's in the process of sorting out his bank details to set up an account with us, but he's desperate for some A-frames, galvanised post supports and some decking. I've made the order out, it's ready for loading at the back. When he phoned late yesterday, he gave a delivery address on a large warehousing site that's no longer used. Unit 4 is the drop off point. He said it would be safe there and he'd arrange collection with one of his drivers. Something about his own premises being a bit overcrowded at the moment. The door to the unit will be closed but unlocked, so if you can sort that, it'll be good. I always welcome new customers, you know that!"

Tom took the schedule, tucked it inside his overall, and went out into the morning air to drive his van to the rear of the building. His load for that day was on a pallet, clearly marked TB with the date. Tom slipped on his protective gloves and began to slide items into the Boxer. Ten minutes later he was done. A quick trip to the Gents before he left, then he'd be on his way.

At 10.57 by the van's dashboard clock, Tom was driving along a narrow, potholed track to the Whitworth Industrial Estate. This place had been run down for several years, with weeds growing in cracks in the tarmac and paint peeling off the sides of the warehouses. He slowed. Unit 1 came up on his right - hand side, then Unit 3. He glanced to the left and saw the even numbers. Unit 2, then Unit 4. Two doors, each about three metres wide, filled the centre of the front face of the building. The doors were the slide-type, but the bottom runners were rusted. Tom wondered if they'd move a centimetre, never mind a couple of metres to get his delivery inside.

He parked as close to the doors as he could, being careful of the potholes in the road surface along that part of the industrial estate. This wasn't the time to be breaking a shock absorber or putting a leaf spring through the bodywork. The back doors of the Peugeot van were about four metres from the warehouse – close enough to drop off his load and be on his way.

No sooner had Tom opened the van doors when he heard the sound of a vehicle approaching. An SUV, silver grey in colour. Tom turned and saw the dust kicked up by the wheels. A minute later the SUV, a Tesla, stopped in front of Tom's van.

"Good morning," said the well - dressed man who spoke with a slight foreign accent. He was about six feet tall and wore Ray-Ban sunglasses. His blue eyes were hidden behind the shades. "What's all this? A delivery?" Tom cleared his throat.

"Yes, a load consisting of A frames, galvanised post supports and decking for Unit 4, Whitworth Industrial Estate." The man came closer to Tom and looked into his eyes.

"What's your name?" asked the man. Tom told him. First and last. "This unit belongs to me and I didn't order any stuff from you. Which company is it?" Tom gave him the name - Corbett and Perkins. "No, there's some mistake here." Tom was confused.

"Haven't you just set up an account with us? You placed your order yesterday afternoon?" The fair - haired man was half an arms-length from Tom's face.

"Now you just listen to me. I've told you once. Get your van and your delivery off this estate now! I don't like the look of you, and any more of your lip, you'll get reported to your firm and any professional bodies of which your firm is a member. Understand?" The man seemed to be staring at Tom, not just into his eyes, but at every feature of his face, his sunglasses hiding his penetrating look. For a second, he felt as if this guy was going to nut him.

"OK, OK. I'm going," was Tom's only riposte. He wanted to get away from this situation as soon as he could.

"I'll remember your face Tom Ball. And if I ever see you again around these parts you'll be in trouble. Don't forget that, will you?" Tom was motionless. "Will you!"

Tom turned the keys and put the Boxer into reverse gear. He didn't want to hang about, but he was tempted to clip the front wing of the silver - grey SUV as he made a U-turn. Just a small dent, then say it was an accident. Once he was a mile from the industrial estate Tom pulled onto a piece of spare ground and phoned his boss.

"Hi, Harry. I thought you might want to know that some guy turned up at the Unit 4 place and has made it clear that he didn't order anything from us. I was about to start unloading but thankfully I hadn't dropped any items off. He was a right nasty bastard."

"Well, funny you say that, Tom, but I checked his bank details and they've never heard of him. No one named Graham Ellison as a customer. I rang the telephone number that registered on my office phone when he called and it has a voice message saying 'this number is no longer in use.' This is a scam, Tom."

"But why go to this trouble to pretend to set up an account and order some stuff from us, only for him to deny he'd ever done it?" asked Tom. "He could have let me deliver the items and removed them, then sold them on." Phillips paused a moment.

"Did you get this guy's name, Tom?" He looked down.
"No, I didn't."
"So, we don't actually know who he was, then?"

"Gertrude, we could make this our little secret, couldn't we?" said Tom after their evening meal. The plates had been taken into the kitchen and Tom had offered to wash up. He would have put things in the dishwasher, but it needed a spare part for the motor. He'd get the item from work tomorrow, and remember to pay for it. He and Gertie were sitting in the lounge, the radio turned low.

"What's that, Tom? What little secret?" Tom had to remind her yet again. He realised things might get a bit tough, what with Gertie's memory being what it was . . . and getting worse.

"You know," he replied in a condescending manner, "you and I getting together as in *getting married*." He gave his remarks time to sink in. "I'm now a single man, you're a single woman, and I'm not bothered about our age difference anyway." Gertie put her copy of the Radio Times down.

"Oh, that. Well, yes, I suppose so, but why does it have to be our little secret, Tom? I'd like to invite some of my W.I. friends – you know, make it a happy event. And of course, the three children." Tom smiled, with difficulty. 'I'm not having all that rubbish,' he thought. He had to come up with a plan, and now. This could go on and on like Coronation Street if he wasn't careful. He took her hand.

"Listen, Gertrude . . ." He paused. "Would you mind if I called you something else? Gave you a pet name?"

"But I'm not a pet, am I?" Silence between them. "Of course, you're not a pet, but a pet name means something, sort of, well, affectionate. Between a couple. Between us." Tom didn't want this to be like toothache, he wanted to get it over with.

"What have you got in mind, then?" Tom looked into her eyes.

"Gerbil." The word hung in the air. Gertrude's face was stony.

"Gerbil! Why Gerbil?"

"Well, because it's close to your own name, and gerbils are the cutest little animals!" Tom balked at his lies. Gertie turned to look at him.

"Oh, Tom, that's one of the most beautiful things anyone has ever said to me!" She leant over and kissed him on the cheek.

"Good, so that's that then! Gerbil and Tom! We make a good pair, don't we Gerbil?" Gertie laughed, and Tom joined in – forcing laughter like an am-dram actor. "Why don't we celebrate with a drink? Can I get you a glass of prosecco, Gerbil?" Gertie nodded and beamed at him.

"That will be wonderful. Then we can start writing down our plans, can't we? There's a pad in that drawer over there, and a biro on the table here. Get me that drink and we'll sit together and begin with a date, then the guest list." Tom went into the kitchen and opened the wine. He yanked a ring-pull from a can of beer and took a swig.

'Guest list, my backside,' he whispered as he put the drinks on a small tray. 'No guests, Gertie, my dear. Just us two.' Tom knew he had to plan this carefully. And had to lie.

"Here we are, Gerbil, a prosecco for the lady of the house." Tom put the glass next to Gertie's chair. She smiled.

"You can write things down, Tom. My writing isn't so good these days." He picked up the biro, a Parker, and took the pad out of the drawer. Gertie sipped her wine, and then began.

"Right, let's plan for the first week in December. We should choose a nice spot, you know, a decent hotel somewhere." Tom's hand moved across the page. "Then we'll have the list of guests. Can you jot down three of my friends from the W.I? Iris, Heather, and Ruby. Then there's Michael, Kathryn and Diane . . . oh, and let me see, two other people I know whose names I can't remember just now." Tom's hand eased down the page. "I think that's it, Tom. Could you see to all of that for me? It would be good if you can. I know I can rely on you, Tom. You're good to me."

Tom tore the page from the pad, folded it twice, and put it in front pocket of his jeans.

"Leave it to me, Gerbil. I'll get onto that tomorrow. There's no need for you to worry about a thing."

Gertrude said she was feeling tired and wanted an early night. The wine glass was empty. She said goodnight to Tom and kissed the top of his head as she left the lounge. Tom remained sitting. He took a glug of his beer, and removed the notepaper from his pocket. He unfolded it and looked at the sheet.

It was blank and he smiled.

77

Liz woke and rubbed her eyes. The radio alarm showed 07.32 and she was alone. It had been another lovely evening with Robbo and he'd stayed over. Liz got out of bed and slipped on her dressing gown. A few brushes of her hair made her look presentable in case Robbo was still in the bungalow. She pinched her cheeks three times to give them some colour, then heard the sound of a boiling kettle and the clatter of mugs. He was in the kitchen! Liz went downstairs ready to meet the day.

"Good morning, gorgeous!" said Robbo. "Sweet dreams?" He kissed her on the mouth and she purred like a cat.

"Yes. I dreamt I'd met this wonderful man who complimented me on my food and wine choice, then whisked me off to bed!" Robbo laughed; his white teeth sparkled in the sunlight.

"Ha, ha. Pull the other one. Anyway, I've made coffee. Can I get you a mug?" Liz nodded. "I found your toaster and I've had a couple of slices. Hope you didn't mind. And the marmalade was lovely. Would you like a slice?"

Minutes later they were sat at the table chatting about the previous evening. Robbo told Liz how much he'd enjoyed the king prawns and the coq-au-vin. The two bottles of Malbec had been emptied and now stood near the back door ready for the recycling bin. He pulled her leg about her choice in music, saying he preferred the likes of Billy Joel rather than old stagers such as Don Williams.

"There's nothing wrong with Don Williams!" she retorted. "I happen to like mature American country singers. They sound so much better than these current ones who can't sing for toffee!" He laughed and threw his head back. Liz noticed he had a tooth missing.

"OK, OK. The next time you come I'll ask *Alexa* for Billy Joel's greatest album." Liz finished her toast which had a little too much marmalade on, but she'd let it pass this time. Looking at his gold watch, Robbo stood up.

"Listen. I must go. I've got a client in at eleven to view some paintings. He's got a budget of two million and is looking for a decent oil." Two million! Liz wasn't sure how many zeros were in two million and she wasn't going to ask. "I've showered and borrowed some of your deodorant so I probably smell OK. Glad I brought a shirt and pair of boxers. I'll use the spare toothbrush and be on my way." Robbo left the kitchen. Liz pondered on this guy who'd recently come into her life. He had a way about him, a bit of a swagger, a sense of humour, and a nice car. And what a job! Working in the city and talking with pop stars and celebrities from sport and show business. Helping them buy oil paintings worth a load of cash!

When she thought about it, she didn't know such a lot about Robbo. Did he have a circle of friends, a family somewhere? It would be nice to meet them sometime – just out of curiosity more than anything. She knew this wasn't going to last forever, but Liz saw no harm in having a bit of fun while her ex-husband was living a comfortable life with his 'mother figure' next door. Robbo had made her feel alive . . . something she hadn't felt with Tom for ages. Liz was lifted out of her thoughts as Robbo put his head around the kitchen door.

"Well, I must be off. No peace for the wicked." She moved closer and kissed him. Robbo smelt of her eau de Cologne – acceptable these days for a man. The tang of minty toothpaste hit her.

"When will I see you again, Robbo?" Liz hoped it didn't sound like a begging question.

"I'm not sure, Liz. I've got an assignment in Edinburgh tomorrow for a few days . . . a large art gallery up there are holding an international exhibition. Then I may have to go to Paris next week. So, I'm afraid the answer is I don't know. But you've got my number. Call me when you can, and if I don't answer, leave a message."

Robbo knows how to treat a woman, thought Liz. So considerate, so thoughtful. She hesitated with her next sentence. Didn't want it to sound cheesy.

"Missing you already," she uttered, then instantly regretted it. "Well, you know . . ."

Robbo stood on the door step and turned.

"You must meet a family member soon," he offered. This was exactly what Liz had been thinking only minutes earlier.

"Oh? Your sister, mother, father?" she asked. Robbo smiled.

"No. My dog. I've got a Cavalier King Charles." Liz held her hands to her breast.

"Oh, how lovely. What's its name?"

"He's called Carisbrooke," replied Robbo as he walked away down the footpath.

78

Mike finished counting the money. Most of it was in £20 notes. Herring had made it clear he wanted cash – his favourite means of dealing with his expenses. Credit and debit cards left a trail and apps on a smartphone did the same. Cheques were about as useful as an ash tray on a Harley Davison . . . taking time to clear and all that guff. Herring didn't have an *Alexa* device, convinced that as soon as he connected it up some investigation body like MI5 would be listening in to his every conversation, and monitoring his activities. Pyong helped, and counted the notes into bundles of one thousand pounds with an elastic band around each one. The ten bundles were piled up and then wrapped in a sheet of the local newspaper, nice and tight, with Sellotape around the lot. Crossways and lengthways. It looked like a paper mache brick.

"We'll put this in with the dog food," he said, once they were satisfied with the package. "When Herring has done the job, I'll give him this. I know he won't count it there and then. He trusts us, I hope, and he knows where we live. He'll be back if he has a complaint." Pyong forced a smile. This gave her an uneasy feeling as Mike expected. He looked at her.

"Listen, Pyong, this will soon be over. I don't want you to feel you're directly involved. Herring will let me know how and where he wants to meet to pay him. It'll be somewhere open and I'm guessing he'll want the package in a plain, plastic carrier bag." Pyong touched Mike's arm.

"What then?" she asked.

"Well, nothing really. Tom Ball will disappear and mother can get back to her normal way of life. If she needs a plumber, I'll tell her to phone me." He paused. "We'll also need to practice how we respond to questions . . ."

"Like what?" Mike continued.

"When it becomes public that mother's live-in lodger has gone – and we don't know if a body will be found – folks will ask questions. If Herring dumps the body in the river, for example, and it washes up on the coast, then the police will be involved and we'll be questioned . . . at least I will."

"What about Kathryn and Diane? Are you going to talk to them, you know, about getting your story straight?" Mike sensed his wife was trying to be helpful here.

"Good point. Yes, we don't want to be giving Essex CID a different take on how we saw mother and Tom's relationship heading. Be best if we all felt equally strong about the situation. I'll call them later and have a chat. May be best if we meet up together again soon."

Pyong cleared away the Sellotape, scissors, and rest of the newspaper. A few elastic bands were put into a lidded pot on the window sill. Pyong was about to fold the newspaper when she spotted an article.

HAVE YOU SEEN THIS MAN?

Essex police are looking for this man in connection with the theft of a motor vehicle in Benfleet Road, Saffron Walden on 26 May. He is six feet tall with blue eyes and ginger hair.
If you think you can help the police, please call Crimestoppers on 0800 555 111

Pyong glared at the photofit picture. His face looked familiar. She called Mike who was now attending to a German Shepherd dog with pus oozing from a wound.

"Mike! Come here when you've minute!" she bellowed from the kitchen. A few minutes later Mike was there.

"What is it? You sounded desperate." She showed him the newspaper page, bottom left - hand corner.

"Look at this. Does he look familiar to you?" asked Pyong. He had a long look at the photofit.

"No, can't say that he does. Look at that hairstyle! He could be any of a number of people I know. Mr Percival, the butcher? Clarence Jeffries, the solicitor. Owen Rafferty, our dentist?" Pyong took another look.

"I have seen that face somewhere before. I'm certain I have."

79

Gareth White was on the phone to Saffron Walden police station. He'd been waiting for over four minutes before a breathless DS Hayman took the call from the main desk.

"Hello, Mr White. Sorry to have kept you waiting but I was outside attending to a matter. What can I do for you?" White cleared his throat.

"I took my car in for a service this morning to our local Merc dealer. They rang me five minutes ago to say they'd found a tiny, gold crucifix lodged under the floor mat on the driver's side.

"Ah, and your cavity wall insulation salesman was wearing a thin gold chain according to your wife, if memory serves. Can you ring your dealer and ask the service manager to put that crucifix to one side? Let him know I'll be there to collect it. Is it the garage on Radcliffe Road?" Gareth White confirmed it was. "OK. I'll go there and pick it up now. I'll keep you informed. Thanks for the call, Mr White." Hayman rung off. He grabbed his jacket from the back of the chair, snatched his car keys, and headed down to the car park. Getting into the standard provision vehicle, a black Ford Focus, Hayman entered the Merc dealer post code into the satnav, tapped Start, and drove out of the station as the barrier lifted slowly to let him out.

'How the hell have Forensics missed that?' he said aloud as he changed up a gear.

DS Hayman was no jewellery expert, but he felt certain that with the crucifix found in the car, there just might be a jeweller in the area who could help.

Chris Hayman parked the Focus in the Visitors area of the forecourt. He entered the premises through the double glass doors signed Reception and headed for the desk. A blonde girl in her twenties occupied a swivel chair, partly hidden behind a computer. Her lapel badge showed Jill. She looked up as the detective approached. Before he could speak, Jill smiled and looked up at him.

"Are you Detective Sergeant Hayman?" He nodded. "Mr Jones, our service manager, is in his office. Please follow me." Jill strode briskly towards a waiting area with a coffee machine and three - seater leatherette sofa. She knocked on a dark brown door near the coffee machine, then heard Jones say 'come in.' Jill ushered the detective in.

"Hello sergeant. Dave Jones. Please take a seat." Hayman sat on an upright, chrome and canvas chair. He'd expected more from a dealer in prestige German cars, but it was comfortable. "You've come for the crucifix . . . it's here." Jones opened a drawer and took out the postcard sized poly bag. "One of my mechanics spotted it just under the carpet in the driver footwell, but in a recess where the rubber buttons of the mat fit tightly. It could easily have been missed. One of the oddest things we've found in a car!"

The DS looked at the little gold cross through the bag material.

"Thanks, Mr Jones. I won't take up any more of your time." Hayman turned to leave.

"May I ask what a detective sergeant wants with that?" enquired Jones.

"Well, I can't say too much, but this is likely to lead us to someone who stole Mr White's Mercedes Benz a few months ago." Jones put his hand out.

"Oh, right. Good luck with that, sergeant. I hope you find the thief."

Half an hour later Chris Hayman and DC Grayson were comparing notes in a small meeting room at Saffron Walden police station. Grayson had got two coffees for them. Hayman put the poly bag on the desk and both looked at it for a few minutes.

"That gold crucifix may not be a common style," said the DC. He took a magnifying glass from a drawer. "It has the letters IHS on it in blue. Looks like they could be in enamel," Grayson said, then took a quick sip of his latte.

"Well, IHS is the Latinised version of the Greek letters iota-eta-sigma which are the first three letters of the name Jesus in Greek," commented the DS. Grayson should have known that, being a Catholic, and he blushed slightly. He didn't realise that his sergeant was such an academic; he had a B.A. degree in something. "Can you get onto a couple of jewellers in the town, see what comments they might have on it? Bye the way, any news on Barclays Bank?" Grayson finished the remains of his coffee.

"Yes, I was coming onto that. I had a call from the manager at the Victoria Street branch. He'd asked his staff to keep their eyes open for a woman wearing red leather gloves. The woman called in the day before yesterday. Let me see . . ." Grayson flipped open his notebook. "Here we are. A Mrs Heseltine. First name Alice."

"Hello, can I ask . . . are you licensed for weddings?" Tom Ball was talking to Kira, the receptionist at a hotel in Walton-on-the-Naze. His plan was to take Gertie to the Essex coast, which he knew she loved, but not back to the Brompton Court hotel. It had too many memories for her, and she knew some of the staff. That would never do for Tom; he wanted anonymity. Walton was about ten miles further north along the coast, a picturesque little town with a long beach. The sea front residences were mainly blocks of flats and detached bungalows, almost all of them painted white.

"Yes, Montfort Hall is licensed to hold weddings. We received our license on the first of June last year. Are you wanting some information?" asked Kira. Tom checked the list in his hand.

"Well, yes. My partner and I are keen to get married. It will be a small, private affair . . . in fact, just the two of us. We'd like to stay two nights on a full board basis mid - week, and have a special dinner on the evening of the wedding. Can you tell me what you'd charge for that?" Tom heard a rustling of paper, then a brief pause.

"It depends on when you want to get married, sir. We have peak periods, for example May to September are quite busy. Do you have a date in mind?"

"As soon as possible actually. Do you have anything this month, or into November? It certainly must be before Christmas." Another flicking of paper sound, probably the pages of a desk diary being turned.

"We can do Tuesday and Wednesday, the 23rd and 24th of November, or, let me see . . ." Tom interjected.

"That's fine! And the cost?" Another pause. Tom wondered if the receptionist had any details on her computer, or was it all in ledgers like a Dickensian funeral parlour?

"For what you want, sir, we're looking at £410 including the registrar's fee, and dependant on what you wanted for your 'special dinner' on the second night. There'll be a deposit to pay to secure the booking." Tom wanted to get on with this. Get a date fixed, then tell Gertie he was taking her away for a couple of days to a smart hotel for a nice break. It would be a lovely surprise for her, and he prayed she wasn't going to miss the hangers-on that she'd blathered about earlier.

"OK, what's the deposit?" Kira explained that the standard rate was 20%. It seemed high to Tom, but he needed to get this done.

"Right. Do you take credit cards?" Kira took Tom's and Gertie's names and dates of birth, along with Gertie's address, then the card details. £82 was taken from Tom's credit card.

"That's all gone through, Mr Ball. We look forward to welcoming you to Montfort Hall on 23rd November. We have a standard range of floral displays that come with the wedding package, but if you want any special flowers, please give us a week's notice. Do you have any other specific wishes at this stage?" Tom didn't. He just wanted this over and done with. He now had just under four weeks to wait before the wedding. Enough time to keep Gertie sweet, and plan the best time to share the news about a 'break away' to the coast.

All he had to do now was carry on as normal, avoid Gertie's children if possible, and continue to keep a lookout for Jamek Ingherr. He'd also pop next door to see Liz and dig out one of his suits. Maybe a decent shirt and tie, too.

He wanted to look his best for his wedding day after all.

Sitting in his office, DI Sandy Matthews was trawling through the list of respondents with DS Chris Hayman following their communication tactics using the photofit image of Cavity Wall Man. Eighteen replies, all phone calls, and a mix of 'it was definitely him in the supermarket' to 'it might have been that man but he looked away as I passed him.' Half from the TV news item, the rest from the three regional newspapers. Matthews had done this before with previous investigations and he guessed that about three quarters were a waste of time. Those who wanted some attention in their sparse, empty lives, those who felt they had important information – because they always thought that, and those who were pure time wasters.

'It was him, I'm sure, but he was under six feet tall . . . Yes, it was him, but he had darker hair . . . I'm certain that was the man, but he had brown eyes . . .' The DI sighed.

"What do you make of these, Chris? Looks like a poor response overall." Hayman scanned the two sheets of A4.

"I think those numbered four, seven and eleven sound genuine so I'd like to think we followed those up. There are four others that
may be worth checking out if those first three don't provide anything." Matthews felt his DS sounded like a punter on race day at Ascot. He nodded.

"I agree, Chris. Can you put those three onto a separate list? I suggest you and DC Grayson chase them up as soon as you are able. Get the usual details, you know date, time, place, any other aspects that might help – all that." Matthews knew he didn't need to remind his efficient sergeant, but this was an important enquiry. If Cavity Wall Man could be found it would get the DI's boss off his back.

"I'll get onto that, sir, and while we're at it, Grayson and I will follow up on Mrs Alice Heseltine. You know, the red leather glove lady who withdrew one thousand pounds from Barclays a few months ago." The DI frowned.

"Hang on! Heseltine? Now that's not a common name, is it? We didn't ask Nigel Heseltine about his wife, did we? Is she the one you're talking about?" Hayman assumed that Alice was Nigel's wife, but he would check the address. "If it is, ask her if she knows anyone named Jimmy, the name on the envelope in the Merc. But be careful, we don't want to give too much away at this stage." Hayman got up. "Ask her if she has seen the photofit picture, too. If so, does she recognise the man? Another thing, Chris, do some probing on her husband. I didn't trust him when we spoke with him in the back of the car at the golf club. His replies to my questions about his relationship with Peter Dobson seemed too rehearsed, too knee-jerk. Find out what you can on his background – previous jobs, friends, etc." The DS gave his boss the 'I'm on the case' look as he left Matthews' office.

Hayman walked down the open office to the desk of DC Cameron Grayson who was engrossed staring at his computer screen.

"How's it going, Cam? Any news on the 'red gloves' woman?"

"Yes, here's her address in Saffron Walden. House name 'Jacaranda' at post code CB10 7HN. Before you ask, it is the same as Mr Nigel Heseltine that you and the DI saw at the golf club. It's got to be his wife. Do you think she's involved, sarge?" Hayman couldn't rule out that Mrs Heseltine *did* have something to do with the Dobson case. Maybe she withdrew the cash to give to her husband, but how did it end up in the Merc? Nigel Heseltine had a motive connected to the election of a new president at the golf club as Dobson was favourite to get the position, but was his wife a party to this matter? Perhaps the cash was stolen from the Heseltine household by the car thief, who then left it in the car when it had been abandoned on the disused industrial estate? If so, it had not been reported to the police, and the name Jimmy on the envelope may not have a connection to the Heseltine's at all.

DS Hayman knew he wasn't going to rush to any conclusions, he'd tread gently, and 'piece together the jigsaw' before getting back to DI Matthews. But there was one thing he did know, and that was that Alice Heseltine had *not taken* a DNA test. The envelope and blonde hair found in the envelope were still archived at the police station.

"Come on, Cam, time to pay the Heseltine's a visit!"

82

"Hello, Robbo. It's me. I'm sure you're busy but I thought I'd ask you what you're doing tomorrow evening. I've bought a leg of lamb which I'm going to cook slowly and make a jus with red wine. It'll come with all the trimmings. Anyway, give me a call when you've time. Bye."

Liz put the phone down. In truth, she hated leaving messages. One small slip with a word, or the wrong intonation, and you couldn't take it back.

When would he phone her? Hell, she was a grown woman, but she felt like eighteen again. Liz had never wanted to get involved with anybody. She wasn't looking for a man, but when she thought about how it had happened – with Robbo seeing her in the Cowherd's Arms pub on her night out with Mary, and Terry Williams passing on the information – she put it down to fate.

Liz had read about things like this happening in her women's magazines. Various letters from females of all ages . . . even a woman of 85, for goodness sakes! But then she thought of Gertie next door. Although Liz wasn't sure of her age, Gertie had to be 80 if she was a day, and there she was with her ex-husband who hadn't reached forty, yet!

Liz pulled herself together. She wasn't going to spend the day hovering by the phone. But wherever she went, Liz would carry her mobile with her . . . garden, loo, grocery shopping, everywhere. She didn't want to miss his call.

She imagined him arranging a deal with some overpaid footballer or screen actor for the purchase of an oil painting or sculpture, talking in hundreds of thousands of pounds – even millions – then going out for a champagne lunch to celebrate. The art gallery director slipping Robbo his commission on his return. 'Here's a cheque for ten thousand' or 'I've transferred ten grand into your bank account, Robbo.' Oh, how nice it must be not to worry about money. But then, the plans of Liz and her now ex-husband were exactly that. They had worried about paying for things, and needed to pull their horns in for years. Over half of her wardrobe came from charity shops, and some of her dresses were cast-offs from her sister, Mary. How would it feel to walk into M & S or John Lewis and pick what you wanted without caring how much an item cost?

That's why Tom was doing what he was doing. Liz brought herself back down to earth. Maybe he wasn't having a great time, putting up with the foibles of an old pensioner? But their plan was still going ahead, so Liz persuaded herself that she ought to bear that in mind, and that eventually she and Tom would be reunited. Liz thought of 'Loadsamoney,' the character played by Harry Enfield on his TV comedy show – a cockney lout always seen with a bundle of cash in his hand.

Tom would leave the builder's merchants, set up his own business, buy a decent car, and they could move to a smarter part of Basildon. A four bedroom, detached property with a double garage and nice garden . . . begin to socialise more, and tell neighbours where they were going for their next cruise, or the log cabin they'd bought in a prestigious area of the Peak District.

Liz was putting two sheets, a few towels and some other items into the washing machine
when her mobile let out the ringtone. Her heart missed a beat . . . was it Robbo? It was!

"Hi, Robbo. How are you? Been busy?" She couldn't think of anything else to say. Did it sound too corny?

"Hello Liz. I'm fine thank you. I got your message, and thank you for your consideration regarding the lamb. It's a meat I love as you know. Listen, I've got a better idea." Liz waited. It seemed an eternity. "There's a restaurant I know that you'll love. Tomorrow evening. Are you up for it? If so, I'll text you the details." Liz's pulse rate was up, she could tell.

"Yes, that'll be fine. I'm free!" With that Robbo ended the call. No 'goodbye' or 'see you then.' But she realised that was the way he was. Forthright and straight talking, but he was probably in the middle of some tough negotiations so it was good of him to make the time to call. The lamb went back into the fridge – it would keep for another time.

Liz switched the washing machine on and it burst into life, swirling suds hitting the round glass door with venom. It was time for coffee, but before she had time to fill the kettle, her phone pinged. A message from Robbo!

Hi Liz. Meet me at the old abandoned Magdalene abbey at 7 pm tomorrow. Take a taxi. I want to show you something before we
go to the restaurant. I've booked a table for 8 pm. R x

How romantic, thought Liz, a surprise meeting before dinner. At the old abbey, too! She hadn't been there for ages. But she didn't want all this to get too much for her, become consumed with Robbo . . . it wasn't going to last forever. With a job like his, he probably had a few 'lady friends' that he wined and dined from time to time.

No. She and Tom would be getting together again in the not- too- distant future and this was just a pleasant interval. That's how she'd consider the matter. Liz had to, otherwise it would drive her insane. However, she wanted to get to know Robbo better, and a meeting before dinner would give her plenty of time to probe a little. Nothing too demanding, but at least she would like to know about his background – school, college, parents, siblings, hobbies, and interests – that sort of thing. And most importantly, his real name! Robbo sounded nice and friendly, cosy even, but Liz had to ask him about the name on his birth certificate. He knew hers, after all - Elizabeth Vivian Gallagher. She even wondered if he'd begin to call her something else – Lizzie, or Viv, but did she really want to get on such terms with him? She wasn't sure.

Liz finished her coffee and made up her mind to get on with some housework – it would take her mind off things until tomorrow evening. She'd promised Mary that she would phone her, and Liz also wanted to go through her wardrobe to find the nicest dress to wear.

She'd polish her smartest black leather shoes, and sort out some jewellery. There was the elephant brooch with paste diamonds, and a necklace her mother had given her a long time ago. The earrings had to be just right . . . not too long and dangly, not too small, and there was one thing that was certain.

Liz Ball was going to be as pretty as she could be. As pretty as a picture.

The two detectives went to see Alice Heseltine. Her story was straightforward. She had withdrawn one thousand pounds from her own Barclays account on or about 24 May because she intended to buy her husband a present. She wasn't sure of the date, but could check her bank statement if it was important. He'd been talking of getting an automatic grass mower and she wanted to treat him, there being one in stock at the local garden centre. It was their wedding anniversary on 29 May and she decided he deserved it.

When she left the bank, she went to two more shops. The Barclays envelope containing the cash was in a cotton shoulder bag, but when she got home it was missing. Mrs Heseltine said she was too embarrassed to tell her husband, but as it was from her personal account, she was sure he wouldn't find out. She still hasn't said anything to him, she confessed to the police.

As far as she was aware, she hadn't written anything on the envelope and did not know anyone by the name of Jimmy after Hayman had shared the name with her. The first she'd heard about Peter Dobson being killed in an RTA was when her husband received a telephone call whilst they were away in Cromer for the week-end. She was very saddened to get the news.

Alice Heseltine suggested that whoever took the money could have been the car thief. A pure coincidence, she had proposed to the detectives.

As far as the photofit image was concerned, she had seen it on local TV news, but was busy doing something else at the time. After glancing at it, she did not recognise the man shown.

DS Hayman asked Alice if she was agreeable to take a DNA test. She was, and then added 'since I've nothing to hide.' An appointment was made for Mrs Heseltine to go to the station tomorrow to provide a sample of saliva.

The sergeant mentioned the fact that it appeared a Mont Blanc pen may have been used to write on the envelope containing the cash, and did she ever use her husband's Mont Blanc pen? Alice looked surprised, until Hayman explained that a previous enquiry revealed that there were two golf club members who owned such a fountain pen. She simply replied that it was more than her life was worth to use Nigel's fine pen.

Alice Heseltine apologised to the two policemen, but there was nothing more she could add at this stage. With no tea or coffee being offered, and certainly no scones, Hayman and Grayson had got up and left the Heseltine home. Sitting in the police car a few minutes later, the DC spoke first.

"Nice place, sarge. They must be worth a bob or two?" Grayson didn't know the origin of that phrase, but he was aware what it meant. His dad used to use it when Grayson was a kid.

"Dead right, Cam. What did you make of our Alice, then?" Hayman turned the car key to warm the engine, and then let it idle.

"I'm not sure. Her story is plausible, but it's a million to one chance that whosoever stole the money – if it was stolen – was the same person that took the Merc." Hayman nodded.

"Yes, I agree. Assuming it wasn't stolen, do you think our Alice withdrew the money to give to a hit man? Someone she, or her husband, or both, paid to follow Dobson and run him off the road late at night after the party for the golf club groundsman. And she could have used his flashy pen when he was out?"

"Well, the perp was the guy seen on CCTV, with the expensive trainers, who we have named Cavity Wall Man. He has to be the one who caused Dobson's death. Let's hope that we get some decent leads on him." The sergeant gripped the steering wheel.

"I've left DC Jackson poring over the names. DI Matthews is happy for Jackson to work with us. He's the new recruit straight from police college – it'll give him something to get his teeth into. We had three decent leads, and a few others that might take us somewhere. Maybe you and Jackson could also check a couple of jewellers as we said earlier? See if they can throw any light on the gold crucifix. It doesn't belong to the White's so we must assume it's from the car thief." Grayson smiled at his sergeant.

"Yes?" asked Hayman, recognising the look in Grayson's eyes.

"Well, I popped out for ten minutes this morning. Went to that jeweller's across the road. Pomfret and Son. They're pretty upmarket, I think. Anyway, Mr Pomfret had a good look at it with his eye loupe magnifier, and guess what?"

"Go on, Cam, surprise me," replied the DS with a hint of sarcasm.

"Going by the colour of the gold, the style and the lustre, he's 99% certain it's from South Africa."

Mike, Kathryn and Diane were sitting in a small café in Ingatstone at a table away from the other customers. The town, just off the A12 between Brentwood and Romford, and not far from Chelmsford, was convenient for the three of them. Mike had suggested the meeting to go over the final details about Tom Ball. Mike had already outlined the facts with his sisters, but they all needed to be certain that they were 'singing from the same hymn sheet.' It was waitress service, and after they'd ordered their different coffees and a pastry each, Mike began.

"Listen," he said, leaning forwards and knitting his fingers. "If the police come knocking when Tom has gone, we all need the same story. OK?" The girls nodded, Kathryn a little reluctantly. The closeness of the evil deed was beginning to get to her. "Right, so here's what I think we say . . ." And so, Mike laid out his thoughts, in a quiet, unassuming way.

When Ball went missing, a number of people would begin to ask questions and inevitably Essex CID would get involved. Those who would query his disappearance would include their mother, his workplace, and his ex-wife, Liz Ball, to mention but three. Of course, there would be others, but they were the main ones.

The three siblings would tell police that none of them were in favour of Tom being with their mother, but in her interest, they wished her well if that was what she wanted.

None of them had wished any harm on Tom, and he seemed to be an honest and hard - working man who cared for people and gave his time to others.

They knew that their mother had gone to Clacton-on-Sea with Tom for a couple of days, and considered that Tom had been the perfect gentleman. He looked after their mother, and even paid for the hotel.

At 81 years of age, their mother was getting on in years, but since her divorce from their father, Nigel, she had lived a fairly lonely existence of which they had their concerns. Mainly for her safety.

Did the three of them feel that Tom Ball was 'taking advantage' of their mother? Only slightly.

And the last time they saw Tom Ball? It was when they'd visited their mother's house about three months ago. He was at the property and Gertrude had introduced him to them.

Did their mother talk about Tom to them when they phoned her? No, she said very little about him.

How well do they know Liz Ball? Hardly at all, except to shout 'hello' over the fence if she was in her front garden.

Did any of them ever have a conversation with Tom? Nothing more than a few sentences.

Had Tom Ball ever mentioned that he had any friends or acquaintances in the Basildon area? No, not that they could recall.

Do they have any idea at all where Tom Ball may have gone to? No, none at all. They believed he was divorced from Liz, and may have left the area.

Was Tom Ball the type who would harm another person, or bear any malice against another, and in particular, their mother? No, certainly not.

If you can think of anything which might help us in our enquiries, you will be sure to let us know? Yes, of course, absolutely.

During Mike's soliloquy, the girls had munched on their Eccles cakes and sipped their coffee whilst listening carefully to what he was saying. Regular nods of heads suggested his words had sunk in. Mike had taken bites of his millionaire's shortcake in between parts of his 'speech,' and was now finishing his Americano.

"Have I left anything out? Kath?" Kathryn's eyes searched the café, looking for any inspiration.

"No, I don't think so." Mike turned to Diane.

"Di. You?" Diane wiped her mouth with the paper serviette.

"When does your contact get paid?" she asked in a whisper. Mike poked his teeth with a fingernail, then licked his lips.

"I think I mentioned that. Anyway, it's half when he gives me the nod, then the other half when he's finished the job. He'll want five grand any day now, I would think. I'm not to ask him any questions – his insistence."

"So, Tom Ball goes off into thin air and we never see him again?" queried Diane. Mike smiled and nodded. "Then the police come asking questions?" she added, tremulously.

"Look, there's no need to worry. Our hands are clean! There's no way his disappearance can be linked to us. I'll meet my contact in some outdoor run of the mill place, avoiding any CCTV cameras, hand over the payments wrapped in newspaper in plastic carrier bags on the two occasions, then we never see him again. Job done!" Kathryn sighed.

"You make it sound so simple. Hell, I hope it's all as easy as you're making out." Mike squeezed her hand.

"It will be, sis, it will be." He reached out for Diane's hand, too. She took it as if they were in prayer. "We stick to the same story, stay calm, and wait. When the police come calling, we stay composed, relaxed, and act normal. OK?"

Kathryn looked at her watch.

"I need to go," she said anxiously, and rose from her chair. Diane did the same.

"Everything will be fine. Trust me," reassured Mike, keeping his voice down as the girls left the café.

"Any news on the follow – up to the photofit pictures, Chris?" DI Sandy Matthews wanted this matter put to bed. There were other pressing matters to concern him, and the sooner they found the car thief and got him to court, the better.

"Yes. DC Grayson has been in touch with all three of those informants who thought they knew who the person was. Trouble is, all three give different names. Grayson has spoken to each one over the phone, and double checked the details given to him. One is a plumber from Saffron, another a teacher from a secondary school in Billericay, and the third is a retired accountant that lives in North Benfleet."

"Who is the retired accountant? They're usually pretty accurate about things." Hayman shuffled some pages of a desk note book.

"Ted Mortimer of 14, Willow View Road. Do you want us to pay him a visit, sir?" asked the sergeant. The DI nodded.

"Yes, and the other two. Just in case. You never know. What about the other feedback? There were another handful who reckoned they'd recognised the man in the photofit." Hayman confirmed that they were already planning to contact those, too.

This was a perennial problem with photofits. People looked at the image and saw what they wanted to see. Interpreted the eyes, the mouth and nose, the hair style and suddenly somebody in their head came to the fore and bingo! 'It's him, I'm sure of it!'

The ideal scenario was when at least five people gave the same information, and a name – or at least an address. Then it was worth getting a bit excited about the perp the police wanted to bring to justice. Otherwise, it became a drudge . . . and this was getting that way. Any self-respecting detective always hoped for a lead out of nowhere – the sort that was worth
following up when somebody phoned the station and began 'I don't know if this is of much help, but that photofit picture just could be my neighbour.'

But the DC and Detective Sergeant Hayman had to follow up on all the leads. If they decided one wasn't worth pursuing, and it turned out to be the perpetrator of the crime, there'd be all hell to pay. So, it had to be done. Stones being unturned, and all that.

"OK, Chris, well, you'd better get on then," said the DI. Hayman left the office of the inspector with a purposeful stride.

Within minutes, Hayman was talking to DC Grayson and they were planning their next move.

86

Tom had been to see Liz to choose a suit from his wardrobe. She wasn't surprised when he rang her bell and briefly explained the purpose of his visit. She'd pulled his leg about looking his best on his special day, and from her comments, Tom decided that Liz didn't have a real problem with his plan.

"You could take another suit as well as the charcoal grey one. You never know when you and your new wife might want to go somewhere special, or attend an event such as a family party or anniversary?" She had smiled at him.

"You mean for one of my children?" How strange that sounded to both of them, and the question hung in the air for a few seconds.

"Isn't it odd, that one can go from having no children to having three in the blink of an eye? Once you've said 'I do,' and gone through the 'for richer, for poorer' palaver, you instantly become a father of three!" Tom hadn't seen it like that before, but she was right. A father overnight, as it were.

"Where's the wedding, then? Some posh hotel – a five - star venue?" Tom had hesitated. Should he tell Liz? Perhaps she would jeopardise the proceedings . . . turn up and shout her protestations from the back of the room, or go round and tell all the guests that her ex was a real bad man, and that Gertrude didn't know what she was letting herself in for? Because Tom and her had all this planned, he felt an obligation to share the details with Liz.

"A small three star in Walton. The Montfort. And it's just Gertie and me. No guests." Liz sounded surprised.

"What! Is that all? What do the children make of those arrangements?" Tom had to tell her that he was organising the wedding, and it was going to be a quiet affair. The two of them, plus the registrar and a witness. He didn't tell Liz that Gertie wasn't aware of his plan. This was quickly followed with an assurance that it wouldn't be long before Gertie passed away and he'd be rich. Then he and Liz could re-marry and share the benefits of Gertie's Will.

"She's made her Will out with the British Heart Foundation! She went to the place in town and saw a solicitor acting for the BHF. It's all sorted, and everything is left to me!" Liz gasped.

"What? It's all done, then?" Tom had chuckled.

"Like taking candy from a baby," he added. "When you look at the fixtures and fittings in her house, you've got to be talking two million I would say. Liz whistled an out of tune whistle.

"Good Lord! Two million!" Liz sat down on a kitchen stool. "Think what we can do with that!" She was warming to Tom's comments. "But . . . how long will it be before we can get married again? That's the fly in the ointment." He rested his hand on her arm.

"I don't know. Nobody knows, but there is one thing that I haven't mentioned." He got Liz's attention.

"Yes?" She stared into his eyes.

"Gertie has a heart problem. She has a pacemaker fitted, and her consultant has told her to avoid stressful situations. A loud bang would probably be the end for her! Gertie needs an assessment soon." Tom looked serious for a second. "But she won't arrange that before the wedding. I'll put her off as long as I can." He paused. "I was thinking, something like the accidental bursting of a toy balloon in her ear might do the trick?" Liz had quickly stood up.

"You wouldn't, would you?" she demanded, suddenly coming to Gertie's defence.

"Me, why no, of course not," Tom replied, having looked away into the back garden.

"When is the wedding date?" Liz had asked, turning the discussion away from the subject of Gertie's possible demise. Tom confirmed it was to be Tuesday, 23rd. November. "And what would you like for a wedding present?" joked his ex-wife.

"I'll give it some thought," he laughed. "Nothing too expensive," he added.

"Well, I'm prepared to go up to a tenner," Liz offered. "Anyway, I'm busy and you're taking up my time. Go and choose your suits, and a decent shirt or two, and clear off. I've got things to do."

Tom wasn't sure for a second if Liz really meant that or not, but he took the hint. Raking about in his wardrobe, he pulled out two suits on hangers and laid them on the bed. Then he did likewise with three shirts – two white, one light blue. Not forgetting ties, he chose three of his favourites and rolled them around his left hand. Shoes were another necessity, and he bent down to rake among the bottom shelf where he normally kept his shoes. There were a nice pair of black leather ones, and a solid pair of dark brown shoes. As he picked up one of the brown shoes, he spotted something else. A black handbag.

'Blast' he breathed under his breath. Tom had always meant to get rid of that - the initials J T clearly visible on the side of the flap. Julie Thornton. Had he kept it as a souvenir? That night he'd met her in the club with his mates, and she would have been all right, but she was a girl who teased men. It didn't matter now. The damn thing shouldn't be there! Tom picked it up. He'd slip it under his suits – Liz would never see it – and it will go to the household skip at the civic amenity tip.

"You've taken your time," exclaimed Liz as Tom got back down stairs. "Here, let me help you with your clothes." He backed away quickly.

"No!" he barked. Liz had been taken aback.

"All right, all right. Stay calm. Bloody hell, what's got into you? Wedding nerves?"

Without another word, Tom left the bungalow.

87

It was eerily quiet. The sun was low in the sky, and its rays made the stone of the abbey look amber in colour. Liz had paid the taxi driver, who driven off mumbling something about 'who the hell wants to be out here?' But Robbo had suggested meeting here, and she trusted him. He must have something to show her, but what could it be? This place was a thousand years old, and Liz recalled that it might have had something to do with Richard the Lionheart.

Liz looked at her watch. 6.55 pm, and she was certain Robbo would be there by 7.00 pm. He was a man of precision and accuracy, and so far, he hadn't let her down. Perhaps he couldn't pick her up at home because he'd been busy . . .negotiating with a film star for the sale of an expensive painting or sculpture.

She was feeling happy, and her dress fitted her nicely. The earrings were just right, and her perfume was an expensive Gucci one that her sister, Mary, had bought her for Christmas last year. A dilapidated wooden bench at the front entrance to the abbey beckoned her. She may as well rest her legs until Robbo arrived. Choosing the cleanest part of the seat, Liz sat down carefully. But no sooner had she pulled her lace shawl around her shoulders than she heard the distant sound of a car approaching. She turned to see Robbo's silver SUV raising dust along the track from the main road. He got out of his car holding a bunch of flowers.

"Liz, sorry to have kept you waiting!" She didn't look at her watch, but it couldn't have been more than a few minutes after seven o'clock.

"Don't be silly. This is a lovely place!" she said softly. "I expect you've been busy?" Robbo handed her the flowers with a sweet smile. "For me? You shouldn't have." He was dressed in a dark suit and storm grey cotton, rollneck shirt. He could have passed for James Bond, thought Liz.

"I have, but don't ask why! You look gorgeous, Liz," gushed Robbo. She wasn't sure how genuine he sounded, but his comment was welcome. She moved closer.

"So, why did you want to meet me here?" He sat down next to her.

"Well, you may not believe this, but this is where my parents came thirty years ago. They were on holiday in this area. My mother told me when I as about fifteen that I was conceived at Magdalene abbey. Right here! In fact, she mentioned a stone altar in the abbey. Come, let's take a look." Robbo held his hand out, and Liz took it.

This sounded a bit bizarre. Asking Liz to get a taxi out here, and then telling her this is where he was conceived! She wasn't going to query it right now, but her mind was beginning to wonder if he had some ulterior motive? This place was miles from anywhere – there probably wasn't even a phone signal. Hell, what if she needed to call for help?

"Are you OK? You've gone pale. Are you feeling all right, Liz?" He sounded genuinely concerned, but then he would be if this was some kind of plan.

"No. I'm fine. Let's keep going . . . find your altar." Liz had to stay strong. Robbo had her hand in a strong grip.

"There it is. Look! A stone altar, or at least a flat stone slab. Maybe the word 'altar' is taking it a bit too far? Let's take a closer look!" Liz resisted the tug of his hand.

"Robbo. I don't want to go any further. Please!" Liz let out a gentle whimper – quite unintentionally, but it was there. "Please. Let's go, get away from this place. I'm feeling unsettled."

He looked deep into her eyes and turned to face her.

"OK. OK. Don't worry. We can go. The restaurant, La Fourchette, is about twenty minutes from here. It won't matter if we arrive a little early – the table will be reserved for us." Liz suddenly felt better. Felt relieved. "Come on, let's go. I don't like to see you like this." He led the way back to his car and Liz followed. She wasn't sure, but it sounded as if he mumbled something under his breath.

On the journey to the restaurant, little was said. Liz was thinking about the stone walls of the abbey that seemed to envelop her like a tomb. She told herself not to be silly, but she had experienced an odd feeling.

Robbo pulled the SUV into the car park and came to a stop beneath a cast iron lamppost. Another car pulled in behind them but stopped several spaces away. He undid his seat belt and suggested Liz go ahead of him as he had to make an important phone call. It would take two minutes, he reassured her.

"The table is booked in the name of Robinson," he said as she got out. "Order a bottle of their 2015 Rioja," he shouted as she walked to the front door. Inside Liz was met by a tall, handsome waiter who checked the reservation and took her to their table.

"Is madam waiting for her partner, or do you want to order a drink now?" he asked. Liz asked for the Spanish wine, and a gin and tonic. She wasn't sure what Robbo wanted, but he'd be in very soon. Before she had time to start to look at the menu, her drink arrived, followed quickly by the Spanish red.

This place looked expensive, and Liz began to wonder if she was underdressed. The menu was extensive, with no prices shown against any of the dishes. The type of restaurant where it would be unbecoming to enquire about the price of the lobster thermidor or the venison steak. Liz didn't want Robbo to think she was greedy, and she'd have to go with her instinct about how expensive a dish may be.

Glancing at her watch, Liz noticed it was now 8.15 pm. The waiter hovered.

"Is sir joining madam soon?" he asked as politely as possible. Liz wondered where the hell 'sir' was?

"I'll pop outside to see if he's finished a phone call he had to make," she replied. With that, Liz left the restaurant and walked across to Robbo's car. Being dark, it was difficult to see if he was still in the driver's seat. She went around to the driver's door and opened it.

The interior light came on, but the Lexus was empty.

DS Hayman and Detective Constable Grayson had interviewed several respondents to the media request for information on the man shown in the photofit picture. The three favoured replies, including Ted Mortimer, the retired accountant, hadn't revealed much. His statement was followed up, and the name of a man that he'd provided had a cast iron alibi – he was out of the country. Unfortunately, there was limited overlap on the other information, and when questioned, there was variation on the height of the person, where they had been seen, their hair colour, whether they wore trainers or leather shoes . . . and eye colour was anywhere between light brown to dark blue. Hayman was always suspicious of anybody stating eye colour. 'How the hell could you know somebody's eye colour from ten paces away?' he'd query.

The gold crucifix held the possibility of identifying the car thief. Hayman wasn't sure if his boss would approve another press release on that alone. If the photofit didn't throw up any clues, what hope did a little cross have? One proposal from DS Hayman was to call on a number of jewellers in the Saffron area to see if they could recall selling that crucifix to anyone? And with it very likely being South African gold, Hayman hoped that would focus the mind of any jewellery outlet in this part of Essex. His plan was to get DI Matthews to give the OK for a couple of DCs to spend a day talking to jewellers, taking a blown - up photo of the crucifix as a prompt tool.

The spearmint chewing gum wrapper found in the stolen Merc had been logged and was still bagged as possible evidence. But how many people chewed gum these days? Chris Hayman had checked some stats on gum, sales were
down by twenty per cent compared to five years ago.

The detective sergeant wasn't giving up, though. In his job, 'lady luck' played her role from time to time, and Hayman always hoped that she'd smile on him.

The DS knocked on DI Matthews door, proposed his plan, and came out after minutes with a clear idea on how his next 48 hours would look. A cup of coffee consumed, he'd spoken with DC Grayson and DC Jackson on the plan of action – jeweller's visits with the photofit picture and gold crucifix image, asking lots of questions. He told them he was going to talk to Mrs Alice Heseltine again to double check her story.

There were aspects of her statement that had left the sergeant feeling somewhat uneasy.

89

Tom Ball was in his room at Gertie's house. He had hung up the suits and shirts. However, he still had the handbag, now empty. Why had he kept it so long? He'd been foolish – a key piece of evidence in the case of Julie Thornton's murder. But sometimes murderer's need to keep a reminder of their conquests. Something to hold, and look at, to bring back the memories of the moment it happened.

Julie Thornton had it coming, some had said. Leaving little to the imagination, she'd dress in a low- cut top, mini-skirt, and high heeled shoes. Stockings were obligatory, but some of the lads that got down the Pink Pelican club liked to think about the bare flesh above the stocking top – and Julie played along. Tom had only offered to walk her home to save her spending money she didn't have on a taxi. But she'd egged him on, flirting with him, teasing him about his masculinity. OK, a joke was a joke, but that night Julie took it too far.

Tom Ball still had a length of flex in his jacket pocket from an electrical job he'd done for a neighbour only minutes before he left for the club that night. It had come in handy for tying Julie's wrists together before he hit her and heaved her lifeless body into the ditch. A late passenger train thundered by as he'd pulled the knife from her neck and he'd prayed nobody had seen him.

He recalled being disgusted at the clothes she wore that night, and after killing her he removed her top and bra, followed by her mini-skirt. As he walked away, he nonchalantly threw them alongside the ditch as he left the scene of the crime.

Tom picked up her handbag, he can't remember why, and further down the railway track he emptied the contents into a large
drain. Mobile phone, purse, handkerchief, lipstick, comb, and a few loose coins. They would be washed away the next time it rained heavily.

He'd stashed the handbag in a plastic carrier bag with a view to taking it to the civic amenity tip soon. But that never happened. He loved touching it from time to time, recalling Julie Thornton and the way she was dressed. And there it was, in the bottom of the bloody wardrobe where anyone could have seen it! He cursed himself . . . but he now had a chance to get shot of it.

Taking the initials J T from the flap would be a start, then with a Stanley knife, cut the damn thing up and feed bits into different bins at the tip. Sod the signs . . . Household Waste, Card and Paper . . . he'd mix and match a bit. Let the operatives at the main waste recycling facility worry about a few bits of black leather mixed in with other stuff.

"Thomas. Are you there?" Gertie's dulcet tones filtered up the stairs. "Your dinner's on the table in ten minutes. Don't forget to wash your hands! I've got a nice bottle of Merlot opened and breathing."

'Opened and breathing,' thought Tom. 'You won't be open and breathing for much longer, my dear.'

Now was the time to let Gertie know that he had booked a surprise break for just the two of them. Walton was a lovely place at this time of year, and a walk along the sea front was so bracing. He'd tell her it was to be a surprise, just mention a nice hotel on the Essex coast for a little rest and recuperation. But it would be an idea to take something special to wear – a white dress and white shoes with a medium heel? She would be thrilled at the idea.

Then he'd choose the right time on their first evening at the hotel to mention the wedding ceremony, becoming joined in holy matrimony, and having their short honeymoon immediately after the event.

Nothing could go wrong, Tom decided, he'd planned this nicely. It would go like a well - oiled machine.

As Tom was washing his hands, his sister-in-law, Mary in Southend, was scrolling through photos on her mobile phone. She stopped flicking her finger across the screen when she came to a photo that she'd taken a few weeks previously.

A black leather handbag with the letters J T on the side.

"You arrived here at about half past seven. Mr Robinson stayed in his vehicle to make a phone call, you say, and you went into the restaurant to wait for him?" Detective Sergeant Norman Arnold from Basildon CID was talking to Liz in a quiet corner of the bistro. Liz nodded. "You say you waited for about fifteen minutes before you went out to look for him?" Another nod. "And you saw nothing at all to arouse any suspicion about what may have happened to him?" Liz wiped her nose.

"No. As I've told you, the car was empty. Robbo wasn't there. I called out for him, but he was nowhere to be seen. Another person came over to see if I was OK, and they suggested I phone the police. The head waiter was good enough to do that for me."

"Well, it's only two hours since you went out to find him, so we shouldn't be too alarmed," offered Arnold. He knew that a couple of hours was not long, but under these circumstances he was concerned but didn't show it. "Any idea where he might have gone . . . back home, or to a friend's house, maybe?" Liz shook her head.

"My detective constable, DC Clarke, has had a good look at the vehicle and there are no signs of ownership. The boot is empty, as well as the glove locker. Nothing in the door pockets. Not even a packet of mints or a parking disc." Arnold paused. "If you don't mind me asking, Mrs Ball, but how well do you know Mr Robinson?" Liz gave the Sergeant as much information as she could, including a description of Robbo, and the fact that he lives in Great Dunmow and works for an art gallery in London, and has a dog that she had never seen whose name she couldn't recall. She told the police Robbo has a slightly foreign accent, but you had to listen carefully to pick it up. It was about as much as she had on him, well aware now that she barely knew Robbo at all. Arnold asked about Liz's personal situation and she gave him the bare, essential details about her divorce from Tom.

"If your ex-husband knew about Mr Robinson, do you think he may have been involved?" Liz told the DS that she was certain Tom knew nothing about Robbo, who'd always park his Lexus in the next street, and had been discreet during his few visits to her home. "OK, well we'll put out a missing person's report, but if Mr Robinson gets in touch with you, please let me know immediately. Here's my card." Arnold paused, then the pair went outside. "We can give you a lift home if you like? Or I'll call a taxi for you?" Liz opted for the offer of a lift. The DS opened the back door of the black Ford Mondeo for Liz and she got in.

"I'll just have a word with the staff, but my detective constable will stay with you." Arnold walked back to the front door as the detective got into the driver's seat. Inside the restaurant,
Arnold asked for the manager who appeared in seconds. He took him to one side.

"When did Mr Robinson book the table?" The day before, around noon.

"Did Mr Robinson leave any credit or debit card details?" No, he was going to pay in cash.

"Perhaps a contact number for you to get in touch with him?" Yes, a mobile number. The waiter checked the table booking diary. He gave Arnold the details.

"Has Mr Robinson ever booked a table with you before?" No, the name wasn't familiar.

"How did his lady guest seem when she came into the restaurant?" Calm, relaxed, happy.

Satisfied with the comments, DS Arnold told the manager that the unlocked Lexus SUV would be marked with blue and white police tape for now, and he'd arrange for a tow truck to remove it from the car park as soon as possible.

Nearly an hour later Liz was settled in her lounge at home, a mug of coffee and a large brandy by her side. She had changed out of her dress and into a pink, fleecy cotton top and a pair of cargo pants. The unmarked police car had gone, and Liz was alone to reflect on the evening.

The plan for the evening had come undone. She'd so looked forward to going out with Robbo, meeting him at the old abbey, a table for two in what seemed a lovely place to dine, and maybe he was going to stay over for the night. But one of the questions posed by the detective came to mind. 'Did your ex-husband know about Mr Robinson?'

Did he? Liz thought about it. If Tom had found out that she was seeing another man, how would he take it? Her opinion of Thomas Ball was that he was harmless, and would never try to do anything to Robbo, let alone drag him from his car and make him disappear into thin air! She wasn't going to ask Tom, that would give the game away.

By the time Liz had finished her coffee and brandy, her head was in a spin. And it hit her again – her knowledge of the man who called himself Robbo was superficial.

Back at the station, DS Arnold checked the mobile phone number he'd obtained from the restaurant. It was a pay-as-you-go phone, and when he tried the number, it only rang ten times before ringing off.

After five attempts he gave up.

91

"I fancy a couple of days away. Maybe the seaside – get some fresh air, go for a stroll along the promenade. What do you think, Gerbil?" asked Tom part way through their evening
meal. He hoped his tone and delivery of the question had hit the right note.

"Oh, yes! That would be lovely, Tom," said Gertie enthusiastically. "Where to?" Tom sipped his beer. He fancied a long drink, and Gertie could have the merlot.

"I'd like it to be a surprise! You know how you enjoy surprises!" Gertie's face beamed.

"Oh, yes. That sounds exciting, Tom. I tell you what, you pick the venue and the date, then let me know when we're going. Give me time to get my wardrobe together." Tom saw this as his chance to mention her clothes.

"Agreed. But I'd suggest you take something special, Gerbil. That white dress is nice, the one with the sweetheart neckline and light brown belt. And you've got a pair of shoes, the white leather ones. We could have a really nice dinner on the first night we're there. Sort of celebrate us being together for so long . . ." Gertie put her fork down.

"Hmm. How long is it now?" Tom decided to test her memory.

"How long do you think it's been since I first came to stay?" She looked vacant for a few seconds, glancing at various things in the room as if searching for some kind of inspiration.

"Oh, about three years now, I think." That comment took Tom by surprise. It was closer to seven months. Certainly not three years! He wasn't going to spoil the evening.

"A bit less than that, Gerbil, but you're not far off. More wine?" He leant across and topped up her glass.

'This old bird hasn't got a clue,' Tom said to himself. There was a hint of guilt as he confirmed how easy this was going to be. Soon they'd be married, Gertie would pass away, Tom would go through the grieving and all that, then he and Liz would start going out in public together and re-marry. Simple.

"OK, but let's keep this a secret, shall we? Just you and I will know about it. It'll be like a scene from one of those films where the couple go off and nobody knows where they've gone!" Tom made that up. He couldn't think of any film like that, but it sounded good. Gertie tittered, and her eyes lit up.

"It's a deal! But don't forget to let me know *when* we're going, will you?"

The meal was finished and Tom offered to do the clearing up. He'd slip the plates and cutlery into the dishwasher, then rinse the glasses in the sink. Just as easy to dump everything in the Bosch machine and switch it on every week instead of standing in the kitchen letting his varicose veins get worse.

Gertie went into the lounge, flicked open the latest copy of *Life* magazine that Tom had bought and began to scan the pages, stopping at articles that attracted her interest. Tom hadgone up to his room to watch a TV station showing evening horseracing from Leopardstown. He had a vested interest as he'd backed two horses in each race. With any luck he estimated he could be up by a couple of grand by the time the last race was run.

Gertie closed her magazine, and looking across to the chair where Tom usually sat, noticed his mobile phone on the small table next to it. Gertie did have her own phone, which she rarely used, and Mike had tried really hard to get her to use it more. Out of curiosity, and partly boredom, Gertie picked up Tom's phone. She knew that it was wrong to go through other people's things, it was how she was brought up as a Catholic, but she tapped the screen and suddenly the time and temperature showed up in big numbers. 20.05 and 16 C.

There lots of little coloured squares everywhere. Gertie put her finger tip on one and tapped. Suddenly a list of messages came up. There were things that didn't make sense, but there was one caught her eye. Gertie tapped again.

Dear Mr Ball. This confirms your reservation at Montfort Hall for the nights of 23 and 24 November. We look forward to welcoming you both on what we hope will prove to be a wonderful occasion. Regards, Kira.

How exciting, thought Gertie. And how quick Tom had been in booking a hotel so soon after they'd discussed it over dinner. He was thoughtful. Gertrude knew that. She tapped on a triangle at the bottom of the screen, then again, and all those coloured squares came back on. Gertie put the phone back in the exact position whence she'd got it. She wasn't going to tell Tom she'd seen it. No, Gertrude would play along and pretend she knew nothing of it.

But as the evening passed, and Tom stayed upstairs, Gertie had to tell someone before she burst with excitement. Going into the kitchen, she quietly lifted the house phone from the wall bracket and dialled a number. She kept her voice down as the call was picked up after three rings.

"Hello," she whispered. "Tom's taking me to Montfort Hall on the 23rd. of November for two nights! Isn't that exciting! It's going to be a wonderful occasion. I can't wait!"

92

DS Chris Hayman and his two detective constables had drawn a blank. There simply wasn't enough evidence from any of those who'd responded to the media coverage of the car theft and subsequent manslaughter of Peter Dobson to charge anyone. The mention of the expensive trainers, gold crucifix and even the chewing gum wrapper had not been sufficient to get a hit.

Eight jewellers had been seen, with three of them confirming they had sold similar crosses to that shown in a photograph presented to them, but not within the last twelve months. Four agreed that it could be South African gold, and even purchased outside of the UK. One remarked that it looked 'Italian.'

Hayman began to wonder if Kate White had been sure about her description of Cavity Wall Man? If he'd been in her home for, say, three minutes, did she really get a good enough look at him? She reported having a cake in the oven, so maybe her mind was on that?

If somebody is going on about a subject you're not really interested in, how much notice do you take of their appearance? Probably about as much as the mumbo jumbo coming out of their mouth? The DS always wanted to make a good impression, but this dead end was becoming frustrating for him. He knew DI Matthews would want an update shortly, and Hayman wanted to be able to report some positive news. He needed a break, a nugget of information that would lead him to the car thief and the subsequent events on that fateful night of the golf club party.

"Sarge, it may not be relevant, but I've been looking at some items for sale on that Marketplace section of Facebook." The DS hoped this would be useful . . . his DC spending office time searching for something to buy on social media!

"Oh? Looking for early Christmas gifts, are we, Cam?" retorted Hayman with a grin.

"No, sarge. But you know that the CCTV footage showed the car thief wearing those upmarket trainers, well I decided to take a look on Marketplace, clicked on Apparel, then Footwear, and scrolled down the screen, seeing what was there." Hayman urged Grayson to get to the point. "There's a pair of Nike Men's Air Max 90 for sale. Fifty quid. There are three photos of the trainers. In good condition, too. I could be wrong, but these could be the same pair worn by the perp?" The DS sat back on his swivel chair, hands behind his head.

"It's a slim chance, Cam. If the detective inspector knew you were using Facebook, he'd probably give me a rollocking, as well as yourself. But . . . OK, take a look. Send the seller a reply and ask if they're still available. Go check them out, but keep this to ourselves. If it's not what we're after, nobody else needs to know. All right?"

DC Grayson turned to go. "Cam," said Hayman softly. "Good work."

Mike Heseltine was making himself a cup of coffee at the kennels when there was a knock at the front door. A neighbour, Janette, from over the back fence, was asking if Pyong was OK as she hadn't seen her for a while.

"It's been quiet since Pyong left for Thailand," replied Mike. "A week ago, she received a phone call from her sister in Bangkok to say that their mother, Wan Lee, had gone into hospital." Pyong was one of seven children, and her father had died four years ago. Her mother was frail, and since the death of her father, had slowly deteriorated. Pyong estimated her mother weighed no more than five stone, and had been a cigarette smoker for many years.

"Oh, right. It's just that I wondered if she'd gone down with something. There's some bug going around, apparently. Anyway, give her my love next time you speak to her." With that, Janette turned and was gone.

Although the kennels were full, Mike was able to manage on his own. He'd developed his own routine, rising early to prepare the food for the dogs, taking four together for a morning walk, cleaning out the individual kennels as required, and fitting his meals, or rather snacks, in between. This had given him extra vigour, somehow, and he was feeling as fit as he had been for a while. Mike had bought himself a see-through, plastic tablet box from Boots. This helped with taking his propranolol and antidepressant which Dr Ranji, his psychiatrist, had prescribed, plus a multivitamin and the low dose aspirin. Sometimes, Pyong had to remind him to take the propranolol. When he forgot, his head was all over the place. He'd have angry mood swings and if he didn't be careful, he'd suddenly realise he was taking his frustration and anger out on the dogs.

But right now, he was feeling fine. The settled weather helped, too. There hadn't been any rain for a week or so, and the temperatures were holding up for so late in the year. One bonus was the dry grass in the large paddock where he exercised his pack. Wet dogs became smelly, and needed extra bathing, especially before their owners came to collect them!

He hadn't heard from either of his sisters lately, nor had James Herring phoned him. Things seemed quiet. He even rang his own home number from his mobile to check that it was still working. Pyong had told Mike she'd phone him that evening at about 6.00 pm UK time. With the seven - hour difference, Pyong would be making the call at around 11.00 am local time. He must remember to ask how Wan Lee is, and her siblings, as well as Pyong herself. He was worried that Wan Lee might die whilst Pyong was away, but the funeral ceremony was a relatively quick affair with Buddhists, so she wouldn't be out there too long.

Mike had been out a couple of evenings ago. He fancied a drink and some fresh air away from the canine smells and odour of dried dog food, so took off and drove into the country. A pub that he hadn't been in before had flashed a welcome sign, and he'd stopped for a pint of local ale. The handful of people in there seemed friendly enough, and a pint was enough for him. He certainly didn't want to get stopped for drink-driving.

Sometimes he thought how things would have been if he and Pyong had kids, perhaps a boy and a girl, who could help out with the business . . . even take it over when he and his wife hung up their dog leads? But it wasn't to be, so he didn't spend time agonising over it. 'What will be, will be,' as his father used to say when they'd lived in South Africa.

Mike checked the time. The large wall clock showed 5.05 pm so he'd better get some of his 'guests' exercised before it began to get dark. The clocks were due to go back an hour soon – it was a time of the year Mike didn't look forward to. Turning on the lights at four o'clock in the afternoon was not fun, and the evenings became too long.

Never mind, he told himself, time to crack on. He'd get the leads and take out half of the dogs now, the rest after his light evening meal – maybe an omelette.

The floodlights that they'd installed around the paddock perimeter six months ago had been a boon, too, allowing the dogs to be exercised until late.

Then, when all was sorted in the kennels, he'd settle down with a few magazines. The ones Pyong hadn't seen.

Those he kept stashed in a locker in the work area.

Magazines for which only he knew the code to the padlock.

94

Tom was feeling in a good mood. He'd upped his daily delivery rate, enough to earn him a bonus of £500. He had gone from an average of eight drops a day six months ago to eleven currently. With that, and his plans to go away to Walton with Gertie for their wedding, he was 'as pleased as punch.'

That said, Tom continued to be vigilant when it came to keeping a lookout for Herring. He hadn't seen anybody so far that resembled the photo sent to him on Facebook by Patrick Murray. There had been one new customer who had a high forehead and thick eyebrows, and Tom was instantly wary when he saw him. But after dropping off a load, and a brief chat, the customer turned out to be a bit of a ponce, with a voice higher in key than Joe Pasquale. Nonetheless, he would continue to be aware of his surroundings.

Tom was also considering his situation with *Hightrack Express*. He'd had a flutter on the Leopardstown meeting, estimated he'd be up by a couple of grand after that, but some of the donkeys were still running! Tom wondered if he was losing his touch? There was over thirty grand in his account. He may as well take it all out, and spend a bit before he reaped the benefits of Gertie's Will – and the potential resale value of the paintings in her home, apart from *The Infant Urchin* he'd shown to Mr Pugh, the chap in the Cholmondeley antique shop. £30 to £50 at auction, he'd said! Tom knew Pugh was mistaken. It probably was a genuine Joseph Reynolds and could tip the scales at a million pounds or so.

Once they got to Walton for the wedding, he'd want some cash to pay for that, along with a few bottles of champagne. It would never do if his wife to be thought he was impecunious.

Then there was the handbag to dispose of. He did not want Gertie to see that . . . she'd be putting her nose in.

'Where did you get that from? Who does it belong to?'

Tom was looking to his future, needed to get things sorted out in his life. Right now, there were too many potholes in the road.

They needed filling in so he could move on.

95

DC Cameron Grayson had some news for DS Hayman, and approached him before the sergeant could take his first caffeine surge of the day.

"Sarge, I've checked out the Nike trainers. I messaged the seller with the usual 'Are they still available.' Someone calling themselves The Lone Ranger replied with a 'Yes.' I asked the seller if I could look at them, and they replied with an address in Harlow. I made a note of it. Can I have your approval for me to go over? Maybe this evening?"

Hayman gave a slight sigh.

"Cam, we need to be careful here. It's police business, but yet it isn't, if you get my drift. I suggest you go ahead,

but let's keep this between us for now. No one else, right? If the trainers lead us to the car thief, we can let Matthews know. If not, you'll need to be able to state that you were doing it on a personal basis.
OK?" Grayson slipped his hands into his pockets.

"That's OK, sarge. The trainers are my size, so if I say I'm doing it purely for myself, can't I?" Hayman nodded as if to agree.

"Go for it. The sooner the better." Grayson suggested he make a Facebook request now to drive to Harlow that evening and check out the trainers. "By the way, Cam, the Super wants me to put DC Jackson on another case so you're on your own."

So, that was that. A long shot, but if it could be proven that the shoes for sale on Marketplace were the same as those used by the car thief, it would be a breakthrough. And it could lead to further information on the case.

The day wore on, and the detectives were busy on several fronts. DS Hayman often equated their roles to that of the 'plate on a stick' act in the circus. Half a dozen plates, each spinning on a thin rod, some slowing down, others needing to be turned in a corkscrew manner to keep them aloft. Their work was nothing like what was portrayed on TV. A whole two - hour *Vera* programme where DI Stanhope and her sergeant spent weeks following up on one case, trying to find the culprit, and it turned out to be someone that didn't really fit in until one key piece of information a few minutes from the end meant that person was likely to be guilty!

Cameron Grayson had messaged The Lone Ranger and arranged to call at his address at 6.00 pm. At five o'clock, the DC left Saffron Walden Central and headed to Harlow via the M11. He didn't break the speed limit, but kept to 70 mph on the motorway, before leaving at junction 7. It was 5.55 pm when he rang the bell.

"Hi, I guess you're The Lone Ranger?" asked Grayson with a wry smile. The seller nodded.

"But you're not Tonto!" retorted The Lone Ranger. Both had a chuckle. "My name's Rick."

"I'm Cam and I've come about the trainers." He was invited into the kitchen of the maisonette which had the air of a bachelor pad. Rick picked a box from a lower cupboard, and lifted the lid.

"Here we are. Nike Air Max 90. I paid a guy £75 for these two weeks ago. I've worn them once!" Grayson removed one from the box and looked at the sole. There were tiny fragments of what resembled dried soil and grit in between the criss-cross rubber pattern of the tread.

"Why are you selling, Rick, if you've only had them for a fortnight?" Grayson slipped the trainer back into the box.

"Thing is, I didn't tell my girlfriend I'd got them and she bought me a pair a few days later! Doh! So, these are surplus to requirements." Made sense . . . if it was true. The DC noticed Rick was wearing a thin gold chain around his neck, his shirt collar open, a couple of buttons undone. Was he talking to the car thief? Was this the man who'd stolen the Merc and driven Peter Hobson off the road? Essex wasn't a large county. It wouldn't take long to travel from Harlow to Saffron, steal the car, nudge Dobson's vehicle on that S-bend and send it into the ditch. The Merc was found abandoned later, so if it was Rick, he could have driven to Saffron, done the job, then driven back to Harlow . . . or, had somebody else drive him there and back?

Grayson scanned Rick's face without wanting him to think he was gay and looking for a date. There was a hint of the photofit picture, but not enough for Grayson to think 'this is him!' for definite.

"Well? What do you think? You can have them for forty quid cash. I've got two other people interested," said The Lone Ranger, clearly wanting a sale.

"And you said you'd bought them off a guy. Was he local, as a matter of interest?" Rick shuffled his feet, then scratched his nose.

"Er, yes. Brentwood way. I don't recall his name. He'd put them on Marketplace on Facebook, too. I could check my messages if you
like. Why do you ask?" Grayson had to be careful here.

"No, it's not important. A mate of mine bought a similar pair a month ago from a guy in Basildon. You just never know if these things have been nicked, do you?" he lied.

"I'll take them, Rick," smiled the DC. They're my size. I won't try them on. I'm sure they'll be fine!" Grayson took out his wallet and pulled four ten - pound notes out. "Here we go. Forty quid." Rick handed the box to the DC and showed him to the door.

"Cheers, Rick," shouted Grayson as he walked away. He had been tempted to ask Rick if he was religious. Grayson had spotted a wooden cross on the wall in the hallway.

He wondered if Rick might have lost a gold crucifix? But asking *that* question when buying a pair of trainers would have been over the top.

It would keep for another day.

And if Rick had only had the trainers for a couple of weeks, he couldn't have been the person seen on the CCTV footage stealing the Mercedes Benz.

DS Norman Arnold had been back to see Liz two days after the disappearance of Robbo. He'd asked her for a contact phone number for him, and Liz gave the sergeant the same mobile number that Arnold had obtained from the restaurant. He'd tried it half another half a dozen times without success.

Liz was asked if she had any photos of Mr Robinson? The answer was a simple 'no.' Neither of them had used their phones to take a selfie, or a photo of each other. The DS reconfirmed the basic description of Robinson - about two metres tall, with blond hair and blue eyes.

Could she try to remember the name of the art gallery in London? As hard as she tried, Liz could not recall whether Robbo had actually mentioned the name of the gallery. Liz told the DS that Robbo was involved with the sale of expensive paintings and sculptures to footballers and film stars, but of course, he wasn't allowed to mention any client names.

And his home? Had Liz ever been to visit him? No, she had never been invited to his property near Great Dunmow.

His car? Well, the police now had the Lexus SUV in their pound and had thoroughly inspected it. Fingerprints had been taken from the vehicle's steering wheel and driver's door handle, but nothing was found inside. When quizzed on the oddness of that, Liz had never thought about it – why should she? Getting into his car wasn't about prying as to what was in a glove locker, or a door pocket, or tucked above the sun-visor.

Arnold asked about a dog that Liz had mentioned. No, sorry, but he had never brought the dog to her place, nor had she seen it elsewhere. Was it a German Shepherd? Liz was certain it wasn't . . . perhaps a Golden Retriever, or a Bull Mastiff, maybe? No, none of those. There was a royal name in there somewhere . . . a prince something, or a queen thingummy? Liz closed her eyes. Yes! A King Charles. That was it! A Cavalier King Charles spaniel!

DS Arnold added that to his notes. Hell, of all the evidence to try to ascertain the identity of the missing person, his best shot is a bloody spaniel! But it was better than nothing. He knew little about dogs, but it sounded as though it could be registered with a body such as the Kennel Club? He'd have to do some canine detective work. Perhaps he could call for 'Lassie' to assist him, he'd chuckled to himself later.

The detective sergeant asked about the age of Robbo. Liz guessed at 35. Then a few more questions, including one about their relationship. Liz explained that she was now divorced and therefore a free agent when it came to seeing other men. The DS asked where her husband was, and she had to tell him. His eyebrows rose a centimetre when Liz told the sergeant that he was living next door with a lady who was about 80. It reminded Arnold of Elizabeth Taylor and her younger beaus. Bungalow Bill was one – 'plenty downstairs but nothing up top' was how one tabloid had put it.

Arnold asked one last question. Robbo's name? How come Liz didn't know him as anything else but Robbo? She hadn't thought to question it. He'd invited her to call him that, and it seemed all right. His surname must be Robinson. That's what he used to book the bistro table. But the DS, with ten years of service to his name, wasn't that green. He'd done the exact same as a teenager in Harwich, dating a girl named Samantha and telling her he was known as 'Normie' to all of his mates.

DS Arnold closed his notebook, thanked Liz Ball, and left her home. He had little to go on, and Liz felt as if a cloud had been lifted from over her after all the talk about Robbo. She needed a coffee, a strong one. Nursing the mug in her hand, she sat at the kitchen table and reflected on the last few days, wondering if she ought to have got involved with Robbo, or whatever his name was, at all?

Where the hell had he got to? How does someone just disappear from their car at a time like that? The table reserved for them, a quick phone call to make, the wine ordered, a nice evening ahead . . .

'Where are you?' Liz screamed at the top of her voice and threw the mug across the kitchen floor, shattering into pieces on the tiles, coffee seeping into the grouting.

If there was a time to cry, it was now.

And she did.

97

"Come on, Gerbil. Let's get going!" hollered Tom from the bottom of the stairs. It was mid - afternoon, and he was keen to set off for Walton-on-the-Naze. Gertie had finished her packing, after lots of umming about what to take. Tom had confirmed the need to take some smart clothes, including the white dress and white shoes in which he thought she would look lovely on their wedding day.

A picture! Tom suddenly realised that he hadn't asked for a photographer. However, the less coverage this event got, the better. Why bother telling anybody about their wedding? For Tom, if he was honest with himself, it was all a bit of a chore. They'd get a certificate to prove their union, and that was all that he wanted out of this charade. For that's all it was . . . a damn charade.

"I'm ready! Can you come and pick up the suitcase, Tom?" He trudged upstairs, lifted the large, old-fashioned case up, and slowly went back down to the hall. The case was heavy, and it looked as if it had been on many trips – the wrap-around wooden strips were well battered, and several faded stickers covered the sides. Hong Kong, San Francisco, Colombo, Sydney. Gertie had certainly been to some interesting parts of the globe! He could use her travels as an opener over dinner if conversation became a little slow.

Tom pushed the suitcase, and his own case, into the back of the Peugeot van. He'd cleaned and vacuumed the interior the day before to make it as presentable as possible. A new pine air - freshener was dangling from the rear - view mirror. It wouldn't be long now before this van would be history for him, and a new, gleaming BMW or Audi would be his. Full spec, with leather, heated seats, motion sensors, cameras front and rear . . . the works.

Tom checked the front door to ensure Gertie had locked it, then opened the passenger door for her and she got in. He turned on the sat-nav, stuck to the windscreen with a rubber sucker, then entered the post code for Montfort Hall. 57 miles, one hour and seven minutes. Fine. They'd stop off on the way for a sandwich and cup of tea, arriving at the hotel late - afternoon.

Thankfully it was dry and the weather forecast was good, with a HIGH over the UK for the next few days. Tom had thrown an umbrella in, as well as two raincoats, but it was doubtful they'd be required. Within ten minutes they were out of the town and heading for Chelmsford, where they'd pick up the A12 to Colchester, then south east toward Walton-on-the-Naze.

"This is a lovely surprise, Tom. I can't thank you enough. I get bored seeing the same walls every day. It's good to get out for some fresh air. I can smell the pine trees already." Pine trees? Should Tom put her right – it was the air freshener Gertie was noticing. No, best leave it.

"Yes, that's right, and soon it will be sea air! Walton should be nice this time of year. Brisk and bracing along the seafront."

Soon Tom noticed a sign for *Garden Centre & Tea Room 2 miles.* He wanted a pee, so persuaded Gertie that it would be a good place for a break. She agreed. He pulled the van into the car park, coming to a halt near the *Plant Pots Half Price* sign. He whipped round to Gertie's door and opened it for her. She eased out, but needed Tom to give her a hand.

"My hips! They're not getting any better," gasped Gertie, getting her breath as Tom closed the van door behind her. Hips? Tom couldn't recall Gertie mentioning hips before. All part of the downward health spiral when we get older, Tom decided. If it wasn't hips it was back pain, but if not that, probably eyesight or deafness.

"Come on, Gerbil, let's get inside and order a pot of tea. We might have a cake, as well!"

The pair took a seat by a window. Tom went to the counter, ordered a pot of tea for two, and two slices of carrot cake. He knew for definite that his bride-to-be enjoyed a decent carrot cake. Minutes later he was lifting the teapot and crockery off the tray, along with the two cakes.

"My, my, that looks good!" she exclaimed. Tom did the honours and poured the tea. Milk first. Then they tackled their cakes, using a small fork, which helped make eating the fruity slice much easier.

The couple chatted about the garden centre and the weather. The café wasn't busy, but suddenly there was a clatter of dishes as a waitress stumbled with a tray loaded with crockery. Gertie gripped her chest and let out a loud gasp.

"Gerbil! Are you alright?" asked Tom, jumping off his chair and moving quickly round to her side of the table. Gertie was slumped forwards, her plate now on the floor. He eased her back slightly and held the back of her head. A couple at the next table asked if they could help, but Gertie eased herself up.

"It's OK. It was just a twinge. No, please don't fuss. I'm fine." Tom thanked the couple, an
elderly pair, most likely pensioners. Tom leant closer to Gertie.

"Are you sure you are OK? Do you want me to call an ambulance?" She shook her head.

"No, no. It's nothing. Why don't we go now?" The half-drunk tea, and partly eaten carrot cakes were left. Other customers stared at Tom and Gertie as they left, wondering if they should help. Nobody did.

A few minutes later they were both back in the van. Neither needed the toilet after their tea, and Tom reset the satnav for the hotel. The rest of the trip was done in silence, Tom glancing at Gertie from time to time to ensure she was alright.

'Bloody hell,' he thought. This is the last thing he wanted to happen. Of course, he'd assumed that it would all go perfectly, but sometimes life threw you a fast one outside off stump that you left or tried to hit. No matter. Gertie was resting her eyes, and as soon as they reached Walton, Tom would get Gertie to the room and tell her to rest. She had to be well enough to get through the wedding ceremony tomorrow, just had to be!

*

It was a little after five o'clock when Tom parked up at the Montfort. Gertie looked sprightly enough and seemed to cheer up when she looked across the road at the sea.

"Oh, Tom, this is lovely!" He said nothing, and proceeded to get the luggage from the van as Gertie slowly made her way to the front steps of the hotel. Once they were both inside, they were greeted by Kira at reception.

"Mr Ball?" Tom nodded. "Good. Now, everything is in order for tomorrow . . ." Tom cut her off. He didn't want Gertie hearing anything about 'tomorrow.'

"Kira. Sorry to interrupt you, but could we check in straightaway? It's been a long journey and Gertrude, here, would like to rest. I'll come back later to talk to you." Kira was slightly taken aback, but stayed calm as she asked

Tom to complete the registration form. Then she handed him the keys.

"Room 103. On the ground floor, along that corridor there." She pointed across the foyer. "Dinner is served in the restaurant from 6.30 until 9.30 pm. Breakfast from 7 'til 10. If there's anything you need, please contact reception." It sounded like her patter to every new customer. Tom thanked her, and then he and Gertie made their way to room 103.

Tom suggested Gertie rest for a while, and he'd unpack for both of them. She smiled as she kicked off her shoes and eased onto the left side of the double bed. Tom drew the heavy curtains, but allowed a narrow chink of light into the room. By the time he'd finished hanging up his suit and shirts, and Gertie's dresses, there was a gentle snore. Gertie was fast asleep, her heavy breathing filling the room.

He'd noticed the bar was open when they'd arrived, so he was going to get a pint after he'd spoken to Kira. All he had to do was to make sure that Kira didn't mention the plans to Gertie. But he wasn't going to say that in as many words. Kira would think it odd that all this was going to be a surprise for his future bride. The best thing would be for Tom to keep Gertie away from reception.

"I'm sorry if I was a little sharp earlier, Kira. I didn't mean to come across like that. It's just that Gertrude was very tired, and I felt a lie down for her was the best thing." She smiled her hotel reception smile, learnt during her training.

"Don't worry, Mr Ball. I understand." Kira shuffled some papers. "Can I remind you about tomorrow, then?" Tom nodded and smiled. "The actual wedding is scheduled for 11.00 am, with the registrar and witness arriving at 10.40 am. The Belmont Suite along the corridor is where it will take place. Can I ask you to enter the Suite at 10.55 am precisely?" Tom nodded again. "We've made some catering arrangements next to the Suite – champagne and a variety of sandwiches. You did say you didn't want to go over the top?" Tom smiled.

"Can you confirm how many guests you will have at the ceremony?" He frowned.

"Guests? None, actually. It's a private affair." Kira's eyebrows raised, but it wasn't for her to question the customer's decisions. It was her turn to smile.

"Very well. I think that's all for now?" Tom gave her a wink and headed for the bar.

An hour and half later, Tom went back to the room to find Gertie still asleep, her breathing shallow. He was about to rinse his face in the bathroom when the room telephone rang. He grabbed it quickly in case it woke Gertie.

"Hello?" he said quietly.

"Mr Ball, it's Kira here. A gentleman has just been to reception to say that a white Peugeot van parked in our car park has two flat tyres. Looking at your registration form, I think it's yours."

Two flat tyres?

"Ok, Kira, I'll take a look. Thanks." If Tom and his bride were going to use the van tomorrow, the last thing he wanted was to start messing about with dirty wheels. In any case, he only had one spare. Tom slipped on his jacket and closed the room door as quietly as he could. It was now dark outside, but one tall security light gave Tom some vision as he walked across to his van. Bending down, he could see both back tyres were as flat as pancakes. It was difficult to tell if they'd been punctured. By feeling for them, he knew the valve caps were in place, but someone could have let them down and then replaced the caps. This was a bloody nuisance for Tom. There was no option but to ask Kira for details of the nearest garage that could come and repair the tyres – whatever the issue was. Tom was about to turn when he sensed somebody next to him. He felt an arm around his neck, strong and firm, then a scratch on his skin.

In less than a heartbeat his world went black.

98

DS Norman Arnold had drawn a complete blank on Robbo Robinson. The registration of the Lexus, DBZ 2345, was false. The number, originally from Northern Ireland, did not match the VIN (Vehicle Identity Number) for the car. Further enquiries showed that the Lexus had been registered in Wimbledon and stolen in central London ten months previously. Not only that, but its colour was first listed a Huckleberry Blue, and it had undergone a respray.

He'd phoned several art galleries in London, but nobody had heard of a Mr Robinson. The electoral roll for Great Dunmow had revealed six male Robinsons but none were known as Robbo. Without a first name to go on, it made the enquiries more difficult.

Two Kennel Club groups were identified in the Great Dunmow area, but neither had a King Charles spaniel registered with them. So, who was this Mr Robinson? Arnold considered social media. Most people these days had the world know about their business via Facebook or Twitter or Instagram, didn't they? But he knew that if he simply typed Robinson into the search engine he'd be drowned with names! Without a first name it would be futile.

If Robinson was dead, it would help if they had a body. Dental records, any surgery marks on the torso, scars, piercings? Had he left the country after abandoning the car at the bistro and given up on dating Liz Ball? If so, how had he got away from what was a fairly remote location?

Nobody saw Robinson being picked up by a taxi, although one diner stated that he thought saw a car's headlights in the gloom of the car park, but couldn't be sure if it was leaving or arriving.

There was nothing more DS Arnold could do other than register Robbo Robinson as a 'missing person,' and hope that within a few days somebody would report a man missing - a husband, a brother, a nephew – anyone. Until then, Norman Arnold would get on with his job as a detective and play the waiting game. But that afternoon the police station sergeant on duty at the desk took a phone call.

"Hello, yes, my name is Mrs Jones. I'm not sure if I'm being over the top here, but there's dog barking next door. It's been making a noise since last evening. It's not right. The owner always cares for that dog, a Cavalier King Charles spaniel. And I haven't seen Mr Herring since yesterday. I thought I'd let you know."

The desk sergeant, Ronnie Olney, took the full name and address of the caller and thanked her for letting the police know. Olney rang through to the desk of DS Arnold.

"Norman? You asked me to let you know if there were any phone calls that might be of interest. Not sure about this one, but I think I may have one for you."

"No. I haven't seen Mr Ball," explained Kira at the hotel desk. "I told him a man had reported his van as having a couple of flat tyres, and he went outside to take a look. I don't remember him coming back into the hotel, but I had a couple of jobs to do in the back office so could easily have missed him." Gertie fidgeted with her cardigan buttons.

"But it's nearly eight o'clock and we were supposed to be eating by now. Do you think we should call the police?" Kira shuffled uneasily on her stool. The hotel in a quiet place like Walton-on-the-Naze had never had any issues with the police, she told herself. What would it do for business if it got into the newspapers? The owner, Mr Whitmarsh, would be most displeased.

"I suggest we don't do that, yet. Why don't you go into the dining room and order something while I ask one of the porters to go outside and look at Mr Ball's van. He might even have tried to arrange things himself — maybe with a garage or the AA or something? Mr Ball might even end up coming through the front door any second now!" Kira knew she was trying to delay matters, but Tom Ball could be anywhere as far as she was concerned.

"Oh, very well, but if he phones, let me know immediately, won't you?" Kira smiled. Gertrude wandered off to get something to eat, but she wasn't feeling very hungry. Might was well look at the menu, though, as they had another night there and Tom had promised her a lovely evening meal after the wedding ceremony.

Sitting alone after ordering a prawn risotto and a glass of chardonnay, Gertie thought about the guests that would be there in the morning. The three children, and her friends from the W.I. - Iris, Heather and Ruby. But she'd forgotten to give Tom the two names of her other friends, and right now she couldn't recall who they were. Ah, well, that would be eight of them in total. It would be a nice gathering, Gertie decided.

She picked at her risotto, impaling a prawn here and there on her fork, followed by a small portion of creamy rice. Glancing at her watch, Gertie noticed the time was now 8.35 pm. Even if Tom had gone to get the tyres done, he ought to be back by now. With two flat tyres, he wouldn't have driven anywhere – he'd have to wait until someone arrived to do the job in the hotel car park.

A porter had spoken with Kira. There was no sign of Mr Ball in the car park, and the Peugeot van still had two flat tyres. It wasn't looking good for the hotel. A police car in front of the main door, a couple of uniforms searching around, nosy folks peeking through their curtains and trying to guess what was happening. No, not good at all.

"Well, what news have you got for me, young lady?" asked Gertrude in an anxious tone. Kira stiffened.

"Er, none at the moment. I propose that we wait until ten o'clock before we do anything else, don't you?" Gertrude leant across the desk.

"Now you listen to me, young lady. First of all. Do not patronise me. Secondly, I don't like your tone. I'm telling you *now* to call the police! *If you don't do it, I will!*" Kira blanched and dropped her ballpoint pen. Whitmarsh, the manager, was in the back office.

"Can I help you, madam?" he asked as politely as he could after hearing Gertie's anger. She repeated her demands to Whitmarsh. Call the police now! The manager had no option, as one or two hotel guests were coming out of the dining room and slowing down to listen.

"Madam, may I suggest you retire to your room and we'll handle this from now on. I'll arrange for a member of staff to bring a drink to your room. What would you like?" Gertie calmed a little, her breathing becoming easier.

"Very well. A large Remy Martin would be most agreeable," she said. "And don't be long about it!"

Minutes later a waiter delivered her brandy on a tray. She placed the glass on the bedside table and kicked off her shoes. Sitting in the single, uncomfortable armchair, she couldn't help but wonder where Tom had got to? And on the eve of their wedding day! He'd turn up, she was certain of that, but when? Tonight? In the morning?

Tomorrow afternoon? Had he got cold feet, she wondered. Was all this bravado simply too much for him, and he really wanted to go back to Liz?

This was becoming unreal – Gertrude wondering if she was dreaming, and that any second Tom would shake her gently and wake her up! But no, it wasn't a dream . . . more of a nightmare now. Her room telephone rang and she picked up the receiver.

"Hello, Mrs Heseltine. It's Mr Whitmarsh here. I've phoned the police and someone will be here in half an hour. The nearest police station is in Clacton, I'm afraid. Can I get you another brandy?" Gertrude nodded absentmindedly at the phone and then said 'yes.'

Forty minutes later, two uniformed constables of Essex Police were talking with Gertrude in her room. They asked her to provide as much information as she could, beginning with what she was doing at the hotel, and information on Thomas Ball.

"Well, officer, it's like this. He was my next - door neighbour, did some jobs for me, then we decided to get, er, married. Yes, that's it." Gertrude stumbled slightly and then gripped the side of the bed. "We decided to get together in wedlock – a union, you know." She slurred her words as she eased onto the bed and lay her head back. Ten seconds later she was snoring gently. The two constables looked at each other and one shrugged.

"Nothing more we can do here, Harry. Best come back in the morning when the old lady has come round."

Both brandy glasses were empty.

DS Norman Arnold had telephoned Miss Hayes who'd reported the barking dog. Arnold considered it a long shot, but with so little to go on, it was worth an hour of his time.

A dog left on its own for more than 24 hours always warranted a look-see. Its owner could be collapsed indoors, or dead in the garden, without a neighbour or anyone knowing.

Miss Hayes lived in Wickford, a twenty - minute drive from Basildon. Liz Ball told the sergeant that Robinson lived in Great Dunmow. The chances were that this wasn't a dog belonging to him, but as usual, Arnold kept an open mind until proven otherwise. He'd called Hayes before he left the station to confirm she was at home. After parking on Suffolk Road, the DS found number 16 and rang the bell. After straightening his tie, the door opened. He flipped open his warrant card.

"Sergeant Arnold. Do come in." Miss Hayes led the way into a sitting room which reminded the detective of a scene from a TV period drama - glass lamp shades with beaded tassels, deep pile carpets with whorled patterns, and a large Ferguson radio the size of a coffin. The DS declined the offer of a seat.

"I won't keep you, Miss Hayes. You spoke to our desk sergeant yesterday about a barking dog – next door, you said?" She nodded. "I can't hear it just now. When did you last hear it barking?" Five minutes ago, she replied. "What can you tell me about the owner of the property next door?" Miss Hayes told Arnold about Mr Herring, who was renting the terraced house.

James Herring had moved into number 18 about a year ago. He rented a garage at the end of the road where he parked his car. He had a slight foreign accent, possibly east European, but Hayes wasn't certain about that. She had occasionally spoken to him over the back fence, but he kept himself to himself, often reluctant to say much.

"Mr Herring, you say?" Arnold was disappointed that it wasn't a Mr Robinson. "With a slight accent?" Miss Hayes nodded. "Can you describe the man for me?" Hayes told the detective that Mr Herring was about his height (Arnold is six feet tall), with fair hair and blue eyes. "Did you ever see his car?"

"Yes, he'd park it out front sometimes. Bright grey colour, sort of big and square." Arnold realised that this lady knew very little about motor vehicles.

"Did you notice the registration plates at all? Can you remember any letters or numbers on it?" Hayes screwed her eyes up as if cogitating. She told Arnold there was a Z and she recalled the number 2.

"And he was renting the property. Do you know who from?" Hayes told the DS that it was an estate agent in town dealt with the lease to number 18. The agent was A. C. and D. J. Alderson in River Lane. At that point the dog began barking.

"Well, Miss Hayes, you've been very helpful. I think we need to get the dog seen to by the RSPCA as soon as possible." He paused. "Do you know where Mr Herring worked?" She frowned.

"As far as I knew, he didn't have a job. He'd come and go at all times of the day and night. But he was always polite."

Norman Arnold thanked her again as he left. Five minutes later he was parking his unmarked car in River Lane close to Aldersons Estate Agents. The office was empty apart from one girl named Patricia sitting at a desk with a large computer in front of her. Arnold introduced himself, flashed his warrant card, and asked about James Herring. Patricia checked her computer listing for a Mr Herring without success. The DS gave her the address and she went into the *Address List* file. 'It's rented by Jamek Ingherr,' she told him. This was getting more of a puzzle, thought Arnold. But Patricia obliged by answering his questions, and after checking with David Alderson over the phone, gave the sergeant a key to the property at number

18, Suffolk Road. Patricia told the detective what information the agents had on Mr Ingherr.

He paid his rent quarterly in advance – always cash, registered his nationality as Serbian, and gave his date of birth as 12 November 1990 which made him 31. They had digital copies of a Serbian driving licence and his passport on file. The rental agreement began thirteen months previously and was open-ended, but with a three - month notice period on either side.

He asked Maisy to send the driving licence and passport images to an email address at Basildon police station. Once outside, Arnold phoned the station and asked DC Clarke to contact the RSPCA and get someone from their nearest branch to meet him at number 18 as soon as possible. He also wanted Clarke to be with him when he entered the property in Suffolk Road. Two pairs of eyes were always better than one.

Fifteen minutes later, as Arnold sat waiting in his car, the RSPCA van arrived, followed a few seconds later by DC Gary Clarke.

The two detectives each donned a pair of gloves, and the three entered the property slowly, not wanting to alarm the spaniel. The RSPCA officer took charge of the Cavalier King Charles which looked in a sorry state, and DS Arnold gave the officer a contact card, asking him for an update on the dog when he was able to report on it. Minutes later the RSPCA van pulled away.

The DS and Clarke began to take a look around the house. An hour later they'd got a laptop computer bagged, as well as a Glock 9mm handgun. The wardrobe held few clothes, and most drawers were empty. Mr Ingherr certainly travelled light.

"Well, Gary, there's one thing I'm certain of. Our Mr Robinson is definitely Jamek Ingherr. All we have to do now is find him. He's got a few questions to answer!"

101

DC Cam Grayson had shown the Nike trainers to his sergeant, Chris Hayman, who'd then arranged for Forensics to take a look at them. Minute scrapings of dirt from both soles of the shoes had revealed tiny fragments of silica and several plant seeds, almost imperceptible to the naked eye. The sole of the left shoe also traces of excrement. The wearer of these shoes had probably stood in some dog excrement on the pavement! That made Hayman chuckle when he read the report from the science boffins, especially as he wouldn't have been able to spell 'excrement.'

Further analysis showed that the seeds were from the geranium genus, Pelargonium, and the silica was a type used in the manufacture of high - quality paving stones. It didn't take the detective sergeant more than a few milliseconds to ask himself the question 'do the paving stones on Mr White's drive have the same type of silica, and do the Whites have any pelargoniums in their garden?' He couldn't recall seeing a dog at their house, but the wearer of the white trainers could have picked the poo up anywhere.

Hayman spoke with his DI, Sandy Matthews, and told him of his thinking; more the logic of it all. Matthews gave his DS the go ahead to check out the aspects of the Forensics analysis.

Two hours later, the science guys were able to confirm that the tiny dirt pieces from the Nike trainers did in fact have pieces of silica identical to some scraped from the paving stones on the drive where Mr White parked his Mercedes. Not only that, but the seeds in those dirt pieces were the same as the white geraniums in the border on the drive. And no, the Whites *did not* have a dog.

Before DI Matthews proposed it, Hayman was already planning to go back and see The Lone Ranger – Rick – and ask him about the man from whom he bought the Air Max 90 trainers two weeks previously. If the seller had owned these since 26 May, the date the car was stolen, or before, then he had to be the car thief and the killer of Peter Dobson.

And there was a bonus on the horizon - the gold crucifix found under the driver's door mat when the Merc was serviced. If the owner of the trainers had also lost a crucifix . . . bingo! The prosecution could have a field day with the evidence.

It was time Chris Hayman had some luck.

He hadn't had a win with his lucky Thunderball numbers for over four months now.

102

Gertrude Heseltine jolted herself awake. She checked her watch. It was 8.45 am and she was fully dressed. Gertrude couldn't remember going to sleep, but had a vision of two men in her room asking questions. She eased off the bed and, after opening the curtains, made her way to the bathroom. When she looked in the mirror, she got a shock! Her hair was frizzy, her eyes puffed with dark bags underneath.

Gertrude tried to get her head around events of the last fourteen hours. After rinsing her face with cold water, she put the kettle on and made the effort to get some coffee. Two sachets. It wasn't until she began to sip her black coffee that aspects of her arrival at the hotel started to fall into place. Two paracetamol tablets were swallowed mid-cup.

Tom! Yes, that was it. He'd gone missing last evening. The girl on reception was rude, and couldn't help, but the manager did say he try to do what he could to find Tom. When she'd tidied herself up and made herself presentable, Gertie would go to reception to find out what was happening.

Then she suddenly realised that it was her wedding day! Good grief! The guests would be arriving soon for the ceremony, except that nobody had told her what time that was to take place. So, there were several questions for the receptionist, whose name she could not recall.

'Where's my husband-to-be, what time do we get married, when do the guests arrive, and what's happening about a reception?'

Gertrude could remember that Tom had gone out to look at the van tyres since somebody had mentioned that there were two flat ones. However, she could not recall that Tom had come back to the room. He said he was going to the bar for a drink. Had he met someone there? Maybe had one too many? He was probably sleeping it off in another hotel room! But, not to worry, all would be revealed when she asked about Tom, and the other queries she had.

Gertrude tidied herself, brushed her hair, and applied some make-up. Her dress didn't look creased despite sleeping in it, and her shoes appeared clean. She did a semi-twirl looking in the full-length mirror, pinched her cheeks for some colour, picked up her handbag and left the room.

At reception she noticed two policemen chatting to the rude girl behind the desk. Gertrude interrupted.

"Excuse me, young lady, but do you know of the whereabouts of Thomas Ball?" Kira turned toward Gertie.

"Good morning, Mrs Heseltine. I'm glad you've come to see me. I was just about to phone your room." Gertrude glanced at the two uniforms. "These two officers have returned to ask you some questions. They were here last night, but it seems you were tired and fell asleep. Mr Whitmarsh isn't here yet so you can use his office." Gertie raised her eyebrows, but one PC gestured for her to follow the other officer.

"This way, Mrs Heseltine. This won't take long." Once inside the manager's office, all three sat down and the two policemen removed their caps. One began by asking Gertrude to tell them about herself and Tom Ball, and what led to the two of them being at Montfort Hall.

She cleared her throat, gave their full names, and then started to tell them about how Tom had come into her life, that she lived alone but was his neighbour, how he and his wife Liz had got divorced, and that after careful consideration, she and Tom Ball had decided to marry. Tom had chosen the hotel, made the wedding arrangements, invited the guests, and after all this was over, they were to live happily as a married couple in her large house in Basildon.

One constable took notes while the other seemed so surprised by her story that he listened with incredulity to her account, his lower jaw dropping every other sentence. The first officer raised his biro like a conductor's baton.

"We'll need a description of Tom Ball, Mrs Heseltine. You know, the usual. Height, build, hair and eye colour, any distinguishing features. Oh, and what he was wearing when he went outside to check his van." Gertie obliged as best she could.

"Hold on a second! Are you telling me you haven't found him? Isn't he around anywhere? He can't be far, surely? Thomas only popped outside for a few minutes to look at the tyres!" She tugged her cardigan around her chest. "We're getting married today. You've got to find him."

The note-taking constable reassured her that they would do everything in their power to find Tom as quickly as possible. Gertie stood, assuming they'd finished.

"Mrs Heseltine, has Mr Ball left any of his personal possessions in your hotel room? I'm thinking wallet or mobile phone?" Gertie shook her head. 'Only clothes,' she had told them. She got up.

"Look, I've got things to attend to. The wedding ceremony and my guests. Can't you see how important this is to me, for goodness sakes!" Gertie brushed past both policemen and waltzed out of the room heading straight for reception where a couple were checking out.

"Excuse me, young lady, but I need to talk to you about my wedding plans. Now!" Kira looked up in amazement at the audacity.

"Madam, if you'll just give me a couple of minutes, I'll be with you shortly."

"Couple of minutes! I need to find out the details about my wedding today!" Gertie had her tail up, but thankfully, the manager entered the hotel foyer at that very instant.

"Ah, Mrs Heseltine. Do allow me to help. Let's find a quiet spot over here and I'll order some coffee for us." Whitmarsh winked at Kira. "We want to do everything we can to make your day as special as it deserves to be." The hotel manager winced inwardly. This old crone was giving him a headache. Kira ordered the coffee as soon as her guests had departed, and felt relieved that her boss was handling this annoying woman. The coffee arrived - on a tray brought to them by a waiter, in a silver coffee pot, with a cut glass milk jug and sugar bowl. A plate of chocolate biscuits was put onto the small, round table. Gertie smiled. Whitmarsh hoped to placate Mrs Heseltine.

While the two of them talked, the police officers were searching the hotel grounds, although the area wasn't large. They had been around the Peugeot van, which they found unlocked, and had looked underneath it. There were no signs of a struggle, no blood marks, and no unusual objects found in the immediate area. One of the constables had spoken to his sergeant who decided it wasn't justified to send any other officers to the hotel. It was not a crime scene – a man had simply disappeared, and there were no suspicious circumstances. Essex Constabulary weren't made of money, the sergeant thought.

Whitmarsh had given Gertrude the wedding details. It was now nearly ten o'clock. Only an hour to go to before Gertie and Tom would be taking their oath.

"What do you mean there are no guests? Of course, there are. My three children, and some friends!" Gertie rose. "I'm going to make a telephone call to my children now and sort this out. There's some misunderstanding here, and it's probably your fault!" She was fuming. Whitmarsh stood.

"Mrs Heseltine, if I may make a point?" Gertie stared at him.

"Yes?" she barked.

"Without a bridegroom there is no wedding." That was such an obvious statement that it didn't register with Gertie for several seconds.

"Can I use a phone. I want to call my son, Michael. Please." A minute later, Gertie was in Whitmarsh's office, sitting at his desk. The manager dialled the number which Gertrude showed him in the back of a little notebook she had in her handbag. A soon as she spoke, Whitmarsh made an exit.

"Hello. Michael? It's mother. Are you coming to the wedding today?" she blurted out. There was a pause.

"Wedding? No. I haven't been invited to any wedding. Where are you now?" She told him.

"What about the girls, Kathryn and Diane, are they coming?" Mike didn't think so.

"What's going on there? Where's Tom? Is he with you now?" Gertrude explained the situation.

"Missing? He's gone missing? What – on purpose . . . has he left the hotel?" At that stage, Gertie broke down. Tom had gone, her three children didn't know about an invite to her special day, and the chances were that her WI pals weren't coming either. "Mother, are you still there?" Mike asked after a long pause.

"Yes, I'm here." She blew her nose. "What am I going to do now, Michael? You need to help me. Please."

"Right. Listen to me. I'm coming to the hotel to collect you. Now. Pyong isn't back yet, but I can leave the dogs for a while. Stay there and remain calm. Pack what you can and check with reception if I'm not there by noon. If there's a problem, I'll leave a message at the hotel for you. Otherwise, look after yourself and wait somewhere safe in the hotel. Do not go outside." He hung up. Gertie sniffled as she opened the office door.

"Ah, you'll be Mrs Heseltine?" said a chubby woman with grey hair and horn-rimmed spectacles. "I'm the Registrar for the district. Can I say how pleased I am to be joining you and your partner in matrimony today. Will you be ready for the service at eleven o'clock?"

Gertrude swooned, tried to grab the edge of the reception desk, but missed. She fell to the floor.

Luckily the carpet was thick enough to break her fall.

"Good afternoon, Mrs Ball. May I come in?" Liz opened her front door wider. DS Arnold stepped inside. "I want to give you an update on Mr Robinson." Liz led the way into the sitting room.

"Have you found him? Is he alright?" Liz looked both anxious and agitated. The police seemed to be dragging their feet in terms of finding where Robbo was. It was four days since he'd disappeared. Liz offered the sergeant a chair, and they both sat down.

"Well, I've got to let you know that Mr Robinson isn't his real name He is a Serbian called Jamek Ingherr who is renting a property in Wickford, just north of Basildon. He has been driving a stolen vehicle and using false number plates. It would seem he does not work in an art gallery, and he owns a King Charles spaniel which is now in care with the RSPCA. A neighbour told us he calls the dog Carisbrooke – don't ask me why." Liz chipped in.

"OK, that's hard to absorb right now," offered Liz, trying to take in what Arnold was telling her and holding back a tear.

"I'm sure it is, but I'm afraid he's clearly been posing as somebody different. Do you have any idea why he would do this?" Liz couldn't think
of a motive. The DS asked Liz how she had first met Ingherr.

"He saw me in a pub one evening, The Cowherd's Arms, when I was having a drink with my sister Mary. She lives in Southend and was staying over with me for a couple of days. I wasn't aware that he was watching me, but a guy called Terry Williams who's my husband's book-maker told me that this man, Robbo, would like to get to know me. The landlord said he was a regular customer at the Cowherd and a bachelor. I got his number and gave him a call."

"Then what happened?" probed the detective.

"Well, we met for coffee one day, and then he suggested going out for a meal later in the week. To the bistro where he disappeared. It sounded a lovely place." Arnold paused.

"If you were honest with yourself, Mrs Ball, would you say you were taken in by Jamek Ingherr?" Liz had to agree – she'd believed everything the man had told her. The dealings at the art gallery, meeting famous people . . . it was all a sham. But why? "Do you think Ingherr wanted to get to know you so that he could find out more about your husband? Maybe he was planning something?" Liz laughed.

"I don't know why he'd want to know more about Tom. He never really asked me much about my husband, although, come to think of it, he was starting to enquire about his place of work and what job he had."

"Did you tell him?" Of course, she did. It was an innocent question. "Were there any outcomes from that?" probed Arnold. Liz tried to think.

"I remember that he did tell me of a delivery he'd made to a new customer on a deserted industrial estate. When he turned up at the address the guy said he did not order the goods and told him to clear off. He was very aggressive, apparently." The DS thought about this.

"If it was Ingherr, it may have been that he wanted to get a good look at your husband, close up and in the flesh. It would be an easy ploy to give false details to your husband's work place and order something, delivered to a place on a disused industrial estate." Liz hadn't thought of that. "There's something that I need to let you know, Mrs Ball." Liz took a deep breath, expecting some news on whether they had a lead on Robbo (she was still thinking of him as Robbo).

"We don't know where Ingherr is right now, but we've taken a look at his laptop computer and I want to make you aware that he is an assassin, hiring himself out at great cost anywhere in the world. He has used several different names, and most recently we believe he was involved with the killing of a Sicilian business man in Santa Cruz on the island of Madeira." Liz gasped. Had she been close to somebody like that. My God, it didn't bear thinking about! "My point is that you need to be on your guard, Mrs Ball. And so does your husband. Until we find Jamek Ingherr, both of you are in danger." Liz felt herself beginning to sweat, giving her a cold clammy feeling.

"I suppose I'd better contact Tom. He's away at the moment but I'll give him a ring."

"We're going to put a police patrol on this property for the next seven days. It will be discreet, but there'll be one or more officers in the immediate vicinity to keep an eye on things." Arnold allowed that to sink in. "And you told us that your husband is living next door with Mrs Heseltine?" Liz gave an embarrassed nod. "We shall need to speak with Mrs Heseltine and your husband. Do you know when he gets back?" Liz felt she had to tell Arnold about Tom's situation. She went on to explain that he was getting married to her neighbour – a comment that took Arnold by surprise but he stayed composed.

"Yes, I know. It sounds silly, but we're divorced and they get on really well together, so, there you have it." Liz said it in such a way that the DS knew she didn't want to talk about it any further. Hell, if this policeman knew the real reason behind the wedding, Liz would be down the station right now, answering questions and the interview being recorded! DS Arnold stood.

"I'll be off, Mrs Ball. You've got my number. If the so-called Mr Robinson calls you, I suggest you make some excuse as to why you can't see him, then let me know immediately. In the meantime, call me if there's anything you want to discuss." Liz showed the detective to the door, said goodbye, and closed it firmly. Before she spent too much time thinking any more about Robbo, she had to call Tom. Glancing at her watch, Liz realised that by now Tom would be celebrating his wedding to the new Mrs Ball. Gertrude Ball. She quickly let the thought wash over her.

Liz picked up her mobile phone and called Tom's number.

'Hi, it's Tom Ball here. I'm sorry I can't take your call right now, but if you leave a short message and a contact number, I'll return your call as soon as I can. Thank you.'

Liz didn't leave a message. How on earth was she going to put DS Arnold's news into a short voice message? She paced the kitchen floor for five minutes, then tried again. Tom's voice
kicked in again. Liz was *not* going to leave a message – she had to talk with Tom, and soon. One more time, she decided. Liz punched in the numbers.

Somewhere in the boot of a car, Tom's phone beeped again. But he didn't hear it.

104

DI Sandy Matthews had given his detective sergeant permission to use DC Grayson to follow up on the guy who'd sold the Nike trainers to a man called Rick, aka The Lone Ranger. But again, Matthews emphasised that it must be kept low key. If this was a wild goose chase, and it became known within the station, both Hayman and Matthews would end up looking complete fools. They be ribbed for ages afterwards. But if it turned out to be successful, then Matthews would get a congratulatory slap on the back from Superintendent Charlie McLaughlin. And that was a rarity from the dour Scot.

Chris Hayman asked Cam Grayson to find out who'd sold the trainers to Rick. He didn't need to know the method. 'Just do it,' he'd instructed his DC.

He next evening Grayson drove out to Rick's home and hoped he'd be in. He didn't want to phone or message him in case Rick became suspicious, or to give Rick time to cover his tracks if there was anything dodgy in the deal. No, better to strike unexpectedly.

Grayson pulled up outside the house, and noticed a car on the drive and the garage door open. Somebody was in. Still dressed in a suit, the DC took his warrant card out of his pocket as he approached the front door. He rang the bell and waited.

"Hello?" said the woman. Grayson asked if Rick was available. She half turned and called his name. "He won't be a moment. If this is about that fly-tipping last week . . ." The DC cut her off.

"No, it's nothing to do with that," he replied. Rick came to the door. Recognising the caller, he spoke cheerily.

"Ah, it's Cam, isn't it? Something wrong with the Nike trainers, then?" Rick's wife wandered off, not interested in his buying and selling activities.

"Hi, Rick. No, it's not that, but I do have a question about them." Grayson showed Rick his warrant card. "I'm Detective Constable Cameron Grayson with Essex CID. The police have an interest in finding out who owned those trainers." Rick looked surprised. "I can't give you any details, Rick, but if you could let me know who you bought them from it would help in our enquiries." The DC smiled to soften the seriousness of the question. Rick invited him into the hallway, and asked him to wait a moment
while he grabbed his laptop. Seconds later it was switched on. Rick went onto the Facebook site, then hit Marketplace and found his buying and selling history.

"Let me see . . . here we are." Grayson leant forward and peered at the screen. "This is the guy. Mickey Heseltine. Now, if I can find the message . . . yes, here it is. I told him I was interested in buying them and he was happy for me to call by his place. Yes, here, look. 30, Andrews Road, Brentwood. I didn't get to see much of his place – it was getting dark. He brought the trainers to the door and we did the deal on the doorstep, then I drove away." Grayson noted the address.

"Thank you, Rick, you've been helpful. Do me a favour. Don't tell the guy that the police have been asking about these."

"Why should I? It's history now. You've no need to worry on that score," added Rick. With that, the detective left Rick's property, got back into his car, and headed home. He'd have that address to follow up in the morning. Cameron Grayson had to trust Rick that he wouldn't forewarn the seller of the Air Max trainers that HM Constabulary were interested in his footwear. But he felt deep down that Rick was an honest guy and would stick to his word.

*

The next morning DC Grayson was waiting at his desk, eager to speak with his sergeant. At 8.40 am, Hayman walked in carrying a cardboard cup of coffee. Their eyes met, and the DS knew Grayson had some news for him.

"Morning, Cam. Well?" The DC brought his boss up to date on the visit to see Rick, and the fact that he had an address in Brentwood of the guy who sold the white trainers.

"Look Cam, I don't want to pour cold water on this, but we should both be aware that this Mickey guy may not have anything to do with the theft of the Merc. OK? He could have bought them off somebody else." The shoulders of Grayson slumped.

"Don't say that, Sarge, I'm pinning my hope on the fact that this is the car thief. I can feel it in my bones!" Hayman patted his DC on the back.

"Well, let's hope so. Come on, let's pay the guy a visit. I'll just phone DS Karl Wilson at Brentwood Central to let

him know what we're doing. They like to be informed."
Ten minutes later, Hayman and Grayson were driving to Brentwood. The DC was behind the wheel of the unmarked Mondeo. He set the sat-nav to Andrews Road, eased the car into first gear, and pulled out of the station car park.

It was a clear drive to Brentwood, and the two detectives were soon pulling up in Andrews Road outside a detached property that had a large board at the entrance, the word *Pooches* in bold letters. Below that it read M & P Heseltine Proprietors Telephone Brentwood 01277 228445. Haywood rang the bell. The long chime could be heard from the doorstep. Hayman reached for his ID as somebody approached. The heavy wooden door swung open.

"Good morning," said the occupant. "Can I help you? I'm afraid we're full this week." Hayman flashed the Essex Constabulary warrant card.

"Mr Heseltine? Mickey Heseltine?" Mike nodded. "We're here to ask a couple of questions. Do you have a minute?" Mike rubbed his hands on an apron he was wearing. A dark blue and white striped butcher's apron in need of a wash.

"What's this about? Is it my wife? Is she all right?" Grayson chipped in.

"No, it's not about your wife, Mr Heseltine. It might be easier if we could step inside?" Mike stood back to allow the officers in. Hayman resumed the conversation.

"Did you own a pair of white Nike Air Max 90 trainers that you recently sold on a web site?" Mike licked his lips; his mouth felt dry.

"Er, yes. To a man from Harlow, I think it was. What of it? They weren't stolen if that's what you think." Hayman reassured him that it wasn't the case.

"How long had you owned the trainers before you parted with them, Mr Heseltine?" Mike looked a little irritated.

"They were a birthday present from my wife. My birthday was on the fifth of May. Why?" Grayson moved in front of Mike, who was now rubbing his hands again on the apron.

"We have to tell you, Mr Heseltine, that someone wearing a pair of white trainers like the ones you sold was caught on a CCTV camera in Saffron Walden on 29 May. The trainers that you owned had minute particles lodged in the fine cracks of the soles. These match with tiny fragments of silica and plant seeds found at the house from where a car was stolen. In addition, there were very small, dry, dog excrement particles." Both detectives stared at Heseltine.

"So what? When I wore them there was a good chance that the soles would pick up fragments of all sorts. Surely." Hayman gave him a questioning look. "And I have dogs here, so stepping in dog faeces comes with the territory. You're not suggesting I stole a car from Saffron Walden, are you? I've never been to Saffron Walden!" Neither of the two policemen made a comment.

"Do you own a gold crucifix, Mr Heseltine?" asked Hayman.

"What the hell is this, Detective Sergeant? Ridiculous questions about a pair of trainers, and now a personal query about a crucifix!" The DS backed off.

"I take that as a 'no,' then? Do you mind if we took a quick look around, Mr Heseltine?" Mike didn't like that – a request completely out of the blue to nose about his premises.

"Look, my wife is away at the moment and I'm running this place on my own. I've got over twenty dogs to feed, exercise and clean out. Now is *not* a good time!" Mike was getting flustered.

"When is a good time?" asked Grayson. Mike politely suggested that they leave him to get on with the morning's work, and call back at 3.00 pm that afternoon. The two detectives looked at each other and nodded.

"Yes, that's fine Mr Heseltine. We'll come back at three," replied the DS. "By the way, you asked about your wife. If we'd come with news on her. Is your wife all right?" Mike explained the situation with Pyong's mother in Bangkok. "Is that your van and car on the driveway?" Mike nodded. "And I assume you use both of them – business and leisure?" He nodded again.

"Yes, of course. The van to collect and deliver dogs, and the Nissan Qashqai at other times. Is that a crime?" Hayman assured Mike that it wasn't as Mike slammed his door shut.

*

The two detectives pulled into a layby a mile down the road. A greasy-Joe caravan had the front hatch open and was serving the basic traveller's fodder. The smell of fried food wafted in the air.

"Fancy a bacon sarnie, sarge?" asked Grayson. Hayman smiled and licked his lips mockingly. "On me, then." The DC strode to the caravan, ordered two bacon sandwiches and two teas, and slipped the guy a fiver. The bill was £4.80 - Grayson told him to keep the change as he pulled two napkins from a dispenser.

"What do you make of our Mr Heseltine, Cam?" asked the DS munching into his snack, brown sauce nearly dribbling down his chin. Grayson chewed for a few seconds, took a sip of tea, and then spoke.

"I think he's lying. About not being in Saffron. You could tell by his enthusiasm in replying. Not a 'yes' or 'no,' but the need to *explain* things. I think I'd buy the part about his wife giving him the trainers for his birthday, and if that's true, then he *did* own the Nike's before the death of Peter Dobson. I'd say it was too much of a coincidence for those trainers to have both silica fragments and geranium seeds lodged in the soles. Hell, how many properties have that combination? And as far as dog shit goes, yes, that fits in with him wearing them at his place." Hayman had finished his sandwich, wiping his mouth afterwards.

"Did you notice the registration number of the Qashqai?" Grayson shook his head. "DP 66 UBT. Put a check on that to make sure it's his car. And there's another thing we can do now." Grayson squinted. "Ask Kate White to take a look at Mickey Heseltine in the flesh. He's got dark hair, but Kate told us the cavity wall insulation man had a ginger mop. I think that's how she described it. And remember she said he had an accent. I detected a hint of South African with Heseltine. Did you pick it up?" Grayson shook his head - slightly embarrassed.

"How do we get Kate White to see Heseltine, sarge?"

"We bring him in. After we've checked his kennels place later, we'll find a reason to ask him to accompany us to the station. If Mrs White can be there at the same time . . . voila! Even if she's behind the one-way screen, she may recognise him." The DC admired the somewhat underhand tactics of his boss.

"One more thing, Cam. If it was Heseltine that stole the Merc in Saffron, I'd guess he drove there in his Qashqai. Can you get any cameras between Brentwood and Saffron to do ANPR checks twelve hours either side of 2340 hrs on 29 May when the car was stolen?" Grayson had his notebook out – no way could he recall all of this. "And one more thing. Get ANPR checks for the day our Cavity Wall man called on the White's. Wednesday, 26 May." Both detectives stuffed their used napkins inside their cardboard cups and Grayson tossed them into a rubbish bin from ten feet away.

Before they set off, Hayman finished the discussion by saying that he would phone DS Karl Wilson at Brentwood Central to update him on their visit to Pooches while his DC was driving, and ask if he could spare two uniformed officers to assist with the mid - afternoon visit. Hayman had a feeling that it could turn out to be very interesting. The sergeant also phoned Kate White.

"Hello, Kate. It's DS Chris Hayman. Do you think you could get to Brentwood police station at, say, four o'clock today?"

"Sergeant, it would be my pleasure. See you later."

Kate would find her newest suit and make sure she looked her best.

As soon as Hayman was back at the station, he called Sandy Matthews.

"Any news, Chris?" asked the DI.

105

Gertrude was asleep on her sofa when the telephone rang. She had been dreaming, but was suddenly awake at the thought that it was the police with some news on Tom. But by the time she had got on her feet, stumbled on the way to the hall, the telephone stopped ringing. Slightly out of breath, Gertrude went back into the lounge and sat in an armchair.

One of her children had told her about dialling a four - figure number that would let her know the number of the caller, but she couldn't remember what it was, so she'd have to leave it. The person calling would ring back, she thought.

Gertrude rested her head and reflected on the past two days. She was grateful that Michael had been able to collect her from the hotel in Walton-on-the-Naze, and paid the bill for her stay with Tom! Michael had double-checked the hotel room. There was nothing left; all of her and Tom's belongings had been packed and loaded into his car, and the police had removed Tom's van to a pound in Clacton.

When Michael had got her home, he'd stayed for half an hour to make sure his mother was OK. Liz Ball wasn't in at the time, she'd been having coffee with Stella, one of her Wednesday coffee morning friends. Liz had arrived back home at about two o'clock, and after doing some washing, decided to hang a few clothes out before the sun finally went down. From the back garden she noticed Gertie through the kitchen window. There was no sign of Tom, but at least they were back from the so-called honeymoon, so Liz thought she'd call and see how it had gone. She still hadn't been able to contact Tom, and realised that it might seem a bit odd, enquiring after her ex-husband and his new wife, but she liked Gertie, and she wouldn't stay long.

Liz rang the bell. Then again. Gertie's hearing wasn't brilliant. On the third ring the front door opened.

"Hello, Gertrude. I just thought I'd call to see how things had gone for you?" Gertrude turned away from the door and walked back inside. Liz decided to follow. Gertie dropped into an armchair and sighed heavily.

"Is everything all right, Gertrude?" asked Liz – concerned. Gertie pulled a handkerchief from her sleeve.

"No," she replied quietly. "Tom has gone missing. We didn't get married. There wasn't a ceremony." Liz took a seat next to Gertie.

"What do you mean 'gone missing?'" The air was heavy as Gertie lifted her eyes to meet those of Liz. This would explain why Tom hadn't returned any of Liz's calls.

"What I say. *Gone missing*. We arrived at the hotel and checked in. I had a rest. Somebody had told the receptionist that Tom had two flat tyres on the van. He went out to have a look. I got up, not knowing where Tom was, and then enquired at reception. They hadn't seen him since he walked out of the main door of the hotel. The police were called. Two officers searched the area. Nothing. I had dinner on my own, hoping Tom would walk in at any second. The police asked me questions, but I'd had a couple of complimentary brandies and fell asleep. In the morning there was nothing for it but to ring Michael and ask him to come and fetch me. None of the guests turned up. What else could I do? I'm sorry." Liz was shocked to hear this, and found herself gripping the sides of the armchair for support.

"Haven't you heard anything since?" enquired Liz. Gertie shook her head, then wiped her nose. "We've got to call the police!" suggested Liz. Gertie was silent, still coming to terms with what had happened. Liz then relaxed a little. Robbo had gone missing, only for her to be told that he wasn't Mr Robinson, and he'd been involved with some murder in Madeira, and Robinson wasn't his real name! And now her ex-husband was missing!

"Shall I make us a pot of tea, Gertrude?" offered Liz. Gertie smiled. It meant 'yes.' Liz went into the kitchen, found everything she needed, and took a tray back into the lounge five minutes later. There wasn't any conversation. Both thinking and wondering about things. Gertie wasn't aware of Robbo, but Liz now had the burden of two men in her life that had disappeared. Liz felt she ought to lighten the mood.

"You read about things like this, Gertrude. People who wander off, and then a few days later are found again. Or, they come back having had a change of heart about leaving." She paused. "Don't you think that Tom has simply gone off somewhere, maybe to think things over, and when he's done, he'll just turn up with some explanation. Or maybe, you know, he went to a garage to get the tyres seen to, fell over and had an accident, and he's in a hospital bed with a broken leg?" Both sipped their tea.

"Just before Michael and I left the hotel, one of the policemen told me that they asked every hospital in the area if anyone matching Tom's description had been admitted. The answer was no. The hotel receptionist gave Tom a garage phone number, but she didn't know if he called them. Michael made a call to the garage and they hadn't heard from Tom. It's a mystery, Liz." Gertie paused. "I don't think it will help if we phone the police. They're on the case, and I was assured everything would be done to find him. They've got my number. The police will call when there's news."

For the moment, Liz had no words to say. What the hell was happening to her? If Tom doesn't marry Gertie as they had planned, the whole affair could go bums up. If he did come home, would the wedding still go ahead? Maybe Gertie would have further thoughts – dismiss the whole idea after all. Ask Tom to leave her home and then Liz and Tom would remarry. Wouldn't they? At that moment, if Liz was honest with herself, she wasn't missing Tom as much as she thought she might. It was a strange feeling she had, but living and managing without him, then seeing Robbo, had made her feel liberated.

If Tom never turned up at all, would she miss him? Well, a little, she told herself. But she'd have to manage on State handouts if Gertie's fortune wasn't forthcoming - start working full time.

"Have you finished, Liz?" Gertie was hovering over her with the tray. Heck, Liz had been 'away with the fairies' in her head and flinched at Gertie's offer of taking her teacup.

"Oh, yes. Thank you. I'd better be going, Gertrude. I've got some washing out and it's coming in a bit cloudy. It might rain later."

Once back home, Liz couldn't settle. Her head was spinning. A thought here, another there. What if . . . how's about . . .when might it . . . why did that? When the washing was folded away for tomorrow's ironing, she checked the fridge. Two bottles of prosecco. Under the sink – a full bottle of whisky. Hunger had deserted her, so she could not be bothered to make herself a meal. The tea next door had filled her a little.

Liz poured a large glass of wine and went into the living room with the bottle. She spoke to *Alexa* and requested easy listening music and *Alexa* obliged instantly. That's all she wanted right now. No news about Brexit, or politics or an earthquake in the Philippines. As Matt Monro was singing *Moon River*, she sipped her wine and began to think.

Why worry about Mr Robinson? Why worry about Mr Ball? Liz even questioned her feelings for men. Was she reaching some stage of a female development crossroads when her libido was undergoing some cataclysmic change? Did she really want to live with a man again?

The second wine bottle was empty and laid on its side next to her chair, the glass broken on the floor. Liz Ball was well and truly out.

She wouldn't know anything until late the next morning.

Two uniformed PCs had parked their car well away from the kennels. DS Karl Wilson from the local station had turned up, but was leaving the questioning to Hayman and

Grayson. DS Hayman asked one of the two uniforms to go around the back of the property in case the owner made a run for it. The second one would provide a presence at the main entrance. Wilson remained in his unmarked car at the end of the short drive, but had sight of the front door of Pooches. It was 2.57 pm by Hayman's watch - a good timekeeper. Grayson rang the bell. Seconds later the door opened.

"Mr Heseltine. May we come in?" Mike led the way into a large reception room, full of dark brown furniture and copies of *Horse and Hound*. They weren't offered a seat, and Mike glanced at his watch as if to indicate that he didn't want this to take up too much time. Hayman spoke.

"Mr Heseltine. Could you tell us how long you've owned the kennels?" Six years was his reply. "And I detect a slight accent. Where are you from originally?" He was born in South Africa. "What about your parents? Where do they live at the moment – assuming they're both still alive?"

"Hang on. What the hell is this about? You've no right asking me questions like that, and you know it! My ownership of this business, where I was born, my parents . . . this is bullshit!" The effect was exactly what Hayman wanted – a reason to ask Heseltine to accompany them to the station for further questioning. DS Wilson's Inspector had agreed that the owner of the kennels could be taken to Basildon for that purpose, maintaining police protocol.

"I'm afraid that we're not satisfied with some of your previous answers to the questions we asked this morning. You're going to have to accompany with us to Basildon police station where we can go over some more questions," said Hayman. "It won't take long." Heseltine was taken by surprise. "We'll pull the car up to the door so that hopefully the neighbours don't see anything, and we can get on our way. Do you want to use the toilet before we go?" Mike shook his head. "Do you have any medication you need to take with you?"

"I've got some tablets I have to take soon, and I want my mobile phone," demanded the kennels owner. Hayman agreed to that, but the DS would carry it in his jacket pocket. Grayson had gone to bring the black Mondeo to the door. The DC made sure Mike locked the front door, and then slipped a pair of handcuffs onto him. 'Routine,' he whispered. Heseltine was put into the back of the unmarked car while Hayman went to speak with Karl Wilson, letting him know what was going to happen. The two uniforms were relieved of their immediate duty and walked away to their blue and yellow checked Ford Focus estate.

Minutes later, with Grayson sitting in the back of the Mondeo alongside Heseltine, the car occupants drove back to Basildon as quickly as possible, and in silence. On the way out of the property, the DC had spotted a packet of chewing gum on a side table. He deftly collected it as he walked past, knowing that a wrapper of spearmint gum had been found in the stolen Mercedes. Was that one more thing to pin on Heseltine?

Once back at Basildon Central, the three of them were soon in an interview room. Heseltine had been offered a drink but had refused. Grayson brought in two coffees shortly after Hayman had returned following the collection of a folder. Inside that folder were several photographs. Two from the CCTV of Gareth White's neighbour showing the Mercedes being taken, the gold crucifix, the Nike trainers, a chewing gum wrapper, microscope images of silica fragments and geranium seeds and the front of the envelope found in the stolen car – the name Jimmy clearly visible.

The DS had briefed DI Matthews, and the Inspector was comfortable with Hayman and Grayson talking to Heseltine at this preliminary stage.

One by one Hayman showed Mike the photos, each with a question.

'Is this you wearing a hoodie and white trainers stealing that car?' Reply 'No.'

'Do you own, or have you ever owned, a small gold crucifix?' Reply 'No.'

'Did you sell this pair of trainers to a man in Harlow?' Answer 'Yes, what of it?'

'Do you use chewing gum?' Answer 'No, but my wife does.'

'Have you seen this envelope before?' Reply 'No.'

The DS closed the folder. Grayson took the packet of chewing gum from his pocket.

"I picked this up in your house, Mr Heseltine. It's the same type of gum of which a wrapper was found in the stolen car. What do you have to say to that?" Mike told them again that his wife bought chewing gum occasionally, and finding the wrapper in the car could be pure coincidence.

"And the soles of your trainers showed silica fragments and geranium seeds that match those at Gareth White's house. Any comment on that?" He'd worn the trainers to a couple of garden centres and been on footpaths and driveways. So what?

"Do you know anyone named Jimmy, the name on the envelope?" Not that he could think of.

At this stage Hayman called an end to the interview but not before asking Mike if he could provide a DNA sample. He realised that refusing might throw more suspicion on him, so he agreed. The DS was aware that they didn't have anything concrete that they could pin on Heseltine right now. It was all circumstantial evidence, and they'd have to let him go. Hayman stood.

"Thank you for your time, Mr Heseltine, I'll arrange for a police car take you home. Can I ask you not to leave the area, but if you do, please let us know? Here's my card. By the way, have you heard from your wife?" Mike told them he was expecting a phone call from Pyong later that day.

Minutes after Heseltine had left the station, Hayman spoke with Kate White who had been watching part of the interview from behind a one-way screen. He then debriefed Matthews on the interview by telephone, expressing his opinion that the kennels owner was being frugal with the truth.

"Find out more about him," said the DI. "Background, previous jobs, his marriage, any medical conditions. Oh, and check out his DNA against what we have on the envelope. The single blond hair that was found in the envelope hasn't been matched yet, has it?" Hayman shook his head.

"And what did Kate White have to say about Heseltine?" asked Matthews.

"Well guv, we gave her a full minute to watch Heseltine. She's 99.9% certain it's him, our Cavity Wall man. She's mentioned again that when he called at her place on 26 May he had red hair, but I'd say he was wearing a wig."

"And the ANPR checks?"

"Video footage is being checked now. Should have a result in ten minutes or so." Matthews chipped in.

"Chris, you need to know that Essex CID have posted a report on two missing persons on our intranet logged by DS Norman Arnold. A Jamek Ingherr and Thomas Ball. Herring went missing from a night out at a restaurant just outside Basildon, and Thomas Ball from a hotel in Walton-on-the Naze. Ball is living with a woman in Basildon. Her name is Gertrude Heseltine."

107

DS Chris Hayman had been going through what they could find on Mike Heseltine. With DC Grayson still checking ANPR and Mike Heseltine's time line on Saturday, 29 May, Hayman had found that Heseltine's middle name was James and that when he lived in Northern Transvaal, he had been admitted to a mental institution at the age of sixteen. He had a undergone a number of episodes of self – harm, and killed two cats belonging to a neighbour by hanging them by their necks from a tree in the neighbour's garden. On return to England, Heseltine had been registered with a psychiatrist at Broomfield Hospital in Chelmsford and was receiving treatment for anxiety, depression and bi-polar disorder. The DS had managed to talk with Dr Abdhu Ranji, but the psychiatrist reminded the sergeant of patient confidentiality and declined to comment on Heseltine's current state of mind.

Before setting up his kennels business six years ago, Mike had worked at the Logan Veterinary Surgery in Basildon. A call to the surgery by Hayman revealed that Heseltine had started off well but became a poor timekeeper and was often late for work. There were several cases of money going missing, but they couldn't prove it was him. Hayman asked about a gold crucifix, and was told that he did have one on a thin gold chain around his neck which he was asked to remove whilst on duty assisting during operations. And finally, when Hayman enquired as to whether Heseltine ever chewed gum, he was told that he regularly brought spearmint gum to work with him.

Hayman also checked out Heseltine's wife, Pyong, which was more difficult. There was little on her, apart from the fact that she'd met Heseltine whilst he was on holiday in Thailand. She'd come to the UK in 2014, they married in Basildon at the registry office, and they had set up their kennels business a year later.

Pulling other aspects together, Hayman had wondered if the blond hair in the envelope found in the Merc might have belonged to someone not involved with this case. He was proved right. It was a match for the bank employee that had served Alice Heseltine the day she withdrew one thousand pounds.

DC Grayson had done the ANPR checks for the Nissan Qashqai and found that DP 66 UBT had been flagged driving into Saffron Walden on 26 May at 10.14 am. Kate White thought the cavity wall insulation guy had knocked on her door at around 10.30 am. The vehicle had been seen later driving away from Saffron at 11.06 am, and then picked up by another camera at 11.12 am five miles further away.

'And Heseltine said he'd never been to Saffron Walden!' thought Grayson to himself.

DS Hayman reviewed the mis-per data on Jamek Ingherr and Thomas Ball, and was particularly interested when he checked that Gertrude Heseltine was Mike's biological mother. The information on Ball was limited, but he had been logged as living with Gertrude in Basildon.

What was the connection between Mike Heseltine and Thomas Ball? There had to be one, if Ball was living with Heseltine's mother!

After speaking with Sandy Matthews, and bringing him up to date, Chris Hayman phoned DS Norman Arnold at Basildon Central.

"Hi, Norman. DS Chris Hayman here, Saffron Walden CID. I've read your entry on the two missing persons – Ingherr and Ball. I think it might be a good idea to meet. My DI wants to get involved, too."

"OK, Chris, I'll come up to Saffron. Be with you soon," replied Arnold, then ending the call.

Chris Hayman then started to wonder if Jamek Ingherr was caught up in any of this? It had to be Heseltine that stole the Merc and caused Peter Dobson to drive off the road last May. Mike Heseltine's mother is living with Tom Ball, so has Heseltine got anything to do with the disappearance of Tom Ball?

It was time to obtain a search warrant to look at Pooches, see if they could find further evidence on Mike Heseltine's activities during the last few weeks. His computer and mobile phone would inevitably provide some useful information.

Three hours later, Matthews, Hayman and Arnold had gone through the data they had accumulated on Mike Heseltine, Tom Ball and Jamek Ingherr. Ball and Ingherr were still missing, but Arnold had been to see Liz Ball and told his Basildon colleagues that Ingherr, alias Robbo Robinson, had been dating her. Arnold had also discovered that Ingherr's spaniel had been cared for by Heseltine's kennels, the RSPCA having checked the history of the dog via the chip under its skin.

"We obtained a key for Ingherr's place and found his laptop and a Glock 9mm handgun there," volunteered the DS. "We've enough on him from his emails and browsing history to put him away for a long time, but I'll leave the details for now. As far as we know he doesn't have a licence for the gun."

DI Matthews brought Norman Arnold up to date with their work on the Peter Dobson case, their background checks on Mike Heseltine, the Nike trainers, and the interviews with his father and stepmother. Hayman filled in any gaps that his boss had missed, including the likely use of a ginger wig by Heseltine when he first visited the White's in Saffron Walden.

By the end of the afternoon all parties were fully informed of the current situation with what they referred to as the HIB trio – Heseltine, Ingherr and Ball. A search warrant had been obtained to search the premises of Heseltine and that evening Matthews and his detective sergeant would pay him a call.

They hoped Heseltine hadn't wiped everything from his phone and laptop. But even if he had, the police had technological methods of tracing most of what had been existed on these devices.

DS Hayman hadn't been at his desk long following Norman Arnold's departure when Grayson asked if the sergeant had a minute.

"Hi, Cam, anything new?"

"One of the mechanics was giving the Lexus a last going over prior to us returning the vehicle to its rightful owner in London and he spotted something on the underside at the rear of the vehicle." Hayman raised his eyebrows.

"And . . .?"

"It's a tracker, sarge. Maybe someone wanted to follow Ingherr?"

"Come on, boy. Over here. Come on!" shouted the dog walker encouragingly, waving his hiking pole. The dog, standing still, was barking at the long, stone slab. Johnny Laker had parked half a mile from Magdalene abbey on a bright, cold morning, with his Yorkshire terrier, Munchkin. He'd let the terrier off the lead a few yards from the abbey. There was nobody about, and Johnny inhaled the fresh air out here in the open countryside.

"Come on, Munchkin. What are you doing? Come on, time to go," urged Johnny. But the dog wasn't for moving,

and it kept looking across at its owner. There was nothing for it but
for Johnny to walk across to the stone slab and see what the fuss was about. Clearly, something was attracting the utmost attention of his canine friend.

Johnny wandered over and looked down at the one – inch - thick flat stone, the size of a coffin lid. There was a narrow gap at one end. Johnny used his hiking pole to poke in between the slab and the stone trough below it. Using some leverage, he leant on the tough pole and eased it away a few inches. Peering down into the dark crevice he could just make out a what looked like a grey blanket covering something. With the pointed end of the pole, he eased away some of the thick material at one end. He recoiled in fright as a black rat scurried out of the trough and ran away to the far wall of the abbey.

Johnny could make out a human head - tousled blond hair, part blood-covered, and two sunken eyes were staring at him. He tried to push the blanket back over the head with the end of the pole but gave up as the spike poked one eye. Taking his mobile phone from his outdoor jacket he checked for a signal. One bar was showing – maybe he would be able to phone the police?

Johnny got through, and half an hour after he'd managed to blurt out what he'd found, two police cars arrived, the unmarked one carrying DS Norman Arnold and his boss, Detective Inspector Matty Whelan. He explained the circumstances to Whelan, and after the DS had taken some notes, Johnny was allowed to leave, with Munchkin still barking.

Two hours later the body was lying in the mortuary. Initial findings indicated that he had traces of pentobarbital in his bloodstream which would have killed him very quickly. The doctor carrying out the post mortem had bagged the hands to check for fingernail scrapings later. Marks on the arms suggested a fight had taken place and a tiny puncture wound, with perimeter bruising, on the right side of the victim's neck suggested the pentobarbital had been injected in a rough manner. The dentition was checked, with a gold capped premolar tooth in the upper jaw, and two missing lower jaw molars.

By the end of the day, and using dental records, the victim had been identified as Jamek Ingherr. Norman Arnold now had the unenviable task of informing Liz Ball that her gentleman friend was dead.

But what was Ingherr doing laid in a shallow trough at Magdalene abbey, wondered Arnold and Whelan? As far as the DS was aware, Ingherr had collected Liz and they'd driven together to La Fourchette restaurant, and he'd stayed in the car to make a phone call. Maybe they called in at the abbey first . . . for some reason. The detective cursed himself for not asking that specific question. No matter, he'd see Liz Ball very soon and carefully check on that detail.

Who had killed Ingherr? When Whelan and his DS got back to the station, they discussed the case. After several coffees and post-it notes on a board, Whelan had a hypothesis. It appeared to boil down to one prime suspect. Someone who had a grudge against Ingherr, because his ex-wife was seeing him and taking her out. A case of jealousy.

It had to be Tom Ball, who had conveniently disappeared.

Norman Arnold knew that Ball had been to Walton with Gertrude Heseltine. Was his story about two flat tyres on his van a way of confusing the police? He could have deflated them himself. Perhaps he had no intention of marrying Mrs Heseltine, and he'd left the hotel on the evening of 23 November by getting a lift from a close friend.

DS Arnold would alert Essex CID to put an All Points Warning out for Tom Ball.

109

The detective sergeant had been to see Liz Ball, accompanied by a female officer named Ruby with family liaison experience, and delivered the news about 'Robbo.' That was how she preferred to remember him she'd told Arnold. Liz hadn't cried at first, the news having shocked her into a state of disbelief. Ruby made a pot of tea whilst the sergeant talked to Liz.

The DS gathered more information on exactly what happened on the evening they'd gone to the restaurant, Liz explaining their visit to the abbey, and giving the reason why. Arnold took notes.

"As Tom had disappeared from the hotel in Walton, do you think he may have got cold feet and be staying with a friend? Maybe someone picked him up from the hotel, but he wanted to make it look as though he'd vanished? Do you think he's being shielded?" Arnold had asked Liz.

Liz refused to believe that, telling the DS that her ex-husband was intent on getting married, and she didn't know anyone who'd cover for him.

"Assuming your ex knew about Robbo, do you think he would be jealous enough to kill him?"

Absolutely not Liz had replied. He wasn't that type.

"Is Tom on any medication?" Arnold had enquired.

Not at all, just a daily multivitamin capsule and chondroitin tablet for his joints.

"The last time I was here you gave me details of his bank card and MasterCard credit card, as well as his mobile number. I can tell you that neither of the cards have been used, nor phone calls made from his phone since 23 November." At that news, Liz began to sob. Her mug of tea was half drunk, as Ruby consoled her. "And he's still not answering his phone," added the detective. "I hope you don't mind if I bring up something from twenty years ago." Liz knitted her eyebrows.

"Twenty years ago?" she queried his last comment.

"Yes. The case of Julie Thornton. I won't go into details, but we know that your ex-husband was arrested for the murder of Julie, brought to trial and acquitted." The DS paused. "Is there anything you want to tell us about that?" It was an open question, and Liz wondered where the detective was going with this.

"No. He didn't do it, and I'm convinced that it wasn't him. I wouldn't have married him if I did, would I? It was wrong place, wrong time, but I know it wasn't Tom."

The two police officers made a move once Ruby thought Liz would be OK on her own.

"You've got my number. Give me a call if Tom does get in touch. We'd like to talk to him. And thanks, you've been most helpful."

The DS hadn't shared information on the way Ingherr had died. He kept it simple by telling Liz that his body was found by a dogwalker in the grounds of the abbey.

And Liz hadn't asked.

She did not want to know.

110

It was Monday, 29 November and DI Sandy Matthews along with his sergeant, Chris Hayman, drove in separate cars to the kennels on Andrews Road. An hour earlier he'd spoken to the DI at Brentwood Central, Tobias Ryan, to inform him of their plans. Matthews asked to 'borrow' two PC's again, as Hayman had done earlier via DS Karl Wilson. The door was answered by Mike Heseltine after the second ring. Matthews flashed the search warrant and both stepped inside.

"We're here to search your premises, Mr Heseltine," said the DI in an authoritative manner. Heseltine looked surprised.

"What? Look, I've answered your questions at the police station. I've nothing to hide here. You'll be wasting your time!" He was almost pleading – always a good sign when somebody *does* have something to hide! Both detectives, now wearing gloves, began picking up the items they wanted to remove for further inspection.

One uniformed PC kept watch near the front door, whilst the other uniform was at the rear of the property. Laptop, mobile phone, two diaries, a folder containing details of kennel bookings were collected. When asked about other electronic devices in the property, Heseltine told the police that his wife had her own laptop and phone, but she'd taken them with her.

Outside in the far corner of the paddock where the dogs were exercised, Matthews could see the dying embers of a fire, wisps of grey smoke curling into the cold night air.

"Been having a fire then, Mr Heseltine?" asked Hayman. Heseltine explained that there's been a few items of rubbish he'd been meaning to get rid of for a while. Matthews nodded to his DS.

"Go and have a quick look, Chris, will you. And do the usual." The sergeant walked down to the paddock. When he got there, all he could make out were blackened, charred remains – difficult to identify what Heseltine had been burning. He phoned a Forensics 24 - hour contact number and asked if it was possible to send someone to Andrews Road to remove the ash and remnants of a fire. There'd be a half hour wait. Five minutes later he was back indoors as Hayman gave his boss a knowing look.

"Well, Mr Heseltine, we'll take these five items to have a look at, and let you have the property back. Meanwhile, DS Hayman here will wait for Forensics to come and have a look at the ashes. Purely routine," added Matthews as Heseltine remained stony-faced.

"How long will you be with my property?" demanded Heseltine. Matthews smiled.

"When we're finished with them," he replied. "It won't be long."

DI Matthews left with the evidence bags leaving his sergeant to hang about until a colleague arrived to remove the whole of the fire contents. The two PCs were given orders to leave. Hayman made himself comfortable in an armchair as the kennel owner fidgeted with a magazine. A few minutes later, Heseltine walked to the back door.

"I need to check on the dogs. I always do at this time of the evening." Hayman nodded.

"OK, but don't take too long about it," replied the DS. "And please don't go near the fire."

Mike Heseltine left the room and silently made his way to the kennels, several dogs now yapping. Hayman took out his mobile phone and tapped on his email app, followed by Facebook and WhatsApp. He glanced at his watch. The detective suddenly realised that Heseltine had been gone for over twenty minutes. He closed his phone and went outside.

Looking down the side of the house toward the kennels, fifteen yards away, Hayman saw a body hanging from a wooden beam, a small stepladder on its side below it.

Mike Heseltine had hanged himself.

Michael – somewhere far away

I had hoped to get away with all this. But my plans did not quite go how I wanted. When my stepmother first asked me to steal a car, and by the way she always called me Jimmy, my middle name being James, I felt it wasn't going to be difficult. I had done it before in South Africa, just before I'd been sent to a mental institution. That woman in Saffron Walden fell for my story about cavity wall insulation, and I had the ideal opportunity to clone the keys to that lovely car. I was bloody annoyed to have dropped my stepmother's envelope – damn careless – when she'd been to the bank for the cash. The ginger wig I bought had the police fooled. I liked that.

I wasn't sure about the motive for killing Peter Dobson, but father wanted him out of the way so that he could get the role of President at the golf club, and a grand was always going to come in handy. When the police started to ask questions
about my movements last May, I realised they were onto me. By now they've probably got photos of my Qashqai going to and from Saffron on that Wednesday, and even on the Saturday.

Then there were the questions on my Nike trainers. I was careless there, but it just goes to show what these Forensic people can do – bloody silicone fragments and geranium seeds . . . I ask you! They swallowed the story about them being a birthday present. That damned wife of mine would never think of getting me something I wanted. If that copper hadn't seen them on Facebook all this wouldn't have come out. And . . . carelessly, I'd dropped the chewing gum wrapper in the car, and, for goodness sakes, my crucifix! The one I stole in South Africa from that old woman. Careless me.

When my mother told my sisters and I that she had Tom Ball living with her, oddly enough I felt jealous. He was dangerous, and I was convinced that by doing little jobs for her he was wheedling his way into her life. It became clear that after his divorce from his wife, he wasn't for moving on from her lovely home. He didn't care about their age difference, and she went along with it, his scheming with days here and there, a weekend on the coast. Bloody hell!

I bet he was skint, and when he saw how well - off mother was, he wanted part of that. Maybe all of that! That's why we had to eliminate him, and when Mr Herring said he could do it, it made sense to go through with it. But after a while,
when I'd collected the cash together, I thought 'James Herring is demanding ten thousand to do a job that wasn't that difficult to do.' I'd done some research on Mr Herring, and he was a nasty piece of work, I can tell you. I decided that he had to go, and I'd keep the six grand and a bit that my sisters had given me.

After I'd met Herring in the park, and asked about his Lexus car, he was proud enough to show it to me. The tracker I'd bought from amazon was easy to place on the underside at the back when I bent down and pretended to be interested in the twin exhaust pipes. Then, after I had my coffee and doughnut in the cafe, and been accosted by Father Bedworthy, I'd hung around, hiding behind some trees. Herring went back inside the café, then followed the priest. When I saw the news about the murder of Father Bedworthy, I went back into the café the next day and the owner told me a man fitting the description of Herring had asked where the priest lived. It was Herring that murdered him, I'm convinced.

With the tracker on the Lexus, and using the app on my phone, I could check where Herring was going whenever I wanted. He had been visiting Tom Ball's wife at her home, and then one evening I saw he was heading out of town. That got me interested, and I told Pyong I was meeting a friend for a drink in the local. When I got to an abbey, I crept up to the outer wall and hear them talking, him and Liz Ball. He was giving her some twaddle about being conceived there! What poppycock! But, I thought, if I kill him tonight what better place to put the body than where under that slab. It would serve him right!

One careless vet had left a couple of pre-filled syringe of pentobarbital at the kennels. I'd seen him use one on a dog before. It was dead in a minute. So, I took the syringe with me that night, and I thought if I could catch him unawares, I'd stick the needle in his neck and press the plunger. It worked! He was so busy nattering on his mobile phone in the restaurant car park, he didn't know what was happening when I opened the door and dragged him out. A heavy knee on his chest, and the needle went it just below his ear. A few gasps and he was gone. It was a bit of a job heaving him into the back of the Nissan, but I managed. I meant to remove the tracker but I bloody well forgot, didn't I?

**

There was still Tom Ball to think about. I'd made my mind up to get rid of him without telling anyone. It was very handy when my mother phoned me to say that she and Tom were going to Montfort Hall on 23rd of November, and he'd told her it was going to be 'a wonderful occasion.' I sensed then that he had a plan, probably marriage, so he had to go. Telling the receptionist that a van outside had two flat tyres worked perfectly. I'd hidden in the bushes near his van and watched him. I was careful to replace the valve caps after I'd poked the stick into each valve to let them down. Make it look like punctures. That was my opportunity, and I took it. Nobody else about, an arm around his neck, then the syringe. Bingo. He went down like a culled elephant. I'd hope there weren't any CCTV cameras – I couldn't see any – and this time humping the body into the back of the Qashqai was easier than for Herring. I'd heard his mobile ringing in the boot when we drove back to the kennels – I knew I'd have to take that off him . . . and his wallet. Same as I did with Herring.

Once back at my place, I'd dragged the body into the wash-house where I have a big stainless - steel sink and two wall taps to which I can attach hosepipes. The floor slopes nicely, into a drain at the end. With Pyong absent, I had time to do what I'd been planning for some time. It took me over an hour to cut him up. The sharp butcher's cleaver had been invaluable, and the arms and legs came off easily. I cut the torso into chunks, but had to get rid of the guts and offal parts. And the head. They went into a deep hole I'd dug in the far corner of the paddock near to the fire pit. The flesh would rot in time. I wondered about pulling all of his teeth out with pliers – you know, to prevent detection by dental records, but I couldn't be bothered.

I'd often wondered whether my dogs would be partial to a bit of human flesh, and do you know, they were! Scything off the meat from the limbs, I'd put it all into two large plastic buckets for the next day. The bones I'd need to burn – long bones, sternum and the rib cage, shoulder blades – they'd char nicely with a good douse of petrol. By eleven o'clock that night I was knackered. After washing down the draining board, hosing the wash-house floor, cleaning the cleaver and knife and thoroughly rinsing my plastic apron, I was ready for a drink. The skeletal remains went into a big gardening tub where I'd leave them until morning, then make a fire soon . . . maybe soak the bones in petrol or diesel for a couple of days, like marinading. What fun!

I had to play along with my mother, showing some concern about Tom Ball, except that he'd been dog food a while back. I had to do the return journey to Walton when she phoned me. Tom was missing she told me. I bloody know – I killed him! Anyhow, it's good to know he's gone and won't be benefiting from any inheritance. That belongs to me and my sisters – that good-for-nothing wasn't getting his hands on it.

Those prying detectives were finding too many clues. I'd be foolish, or more careless really . . . dropping the envelope, losing that crucifix, the gum wrapper, selling the trainers, not changing the Nissan number plates on my trips to Saffron. And now they've taken my laptop, phone, two diaries and a folder. Everything that I could I've wiped from the computer and phone, but those techie geeks are clever at finding stuff. I can't see any way out of this. Oh, for hindsight! What I would have done differently? Well, it doesn't matter now. The fuel-soaked bones, the ginger wig, a diary they didn't find, and the i-pad hidden under the floorboards . . . they'll all burn and melt nicely in that hot fire, and not forgetting the mobiles and wallets of Herring and Ball. When it's cold I'll rake it over and take the contents to the tip in a couple of heavy - duty bin bags.

I'm going to miss Pyong, too. She was lucky to get a man like me. But for years she'd moaned about me getting things done. *'Let's improve this, shall we build that, blah, blah, blah.'* She made me sick sometimes. It was worse when I'd forgotten to take my tablets, I became so annoyed about almost everything. But I'll have to tell that nosey neighbour over the back fence, if she asks again, that Pyong won't be coming back from Thailand. Not when she's in the chest freezer. I clear the frosting off her face now and again, and her brown eyes stare up at me. She looks as calm and serene as the day I first met her. I couldn't feed her to the dogs – not my Pyong.

I will tell that sergeant I'm going to check on the dogs. The rope is ready, and the stepladder is nearby. I've calculated that I need 35 seconds to do it. A piece of cake, I would say. Well, here goes . . .

One year later

"I am so pleased you decided to move in with me, Liz. Now that we're almost over the deaths of Tom and Michael, I think we should be strong and prepare to move on together. What do you say?" Gertie placed the tea tray next to Liz's armchair. "And, before I forget, with Christmas and my birthday coming up, we should really celebrate. Shouldn't we?"

The two women talked about their future. Liz had sold her bungalow for a good price, and changed all of her domiciliary details and opened a new bank account which contained a healthy amount. That included the sum in Tom's account at the bookies. She had also set up a stocks and shares ISA in her name.

A funeral service had been held for Michael, and a memorial service for Tom, both well attended.

"I want to let you know about my Will, Elizabeth," said Gertie out of the blue. Liz remembered Tom told her it had been done through the British Heart Foundation.

"You've made one out haven't you, Gertrude?" Gertie grinned.

"No! That's what I told Tom, but I never went to see them – just pretended. It kept him happy." That was damned cunning, thought Liz. Gertie was not as daft as she looked. "But now that we are together, I'd like to make a fresh one out – a proper one with a solicitor. Are you Ok if I leave my estate to you?" Liz nodded, keeping her enthusiasm low-key. "And I want to do it as soon as possible. My doctor said my heart could go anytime, or I could live to be a hundred! A gypsy once told me that, can you believe it?"

"But you look healthy enough to me, Gertrude," offered Liz.

"Thank you. My cardiologist reinforced the fact that I need to avoid any surprises or shocks – take everything easy, you know?" Liz smiled.

A fortnight later, after both had been to see Gertie's solicitor, the Will was signed. Liz stood to inherit everything when Gertie passed away.

With a week to Christmas, Liz began to put the decorations up. They'd had a nice tree delivered, and bought forty new baubles, plus coloured lights for it.

Bunches of holly were placed around the house, and Liz inflated a dozen red and white balloons.

On Christmas eve, Gertie was in the kitchen preparing some nibbles and warming mince pies. Liz quietly walked in, and glided silently up to stand behind Gertie.

The large toy balloon made an almighty bang when Liz touched it with the sprig of holly. The bowl of peanuts slipped from Gertie's hand, she fell backwards, and Gertie's head smacked hard on the kitchen stone floor.

Half an hour later Liz was still sipping her champagne and enjoying a mince pie as she looked around the room at the oil paintings and lovely chandelier.

"How nice my decorations look," she whispered. "I suppose I am going to have to make a few phone calls soon. Give Kathryn and Diane the news . . ."

Liz decided to finish her champagne first; she would open her Christmas presents from Gertie later.

"And it would have been Gertie's birthday tomorrow," said Liz to the Christmas tree as she lifted the champagne bottle and topped up her glass.

The End

Acknowledgements

I'd like to thank a number of people for helping me in getting to the end of this novel. As usual, my wife Nora proofread the draft manuscript, printed off by my nephew, Mark. Nora made a number of corrections that I hadn't spotted! She also acted as a 'sounding board' for the idea of the plot, and helped me bounce around some ideas around before the first word was typed.

My grandson, Christopher, assisted me in getting the book from a computer to the printed version. Thanks, Chris! Thanks also go to the author Malcolm Hollingdrake (The Harrogate Crime Series), and retired police Superintendent Graham Bartlett, for their help in addressing some aspects of the writing and police procedures.

Any mistakes or errors are entirely down to myself, and many of the names and places used in this novel are fictional.

If you enjoyed The Ideal Husband, please take a look at my other novels shown at the start of this book.

You can also find me at
www.facebook/com/A.K.AdamsAuthor

Thank you

Printed in Great Britain
by Amazon